ICEPICK

BOOK VI OF THE INSTRUMENTS OF DEATH SERIES

BY PAUL DALE ANDERSON

For Gretta and for Tammy
And for Lizza who urged me to kill again

PART I

Lovers and madmen have such seething brains,
Such shaping fantasies, that apprehend
More than cool reason ever comprehends.
The lunatic, the lover and the poet
Are of imagination all compact:
One sees more devils than vast hell can hold,
That is, the madman: the lover, all as frantic,
Sees Helen's beauty in a brow of Egypt:
The poet's eye, in fine frenzy rolling,
Doth glance from heaven to earth, from earth to heaven;
And as imagination bodies forth
The forms of things unknown, the poet's pen
Turns them to shapes and gives to airy nothing
A local habitation and a name.
Such tricks hath strong imagination,
That if it would but apprehend some joy,
It comprehends some bringer of that joy;
Or in the night, imagining some fear,
How easy is a bush supposed a bear!

William Shakespeare
A Midsummer's Night Dream, Act V, Scene 1

CHAPTER ONE

You know you're in real trouble now. Your hands and face and clothes are covered with blood. It's obvious what you have done. When you hear a police siren coming your way, you naturally begin to panic.

So the first thing you do is get rid of the icepick. You throw it into the river, pitch it underhand up in the air and watch it splash a good twenty feet from where you're standing on the west bank. Then you follow the icepick into the river. The current is exceptionally strong, but you don't try to fight it. You allow the current to carry you downstream, nearly half a mile, before you swim across the river to the east bank.

When you emerge, you are amazed that all the blood has disappeared from your hands and clothes. You turn your hands over in the moonlight. For the first time in years, even your fingernails are clean.

Although your clothes are soaking wet, the night is still warm. You know you'll dry in time. It actually feels good to be wet. Like when you were a kid and ran laughing through the sprinkler.

Running in wet shoes isn't as much fun as you remembered, but because you have on leather Reeboks you pretend to be a jogger as you put as much distance between yourself and the dead bodies as possible. You hear more sirens heading toward the center of town. You run faster. When you reach the South Street Bridge, you slow to a walk. It's necessary to cross the river again to get to your car. You check your watch, a cheap glow-in-the-dark Timex that has survived the swim. The time is now 2:39.

An hour ago you were in one of the downtown dance clubs—a

cozy little place, with a bar on the first floor and a dance floor on the second, called "Upstairs and Downstairs"—polishing off your fifth beer of the evening. The furthest thing from your mind was murder.

What had attracted your attention and held it was this luscious little number in a yellow blouse and red thigh-length skirt. She wore a red push-up bra under the yellow blouse, and you found it sexy as hell. You observed the bottle-blonde move lithely around the dance floor for more than an hour. She wore a yellow thong beneath the red skirt, and you glimpsed bare cheeks as she swung her ass to the rhythm of the music. You were totally mesmerized.

You had never been in this bar before, didn't normally go to bars, but the night was far too hot to remain in your dingy third-floor apartment without air conditioning. Something—maybe it was the full moon—had made you restless, and so you left your apartment around midnight and drove downtown to Third Avenue where the dance clubs stayed open until two. You only planned on drinking one beer, a Stroh's Light, you could nurse until closing. That way you could pass as ordinary. You've never considered yourself ordinary, but maybe tonight you can pretend. What's the harm in that?

You hadn't intended to go upstairs to the dance floor, either, but all the barstools and tables were taken on the first floor and you had no choice. So you followed the crowd up the stairs and the first thing you saw was the blonde.

She really knew how to move. You admired the way her skirt swirled around her bottom, the way her breasts bounced beneath the bra. One or two other men had their eyes on her. But none watched as closely as you did.

You memorized her movements. Tonight, when you return to your apartment and close your eyes, you will still be able to see her dancing.

You killed the first bottle of beer and ordered another. This was turning into a two-beer night. You were starting to feel light-headed. It occurred to you that you hadn't eaten anything at all today, silly you. Your brain craved glucose, and beer provided a few stray carbohydrates that the liver could metabolize to sugars. Maybe you should switch to regular beers instead of lights. Regular beers contain more carbs.

You killed the second Stroh's Light, then ordered a bottle of Miller High Life.

"Miller Light?" asked the bartender.

"No. Regular Miller," you told the bartender. "No, wait. Make it a Heineken."

You continued to watch the girl dance. She really expended a hell of a lot of energy. You noticed she wasn't dancing with any particular guy. She was out there on the dance floor just swinging her hips around every which way, drinking from a long-necked bottle of Dos Equis, and having the time of her life.

The place was packed with warm sweaty bodies bumping into each other both on and off the dance floor. You had to remain standing because there were no empty barstools. When people stepped in front of you and blocked your view, you switched positions in the room. You moved closer and closer to the blonde in the red skirt.

Because the dance floor was filled with dozens of beautiful people, no one paid special attention to the blonde except you and one other guy. His eyes moved from the girl to you and back to the girl again. He was already unsteady on his feet. He and a friend were doing shots of hard liquor and washing the shots down with beer. The friend had a girl the blonde's age hanging onto one arm. She was obviously drunk. Not yet falling-down drunk, but close.

You ordered your fourth beer fifteen minutes before they announced last call for alcohol. The blonde continued to gyrate, and you couldn't help staring. As the yellow thong slid from side to side, you could swear you saw pubic hair. She didn't notice, didn't try to adjust the thong to cover up.

"What you staring at, asshole?" slurred the guy who had been doing shots. You were so busy watching the girl, you hadn't seen the guy move closer to you. You can smell the alcohol on his breath, the sweat on his body, the sickening stench of his after shave. He's a mean looking bastard—big, manicured hair, muscles—and he's drunk and acting foolish.

He has no idea who you are. If he knew, he wouldn't dare address you so disrespectfully.

"That's my girlfriend you're oogling," said the drunk.

"You're a lucky man," you tell him. You can afford to forgive him his indiscretion. After all, he couldn't know who you really are. No one could.

"I seen you stare at the crack of her ass," the guy said. "I should tear your eyes out."

You feel the guy shoving you, pushing you into other people. How dare he do that? Doesn't he know that touching you without your permission is punishable by death?

"Get out of here before I kick your ass good," he snarls through gritted teeth like he's the alpha dog. If only he knew, he would be backing off with his tail tucked between his trembling legs. You think about telling him, maybe even showing him. But you know this is not the time or place.

So you were the one who backed off. You were the one who left the second floor with your tail tucked between your legs and you heard the guy's raucous laughter follow you all the way down the stairs. You went to the bar, ordered another Heineken, and that's when you saw the icepick, its wooden handle sticking out of an aluminum bin filled with chunks and chips of ice. If you lean across the bar you can grab the icepick before the bartender returns with your Heineken.

But it's too late. Alcohol has slowed your mind and movements, making you hesitate a moment too long. The bartender, a bearded guy in his thirties who looks your age, sets the beer on the bar, takes your wrinkled twenty, and goes off to ring it up in the register. That's when you reach out, snatch up the icepick, and hide it inside your shirt before he returns with your change. You tell the bartender to keep a five for his trouble. He throws the tip in the tip jar next to the cash register. If he noticed the icepick was missing, he didn't say anything.

You carefully nurse your fifth beer until they announce last call. You are still standing facing the bar when the blonde, her boyfriend, and the drunk couple you had seen next to the boyfriend come down the stairs and pass you on their way out. You kill your beer and follow them from the club.

Your car is parked in the opposite direction of where they seem headed, so you follow them on foot. When they get into their own cars, you'll have to go back for yours. But they keep walking. They turn right on West Street. You wait until they are almost out of sight and then you, too, turn right on West Street.

You follow them for three blocks to where West Street dead-ends at the river. The full moon casts a silver glow over the entire landscape. You see the two couples reclining on the grass. You watch and wait. It's what you do best. You're a watcher.

You see the boyfriend move his hand beneath the blonde's red skirt and lift it above her waist. He pulls her thong down to her knees. The other couple roll around on the grass fully clothed. None of them notices you as you walk softly toward them.

You take the icepick from your shirt and grip it in your left hand. You think of yourself as ambidextrous, but really you're more comfortable using your left hand than your right.

"I seen you look at the crack of her ass," the guy had said. "I should tear your eyes out."

You go for his eyes with the icepick. He's preoccupied, and he doesn't hear you walking on the grass until you're already on him. When he looks up, you ram the icepick into the guy's right eye. Blood squirts out as the long shaft penetrates all the way to the brain.

You quickly remove the icepick and jab it into his other eye. The girl begins screaming and you notice she has her cell phone in her hand and has already thumbed a button. You ram the icepick into her right eye and then her left eye. She drops the cell phone.

The other couple stop rolling around on the grass at the sound of the screams. They are both drunk, and their reaction time has been slowed by alcohol. The man tries to stand, but his shoes slip on the dewy grass. You rush toward him and jab the icepick into his right eye.

"No!" screams the girl. "Not the eyes!"

She, too, has a cell phone. Don't girls go anywhere or do anything without a cell phone? Does she think the cell phone will protect her? What fools these mortals be! You stab the man in the left eye and turn your attention to the woman.

She drops the cell phone and raises her right hand to shield her eyes. She knows what's coming. You saw the knowledge in her eyes before she covered them with her hands. It takes all your strength to force the metal shaft between the first and second metacarpals. The tip penetrates, sinks into the eyeball, and she stops screaming.

You tug the icepick free, shove the bloody hand aside, and do the other eyeball.

You're covered in blood and slimy fluid that squirted from their eyes. You're breathing hard from the exertion. You step back, take a slow breath, and look at your handiwork.

Now you're in trouble. If the police catch you, they'll lock you up and throw away the key. So you throw the icepick in the river. Then you throw yourself into the river and float downstream.

A police car races past you on the South Street Bridge, red and blue lights flashing. If you were walking in the other direction, cops might stop you and question you. But you are walking toward the crime scene, not away from it. They ignore you.

You reach your car—a red ten-year-old Toyota Matrix you bought used—and you sit in the driver's seat and relax for a moment before driving home.

Vivid images of the blonde girl flood your mind. You know you could have done anything to her and she couldn't have stopped you. You fantasize about some of the things you might have done.

Next time, you tell yourself, you'll do more.

CHAPTER TWO

Andy Sinnott was young to be a homicide lieutenant. Andy was only 31, had been on the force just eight years, and this was his first big case. Like all sworn officers, Andy had gone through the police training academy. Unlike most officers, however, Andy had come to the force directly from college. He had no military experience, and he hadn't been an athlete in either high school or college. He knew most of the men he worked with were waiting for him to fuck up. They didn't think he had what it takes to be head of homicide and he had to prove them wrong.

Andy had something most other officers didn't: education. He had a degree in computer science, plus a masters in criminology. He had also attended the FBI's National Academy, an elite ten-week training course for law officers where he majored in forensics and behavioral science. In his spare time, Andy was enrolled in the FBI's Virtual Academy for Law Enforcement where he took on-line classes. And he had earned a yellow brick at Quantico for successfully completing the FBI's grueling six-mile run through the woods on the yellow brick road built by the Marine Corps. The yellow brick road was an obstacle course designed to train Marine officers. It was probably ten times harder than similar obstacle courses at Army or Air Force bases.

Preparing to pass the yellow brick road had given Andy a love of running. Something magical happened to him about twenty minutes into a long run. Not only did he get a second wind, but his muscles and mind merged. He could think clearer, see things sharper, feel more acutely. Running was the closest to heaven he expected to get in this life. Running turned meek, mild-mannered

Andy Sinnott into a kind of Superman.

"Four victims, two men and two women," said Art Lewinski, the patrolman who had discovered the bodies. "It's not pretty, Lieutenant."

Lewinski was a veteran patrolman, grossly overweight from too many beers and riding around in a squad car all night long. Art had been Andy's training partner before Andy joined Bill Bowers' crime scene team and made detective. He was a good cop, sullied only from having seen too much violence in twenty-six years in uniform. Nothing seemed to faze him anymore. But Art seemed visibly shaken by the condition of the bodies on the grass.

"Eight eyeballs," Lewinski said, shaking his head. "If he wanted to kill 'em, why'd he hafta go for the eyes?"

"Probably because he didn't have a gun," said Andy, stepping over the crime scene tape.

"He didn't use no knife, neither," said Lewinski. "Puncture is too narrow for a knife."

"Has the coroner been notified?"

"Stowe's on his way."

"Anything been touched or moved?"

"Naw. No need to feel for no pulse to know they was dead."

Andy put on a pair of surgical gloves. He always kept a pair of latex gloves in his pocket, as did most police officers in this day and age of AIDS.

"The crime scene boys get pictures?"

"Yeah. And they went over the area for footprints. Looks like the perp went for a swim after he finished."

Two of the crime scene techs were walking up and down the river bank, shining flashlights into the murky water. The river was too deep and too muddy to see the bottom.

Andy knelt by the victims and looked at their faces. They were all young, younger than him, and their lives had been snuffed out in an instant. No man nor woman knew when death would happen to him or her. Death was sneaky that way.

Or, as Shakespeare had Julius Caesar say, "Death will come when it will come."

Death came to these four when they least expected. One of the girls had her panties down around her knees, and she wasn't able to run or put up much of a struggle. The guy nearest to her must have been fondling her when it happened. The perpetrator probably killed the man first, then the woman.

The other couple must have been close enough to intervene, but it didn't appear they had done much of anything. There were two smart phones on the ground—a Nokia and an LG—and Sinnott supposed someone, most likely both girls, had called 9-1-1. Men were more likely to fight or flee. Women were more likely to call for help.

Why the eyes? Sure, the eye was the most vulnerable place on the face. The eye socket was a direct opening into the brain. If you wanted to kill someone quick, you'd go for the eyes. But one eye was enough to cause death. Why stab both eyes? That was unnecessary overkill.

Whoever did this had been quick. Lewinski had arrived on the scene within ten minutes of receiving the call, and Lewinski said the perp was nowhere in sight when he got here. Someone had killed four people and escaped into the river within ten minutes. That was no easy task.

Andy saw the coroner's panel truck stop at the end of West Street. Stowe got out with his black bag containing camera, digital voice recorder, medical instruments and notebook. Andy recognized the driver as Harvey Fredriks, Sally Nolan's new lab assistant. Fredriks unloaded a gurney and four vinyl body bags from the back of the truck.

Doctor Stowe was a forensic pathologist who had interned at the Cook County Medical Examiner's office before accepting a two-year post-doc fellowship out here in the sticks. Stowe claimed he had seen every manner of death imaginable at Cook County. But this was obviously the first time he had seen four bodies with both eyeballs punctured. He carefully examined all of the bodies before taking photographs.

"Dead less than an hour," Stowe confirmed. "No evidence of rigor yet, and the bodies are still relatively warm. Of course, it's a hot night. I would estimate time of death between 1:45 and 2:00 AM."

"That's consistent with the 911 telephone calls from the victims," said Sinnott.

"It appears that the cause of death was a long, sharp instrument inserted through the eye socket into the brain," Stowe added, speaking into the voice recorder. "In 1946, Doctor Walter Freeman, a psychiatrist, and Doctor James W. Watts, a neurosurgeon, pioneered the use of ice picks to perform transorbital leukotomies on mental patients. They later developed orbitoclasts, medical instruments that were longer than conventional icepicks, to reach various parts of the brain. Needless to say, there were serious side effects and even deaths. In this case, if I were to guess, I would say the instrument of death was either a conventional icepick or an orbitoclast. Most likely an icepick, since orbitoclasts are hard to come by."

"An icepick? An ordinary icepick killed four people?"

"To be precise, a man killed four people. The man may have used an icepick to do it. Icepicks are merely instruments or tools that have many legitimate purposes, and homicide is not the primary reason icepicks were invented. Icepicks have to be strong enough to chip away at solid ice. Penetrating an eyeball is relatively easy. It's soft tissue all the way into the brain itself. The killer could have used anything from a knife to a pointed stick to accomplish the same end."

"What about the injured hand on the clothed woman?"

"Ah, yes, obviously a defensive wound. She raised her hand to shield her eyes, but it did her no good. Somehow her assailant missed hitting bones in the hand, and the point of the pick penetrated her hand, went through her eye, and entered the cranial cavity via the eye socket. Either the assailant knew where to aim, or he got lucky. Penetrating the palmar and dorsal of the hand and then entering into the eyeball wouldn't be too hard to do unless reflex caused the hand to jerk away from the eye. It must have happened too fast for her to jerk the hand away. He probably rammed the icepick in all the way with a single stroke. She was dead before she felt the pain in her hand."

"Any evidence of sexual assault?" Sinnott asked.

"I don't think sex was a motivating factor," said Stowe. "Jealousy, perhaps. It appears the big man over there was attempting sex with the petite blonde-haired woman when he was killed. He had her panties pulled down around her knees. But there's no evidence of penile penetration and the man's still fully clothed. I doubt the killer would have assaulted the woman post-mortem unless he was really into necrophilia. Besides, he didn't have time."

"One perpetrator killed all four victims? In less than ten minutes?"

"That doesn't seem possible, does it?"

"If it was one guy, he moves fast. He was gone before we got here. And cops were here ten minutes after getting the call."

"Let me get the bodies back to the lab for a complete examination. You got everything you need? Pictures? Prints?"

Andy called one of the techs over to take sets of fingerprints from the victims. Then Andy searched the bodies for wallets and found the men had wallets with drivers' licenses in the hip pockets of their jeans. He located both of the women's purses and discovered drivers' licenses and cash. The pictures on the licenses matched the victims.

"Seems robbery isn't a motive," he said, handing the wallets and purses to the assistant coroner. "Send me an inventory of the contents as soon as you can, Doc. Meanwhile, I'm going to see if I can find where the killer exited the river."

Doctor Stowe signaled Fredriks to bring a gurney and body bags. Fredriks unzipped the heavy vinyl bags and placed one on the grass next to each of the bodies. Then he rolled the corpses onto the plastic, zipped up the bags, and Stowe helped him lift the dead weight onto the gurney. They unloaded the gurney into the truck, put away their equipment, and left.

Sinnott sent his crime scene people downstream to check both banks of the river. They were searching for prints from a size eleven running shoe, similar to shoes Sinnott himself wore except one size larger. The guy they were looking for was probably about five ten or eleven, maybe a hundred and seventy pounds. Average height, average weight. About the same size as Doctor Stowe. The victims were all Caucasians. The killer likely was, too, since killers and victims were normally of the same ethnic group.

Andy walked north to the pedestrian walkway beneath the Main Street Bridge, crossed the river, and then headed south. He shined a high-intensity flashlight on the mud and grass between the river and the bike path. Andy used the bike path often for practice runs when he trained to run marathons, and he knew the area well. But this was the first time he had been on the bike path at night.

Obviously, the same couldn't be said for other joggers. A woman dressed in shorts and halter ran past him, followed by two men in shorts and t-shirts. Another couple came at him from the opposite direction. The path was ten miles long, seven feet wide, and there were separate lanes for joggers and bicyclists. The day had been too hot for jogging or running comfortably, and the cooler night air seemed the perfect temperature. Andy would have to remember that when he trained for his next marathon.

He put thoughts of running aside as he scanned for footprints. There were lots of prints on or near the bike path, but few coming out of the river. He hoped the killer's wet shoes left marks in the mud along the river's edge. But, as warm as it was, he wasn't sure how long tracks would last.

He was almost to the South Street Bridge when he saw muddy shoe prints emerge from the water. They led up to the bike path, disappearing after a dozen or so steps. There had been too much traffic on the jogging path, and the mud had quickly worn off the running shoes.

But now, at least, Andy knew how the killer had avoided police. He had been nowhere near where police would think to look. Not only was he on the opposite side of the river from the crime scene, he was nearly a mile farther south. He could have gone anywhere from here in the dark, and no one would have stopped him nor questioned him.

Had the killer planned all this out in advance? If the killer was covered in blood and gore as Sinnott suspected, had he known that jumping in the river would wash him clean of evidence? Was he a calculating premeditator? Or had he simply been a lucky bastard?

And was the killer a he or a she? Could a woman even thrust an ice pick with enough force to penetrate a human hand, pass all the way through an eyeball, and enter the brain? Yes, anything was possible. And if jealousy were the primary motive, a woman most certainly could have done it. Andy had seen some brutal cat fights during his time on the street where jealous women literally tore each other apart over a man. And most of those women had deliberately scratched and clawed at each other's eyes. One woman had actually gouged out a rival's eyeball with long hardened fingernails that had been sharpened almost to knife points. It was the one and only time Andy had seen Lewinski get sick and throw up at a crime scene. Andy had fought long and hard to keep his own bile under control that day. Fortunately, Andy hadn't eaten an entire pepperoni and olive pizza before he went on duty. Unfortunately, everyone around the crime scene could tell Lewinski had.

But women didn't usually wear size eleven men's running shoes, and this killer obviously did. Andy signaled his evidence techs with the high-intensity LED flashlight. He ordered the crime scene technicians to get pictures and a full cast of the prints in the mud.

Tomorrow night, after Stowe had completed all the autopsies and confirmed the victims had consumed alcohol, Andy would send cops to downtown drinking establishments with pictures from the victims' licenses. Most likely, they had been drinking somewhere nearby until closing time.

Perhaps some bartender or waitress would recall seeing the victims. That would establish a starting point. Had anyone else been with them in the bar? Was anyone stalking them? Had there been an altercation of any sort? It was a long-shot, but who knows? Best case scenario would be if an off-duty cop were working security in the bar. Most of the dance clubs paid off-duty patrolmen to be bouncers and handle unruly customers. Cops were trained to be observant and could usually spot trouble before it happened. Worst case scenario would be if nobody noticed anything.

Andy continued walking the river banks looking for clues until long after sunrise colored the world bright orange. Downtown became alive with traffic noises and gasoline fumes. Bicyclists and joggers appeared on the bike path. Ducks and geese floated on the water. Businesses began opening their doors to customers. Today promised to be even hotter than yesterday. Life went on for most people, not much different today than yesterday or the day before.

But for the four people murdered last night life did not go on. Nothing would ever be the same for them again. Now they were cold corpses splayed open on autopsy tables as Doctor Stowe removed their vital organs to weigh and measure them. Stowe would saw off the skull cap and extract the brain. He would take special note of how the instrument of death had severed the neural connections that supported life, paying special attention to the damaged temporal lobe located immediately behind the eyeball. Were the pituitary and amygdala demolished? Had the point of the ice pick penetrated all the way to the pineal gland and the brain stem itself? At what point had the brain stopped functioning and life ceased?

And which eyeball had been penetrated first?

If the left eyeballs had been attacked first on all of the victims, that could indicate the perpetrator was right-handed. Conversely, if the right eyeballs were first, the perp might be left-handed. The angle of penetration was important, too. Did the pick come at the eye from the right side or the left? Was the stab made underhanded or overhanded? Each detail was a piece of a giant jigsaw puzzle that Andy could assemble until he had a complete picture of the killer and how the killer operated.

He already knew from the size of the footprints that the killer was average height, between five-nine and five-eleven. He was average weight, too, between one-sixty and one-eighty, because the footprints were not exceptionally deep. He wore running shoes, likely wore jeans or shorts and a t-shirt with a logo on the front or a polo shirt with a lizard above the pocket. He was probably white, because most perpetrators chose victims of the same race. He was relatively young, not too much younger or older than the victims. He had sufficient strength to drive an ice pick through the eyeball and into the brain. And he was quick and agile. He had moved between victims, killing each of them before any had a chance to fight or flee.

He wasn't a thief. He hadn't taken money from the wallets or purses of the victims, nor had he removed jewelry. All of the victims wore wrist watches that were easily pawnable, and one of the girls had a solid gold choker linked around her neck and diamond earrings in both ears. Robbery clearly was not a motive.

So why had he killed four people with an icepick? Most men would have used a gun. But not everyone had access to a gun or knew how to use one. Felons were prohibited by law from purchasing or possessing a firearm. Maybe the killer was an ex-felon. Or, perhaps, the murders were spur-of-the-moment and not pre-meditated. The killer had no time to get a gun. Were these victims targets of opportunity?

If so, had something motivated the killer to pick up an icepick from somewhere? Icepicks were sold in home centers and department stores and liquor stores and drug stores and even some all-night convenience stores. Or he might have stolen one from a bar where icepicks were commonly used to separate cubes of ice that had frozen together.

Sex wasn't a motive because neither of the girls were raped. Or, maybe, sex was the motive and the perp had panicked and changed plans when he saw the girls had phoned for help. Had the killer intended to murder the men and kidnap the girls? Had the girls saved themselves from a fate worse than death by using their cell phones?

Or was the doctor right in suggesting jealousy as the motive?

Andy remembered working a multiple homicide a few years ago when jealousy made a man murder his entire family before killing himself. Investigators discovered that the man's wife had threatened to leave him and take the kids. He suspected she was leaving him for another man and became jealous. The thought of his wife and kids living with another man drove him crazy. Despite an order of protection—the man had often beaten his wife and children and the real reason she was leaving had nothing to do with another man but the safety of her children—the man had entered their home with a tire iron and smashed in the skulls of his wife and three kids before setting fire to the house and himself.

The order of protection was granted by a judge based on a threatening e-mail the man had sent to his wife that read, in part, "If I can't have you, no one else can either." But the man had simply ignored the protection order and entered the house with a key—the wife had neglected to change any of the locks after the husband moved out—and he killed them all in their sleep.

Had the perpetrator seen the men making love to the girls in public and gone into a rage? Was the perp jealous that those men had the girls and he didn't? Or was the perp some kind of religious fanatic who killed all four to punish them for public fornication?

Solving crimes meant asking the right questions. Andy realized he wouldn't be able to find answers on the streets until he knew a lot more about the victims. He climbed into his car, a silver Honda Civic Hybrid he had purchased brand new when he was promoted to lieutenant, and drove to the City-County Public Safety Building.

Andy had a desk, not a private office, in the back of the fourth floor squad room Homicide shared with Violent Crimes. Andy kept his own personal computer, an HP laptop, locked in the middle desk drawer so he didn't need to wait to use one of the two department desktop computers. He logged the laptop onto the PSB wi-fi network and checked his e-mail.

Doctor Stowe had already e-mailed attachments of the victims' drivers' licenses. Andy opened a new Excel spreadsheet and entered data on each of the victims, beginning with information from the drivers' licenses.

Daniel Berger was twenty-nine years old, six-one, two hundred and three pounds, and Berger was the man found near the woman with the red skirt and yellow panties. Andy did a quick records check on Berger and turned up a DUI, several speeding tickets, and a more recent charge of drunk and disorderly that was still pending a court date.

Lila Evans was twenty-five, a natural-brunette-dyed-blonde, consistent with what Andy had noticed at the scene. She was five-six, one hundred and twenty-three, and her record was clean.

Paul Rodriguez was thirty, five-eleven, one hundred and eighty-one. He had black hair and brown eyes. He also had a DUI.

Sylvia Simons was twenty-seven, brunette, five-five, and one-fifty. No record.

All four lived in separate apartments in the same apartment complex on the west side.

Andy saved his spreadsheet, checked his other e-mail, then logged off and locked the laptop in his desk again. He rode the elevator all the way down to the basement. To his right were the police pistol ranges, armory, gym, male and female locker rooms, and building maintenance and storage. Straight ahead were the interrogation rooms and the Captain's office. To the left were the evidence lockers, the file rooms, the crime labs, and the county morgue. He turned left.

Half-way to the labs, he ran into Jon Bradley. Bradley was a friend of Captain Troy Nolan. Troy had introduced Bradley to Andy at Troy's wedding. Both Nolan and Bradley had served in the Army, though not at the same time nor place. Nolan had once mistaken

Bradley for the Pickaxe Butcher and shot and nearly killed him. Later, Bradley had prevented the real butcher from killing Nolan. Troy had helped Jon Bradley get a job working nights in the 911 call center on the eighteenth floor.

"I hear you took the calls last night from both homicide victims," Andy said. "What can you tell me about those calls?"

"The first one was a woman's screams," Bradley answered. He stood two inches shorter than Andy's five-seven, and was even skinnier. "Just screams, nothing else. I heard the second caller plead, 'Not the eyes. No, not the eyes.' Then she screamed, too."

"Were the calls terminated or did the lines remain open?"

"They remained open."

"Did you hear anything else?"

"A grunt maybe. Someone moving around. When I got no response on either line, I moved on to other calls. I dispatched a squad to investigate and sent an ambulance."

"Thanks, Jon."

"Please call me Rat," Bradley said. "All my friends do."

"Why do they call you Rat?"

"Because I'm real small, and because I used to live in the sewers. We made up names for ourselves in the sewers. Rat is short for Sewer Rat."

"Rat it is then. I'm Andy."

"I know who you are, Lieutenant."

"It's a small world," said Andy. "We have a lot in common, including friends."

"You headed for the labs?"

"Uh huh."

"George is there. Harvey Fredriks, I mean. I call him George because he looks like George Washington on the dollar bill."

"You both lived in the sewer tunnels, didn't you?"

"We were neighbors. Now we're roommates. We share a house. When Troy and Sally get back from their honeymoon, we'll have a cookout in the back yard. You're invited."

"Thanks," said Andy. "Let me know when, and I'll try to make it. Assuming, that is, I've caught the killer by then."

"I know you'll do it, Lieutenant. You're real smart."

"Andy, Rat. Call me Andy."

"Right, Andy. See ya around."

George was viewing eyeballs through a microscope when Andy entered the lab.

"Hello, George," said Andy.

George looked up from the microscope. "You must have talked with Rat," he said. "Rat's the only guy who calls me George."

"I met him in the hall. He's an interesting guy."

"You don't know the half of it, Lieutenant. He's a hero. A real hero."

"I heard what he did in the tunnels."

"He and Captain Nolan saved my butt from the Butcher," said George. "Did you know Rat was a hero in the Army, too?"

"No."

"He earned a whole bunch of medals. He was wounded four times. He saved a dozen soldiers by killing two enemy snipers while severely injured."

"I understand you're a physicist," said Andy. "How come you're working here in the morgue?"

"Long story, Lieutenant. I got this job because I have the requisite lab skills. And because both Nolans recommended me."

"So what have you learned about the current murders?"

"Our killer used a cheap icepick made with brittle Chinese steel. I'm surprised it didn't break. Whoever used it knew what he was doing. Straight in and out with a minimum of torque."

"Knew what he was doing? Are you saying he's done this before?"

"Not necessarily. But he has superb fine motor control. I suspect he's familiar with delicate instruments and knows exactly how to handle them."

"Like a surgeon?"

"Like a surgeon. Or maybe a machinist who measures exact tolerances with a micrometer. Or maybe he's an artist or sculptor. Someone with excellent fine motor skills and good hand to eye coordination."

"But not your average Joe."

"No, not your average Joe. This guy has special skills, Lieutenant. Superb dexterity. The ability to improvise. He's highly trained. He thinks quickly on his feet. He displayed perfect hand and eye coordination. Not many people can do that. He's the kind of guy who can chew gum, whistle Dixie, and walk at the same time."

"What makes you think he can do that?"

"He moved fast, didn't he? Not a motion wasted once he began to act. He took out two eyeballs, then moved immediately to the next victim and repeated the process. He punctured eight eyes in under eight minutes. When one woman raised her hand to block the weapon, he didn't pause. He penetrated the hand completely without hitting bone. As soon as he finished, he left. Like a computer running an algorithm, this guy's mind ran his executable program to completion and exited. Job over. Do you want to run the program again? Yes or no?"

"What's an algorithm?" Andy had a bachelor's degree in computer science, and he certainly knew what an algorithm was. He just wanted to see if George really knew what he was talking about or only making things up and using big words to appear impressive.

"A set of step by step instructions for completing an operation in a specified order. We use algorithms in mathematics and computers to solve problems via a well-defined reasoning process. An algorithm is a logical way of reasoning that processes input and analyses data in a specific sequence."

"Are you saying this guy's mind works like a computer?"

"All human minds work like computers. Or, rather, all computers work like human minds. Computers were modeled on our brains. This guy's brain, however, is wired differently than most. He has well-defined connections between parts of his brain that coordinate motor function with sensory input, executive control with the limbic system. He can think, feel, and act at the same time. I'm not able to do that. I know of few who can."

"I don't understand," said Andy.

"The average Joe needs time to think before he can act. One part of the brain—the executive control center—evaluates sensory input by recalling long-term memories and comparing the current situation to others an organism has previously encountered. It recalls sights, sounds, feelings, smells, and tastes from the past and makes a comparison. Then it selects the appropriate action and signals the motor cortex to execute movements. For most people, there is a slight delay time for processing of information. Our killer is able to act and react with the minimum possible delay. It's as if he has parallel processers at work simultaneously inside his brain. He doesn't question his actions as you or I might do. He simply acts. He never stops to think. He never worries if his actions will harm others. What other people think, feel, or do matters nothing to him. He responds automatically to sensory input. He acts entirely on impulse."

George paused to catch his breath. Then he added, "Of course, this is purely speculation on my part. I'm not a medical doctor, a psychiatrist, or a criminologist. I tend to see similarities with things I know. I was once a mathematician and considered myself a scientist. I don't know much about people."

"Sounds to me you know a lot," said Andy. "Thanks for the lecture, professor."

"It did sound like I was lecturing, didn't it? Get me going, and I can't stop. Core dump. Everything I've been thinking about just spills out."

"Has Doctor Stowe completed the autopsies?"

"He's got two sewn up. He went home to get some sleep. He's pulling double duty while Doctor Brightson—I mean, Doctor Nolan—is away on her honeymoon."

"Have the personal effects been inventoried?"

"Yeah. Let me get you copies."

George returned with a handful of printouts. "That includes everything we brought in with the bodies. Clothing, jewelry, purses, wallets, contents of pockets, cell phones."

"Definitely rules out robbery as a motive," Andy said, glancing over the inventory. "Cash, jewelry, cell phones, credit cards, and IDs weren't touched."

"Your techs went through call history on the cell phones. They also got a complete history of internet usage and text messages. I'm sure they'll give you copies."

"You're the only one left in the lab?" Andy asked.

"Your guys went home at seven," George answered. "I'll stick around until noon. I don't have to be back tonight until eleven. We have two medical technologists in the office down the hall who work day shift. They'll come over and offer me a break as soon as they finish what the Doc gave them to do. We're a bit short-handed in case you haven't noticed. Doctor Nolan is on vacation, and so is the day lab assistant. Two other guys quit, and the coroner hasn't hired replacements yet."

"I'm glad you're here, George," said Andy. "You've been a big help. Thank you."

George beamed as if it was the first time in a long time that anyone had praised him or thanked him.

When Andy left the lab, George went back to work examining eyeballs as if he expected to see reflected in the retinas the last thing the victims saw before they died: the face of the killer.

CHAPTER THREE

You finish work at nine PM and return home to your apartment by nine-fifteen. The four walls seem no different than a thousand other places you have lived, and you take no note of the floral pattern on the faded wallpaper. You have lived in this place nearly six months now, paying rent week by week, and those four walls were boring the very first day. Now they are unbearable.

You sit cross-legged on the hardwood floor. There are no rugs or carpets covering the bare floor, no chairs, no furniture of any kind. You rented a cheap one-room unfurnished walk-up on the third floor of an old house, and this is what you're stuck with. The sole bathroom is downstairs on the second floor, all the way at the far end of the hall. When the bathroom is being used by other tenants—there are three people living on the second floor, one person plus the building manager on the first, and the other two small rooms on the third floor are currently unoccupied—you use an empty coffee can. Later, when the bathroom is free, you empty the can into the toilet and rinse out the can in the sink. You are well aware of how the expression "Going to the can" originated. You know lots of other useful things, too.

You know how to live always at the ready. You keep your clothes in two canvas duffel bags in one corner of the room near the only window. Besides what you're wearing, all you own is in those duffel bags. Six t-shirts and two pairs of jeans, six pairs of socks, two pairs of shoes and one pair of boots are neatly packed in one of the duffels along with your shaving equipment—an old-fashioned straight razor, leather razor strap, shaving cup, shaving soap, and shaving brush—plus two towels, one wash cloth, a bar of

Ivory soap, a can of lighter fluid, and a metal drinking cup. Neatly folded in the other duffel are a wool overcoat, two pairs of gloves, a dress-up Sunday-go-to-meeting navy-blue suit, a white dress shirt, two neckties, a handkerchief, and a few odds and ends. You own no underpants because they cramp your style and you don't wear them.

In your front pants pockets are a Swiss Army knife, a silver Zippo lighter, a handful of change, the key to your apartment and the key to your car. In the left back pocket is your wallet with driver's license, a fake social security card, a miniature passport that will get you into and out of Canada or Mexico with no questions, and several ATM cards. None of your identification is in your real name, although the ATM card does link to real bank accounts.

When you close your eyes, you can see the blonde dancing in front of you. She is as real to you as if she were alive. You don't regret killing her, because her death was necessary at the time. She lives on in your memory. What more could she ask for?

You tell yourself tonight is a good night to catch up on sleep you missed last night. You lie down on the bare floor, stretch out your legs, and wait for sleep to come. You never have trouble sleeping. You can turn your mind on and off at will.

You sleep fully dressed in case you need to move fast. Even when you sleep, you remain aware of your surroundings. Should a sound awaken you, you can be on your feet and out the door or window with your duffels—one strapped to each shoulder—in seconds. Your car is parked on the street only a block away.

But tonight your mind remains too active for sleep. Each time you close your eyes the blonde appears.

After an hour of waiting for sleep, you get up and pace the hardwood floor in your Reeboks. The room is only ten feet by twelve feet, and getting smaller by the minute as the walls close in on you. You go around in circles as you pace back and forth, back and forth, back and forth.

Someone in the apartment below you pounds on the plaster ceiling with a cane. It makes you mad, and you stomp your Reeboks down even harder on the bare floor. *Take that, you piss ant. If you pound on the ceiling one more time, I'm going to come down there and pound on your head.* You keep on pacing. Back and forth. Back and forth.

You hear the cane hit the ceiling again. You stomp harder.

He pounds, you stomp. He pounds harder, you stomp harder. It's become a game.

He stops pounding, but you keep pacing. Back and forth. Back and forth. Once you start in motion, you tend to stay in motion.

Now you hear him pounding on the door to your room instead of the ceiling. He's not knocking like a civilized person. He's pounding on the fucking door like a maniac. In a minute, he'll try the door and find it unlocked.

You know you shouldn't let him open that door. You know what will happen if he does.

But you don't care. You've been cooped up all day at work, and now you feel cooped up in this goddamn rat-hole, a piss-poor excuse for an apartment. You know you baited the guy, deliberately stomped your feet on the floor above his head, because you knew he would come up here to confront you.

And you know what you're going to do next, don't you?

You let him open the door.

He's an old guy, barely worth your talents. But you've gone this far, so you might as well go all the way.

"What the hell's going on up here?" he angrily asks before he sees your face. You didn't bother to turn on the single overhead light, and the room is dark. "It sounds like a whole herd of elephants…"

"Cockroaches," you say. "My apartment is filled with cockroaches. They're everywhere. You have them, too? I already squashed a bunch of them, but there's too many for one man to kill them all. You want to help me kill cockroaches? Come on in." You step toward him and he sees your face in the light from the hallway.

You see the fear in his eyes as he starts to back away from the door. Either he's scared of cockroaches or he's scared of you. But you're too quick for him to get away. You lunge forward with the key to your apartment wedged between the index and middle fingers of your left hand. The sharp point of the key enters his right eyeball and the serrations along the bottom edge of the key rip the eyeball apart.

You push the key in as far as it will go. The sheer force of your thrust drives the tip into the brain, severing vital connections with the motor cortex and the speech centers. He can't move, can't speak, can't scream. You feel life leave him as you shove him hard against the wall.

Your hands are covered with sticky blood and gooey fluids that erupted from the punctured eyeball. This time the spray missed your face and clothes.

You extract the key and allow the body to drop to the floor. You wipe your hands on the dead man's clothes. Then you drag the body into your apartment and douse the body with lighter fluid from the nearly-full can you keep in one of your duffel bags. You spray the rest of the lighter fluid on the walls, on the floor. You drop the empty can, pick up your duffels, open the window, and pop the top of your Zippo one-handed. You are half-way out the window when you spin the wheel, the steel wheel grinds sparks from the flint, the wick ignites, and you toss the lit lighter at the lighter-fluid-covered body on the floor. You hear a whoosh! as the body ignites, yellow and blue flames already spreading to floor and walls, and you jump three stories to the ground. You land on the soft duffel bags filled with clothes, roll to your right, and you're off and running toward your car. Behind you flames light up the night sky as the old wood-frame house becomes an inferno.

You are in your car and already two blocks away when the fire reaches the gas lines in the basement. The resulting explosion rocks your car and you have to fight to control the wheel. Fortunately, you are too far away for any of the flaming debris to reach you.

Tomorrow, you tell yourself, you will need to buy a new can of lighter fluid and a new Zippo.

And you'll need to look for a new apartment.

Rat got the first call at 11:16 PM. The caller said there was a huge house fire at 2306 Elm and flames were already leaping through the roof, sparks dancing in the night air. Rat dispatched the fire department with a 10-75.

The second telephone call came in almost immediately. Other 911 call-takers, too, were inundated with calls about the same fire. The threat level had now escalated to a second alarm fire, a fire in progress that could easily spread to surrounding buildings.

When the explosion occurred, it quickly became a full four-alarm fire. Every piece of fire equipment in the area—plus ambulances and police cars to cordon off the area around the fire—was routed to 2306 Elm. Several people who were trying to evacuate the house were reported killed by the explosion, and one caller said he saw a man he identified as the building manger blown to bits running out of the burning building.

Rat knew that block of Elm Street was fire-prone. All the houses on Elm were extremely old, built sometime around World War I, and most were constructed mainly of wood. They were tinderboxes waiting for the first sign of a spark. The hot, dry weather didn't help, either. Temps had been in the mid-nineties earlier today, and the temperature was still above eighty degrees.

There had been another fire only three months ago near the end of the same block, and that house had burned to the ground before the fire eventually burned itself out.

Since there were reported fatalities at this fire, Rat was certain George would be called to the scene along with Dr. Stowe. Andy Sinnott would also be there with his crime scene team. Every available patrolman had already been dispatched.

Rat wished he could be there, too. But he was badly needed here. He had a job to do answering telephones. Right now, his job was probably more important than anyone's other than the firemen. After the fire was contained, others would go to work to recover bodies. The city's chief arson investigator was also on the scene. Until arson could be ruled out, deaths caused by the fire would be considered homicides.

Calls continued to come in from anxious residents in nearby houses who wondered if they needed to evacuate. Rat told them that the deputy fire chief on the scene would decide who to evacuate and when. They didn't need to leave until firemen told them to leave.

One woman who called was wheezing and gasping for breath. She said she was severely asthmatic, and the smoke in the air made it so she couldn't breathe even after using a rescue inhaler. Rat immediately sent paramedics to her residence with emergency oxygen. The woman was taken to Bryson Memorial Medical Center to be treated for acute respiratory distress.

There were also the usual accidents, heart attacks, robberies, and false alarms that happened every night. Just because the big fire on Elm consumed most of the city's emergency resources, it didn't mean the city could neglect emergencies elsewhere. Shit happened, especially on nights when the moon was nearly full.

Eight nearby municipalities sent assistance. Not everyone operated on the same radio frequency nor had the same computer access in their squad cars or ambulances that Rat expected from local first responders. Things seemed to get more complicated as the night wore on.

2306 Elm was a total loss and houses on both sides—2302 and 2310—were consumed in flames, the flames spreading. Several garages and nearby residences had already caught fire, and even grass and weeds and bushes and trees were igniting. Two firemen had just been injured when the burning wooden floor they were traversing to rescue children trapped on the second floor of 2314 collapsed under their weight. Other firemen had to go in to rescue not only the children but their injured comrades as well. By the time they got the children out of the burning building, one child was dead from smoke inhalation and two other children were in critical condition.

To make matters worse, water pressure in the hydrants had dropped. People all over town had been watering lawns for weeks, and water stored in Riverdale's reservoirs was dangerously low even before firemen opened six hydrants to supply pumpers. City engineers were working desperately to divert water from other areas of the city to mains on the west side. Rat wondered why they couldn't just tap into all that water in the river. It would make things a whole lot easier if they could.

By three AM, the fire had consumed five houses, three garages, and killed eight people.

By six AM, the fire began to come under control. Not much was left of the twenty-three hundred block of Elm Street. Nearly eighty people had to be evacuated, and half that number were left homeless.

The State fire marshal had been notified, and the state was sending its own arson investigators after local investigators requested their assistance.

When Rat was relieved by Richard Giolitto a few minutes after six AM, Rat left the call center on the eighteenth floor of the City-County Public Safety Building and drove across the river to Elm Street to see the damage for himself. Barricades and yellow crime scene tape closed off Elm in the 1900 block. Broadcast vans from all the local television stations were lined up on both sides of the street just this side of the police line. The air reeked of smoke, and a gray haze blocked out the sun. Today promised to be even hotter than yesterday. Tomorrow would be the first official day of summer.

Four blocks west, the street was filled with fire trucks and squad cars packed in like sardines. More than a hundred men and women still worked frantically to put remaining fires out. Smoldering embers started new blazes that had to be subdued. Although the night was over, the fire raged on.

Where once century-old houses had stood, now there was only smoking rubble. It was as if a giant fist had swooped out of the sky and smashed the 2300 block flat. Houses directly across the street were fire-blackened and a few had singed roofs. Houses behind, those facing the 2300 block of Maple Street, looked badly damaged. Most would need to be demolished.

Rat didn't attempt to get closer. He had done his part, now it was time others did theirs. He mourned for those who had lost their lives in the blaze, those who had died from smoke inhalation, those who were yet to die from burns over most of their bodies. Rat had lived in Riverdale all of his life, less three years in the military, and he mourned the loss of familiar landmarks almost as much as he mourned the loss of human life. If people were the mind of this city, buildings were its body and streets were its soul. Rat felt this strongly because he had lived beneath the streets of this city for five years, and had wandered the streets above ground nearly every night. Streets had personalities most people didn't see.

Streets were how people moved about in life, and streets were where people lived. Not only were children taught their own names at an early age, they were taught the name of the street they lived on in case they got lost. Home wasn't only where the heart was. Home was the address where one lived.

Rat got back in his car, drove across the South Street Bridge, and headed for his own home at 8617 East Fifteenth Street. He didn't expect George home anytime soon.

CHAPTER FOUR

None of the night bartenders Andy had talked with so far recognized the victims, though one bartender said she couldn't be absolutely certain. Andy was disappointed he had only been able to show the drivers' license pictures to eight bartenders before the police department dispatcher called his cell phone. The next place on the list of downtown drinking establishments, Upstairs and Downstairs, would have to wait because dispatch said someone had just died in an explosion at a house fire on Elm Street.

Elm was only a few blocks north of his present location, but the 2300 block was a good mile and a half farther west. Andy was driving his personal car which had no siren. But he did have high intensity red and blue bulbs installed in his emergency flashers. He turned the flashers on and broke a few speed limits. There was little traffic on the road other than emergency vehicles this close to midnight, but Andy saw a whole shitload of fire trucks and ambulances headed in the same direction he was headed.

It looked like the entire fire department had converged on West Elm. He saw several hook and ladders with ladders raised, a half-dozen pumpers already spraying water on rooftops, dozens of firefighters running around in full gear. The deputy fire chief had just arrived. Police cars were positioned at both ends of Elm Street blocking the street, and patrolmen were busily stringing yellow crime scene tape across the sidewalks. He heard more sirens approaching from all directions.

Andy parked his new Honda in the 1700 block of Elm where he thought it was out of the way and relatively safe. He walked the rest of the way, and it felt good to stretch his legs.

Flames were leaping from the roofs of several buildings six blocks west as fire crews directed sprays from huge hoses. All that water generated lots of smoke but did little to put out the fire.

As Andy got closer, he thought he smelled chlorine like he sometimes smelled in swimming pools, and he realized he smelled natural gas. Because natural gas was colorless and odorless, chlorine gas was often added to give heating and cooking gas a distinctive odor. It was the only way to detect a gas leak without special equipment. Fire and gas were a deadly combination. Gas was evidently leaking from underground lines that had ruptured from the first explosion. Natural gas was feeding the flames. Firemen would fight a losing battle until the gas company shut off the supply to the entire block. And if enough gas accumulated in confined spaces, there could be additional explosions.

Andy called the dispatcher on his cell phone and requested the gas company be notified immediately of the situation. Maybe they had already been informed of the gas leak by the fire department, but redundant requests might impress them of the urgency. "Tell the gas company that they better get the gas supply shut off soon, or there will be more explosions. Tell them if anyone dies in those explosions, I'll hold the company's executives personally responsible for negligent homicide."

Additional fire trucks arrived. Andy noted that several had come from surrounding towns.

Art Lewinski, trying to keep camera crews from several of the television stations behind a barricade, was being inundated with questions.

"Is arson suspected?"

"Is it true several people were killed in an explosion?"

"How many people are dead already?"

Art just growled "Keep back" and "Stay behind the line."

"Lieutenant!" shouted one reporter who recognized Andy. Andy had inadvertently confirmed, simply by his presence here, that there had been a homicide or suspected homicide. Why else would the head of homicide be at a house fire?

Andy let Lewinski handle the reporters. Art hated reporters

with a true passion—"They make me look fat on TV," Art claimed—and he would make sure they didn't cross the line unless it was over his dead body.

The only ones Art let past the barricades were firemen, policemen, paramedics, and the familiar crime scene team, including people from the coroner's office. When Harvey Fredriks and Doctor Stowe arrived, Art waved their panel truck through, and now the reporters were convinced there had been multiple homicides. Plus the arrival of the city's chief arson inspector only added fat to the fire, and they smelled an even bigger story brewing.

It was much too hot for Andy to try to get close to the victims. Andy waited in the 2000 block with Doctor Stowe and Harvey Fredriks, or "George" as Rat called him, for the fires to come under control or burn themselves out. Red Cross and Salvation Army volunteers had set up tables with coffee urns and bottles of water for rescue workers and displaced residents. There was a first aid tent with doctors and paramedics dispensing face masks and bottles of oxygen. The whole scene reminded Andy of a summer street carnival complete with bright floodlights, blinking red and blue MARS lights, raised ladders, lots of noise, and crowds of people. All that seemed missing was cotton candy.

"How many dead?" asked Stowe.

"At least one," said Andy. "I've seen several ambulances come and go with lights and sirens. I suspect other victims are burned to a crisp or buried in rubble. We won't be able to get to them until things cool down."

"What started the fire?" asked George.

"No one knows. I was told it began on the top floor of 2306 Elm around eleven and spread to the other buildings. Several people were killed or severely injured when a gas line exploded in the basement. All the buildings are old, but they were all occupied and most are multiple-family dwellings. Careless smoking might have started the fire if someone dropped a lit cigarette on a carpet. We won't know until the arson investigators get a chance to go through the rubble."

No sooner did firefighters get one blaze under control than another erupted. Several firefighters had to be taken off the line and treated for heat stroke. But the fire raged on through the night, and dawn saw little improvement. It was well after six when the last fire was put out, though hot spots still existed and flared up occasionally. What helped immensely was the gas company turning off natural gas, the electric company cutting power to the electrical wires, and city engineers diverting water from wells and reservoirs to the Elm Street mains.

Andy was proud of the way the entire city had pulled together in a time of crisis. Not just Riverdale, but the whole county and surrounds. Some of the firefighters and equipment had come from twenty miles away. Sheriff's deputies had assisted in rerouting traffic so city patrolmen could respond to other emergencies. Hospitals had sent medical personnel to treat injured firefighters and residents on site. Everyone had pitched in.

Now it was time for Andy to go to work. He joined firefighters and arson investigators looking for survivors. They found evidence of nine bodies, but no survivors.

2306 had burned so hot that three of the bodies were only ash. Doctor Stowe did locate badly-charred pieces of bone and teeth among some of the ashes, but it was impossible to tell if the victims were male or female, much less their ages and identities. Some ashes had been scattered when the floors collapsed or when gas lines exploded. It was impossible to tell for certain how many people perished inside 2306.

The building manager and another man whom witnesses said were attempting to escape the fire when the gas lines ignited were recognizable only from the location of their remains.

That accounted for five of the six reported residents of 2306 Elm Street. One resident—a man—remained missing. Four other fatalities were next-door neighbors—two adults and two children—who must have been asleep in 2310 when the explosion sent flaming debris into the house adjacent to 2306. They awoke to an inferno that quickly engulfed the second floor, cutting off escape. They were badly burned, but their bodies still looked human. Doctor Stowe photographed all of the victims and the areas immediately surrounding the bodies.

Add to the death toll the asphyxiated child from 2614 who had died of smoke inhalation, and the total was at least eleven. No one knew for certain if the man who occupied the third floor apartment at 2306 was home or not when the fire began. He may have been out of the house. Perhaps he worked nights. Unfortunately, no one knew the man's name or what he looked like except the apartment manager.

The building itself, Andy had learned from the chief arson investigator, was owned by an out-of-town real estate trust. Many of the older houses on this side of the river had been bought for next to nothing by rich investors. Even with relatively cheap rents, owners made a killing on each of the properties. It didn't make sense that the owner would burn up a cash cow to collect insurance.

But the inspectors were suspicious because the building had burned so incredibly fast. Some kind of accelerant must have been used to kick off the blaze. If investigators found evidence of arson, then all ten deaths were homicides. Otherwise the ten deaths would be classified as tragic accidents.

Andy sent his team of crime scene investigators home. They could comb the scene thoroughly for clues after everything cooled down, but right now things were still too hot and chaotic. One of the arson investigators, dressed in asbestos protective gear, walked around with a video camera to document the destruction. Andy would automatically get a digital copy if it was determined arson caused the fire.

Harvey Fredriks walked back to his truck and returned with a portable vacuum cleaner that ran on batteries. He vacuumed up what ashes he could find of each of the victims as soon as they cooled, changing the bag and carefully cleaning the hose after each body. He sealed each bag and labeled it with time and location. Doctor Stowe supervised, pointing to places where the ashes of human remains were scattered. Stowe placed physical markers to indicate the exact location of each body removed from the scene. It was a long and tedious process that took hours.

Andy followed the chief arson investigator around as he visually inspected the rubble and took his own set of photographs. This was the first time Andy had investigated deaths at a fire, and he had little idea what to look for. He vaguely knew the investigators were searching for origin and cause: where the fire began and what started it. He told the chief arson investigator he didn't see how they would be able to determine origin and cause from the mess the fire had left behind.

"It helps to have a real good understanding of the chemistry and physics of fire development to determine origin and cause," explained Larry Miller, the city's chief arson investigator. Miller was in his early fifties, looked physically fit, and had short hair and a receding hairline. He wore heavy rubber boots and asbestos-lined gloves. "We find that most fires are simply accidents that were easily preventable. Old newspapers stacked next to a water heater, for example. Fewer than ten percent of all the fires I've investigated in my career proved to be arson. But more than a third had deliberate and significant code violations. I'm not looking for signs of arson right now. I'm looking for fire patterns, what happened when the fire spread. That will lead me back to the origin. Then we can examine the origin for cause. We proceed from areas of least damage to areas of more significant damage. Let's start with 2314 and work back to 2306."

2314 was partially intact. Like most of the houses on the street, this had been a two-story wood-frame building with an attic that had been converted to living quarters. The family that lived on the second floor used the attic as a bedroom for two of their three children. All three children had been asleep when the fire began. Since the attic had no windows, firefighters had to cross the wooden second floor to access the attic. That floor had collapsed and two firefighters had been injured. By the time other firefighters got to the children, one of the kids had died of smoke inhalation and the other two were badly burned. All three children and the firefighters had been evacuated to Bryson Memorial Hospital.

The roof was gone, consumed by flames, and the second and third floors were mostly gone. Miller took pictures of the wreckage from several angles.

2310, like 2306, was little more than heaps of ash. All of the residents had miraculously escaped, though several had suffered second and third degree burns. Miller told Andy he'd interview those people at the hospital later in the day.

2306 was obviously where the fire had originated. It had once been a two-story apartment building that had been converted into an eight-room rooming house. Miller said there had been two large apartments on the first floor, three on the second floor plus a bathroom, and the attic had been converted into three smaller rooms.

Only one of the attic rooms was believed to have been occupied. Several years ago, Miller said, the city issued a building permit to add windows to each of the third floor rooms but not an emergency exit. There had been a back wooden stairway to the second floor but no outside exit from the third, a clear code violation for rooming houses. If anyone had been on the third floor at the time of the fire, they likely perished. If a resident tried to jump from a third floor window, he would have been killed or injured in the fall. There was no sign of a body on the side of the building where the windows were located.

"After we're certain we have pictures and everything has cooled," Miller said, "we'll begin sifting through the ashes for evidence. In many ways, we're like archaeologists digging at the ruins of Pompeii centuries after Vesuvius erupted. We try to reconstruct what life must have been like before a cataclysmic event occurred. Unlike Pompeii, however, few things under the ash have been preserved."

"What's your guess at this point?" Andy asked. "Is it arson or not?"

"Probably not," said Miller. "The buildings were old, the wood was dried out, any spark might have set it off. I'll know more in a day or two. But right now I'd say it was an accident waiting to happen. The state sent some of their boys to help with the investigation. Maybe they'll see something I don't."

"Then I'm not going to stick around," said Andy. "Good luck with your investigation. Let me know your final conclusions."

Andy waved at Stowe and Fredriks as he walked the six blocks back to his car. Lewinski had gone home. Art had been replaced at the barricades by a rookie and his training partner. Most of the reporters had also left, now that the fire was out and nothing but rubble remained. Rubble wasn't as visually interesting as flames.

It was already afternoon when Andy climbed into bed. He intended to grab eight hours of sleep and resume interviewing bartenders around eleven. When his phone rang at 4:29 PM, he sleepily answered it without checking the caller ID. He heard Miller, the arson investigator, tell him they had found evidence of arson after all. "We found pieces of a barely identifiable can of lighter fluid buried in the ashes of 2306," Miller said. "And guess what else nearby?"

"What?" Andy managed to ask through a yawn.

"A Zippo cigarette lighter."

"So?" asked Andy.

"So someone used the lighter and lighter fluid to deliberately set the fire," said Miller.

"Are you sure?" asked Andy, forcing himself awake.

"Sure enough to reclassify the fire as arson," said Miller. "And that makes the arsonist a murderer of at least twelve people."

"Twelve? We only found ten bodies."

"Two additional children died in the hospital from smoke inhalation and burns," said Miller. "And one of the residents of 2310 is so critical the doctors don't think he'll survive."

"Shit!' said Andy, struggling to get out of bed.

You slept in your car overnight. It wasn't the first time you've had to sleep in your car, and it probably won't be the last. The downtown parking deck where you spent the night remained relatively empty until seven, and then office workers began arriving. Parking was by permit only from eight AM until six PM, and you moved out of the lot at 7:30 because you didn't know how often police checked the lot during the day. The last thing you need is for cops to notice your stolen license plates.

So you drive to a shopping mall and park in the large lot that surrounds the mall. Though most of the stores don't open until nine or ten, some employees are already arriving and your car doesn't look out of place in the back of the lot. You manage to get another couple hours of sleep.

Sleeping in your car with the windows rolled down certainly seems much cooler than sleeping in that stupid third-floor attic with no cross ventilation. You learned long ago to sleep where and when you can, and sleeping sitting up in a car seat is really quite comfortable. You've slept in worse places.

You wait until the mall opens at nine. Then you take your shaving gear and a clean t-shirt from your duffel bags, find the men's room, and wash up. There are few customers walking the mall this early in the day, and they're virtually all women. The men's room is empty. You lay out your shaving cup, brush, and shaving soap on the sink. You run the tap until the water is steaming. You wet the shaving brush and use it to lather up the soap. Then you brush the shaving soap onto your face.

You hold the leather strap in your right hand and the open straight razor with your left. You strop the blade against the leather, up and down, one side of the blade sharpening on the upstroke and the other side on the down stroke. Six times is sufficient to hone a carbon-steel edge. Your nimble fingers move the razor with surgical precision.

No one knows how to use a straight razor any more, except maybe a barber or hair stylist. It's a pity. First, Gillette scared men into switching to safety razors by suggesting an open blade could slip and men might accidentally slit their own throats while using a straight razor. Then Wilkinson invented stainless-steel blades and Schick invented double, triple and quarto silicone-coated parallel mini-blades. Neither type of blades could be re-sharpened, and men had to constantly spend money purchasing new razor blades. Electric razors, too, had a limited life. The heads wore out and had to be replaced at least once a year, plus you were dependent on electricity for recharging the batteries. All that wasted time and money.

A straight razor, on the other hand, lasted forever. You could sharpen the carbon-steel edges of a straight-razor with a whetstone once a year. Shaving soap was relatively inexpensive, and a bar lasted months. You could always use ordinary soap in a pinch. Even the soap from the dispenser in the men's room would do.

Plus, a straight razor produces a much closer shave than a safety razor or an electric shaver. That's important when your hair is dark and your beard grows fast.

You deftly slice through the stubble on your chin, down your neck, under your nose. When you first learned to control the razor, you often nicked your skin and had to clot blood with toilet paper. You haven't cut yourself in years because you know how to balance the blade lightly between thumb and middle finger, keeping the blade at the ideal angle, using the index finger only to provide proper pressure, much like using a scalpel. Shaving is an art, and you're an artist.

You rinse your face with tap water and wipe your face dry with your t-shirt. Then you wash the t-shirt in the sink using hand soap from the dispenser. You scrub it with both hands, rinse it, and wring it out. You can place it on the back seat of your car and it should dry in an hour in the hot sun.

You brush your teeth with a toothbrush and water, no toothpaste. Toothpaste isn't necessary to get the teeth clean. You rinse your mouth with a handful of water.

You slip the fresh t-shirt over your head, slide your arms through the sleeves. The t-shirt doesn't muss your closely-cropped hair. When your hair grows out more than half an inch, you simply shave it off. You never have to comb your hair because it never gets long enough to comb.

You wrap your shaving gear in your wet t-shirt and return to your car. You have two hours to kill before you need to be at work.

You watch young moms pushing strollers. It's going to be another hot day and some of these young girls are barely dressed. They don't think there will be men watching them during the day. They're wrong.

You watch a woman who parked in the next row bend over to place infant twins into a double stroller. She may be as young as eighteen, too young to be saddled with children. It's a beautiful day, and she wants to be out and about. She thinks the mall is a safe place. Little does she know! There are *no* safe places.

You watch her walk into the mall, and for a moment you think about following her. But then two other women catch your eye. You watch them walk. They wear short shorts and halters, their lithe bodies bouncing. You memorize their movements, capture their images in your mind like a fashion photographer taking pictures of models. Click! Clickety-click-click! Turn this way, darling. That's right. Now show me some skin.

You become so fascinated by the parade of half-naked women that you lose track of time. The sun is almost straight overhead when you realize it's nearly noon already. Where did the morning go?

Because you didn't bother to look for another apartment, you'll have to sleep in your car again tonight. There's no time to stop to buy a lighter or lighter fluid, either, and you feel naked without your Zippo. After work, you can stop in a Walgreens or CVS and pick up a new lighter and a can of lighter fluid. You don't smoke—you have never smoked, such a disgusting and dirty habit—but you need a good lighter for other reasons. A cheap butane lighter simply won't do.

You turn the key in the Matrix's ignition and drive slowly out of the mall without attracting attention to yourself, turn left on Main Street, and head back downtown.

It's time to go to work.

CHAPTER FIVE

All that was left of the Zippo was a bent metal shell. The cotton stuffing inside the case had burned to very fine ash, and so had the wick. Even the flint was gone. Miller said the flint had probably splintered to pieces from the heat.

But the rest of the lighter remained intact, the once highly-polished chrome badly tarnished and misshapen. The lid was open and Andy could see the steel guts had been blackened by flames

"Where did you find the lighter?" Andy asked, returning the sealed evidence bag to Larry Miller. Andy sat in an uncomfortable straight-backed chair in Miller's rather Spartan-looking office on the third floor of the main fire station. Miller himself looked terrible. He hadn't had any sleep in more than thirty-six hours, and it showed. He still smelled like smoke.

"Buried in the ashes of 2306," said Miller.

"Was the lid completely open when you found it?" Andy asked Miller.

"Yes."

Miller handed Andy another evidence bag. This one contained a hunk of tin that had once been painted yellow with some red and some blue lettering. Most of the colored paint had been burned off.

"That's part of an old Ronsonol can that contained Naphtha. Naphtha is a condensate of natural gas, and it's highly volatile and flammable. Zippo acquired the Ronsonol brand in 2010 and changed the formula, phasing Naphtha out of the formulary entirely. Most lighter fluid is now sold in plastic squeeze bottles, and has been for years. That can is twenty years old or older. They don't make them like that anymore."

"Why does finding a lighter and a can of lighter fluid make you so sure they were used to start the fire? Maybe someone simply had them in his room."

"First, because they were found so near the point of origin. Second, because nothing else that we found could have started the fire. There were no carpets or rugs, no curtains, nothing other than bedding that would have caught fire simply from stray sparks, and nothing that would have caused sparks. The wiring had been replaced recently by licensed electricians, brought up to code, and inspected by city inspectors. Yes, the floors were old wood, but the wood had been refinished and coated with polyurethane. A dropped cigarette or match would have gone out long before the polymer coating melted off and the floor ignited. Some kind of accelerant had to be used to start the blaze, because the blaze burned hot right from the start. I think the accelerant was the Naphtha in that old can of lighter fluid, and I think the initial spark came from that Zippo. Zippos have a windproof shield around the wick, and you can drop or toss a Zippo and the flame doesn't go out. I think the arsonist squirted lighter fluid on the floor and tossed a lit Zippo to torch the fumes. Naphtha also works as a solvent and can break down polyurethane coatings even after the polymer has cured. That would leave the floor vulnerable."

"Can you prove it?"

"Not conclusively. Not yet anyway. My lab people are working on it. When they complete the chemical analysis of the ashes, we'll know more. I have a mobile lab in a trailer at the scene, and we're shipping evidence to the state forensic labs for processing. That can take weeks, even months. Meanwhile, I'm reasonably sure there's an arsonist on the loose that killed a dozen people. That's why I notified you. It's your job, as well as mine, to find him."

"What was his motive for setting the fire?" asked Andy.

"Good question. I have no clue at this point."

"Neither have I," admitted Andy. "I'll send my guys around to interview neighbors. I'll send you copies of their reports."

"I worked with your predecessor, Troy Nolan, on a couple of cases, and with his predecessor, Carl Erickson," said Miller. "This is your first arson investigation, isn't it?"

"I studied the protocol in school," said Andy. "But this is my first chance to put what I learned into practice."

"Leave the rocket science to the scientists. That's what the lab people are for. What you need most are good investigative skills, people skills, and an open mind."

"I'll try to remember that," said Andy.

After leaving the fire station, Andy phoned Betty Halloran, Captain Troy Nolan's secretary in the Violent Crimes division office. Betty only worked until 5:00, so Andy left a message on her machine to alert the department first thing in the morning that the fire had been reclassified to arson and was the scene of multiple homicides that required investigation. Then Andy drove to the fire scene itself on Elm, checked to make sure the barricades and yellow police line tapes remained in place across both ends of the 2300 block, and surveyed the devastation in daylight. The street looked entirely different without all the emergency vehicles, fire trucks, floodlights, and billows of black smoke.

The only vehicle parked on the deserted street was the mobile laboratory van of the city's arson squad. Four men and one woman were working the rubble, carefully poking around in the wreckage. They wore white cotton coveralls, rubber boots, thick gloves, and face masks. They must be hotter than hell garbed in all that gear in 98 degree weather, thought Andy. He was sweating in short sleeves.

Last summer had been hot and dry and the summer before that, too; and this year promised to be a repeat. Violent crimes had a tendency to peak during summer months. It had been at the end of that hot summer two years ago that an insane serial killer the press labeled "the Pickaxe Butcher" had suddenly appeared. Andy had been instrumental in uncovering a link between the victims and the killer that revealed a motive for the grisly murders. Troy Nolan had been head of homicide then, and Andy was only one of Nolan's half-dozen crime scene techs working the case. After Sergeant Bill Bowers, Lieutenant Nolan's chief homicide investigator, was murdered by the Butcher, Andy had been promoted to Bowers' position on Nolan's recommendation. A year later, Andy was made head of homicide when Captain Carl Erickson retired. Nolan was promoted to Captain and replaced Erickson as the Violent Crimes honcho.

This summer was Andy's first as head of homicide. In only two days, even before summer officially began, sixteen homicides had occurred within his jurisdiction. With bodies piling up right and left and no clue where to find the killer or the arsonist, Andy felt totally overwhelmed. He was out of his element, surrounded by a sea of quicksand, and one wrong step would surely doom him.

Andrew Sinnott had never planned to be a cop. He had been a total nerd in high school, one of those quiet guys who spent all his time reading or exploring the internet. He hadn't gone out for sports, hadn't even attended any of the home games during football or basketball seasons. He didn't date, kept mostly to himself, and never seemed to have any friends. Had he really changed so much since high school?

Andy was born an only child, the unexpected gift to two past-their-prime parents who tried to protect him from the real world. He grew up believing Santa Claus and the Easter Bunny really existed—how else could one explain Christmas presents under the tree and colored eggs hidden throughout the house and yard—and it wasn't until he got to third grade that it dawned on him that other kids no longer believed in Santa or the Easter Bunny and he wondered why. It was in third grade that Andy also encountered his first extortionist and bully, a chubby kid named Pete Smith who was a whole year older than anyone else because Pete Smith had been held back to repeat third grade after doing poorly on a mandatory standardized reading test. Pete had great difficulty learning to read, and he consequently made fun of all those who were placed in the first reading group and sat in the front of the classroom. Andy was among those who sat in the front row, and Pete was relegated to the last desk in the back row. It wasn't until years later that Andy learned reading level was not the main criteria for seating. Andy had been placed in the front row because he was relatively short, and Pete assigned the last row because he was older and taller than everyone else.

He had lots of friends, because you were either his friend or you were his enemy, and no one wanted to be Pete's enemy. It pissed Pete off that Andy, besides being such a good reader, hadn't volunteered to be Pete's friend by giving Pete half his lunch. Pete's mother never packed a lunch for the boy, so he strong-armed others into relinquishing half their peanut butter and jelly sandwiches.

One morning, Pete snatched Andy's lunch bag out of Andy's hands when students were lined up outside the classroom waiting for the teacher to open the door. When Andy protested and tried to grab his bag back, Pete hit him in the face and gave Andy a bloody nose.

Andy remembered lying on the floor of the school, blood and snot draining into his mouth, his eyes filled with tears. The other children did nothing to help, and most of the boys and even some of the girls just laughed. It was the worst day of Andy's young life and served as a rude awakening. After that, Andy began paying closer attention to what was going on around him instead of being lost in thought.

Pete's mission in life seemed to be to torment Andy Sinnott relentlessly. Pete made it a point to pick on Andy nearly every day because Pete was four inches taller and a good thirty pounds heavier than Andy. When Andy complained to the teacher, Pete and his buddies ridiculed Andy for being a "tattle-tale," and they simply waited until Andy was walking home from school before beating him up. The system that Andy believed would always protect him failed to do so.

There was nothing that Andy could do but endure the abuse. He became even more of a loner, withdrawing into books. But instead of reading the fantasy stories that had been so much a part of his early childhood, he began reading every non-fiction book he could find in the school library, beginning with the World Book encyclopedia.

By the end of fourth grade, Andy had acquired a basic knowledge of biology, chemistry, psychology, geology, astronomy, and physics. He now knew neither Santa nor the Easter Bunny were real. They were merely myths. He no longer trusted anything his parents told him. He need to discover on his own what was true and what wasn't.

He began to question everything. He wanted to know why and how everything happened, the way everything worked. The more he read, the more he knew he didn't know enough. He felt he really needed to know everything. It was more than curiosity. Knowledge seemed to Andy to be necessary to his personal survival. What he didn't know might hurt him.

Eventually, Pete grew tired of picking on Andy. Andy was far too easy, so Pete began to pick on others. Pete was always getting into fights in fifth grade because he loved to fight. Andy was no fun because he never fought back.

By eighth grade, Pete had become a regular juvenile delinquent who missed days and even weeks of school. Andy learned Pete had been arrested, along with three older boys, for shooting pellet guns at passing car windows. Pete disappeared from Andy's life until high school, locked away in the juvenile detention center for two years of rehabilitation.

Pete returned from juvenile detention even worse than he had been before. Now Pete was not only doing drugs but dealing them. He sold pot and pills, and it was rumored he could get cocaine if anyone wanted it. Pete allegedly had connections with the drug underworld. He was a player in the real world, and he was still a bully.

Andy had long wondered what had made Pete the way he was. Pete seemed to have a need to be the center of attention, and he was seldom without an entourage following him around like lap dogs and sick puppies.

Andy had no such need. Andy was perfectly happy being a loner. He spent hours in either the school library or the public library because people like Pete seldom went near a library. Libraries had been the safest places to be when Andy was growing up.

But now Andy's curiosity got the better of him, and he began to watch Pete carefully from a safe distance. Pete had matured from the chubby kid Andy had known in grade school into a muscular teen nearly six feet tall with thick neck and broad shoulders. He obviously worked out, and he had let his sandy-colored hair grow out long. Pete was even trying to nurture a moustache. He was sixteen, going on seventeen. Andy still remained an awkward fifteen who didn't yet need to shave the soft peach-fuzz above his upper lip.

Pretty girls seemed unusually attracted to Pete's bad boy image, and Pete now had as many girls hanging around him as guys. Andy had started to notice girls a year or so ago, but he had no idea of how to attract them or even talk to them. Maybe he could learn something from watching Pete.

Pete never treated anyone nice, and girls were no exception. He grabbed girls whenever he wanted, touching them inappropriately in public, and none of the girls seemed to mind. Pete was a very physical person. He thought with his hands, not with his brains.

Andy, on the other hand, seldom thought about his own body at all. He knew human anatomy only from what he had studied in books. He knew how girls and boys differed from pictures he'd seen in books, mostly illustrative drawings like Henry Gray's, and he understood the location and function of every part of a human being, both inside and out. But he had never seen a live girl naked, nor had he touched one. He had never even kissed a girl. His mother kissed him on the forehead or the cheek, but he never kissed her back. He knew his mother loved him, and he loved her. Knowing it was enough. Neither had to show it. Like Santa or the Easter Bunny, love was something Andy believed existed but had never seen. Perhaps love was another myth and was only real if you believed in it.

Andy's parents were much older than the parents of his classmates, more like grandparents than parents. Andy's father was a certified public accountant, and his mother was a librarian at the local community college. When Andy was fifteen, his father was already sixty-two, and his mother fifty-five. They understood and expressed love verbally, not physically. Andy had a hard time believing his parents had ever had sex. But he supposed they must have, at least once, or he wouldn't be around to wonder about it. He wasn't surprised he had no siblings.

Andy didn't like to admit he was a lot like his parents, but he was. He understood things cerebrally, not physically. He lived in his head, and his body was merely an afterthought.

Andy had become a whiz with computers, and electronic devices replaced books in his life. Andy's parents were computer-literate and they upgraded regularly. Andy's mother even taught an introductory computer course to freshmen at the college, and she kept young Andy abreast on the latest developments in technology. Andy could use her login and password to access the college's databases, and he had entire libraries at his fingertips. He lived in a virtual world. The real world seemed more myth than reality.

Andy discovered he could track Pete digitally. He began with Pete Smith's birth record. Pete was the youngest of six siblings, all boys. His parents had divorced when he was five. His father had moved to the west coast and died in a boating accident when Pete was eight. Pete's mother worked nights as a waitress at an all-night greasy spoon. Pete's oldest brother was married and had two kids. He was a machinist in a non-union factory in Arkansas. The other four boys were unemployed. They lived at home with Pete and their mother in a rented trailer in a south-side trailer park.

Pete had multiple juvenile arrests, but the detailed record was inaccessible online. Pete's brothers had juvenile records, too. Compared to Andy's, Pete's childhood must have been hell. As the youngest of six boys, he was at the bottom of the pecking order at home. Was it any wonder Pete picked on other boys at school?

His mother must have had both hands full just trying to make ends meet. She worked the 11 PM to 7 AM shift at the diner. Add travel time in the ten-year-old Plymouth registered to her name to the time it took to get ready for work, and she had little time to supervise her children. Andy imagined the older boys were supposed to look out for and take care of the younger ones, but that probably never happened. Meals likely consisted of canned pasta and junk food. If Pete wanted a lunch for school, he had to make it himself or steal it from other kids. Andy already knew which option Pete preferred.

If only Andy had known in third grade what he knew now! He could have asked his own mother to make two lunches—his mother surely would have done that if Andy told her why—and Andy could have given one lunch to Pete. It would have made life so much simpler for both boys, and they might even have become friends. But Andy had no idea in third grade what Pete was going through at home. Andy hadn't been aware that other children had home lives vastly different than his. His world at that time had been limited by his own experiences. It wasn't until he began reading extensively and learned to look beyond himself that he became aware the world was more complex than he had imagined.

Andy continued to learn. Human interactions suddenly become fascinating to watch, and Andy yearned to experiment with real live people. He began by talking with some of his classmates. Andy knew all their names from class, but he had never said more than hello to any of them. He had earned straight As in school with one exception. He had consistently failed in the "Plays well with others" category. It wasn't that Andy was stupid. Far from it. But he was certainly ignorant.

Andy was completely ignorant of social conventions because neither he nor his family regularly engaged in social interactions. Most of what Andy knew he had learned from books, not from people. School for Andy was a place for learning about things, not a place for meeting and talking with other people. Talking to people took valuable time away from reading and thinking. Neither his father nor mother were gregarious or compulsive talkers, and they tended to bury their noses in books or newspapers. Andy's father sometimes followed financial news on cable television, but he also subscribed to *The Wall Street Journal, Barron's, Standard and Poor's*, and all of the weekly business magazines and read them religiously. Andy's parents had few friends outside the workplace. They seemed to treasure their time together so much that they spent their free time at home alone, but they understood each other so well they had little need to speak. It was enough just to be in the same house at the same time. Andy had accepted that as the norm and had thought all households were the same. Now he knew differently.

So, Andy asked himself, was the butterfly finally ready to break free of the cocoon? He knew puberty often caused physical and psychological changes in a person, and he suspected he was no exception. Had he grown wings yet? Could he fly? Or was he still a worm who was nowhere near morphed into anything beautiful?

He decided he needed an icebreaker to open conversation. He didn't watch much television, so he couldn't talk about his favorite TV show. He didn't even have a favorite show, though he did enjoy Nova on PBS. He didn't follow sports, so he couldn't talk about his favorite team. He certainly didn't have a favorite team, though he knew most sports teams were named after animals, such as lions and tigers broncos and bears. Andy barely knew what his high school teams were called, and he had no clue if it were currently basketball, football, or baseball season. He decided the weather was as good a topic of conversation as any. The weather was one of the few things everybody had in common.

Should he walk up to someone and ask, "What do you think about the weather?"

Andy spent two days working out exactly what to say before he finally walked up to a small group of boys getting umbrellas and raincoats out of hall lockers, and said, "This weather really sucks."

"Yeah, man," said Ron Pippel, a boy in Andy's home room. "I second that."

"What did you think about that quiz today in history?" Andy quickly asked Pippel who was also in Andy's American History class.

"That sucked, too," said Pippel.

"Yeah," agreed Andy. "I have trouble remembering dates."

"Join the club," said Pippel. "You can't remember dates? I thought you were supposed to be a brain, Sinnott. I thought you were supposed to know everything."

"Dates throw me," confessed Andy. He really did have trouble keeping dates straight in his head. He had no trouble recalling the details of an event, but the exact date and time the event occurred often eluded him. In fact, Andy wasn't even sure of today's date without checking his watch or cell phone or computer.

Pippel closed his locker and spun the dial. "See you tomorrow in home room," he said as he walked away.

"Hey, Sinnott," called one of the other guys nearby. "Did you understand that stupid homework assignment in physics? Do we really gotta solve those vector problems tonight?"

"No sweat," said Andy. "Just follow the formula in the textbook."

Andy wanted to add that it was easy. Vector analysis wasn't rocket science. But then, when he thought about it, he realized vectors were indeed rocket science. The problems in the textbook, however, were elementary examples that required only simple math, not trig or calculus. "If you run into problems you can't solve, e-mail me and I'll show you how I worked through that particular problem."

"For real?" asked the kid. His name was Jeff Walters, and he was a jock. Jeff had made the varsity football team as a sophomore. He stood half a head taller than Andy, and he weighed nearly twice as much. Andy surmised that math was not Jeff's forte.

"Sure," said Andy. He scribbled his e-mail address in his notebook, tore out the page, and handed it to Jeff.

"Listen," said Walters, coming closer so he could talk softly. "I'll probably need your help with all ten of the problems. Why don't you just e-mail me the solutions? It'll save us both some time."

"I can't do that," said Andy.

"Why not?"

"Because you need to do the work yourself if you want to learn."

"Yeah. Well, do me this favor just this one time. I'll make it worth your while."

"I don't need the money, Jeff."

"I wasn't taking about money. I was talking about favors. You do me a favor, and I'll do you a favor. That's the way the world works, you know. My old man says it's good politics to do favors for other people. He's an alderman and he does favors all the time."

"What kind of favor would you do in return?"

"Listen, I know where there's a big party this weekend." Jeff stood so close now he actually made Andy uncomfortable as he whispered, "There'll be girls there, man, and booze and drugs. I can get you in. Just do me this one favor, Sinnott. I need to pass physics or they'll kick me off the team. I can get you into the party and set you up with a girl. You like girls, don't you? You ain't no fag, are you?"

"No," said Andy. "I'm not homosexual and I do like girls."

"Okay," said Jeff, and he exhaled garlic breath in Andy's face. "Then it's settled. I'll e-mail you tonight and you send me the answers. Friday, I'll tell you how to find the party. You drive? You got wheels?"

"I have a learner's permit," Andy said.

"Yeah, well, you gotta get there on your own. You got a brother with a car?"

"No," said Andy.

"Shit. I'm not picking you up."

"I'll walk," said Andy. "I'm used to walking."

"Then it's settled," said Jeff. "I'll e-mail you about eight or nine. You should have the problems worked out by then, right?"

"Yes," said Andy. "But I'm not going to just give you the answers, Jeff. I'll help you work through the problems, but you need to find the answers yourself."

"Then what the fuck good are you?" erupted Jeff, shoving Andy against his locker so hard his butt dented the door. "I thought we had a deal, Sinnott. You better give me the answers tonight, and the right answers. Or I'll tell everyone you're a fag, a queer. I'll tell them I smashed your face in when you tried to hit on me. You got that?"

Andy expected another bloody nose. It was like being in third grade all over again. He felt weak in the knees, and he almost peed in his pants.

Jeff backed away when a teacher came down the hallway. "You better remember what I said, Sinnott," Jeff snarled before leaving.

That night Andy stayed away from his computer. He didn't want to have anything more to do with Jeff Walters, and he sure as hell wasn't about to give Jeff the answers to any of the physics problems. That was cheating. If Jeff failed physics and got kicked off the football team, it served him right.

The next day, Thursday, Andy stayed home from school. He didn't have to feign illness, he was physically sick, nauseous and diarrhetic, and still weak in the knees. Just the thought of running into Jeff Walters in the hallways made Andy throw up.

Maybe the butterfly wasn't ready to fly. Maybe it needed to return to the cocoon and rethink its strategies.

Andy had asked his mother to drop his homework assignments off at the school, and she did so on her way to work.

He stayed home from school on Friday, too. He devoted the day to reading a social psychology textbook his mother had on a bookshelf. It was thirty years out of date, left over from a class Andy's mother had taken in grad school. Still, he learned some things he needed to know.

Saturday and Sunday were filled with the dread of returning to school on Monday. Andy knew he had to face Jeff sooner or later, and he hated the thought of a humiliating confrontation. He had no doubt Jeff would carry out his threats.

Spring rains had turned the grass emerald green, and the bright colors elicited by the first day of sunshine in a week made Andy's walk to school almost bearable. He saw robins pecking at earthworms in the lawns he passed, heard the sweetsong of mating birdcalls. He thought about the Easter Bunny and mourned the fact that there had been no colored eggs left for him to find in years. He suspected the myth had evolved from birds' eggs found in nests at this time of year when mating was on everybody's mind. Rutting rabbits were symbolized as the Easter Bunny, and brightly-colored eggs were symbols of fertility. Parents had probably created the myth to provide themselves much-needed private time while children were wandering the woods hunting for Easter eggs.

What bothered Andy more than the thought of Jeff's threats was the thought that Andy found Jeff's offer tempting. For a moment, he had actually thought about giving the answers to Walters in exchange for setting him up with a girl at the party. It certainly would have been an easy way to meet girls.

But it wouldn't have been right. Andy's parents had instilled a moral code of right and wrong that made it impossible for Andy to go through with Jeff's deal. If Andy wanted to meet a girl, he'd do it on his own; and if Jeff wanted answers to the vector problems, he'd have to work the problems himself.

And Andy had to face his fears on his own, too. He'd been beaten up before, and he'd survived. So what if Jeff called Andy a queer? Andy knew he wasn't gay, and he knew it shouldn't bother him if anyone else thought he was.

"Sticks and stones can break my bones, but names can never hurt me," Andy sang as he walked to school. Unfortunately, he knew that wasn't true. Names hurt. Sometimes they hurt worse than fists.

Andy opened the door to the school and entered the hallway that led to his locker. He carried his books in a backpack, but he wore a light jacket he needed to stash in his locker before class. No one else was hanging around the lockers this morning. Was Andy late?

When he got to his homeroom classroom, he found the other students already sitting in their assigned seats. Some were talking quietly, and others had a stunned look on their faces.

"What did I miss?" Andy asked Ron Pippel.

"You haven't heard? It was on TV news and in all the papers."

"I don't watch much television," said Andy. "And I seldom read the papers."

"Four students were killed Sunday morning after an all-night drinking party. Toby Rogan, Ailene Southridge, Sharon Millgram, and Jeff Walters."

"Jeff's dead?"

"Toby was driving. He must have been really drunk. He sideswiped a utility pole, bounced back on the road the wrong way, and got totaled by a semi."

That had been Andy's introduction to death.

Andy graduated from high school and attended the state university on a full scholarship. He lived in a dormitory the first two years, then moved into an apartment he shared with two other guys. He lost his virginity to a freshman elementary education major named Dolores Ledbetter. Andy and Dolores dated for two years while Andy earned his bachelors in computer science. Dolores taught Andy a lot about women that Andy could never learn from books. They talked about marriage.

Dolores was raped and murdered while walking across campus one night to visit Andy one month before Andy graduated. Some guy stabbed her repeatedly with a knife, dragged her bleeding body into the bushes, and raped her before slitting her throat. Andy was devastated. Campus and city police had no idea who the murderer was. Andy learned there had been other rapes at knifepoint, but no previous murders. Police said Dolores had died because she fought her assailant. They found skin under her broken red-painted fingernails from scratching the rapist and many of Dolores' wounds looked like defensive cuts. If anyone had heard her screams, no one had reported screams or tried to intervene.

After the funeral, Andy became determined to help the police find the killer. He used his internet skills to learn about trace evidence and DNA, and he began to walk the campus at night looking for the killer. He hadn't thought much about what he would do if he caught the rapist in the act. He supposed he would call 911 on his cell phone and hope the police got there before the rapist completed his act and got away.

Even before Andy graduated cum laude with a bachelors in computer science, he enrolled in graduate school. The only forensic sciences program the university offered was administered by the Department of Pharmacology in the College of Medicine. Admission required more undergraduate biology and chemistry courses than Andy had completed. Likewise, the graduate program in criminalistics required a heavier concentration in biological sciences. The only graduate forensics program he could get into right away was the Criminology, Law and Justice curriculum in the Liberal Arts College.

And the only thing you could do with a masters in criminology was to become a cop.

Andy continued to bug campus police during the two years he spent in grad school. His master's thesis was an analysis of the investigation into the violent death of Dolores Ledbetter.

Rapes declined after Dolores' death, attributed to the increased police presence and vigilance of students. Andy suspected it was more likely the decline occurred because Dolores' killer had moved elsewhere after the murder. If he continued to rape, it was in a different jurisdiction. Her murderer was never apprehended nor identified.

Andy's father died at age seventy, not long after Andy received his masters. Andy had applied to join the state police forensic program, and he received his acceptance letter the same day his father died. He moved home to console his mother, and noticed the Riverdale police department announced openings for sworn officers in the newspaper. Andy applied.

Despite his excellent college record and high test scores on the written exam, he wasn't among those selected. Preference was given to military veterans, and Andy did poorly on the physical tests. He was healthy enough, but he wasn't muscular enough to complete the required push-ups and pull-ups.

He began exercising. He ran a mile before breakfast, worked his way up to a dozen push-ups and sit-ups. He chinned himself on an iron bar in a clothes closet.

Andy's mother died of a broken heart at age sixty-three. She literally had a heart attack and collapsed on the kitchen floor while making lunch. Andy couldn't bear to live in the house after that. He sold the house and prepared to join the state police as a forensic sciences trainee. He had to wait six weeks for the fall class to begin, and he was living in a motel when he received a telephone call on his cell phone from Captain Carl Erickson.

"One of our applicants dropped out, and I have an opening I need to fill right away. Are you still interested?"

Andy said no. He was joining the state police in a few weeks.

"Too bad," said Erickson. "I could really use someone who knows computers and has a degree in criminology. Why don't you come down tomorrow and I'll show you around. I'll introduce you to some of the people you could be working with. Maybe I can change your mind."

Andy had nothing better to do while he was waiting, so he agreed. After meeting Troy Nolan and Bill Bowers, Andy retook the PT test and passed. He joined the police department's new trainees during their first week of training. That had been eight years ago. He spent a year working the streets as a patrolman, and then he became a crime scene investigator in the Violent Crimes division where he learned the nitty-gritty from Bill Bowers.

Bowers and Nolan became the brothers Andy always wished he had. They taught the butterfly to fly. But now Andy was head of homicide, promoted ahead of his contemporaries, and he was up the proverbial creek without a paddle.

Tomorrow Andy would assign people to interview the residents of Elm Street about the fire, but tonight Andy concentrated on the icepick murderer. He still had bartenders to interview. Maybe he'd get lucky. First on his list of bars was Upstairs and Downstairs. He had copies of the victims' photos in his pocket, and he drove downtown and found a parking place on Third Avenue only a block from the bars and nightclubs.

CHAPTER SIX

You finish the day's work shortly after nine. At 9:23 you stop at the Walgreens store on Third Avenue. You buy a new Zippo and a plastic container of lighter fluid. You also purchase a pack of six condoms.

You have nowhere to go, nothing you need do. You can sit in your car until you fall asleep if you want, or you can drive to one of the bars and have a few drinks. You think of the blonde girl in the red skirt. You decide a drink might taste good.

Third Avenue is Riverdale's central north-south thoroughfare. It stretches from the upscale residential neighborhoods of the far north side to south side trailer parks out near the interstate. This Walgreens is on the near south side, just north of the train tracks that separate the inner city from the industrial wastes of dilapidated warehouses and abandoned manufacturing plants. You are only a mile south of downtown and the few nightclubs that haven't yet relocated to the suburbs.

Downtown is practically dead after dark except for a three-block-long strip of bars, nightclubs, and restaurants on Third Avenue between West Street and South Street. Both of those streets run east and west. West Street goes from the river to the far west side of town, and South Street is one of three major thoroughfares that cross the river on bridges built approximately a mile apart. There are other bridges, too, that cross the river out at the edges of the city and in north and south suburbs; but South Street, Main Street, and North Street are the only downtown streets connecting the sprawling municipal, county, state and federal government offices on the east side directly with the commercial skyscrapers and shops on the west.

Main Street has a wooden pedestrian bridge built beneath the bridge itself to connect the grassy knoll along the west bank with the ten-mile-long bike path on the east bank. South Street has narrow pedestrian walkways along each side of the busy roadways on the steel bridge itself. North Street is a controlled-access highway with interchanges to various expressways. The North Street Bridge has no pedestrian walkway at all.

Parking on downtown streets is severely restricted during daylight hours, but parking on streets is allowed after 6:00 PM. You drive around until you find an open spot on West Street, just around the corner from Upstairs and Downstairs. You lock the Matrix because everything you own is in the two duffel bags on the floor behind the front seat.

It's ten o'clock, and tonight the dance club collects a ten dollar cover at the front door. Did you forget that this is Friday night? Upstairs and Downstairs has a live band instead of a DJ on weekends, and they charge a modest cover. You must have known that.

The big guy collecting the cover charge and carding kids is an off-duty cop. You can smell a cop a mile away. Cons swear it's because cops have a distinctive odor, and they're correct. It's the familiar smell of Hoppe's Number 9 bore cleaning solvent and gun oil. If cops spent as much time wiping excess oil off their guns as they spend wiping shit from their asses, they wouldn't smell so bad.

You push past people to get to the bar, but there is a long line waiting to be served. The sole downstairs bartender is the same guy who served you on Wednesday. He's a little taller than you, close to six feet, and he has a dark-brown beard. He's wearing a dark blue polo shirt with "Upstairs and Downstairs" embroidered in yellow over the pocket.

You have never seen this place as crowded as it is tonight. Most of the patrons are female, attracted by the all-male band you hear playing upstairs. Shorts and halters appear to be the uniform of the day, although there are enough short skirts and braless blouses here to make your mouth water. Temperatures outside are still in the nineties, and heat from so many crowded bodies make the inside air conditioning seem non-existent.

Two women are in conversation next to the bar, their breasts peeking out of thin halter tops. As one bends forward to hear what the other is saying, you can't help but notice the display of raw flesh staring you in the face. You've seen it all before, of course, but it still excites you. Is that an exposed nipple you see? It could be!

Life can be so boring, filled with routine, and you crave excitement as much as the women around you crave excitement. It does excite you to see the way they're dressed. Or, rather, not dressed.

You're a watcher, and you watch all the people in the bar with a trained eye. You see a short, thin guy pass the cop at the door with a slight nod and without paying cover, and you know instantly the new guy is another cop. He has light brown hair, trimmed to medium length. He's about your age, maybe a year or two younger. He's wearing gray slacks and a navy-blue sport coat despite the heat. He has a light blue dress shirt open at the collar, probably short sleeved, and you notice the tell-tale bulge on his right hip where he carries a Glock 17 in a clip-on breakaway holster. His shoes are leather Reebok running shoes, similar to the ones you wear.

He, too, is a watcher, and you sense his eyes taking in the crowd. For a brief moment you feel panic, but then you realize he doesn't know you from Adam. You are only one more face in the crowd to him.

He gets in line three people behind you. You reject the idea that he is off-duty and in the bar only for fun. If he were off-duty, he wouldn't be wearing a sport-coat to cover his piece.

The woman ahead of you advances to the bar and you wait patiently for the bartender to fill her order. When it's your turn, you ask for a bottle of Heineken and tip the bartender a buck.

You move out of the way but remain close enough to hear what the cop says to the bartender. You are fairly certain the cop isn't here merely to have a drink, and you're very curious why a detective would wait in line on a hot summer night to speak with a bartender.

The cop orders a plain Coke with lots of ice, watching intently as the bartender chops up ice with an icepick, scoops a handful of ice chips into a tall glass, and fills the glass with soda from a spigot. The cop shows the bartender his badge, takes a handful of computer printouts from his inside coat pocket, hands them to the bartender, and begins asking questions.

"Have you seen any of these people recently?" the cop asks.

"Not tonight," says the bartender, glancing briefly at pictures printed on each of the printouts.

"How about Wednesday night?"

"Maybe. I see so many people, it's hard to remember when I saw them last."

"But you have seen them?"

"Oh, sure."

"Have you noticed anything missing in the last day or so? An icepick, perhaps?"

"Funny you should ask. I thought I had dropped the icepick I keep next to the bar on the floor, but it wasn't there when I swept up after closing. So I got another icepick out of the storeroom."

"Can you describe the icepick?"

"I can do better than that." He holds up the replacement icepick. "Just like this one. We buy them by the dozen because they break."

The cop takes the icepick and looks at the point, the shaft, the wooden handle.

"You'll have to excuse me," says the bartender. "The line is getting long behind you and I've gotta take care of customers."

"Mind if I borrow this?" the cop asks. "I'll return it after I get photos."

"Any other night I'd say yes. But I ain't got time to run to the storeroom for another. Come back after closing and you can have it."

"Thanks," says the cop. He takes his Coke and steps away from the bar.

You watch the cop walk upstairs to look around the dance floor. You wait ten minutes and he comes back down, places the empty glass on the bar, and leaves.

You think about following him to see where else he goes in his search for you. Now, at least, you know what your adversary looks like. This could be an interesting game.

The cop's eyes are a lot like yours, except his are hazel and yours are brown. But the intelligence in those eyes is extremely rare, something you've only seen before in a mirror. He will be a worthy adversary. You need to be careful.

You have encountered worthy adversaries before, but none who proved equal to the task. You are living proof of that. And your previous adversaries, without exception, are no longer living. Last man standing is winner by default.

But the cop is out the door before you can follow, and you decide not to let him spoil any of your planned fun. The night is still young, and there is much yet to see and do. It's time now to go upstairs and watch the dance. When the cop comes back at closing, you can easily dispose of him.

You have an advantage over every cop you have ever met: they always hesitate and you never do. Cops are afraid of making the wrong choices, of shooting an innocent bystander or some such nonsense. You never concern yourself with causing collateral damage. All of the choices you make are exactly the right choice at the time you make them. There is never any doubt in your mind, none whatsoever; hence no hesitation. You are always ready to make your move because you have nothing to lose whichever move you make.

You have no home, no belongings that cannot be easily replaced. Like the lighter, for example. Or the lighter fluid. Or that crappy attic apartment. Or even the wreck of a car you drive.

You have no family or friends. You are not married. You were married once, but it didn't work out. You killed your wife and your infant son, then took care of both sets of parents, hers and your own. Then you killed yourself.

That's what you wanted everyone to think. You left a suicide note and drove your car off a bridge. They dredged the river for weeks before giving up on recovering a body. You are officially dead. R. I. P.

Acquiring a new identity wasn't difficult, but it was certainly expensive. You move around a lot, and you've been careful to keep a low profile most of the time. None of your recent victims knew your name, and you never leave witnesses alive to identify you. Not since you learned how easy it is to kill.

Sometimes, you go months without killing. Once, you even went an entire year. But then something always happens, and your true self emerges from the façade. It's as if you want them to know who you are, what you're capable of doing.

You take your beer and climb the stairs to the second floor dance hall. A four-piece band plays on a makeshift stage at one end of the floor. Tonight's band features a good-looking lead guitarist with a Gibson Les Paul Gold Top, a drummer with a set of snares, cymbals, and a big bass floor model Ludwig with dual kick pedals, a prancing bass guitarist with a Fender Tony Franklin Fretless Precision Bass, and a keyboardist standing behind a Yamaha synthesizer. Their music is far too loud for such a confined space, and it actually hurts your sensitive ears.

None of the women seem to mind, however, and they grind their hips and shake their booties to the beat as if the music stirred something primitive and primal deep within their psyches. The air is rank with sweat and perfume and after shave. So many bodies so close together. When strobe lights begin flashing, you go into sensory overload. You feel a headache coming on and you have to leave.

You go back downstairs and order another beer and a shot of Jack Daniel's. The Jack burns your throat as it goes down, and you order another. It isn't wise to mix hard liquor with beer, but you do it anyway. It's the only way you can control the headache.

There are enough women to choose from on the ground floor, and you don't need to go back upstairs to hunt. You look around for targets, and your eyes fasten on a vivacious redhead. She's part of a group of young women sitting at a table in a corner. There are six other women at the same table with her, empty beer bottles littering the tabletop. They have obviously been here a while, probably before the place started charging a cover at eight. One of the women looks older than the rest, perhaps in her early-thirties, and she is conservatively dressed as if she had come to the bar directly after leaving work in some nearby office building. The others look like they range in age from twenty-one to twenty-six. The redhead looks perhaps twenty-one or twenty-two years of age, wears contact lenses, and has quite obviously gone home to change after work because she is now clad in strapless halter and short shorts like so many others tonight. The halter is red, the shorts white. Her bare legs are quite shapely and muscular and well-tanned, and she has kicked off her leather sandals beneath the table. Her toenails are painted red.

You watch her carefully. She wears a garnet ring the color of her hair on her right hand, but the third finger of her left hand is naked. Her breasts are not large, but they are certainly shapely. Her bare abdomen shows off a red jewel in her navel, perhaps another garnet. She has a small tattoo on her right ankle.

You don't approve of the dangling gold earrings. She has her red hair up in a ponytail, and the earrings make her ears look too large for her face. Except for the earrings, she looks good enough to eat.

She leans back in her chair, her legs stretched straight out. Her tiny breasts push at the red fabric. You decide she is the one you want.

You order another Jack Daniel's and another beer. While the bartender is reaching for the bottle of Jack on the top shelf, you reach across the wooden bar and purloin the icepick from the aluminum bin. You have it safely tucked under your t-shirt before the bartender returns with your drinks.

You melt into the crowd, keeping your eyes on the redhead. Will she leave the bar with her friends? Or will she leave by herself?

You're really feeling the drinks by the time the girls get up from the table around midnight. They came here not to dance but mostly to have a few beers with co-workers after a long week, chat about boyfriends, and perhaps get lucky if some good-looking guy attempts to pick them up. Unfortunately for them, though, they don't look approachable. They selected a table in the back of the bar where they could hear each other talk, they sit in a fairly large group with all the chairs taken, and they don't seem interested in dancing. Besides, most of the people in the bar tonight are women, and the single guys are all upstairs looking to get lucky themselves.

You set your empty beer bottle down on the bar and follow the women outside. Temperatures haven't dropped significantly in the past two hours, and the sudden blast of hot air sobers you up quickly. The off-duty cop at the door is still busily collecting money from people entering the bar, and he doesn't pay any attention to people leaving.

You see the girls give each other chaste hugs at the corner of Third and West. Then they separate and walk to their individual cars. The redhead unlocks a white Kia Optima with her remote. You note the license number before going to your own car. You get in quickly, start the motor, and wait for her to drive past.

When she passes the corner, you pull out and follow. She turns east on South Street, drives across the bridge, continues east for another three miles, and finally parks in the open lot outside an upscale apartment complex. Any worries that she lives at home with her parents dissipate as you watch her enter the apartment building with her own key to the lobby.

You check for security cameras. They seem to be everywhere these days, and you can't be too careful. You see one in the lobby aimed at the entrance. There's another in back watching the pool.

Lights come on in a third floor window, and you see the redhead walk to the picture window and close the blinds. Now you know which apartment is hers. It's the one on the far right.

You open one of your duffel bags and remove a pair of leather gloves. You put the gloves on your hands and wait to make sure no one else is around. It wouldn't do for anyone to see you wearing gloves when the air temperature is nearly ninety. You also want to give the girl a chance to get comfortable before you make your move.

Staying outside the margins of the camera lenses isn't difficult. You are wearing jeans and a black t-shirt—all of your t-shirts are black—and you are practically invisible in the night, despite the nearly full moon. You move like a lengthening shadow from your car to the side of the building.

The drain pipe is aluminum, but it is solidly anchored to the brick wall. You go up the pipe quickly and quietly to the third floor where your feet find the narrow ledge under her window. Had she lived in one of the other apartments, you would have tried another approach.

Since this apartment building has central air conditioning, the window is sealed shut. You peer through slots between the blinds and see the living room on the other side of the window. The redhead must be inside the bedroom or the bathroom or maybe the kitchen, because she's not visible in the living room. You begin to slowly peel the putty off the window frame using the icepick to pry under and around the window itself. You feel the glass loosen from the frame. Balancing on the ledge while manipulating the glass is a challenge. You need to carefully angle the glass inside the window frame. If you accidentally drop the sheet of glass, the noise of shattering glass will alert all the neighbors.

You manage to get the glass inside with little noise and maneuver it cautiously onto the carpet. You gently lift the blinds and step over the sill into the living room.

Lights are on in the living room, the bedroom, and the bath. You peek into the bedroom and find it vacant. She must be taking a bath.

You do not hear running water from a shower, but you do smell lavender soap. She must be soaking in the tub. What could be more perfect than that? She's already naked.

You have the icepick in your gloved left hand as you enter the tiny bathroom. The toilet and a sink are to your left, the bathtub straight ahead. Her red hair is loose of the pony tail, soapy wet with lather. Her eyes are tightly closed as she shampoos her hair, humming softly to herself, totally oblivious to your presence. She doesn't hear your Reeboks advance silently across the tiles. You watch her with fascination. Her breasts are exactly as you pictured them, small but perky. Her nipples are the size of dimes.

You slide your gloved right hand over her mouth to keep her from screaming. The tip of the icepick is an inch from her left eye, and her eyes are wide with fright.

"I love you," you say as you insert the icepick into the girl's iris.

Andy returned to Upstairs and Downstairs at 1:45. The band had finished their last set at 1:30, and last call for alcohol was announced at 1:40. People were leaving in droves, mostly as couples, some in small groups of four or five, and a few individually.

Walt Exeter, the off-duty cop who worked security at the bar on weekends, was herding people out. "You don't have to go home, people, but you can't stay here," he yelled.

Andy waited for the bartender to return from clearing bottles and glasses from tables. There were a few customers still finishing drinks, and the bartender reminded them the bar was required to close promptly at two.

"I'm back to get that icepick from you," Andy told the bartender when the man returned to the other side of the bar.

"It's gone," said the bartender. "It disappeared around midnight. I had to get another from the back. We only have two left."

"Can I still have one? I'll make sure you get it back tomorrow."

"That makes two I've lost in a week," said the bartender. "I break one or two a year, but I've never lost one before now. Let me get you a new one from the storeroom."

He walked from behind the bar to a door on the south wall beneath the stairs. A minute later he was back with an icepick in a plastic blister pack. "Brand new, right out of the box."

"Thanks," said Andy. "By the way, what's your name?"

"Gordy. Gordon Harris," said the bartender, extending his hand.

"Call me Andy."

"This must have something to do with the four people the paper said were killed with an icepick."

"We think your missing icepick was the murder weapon."

"Jesus," said Gordy.

"You might want to make your icepicks less accessible in the future, Gordy. In the wrong hands, they become deadly weapons."

"Back again, Lieutenant?" asked Walt Exeter. "I didn't know you drank."

"I don't," said Andy. "I'm working a case. Say, Walt, have you noticed anyone acting really out of the ordinary tonight? Someone lifted an icepick from behind the bar and walked off with it. You see anyone act strange?"

"We get a few weirdoes in here now and then, but tonight I was too busy to notice. We were packed solid from nine until closing."

"Because of the band?"

"You heard them. What did you think?"

"It's not my kind of music," Andy said.

"They got a following. Two CDs and a third coming out next month. We were lucky to get them for just one night. Tomorrow, we have a local band."

"I'll stop back tomorrow to return the icepick I've borrowed."

"I'll be here," said Walt.

"Do me a favor and pay special attention to single guys. You see anything suspicious, let me know."

"I'll keep my eyes open," said Walt.

Andy drove straight back to the lab with the sample icepick and dropped it off with George. "Let me know if this matches what we know of the murder weapon. I think it's from the same manufacturer. Take some pictures, then get the icepick back to me intact by tomorrow night."

"Made in Taiwan," noted George from the packaging. "I thought it came from China. I guess Taiwan is close enough."

"How is Stowe coming with the autopsies?"

"He's finished all four vics from Wednesday and released those bodies for mortuary pick-up. He shipped some of the remains of the intact burn victims and the people who got caught by the explosion to Bryson Memorial and asked Bryson's staff pathologists to assist. Stowe thinks they know enough forensics to do justice to the people from 2302 and 2310. He's working on the ashes from 2306 himself. We sent ashes from each pile to state labs for DNA analysis. It may take a while to get the results."

"Any evidence of accelerant?"

"Funny you should ask me about that. One of the victims had traces of Naphtha and other hydrocarbons commonly found in lighter fluid. It was almost as if his body had been doused with lighter fluid before the fire began."

"Only one of the victims?"

"Only one."

"Have you identified who he was?"

"Are you kidding? We may never know who they were. All of their identification was destroyed in the fire along with fingerprints. The names of residents were lost when the manager's apartment burned. DNA won't give us a name unless we can match the DNA to effects we've already identified. Teeth might help, if we can match them to dental records. But we'll need names before we can get dental records."

"Is Dr. Stowe in his office?"

"Yes, but he's asleep in his chair. Let him sleep. He worked all night and all day. He's worn out."

"What about you? Did you get any sleep?"

"A couple of hours."

"Go home, George."

"I can't."

"Why not?"

"I have work to do."

"It will still be there in the morning."

"All my life," said George, "I've been intrigued by two questions: How do things work? And why do they work that way? I've applied those questions to inorganic matter mostly. But since I took this job, I've had to deal primarily with organic matter: The human organism and what makes it tick. Why would one human being ever deliberately hurt another? It's unfathomable to me, and it keeps me awake. I've hurt people by omission, I'm sure, but never by commission. In just the past two days, nearly twenty people have died at the hands of two killers, people who deliberately committed acts of violence against other human beings. Both the how and the why bother me relentlessly. I'm not sure I'll be able to sleep until I have some answers."

"You want to know the how and the why," said Andy, "and I do, too. But, more importantly, I want to know who. Who did this? I need to know who so I can stop him from doing it again."

"You think he'll do it again?"

"The icepick killer, yes. I don't know about the arsonist."

"I think I need a smoke," said George. "You want to step outside with me for a few minutes while I puff on my pipe?"

"I should go to my office and check my e-mail and phone messages," said Andy. "I'll walk with you to the elevator, though."

"How long do we have?" asked George when they got to the elevator.

"Before the elevator comes? This time of night, the elevator is pretty quick. It doesn't have to stop at each floor."

"No. I mean, how long do we have before the icepick guy kills again?"

"Good question," answered Andy. "I really don't know."

They stepped into the elevator and rode up to the first floor. George got out, and Andy continued up to the squad room on four. None of his techs were on duty tonight, and the place seemed unusually empty and quiet.

He checked his phone messages first, then his e-mail. Stowe had sent preliminary autopsy results of the four icepick victims as attachments.

His snail mail included a picture postcard from Troy and Sally Nolan in Barbados. "Having a great time. Being married is great. You should try it, Andy. See you in three weeks."

Andy updated his Excel file with the autopsy information. Then he opened a new workbook for the arson victims. He knew he should go home and get some sleep himself. But, like George, some questions nagged at him and probably wouldn't let him sleep.

He knew the killer was average height and weight, probably left-handed, wore size eleven running shoes that Andy's techs had matched to men's Reebok Classic Leather Running Shoes with rubber soles. Andy suspected the shoes were black, not white, the only two available colors. Since the killer had moved fast enough to take out four victims in under ten minutes, the guy was probably under forty and in good physical condition. He was likely Caucasian, because all his victims were Caucasian.

What worried Andy was the killer's efficiency. Anyone that good at killing must have killed before. There were no signs of hesitation or remorse. Either someone had trained the guy to kill, or he had trained himself.

Did that mean the killer was ex-military? Perhaps. Or maybe even an ex-cop.

The guy must have been covered with blood and gore after stabbing eight eyes, but he didn't react adversely. After successfully killing four people, he jumped in the river and made his getaway. Either he had planned all this out in advance, or he was capable of acting coolly under pressure.

And he was still out there. Someone, possibly the same person, had stolen another icepick from Upstairs and Downstairs. Did that mean he was getting ready to kill again? What was his motive for killing? None of the women or men had been sexually assaulted. None of them had been robbed of money or jewelry. So why were they killed? Why attack the eyes?

Obviously, the guy had a thing for eyes. Had he killed these four because they had seen something? Or was he some nut who thought the eyes were windows to the soul and he wanted to shatter their souls?

If he had simply wanted to kill his victims, he could have stabbed them in the throat. If he knew anything about anatomy, and Stowe said the killer did, then he would have known that opening the carotid artery on either side of the neck would have done the trick in seconds.

Why both eyes? They would have died when the icepick entered the first eye and penetrated to the brain. Doing both eyes was overkill. One eye was sufficient and efficient. Both eyes was excessive, indicating obsessive behavior.

Why these victims? Why had the killer chosen to kill these four particular people in this manner at this time? Most murders, Andy knew, were committed by someone who knew the victims previously, had a relationship of some kind with the victims. A spouse, a relative, a neighbor, a co-worker. Unless robbery were the motive, random killings were rare.

So far, Upstairs and Downstairs was the only lead Andy had. Twice now, the killer had frequented the nightclub and stolen icepicks. What was it about that particular bar that attracted the killer back to it? It certainly wasn't the band. There had been no band playing on Wednesday night, and last night's band was a one-time deal. If he simply wanted to steal an icepick, he could have done that at any of a half-dozen bars in the area.

There were two reasons Andy could think of for choosing Upstairs and Downstairs. First, the place was usually so packed that no one would remember the face of one man in the crowd. Second, the place was frequented by young scantily-clad women. Not hookers, like some of the places on the strip. The women who went into Upstairs and Downstairs were clean-cut singles out for a night on the town. They went to the bar to dance, to meet friends, or to have a chance encounter with a single man.

The two women victims knew the male victims fairly well, and they didn't just meet in the bar by chance on Wednesday. All four victims lived in the same apartment complex, likely went to the bar together, and left together. If they had a chance encounter that night, it was only with the killer. So did the killer follow them from the bar? Probably. Did he know them from before? Not likely. Why did he choose these victims and not someone else? What was it about the victims that would have attracted the killer's attention? Was it the blonde's short red skirt? Or was it something about the eyes?

Andy was still pondering those questions when the first of the crime scene technicians arrived for their weekend rotations at seven AM. Andy made assignments to the team when they were all assembled at eight.

There were only two dedicated homicide investigators on the force: Andy and Sergeant Delmar Conklin. Del had been hired to replace Andy as chief crime scene investigator when Andy was promoted to head homicide. Del, 42, had a bachelors in crime scene investigation from a technical college and ten years of experience on a west-coast police department. Prior to that, he had been a U. S. Marine, and he still wore his hair high and tight.

The others on the team were two detectives assigned to the Violent Crimes Division, four crime scene technicians, and one newly-hired criminalist who began work for Violent Crimes barely a month ago. Her name was Linda Davis, she was twenty-six years old, a recent graduate of the University of Florida's Forensic Science Masters Program, and the department's chief rape investigator. She had just completed her ride-alongs, weapons qualification, and introduction to department policies and procedures. Andy had heard she had joined the team, but he had never met her before.

Linda was petite, perhaps five-two, and she looked like a pixie. She had reddish-blonde hair cut short, freckles, and a mischievous smile. Her eyes were hazel like Andy's, and she probably weighed no more than a hundred pounds soaking wet. She wore a white blouse, navy-blue slacks, SAS flats, and a nine millimeter Glock 19 in a holster on her belt. Even the reduced size of the Glock 19 seemed too big for her tiny hands.

"We have two separate crimes to investigate," Andy told his assembled crew. While Captain Nolan was on his honeymoon, Andy was also acting head of Violent Crimes. "You can get the details from the spreadsheets I have posted to the network. I want to break you down into two teams. Del will coordinate the team investigating the arson homicides. I'll work the icepick murders. Davis, you're with me. Del, I want you to interview all of the neighbors. We're duplicating some of the efforts of the Fire Department's arson investigators, but I want to collect our own information. See a guy named Larry Miller at the main fire station to coordinate your efforts with local and state fire investigators."

"You're sure it's arson?" asked Del Conklin.

"Miller found a Zippo lighter and evidence of accelerant at the scene. Fredriks in the Coroner's office found lighter fluid on the ashes of one of the victims. We have no motive yet, but it does look like arson."

"What about the icepick deaths?" asked Richard Pearson, one of the detectives in Violent Crimes. "Any motive?"

"We've ruled out robbery."

"Revenge?" asked Pearson. "Anyone have a grudge against the vics?"

"That will be your assignment, Rich. They all lived in the same apartment complex on the west side. Interview their neighbors and relatives. Find out where they worked and interview co-workers. You know the protocol. Okay, pick your partners and get to it."

Andy's cell phone vibrated in his pocket. Caller ID indicated dispatch was calling.

It was 9:27 on a beautiful Saturday morning, the twentieth of June, the first full day of summer. Any plans Andy had for going home and getting some much-needed sleep had just gone out the window.

CHAPTER SEVEN

"A maintenance man discovered that third-floor window was missing while mowing the lawn this morning. There was no broken glass on the ground, but he could tell the window was gone. The window was double-paned and slightly tinted to protect against UV, easy to see it wasn't there. The maintenance guy notified the super, they tried to phone the tenant, and finally they went up to the third-floor apartment to find out what had happened to the window. The super unlocked the apartment when no one answered his knocks on the door. They found the intact glass on the floor of the living room and checked out the rest of the apartment. They discovered the tenant's body on the bed. She was naked, her eyes poked out, and her ears bloody where earrings had been ripped out of the piercings. The super called 911, and my partner and I were first on the scene."

"Anyone touch the body?" Andy asked the patrolman whose name badge read "Carson."

"Not that I know of. I didn't, and neither did my partner. We took a quick look and sealed off the entire floor until you or the coroner got here. You got here first."

Sinnott, Pearson, and Davis put gloves on their hands and plastic covers on their shoes before entering the apartment. The door opened into the living room. To the left was a large walk-in closet and the entrance to the kitchen, and a bathroom and bedroom were to the right. The living room contained a second-hand sofa, a 52-inch flat-screen television, a DVD player, and a wooden table with a laptop computer and four chairs around the table. There was no stereo, but there were CDs stacked on the table next to the computer. A sheet of double-paned window glass was propped against the wall to the left of the open window. The perpetrator had obviously entered through the open window and likely left the same way.

"What's that smell?" asked Pearson.

"Lavender bubble bath," said Davis.

A trail of dried blood led from the bathroom into the bedroom where a female body lay spread-eagled on the once-white duvet covering a mussed queen-sized bed. The girl was red-haired, about twenty-one, completely naked, and her eyes and ears and thighs had caked blood on them.

"She's been raped," said Davis, reciting the obvious.

"We'll let Dr. Stowe confirm that," said Andy. "Rich, call the techs. Get them out here with the evidence van ASAP. We need pictures, prints, the works. After we look around, you go interview the super and the maintenance guy. Get the tenant's name, when she moved in—I don't think she's been living here long because she doesn't have a lot of furniture—you know the drill. Get any footage from the security cameras. I saw a camera in the lobby on the first floor, and there may be more. Davis, find her purse and see what's in it. Driver's license, cash, credit cards, receipts. Find the clothes she was wearing last. Document everything."

"It looks like she was killed in the bathtub," said Pearson. "Then the perp dragged the body into the bedroom."

Andy went to the open window and looked out. Below the window was a small decorative stone ledge. There was a similar ledge running the length of the building beneath the second floor windows. The ground below smelled of recently-cut grass. Thirty feet away was a paved parking lot with a dozen cars. Beyond the parking area was the street. Across the street was another apartment complex.

"Rich, check with that apartment building across the street and see if they have a security camera. Maybe they caught the guy going in or out of the window."

"Right," said Pearson. "Looks like the perpetrator left the murder weapon behind. There's an icepick in the bathtub."

Andy walked into the bathroom where Pearson was looking down into a tub filled with bloody water and purple soap scum. Barely visible in the bottom of the tub was an icepick similar to the one Andy had borrowed from the bartender at Upstairs and Downstairs.

Andy didn't want to retrieve the icepick until the techs had photographed the scene. "You call the evidence wagon yet?" he asked Pearson.

Pearson took out his cell phone and hit speed dial. He gave the dispatcher the address and asked him to hurry up the techs who should already be on the way.

"Her name is Barbara Ames," said Linda Davis. "Three months shy of twenty-two, red hair, hazel eyes, five-six, one-thirty. Address on the license is different than here."

"Address is probably her parents. She moved recently and hasn't had time to notify DMV."

"I'll check it out," said Davis. "See what I can find out about Barbara from her parents. They'll need to be notified anyway."

"Credit cards?"

"Mastercard. Visa ATM debit card from Chase."

"Anything else in the purse?"

"Checkbook. Credit card receipts. Forty-three dollars, two twenties and three ones. Twenties are new like they just came out of an ATM machine. Some change. Lipstick. Comb. Cell phone."

"Money's not the motive," said Pearson.

"I found her dirty clothes in a hamper in the bedroom. Red halter. White shorts. Red thong. No bra."

Doctor Stowe arrived with Harvey Fredriks. Both men wore surgical gloves and plastic booties. Stowe looked terrible. He hadn't shaved, his long black hair was uncombed, and he had bags under his eyes. He looked twice as old as his thirty-three years.

Andy and Davis followed Stowe into the bedroom. The forensic pathologist set his black leather briefcase that was the size of a small suitcase down on the carpet, took out a digital camera, and began documenting the corpse. He shot pictures from every possible angle, zooming in on the face, the ears, and the genitalia. Then he took out two digital thermometers and measured the air temperature and the temperature of the body.

"She's been dead about nine or ten hours," he said after turning on a digital voice recorder. "Rigor is pronounced. Cause of death is sharp force trauma to the right eye. Stab wound to right eye first, then the left. She was already dead when he stabbed the left eye."

"How can you tell?" asked Andy.

"Her heart had stopped pumping when the sharp instrument penetrated the left eye. Blood squirted out of the right, but only leaked out of the left. I'd say ears were ripped post mortem for the same reason. You find the earrings he tore out?"

"Not yet," said Andy. "We did find an icepick, though."

"Looks like he yanked the earrings out. One post bent and broke off. See the scratches on the left ear lobe? The other post tore through the adipose tissue, severing the bottom of the ear lobe."

"Maybe he kept the earrings as souvenirs," suggested Pearson.

"There are bite marks on the breasts," continued the doctor. "I'll make an impression when I get her back to the morgue. Maybe we'll get lucky and pick up some DNA from saliva on or around the nipples." Stowe took a dry sponge from his bag and gently blotted the breasts. Then he sealed the sponge in an evidence bag and labeled it with a marker.

"Was she raped?" asked Pearson.

"Post mortem penetration. No vaginal secretions evident, no seminal fluid visible. He likely wore a rubber, forced his way in. Harvey, you be careful when you bag her. We want to preserve any hairs or trace evidence."

"Gotcha," said George.

"What do you think, Doc?" asked Andy. "Did the same guy do this?"

"Eyes were done the same as the eyes on Wednesday," replied the doctor. "Except this time the killer left the icepick behind for you to find. None of the other victims were raped. This girl was. Last time, none of the earrings were touched on either of the female victims. This time he rips the earrings out of both ears right after he kills her but before he rapes her. Why? I don't think he stole the earrings. He didn't take the navel ring. Nor the garnet on her right hand. See if you can find those earrings. I bet they're still here. To answer your question, Andy, there are similarities and differences. But, yes. I think it was the same guy. If you find those earrings in the apartment, it will eliminate one of the discrepancies. I don't think this killer takes souvenirs."

Andy's crime scene boys arrived. One immediately began taking pictures while another started dusting for prints. A third mapped the crime scene, inside and out, documenting the location of objects in all the rooms relative to the position of the body.

The fourth crime scene guy, actually a woman by the name of Lorraine Evangelista, began gathering blood samples. She took samples from the floor, the bathroom, the bedclothes. She bottled a sample of the water in the tub. She fished the icepick out of the bottom of the tub with a pair of forceps, bagging the murder weapon, sealing and labeling the bag. She probed the porcelain for other evidence, and discovered a pair of bent 14 karat gold earrings.

Evangelista carefully collected hair from the water. She was an experienced evidence technician, patient and thorough.

"Lieutenant," she asked Andy, showing him the bagged icepick and earrings, "do you want me to drain the tub so we can get prints? Or do you want me to collect all the water first? I have samples, but there's probably some trace left in the water we might want to examine. It's your call."

"Get it all," said Andy. "He killed her in the tub, then dragged the body out and into the bedroom. He had to leave something of himself behind."

Evangelista went out to the evidence van and came back with a sterile industrial-sized stainless steel wet-dry vacuum. While she was sucking up the contents of the tub, Andy called a conference in the hallway with the doctor, Davis, and Pearson.

"You were right, Doc," Andy told Stowe. "We found both earrings in the tub. He didn't want them for souvenirs."

"It's the same guy," said Stowe. "This time he raped, and last time he didn't."

"I think he would have raped last time, too," said Andy, "except he knew the victims had called 911. He didn't want to be caught with his pants down."

"Makes sense," agreed Stowe.

"He's pretty brazen," suggested Davis. "Someone could have seen the open window and called police while he was taking his time in the bedroom."

"Not at night if he turned out the lights in the living room," said Pearson.

"Okay," said Andy, "I think we're done here unless anyone has anything to add. We'll let the evidence boys take care of the rest."

"Evidence techs," said Davis. "Please call them evidence technicians, not boys. In case you haven't noticed, one of them is female."

"Sorry," said Andy. "Force of habit."

Stowe stuck his head inside the door and told Fredriks to "Bag her and tag her and let's get this show on the road."

Andy and Davis did a walk-around outside the building while Pearson interviewed the building superintendent and the maintenance man. Carson had strung yellow crime scene tape around the entire side of the building with the open window. Local media and a few dozen onlookers were gathered in the parking lot.

"He went up the drain pipe here," said Andy. The downspout was pulled slightly away from the building as if it had bourn a heady burden. "This guy must have monkey blood. You can see the indentations in the aluminum where he grabbed onto the downspout, but he must have gone up so fast he didn't pull the pipe free of its moorings. He went up more than three floors, stepped onto that ledge, and kept his balance while crossing to the window. I couldn't do that. Could you?"

"No," admitted Davis. "I wouldn't even want to try."

"He balanced on that ledge and pried open the window. He was strong enough and coordinated enough to take the window out of the frame, angle it inside the living room, and set it quietly on the floor. Anyone else would have dropped it, but this guy didn't."

"What is he? Some kind of Superman?"

"Agile, strong, determined. He's no Superman or Spiderman, but he's not your ordinary rapist, either. He's trained to do things other people can't."

"Like James Bond?"

"Better trained even than Bond. The question is, who trained him? Some government agency? Or did he learn to do these things by himself?"

"Rape isn't a sexual crime as most people think," said Linda Davis. "It about power. Men who rape usually feel powerless around women. They're very fearful of rejection. Consensual sex has too many ego-shattering risks involved to take the chance they could be rejected the way they likely were in the past. So they place their victims in a position where they cannot possibly say no. This guy thinks that holding a woman at gun point or knife point isn't enough. Women might still reject him, might fight him off or run away. He kills them first. Dead women can't fight, can't run, and they can't say no."

"You think that describes our killer?"

"Doesn't it?"

Andy had to think about that. He remembered what had happened to Dolores Ledbetter. Dolores had fought her rapist, and the guy had stabbed her and then raped her. Had the rapist killed Dolores before or after he raped her?

Even if he had killed Dolores after, he had repeatedly stabbed her before raping her and the wounds rendered her completely helpless. Andy's consolation was that police said she was probably unconscious by the time the actual rape occurred. There was blood everywhere at the crime scene, and she had lost so much blood she was barely alive when her throat was cut.

So what Davis said made perfect sense. Andy felt the old anger—anger he had repressed since Dolores was buried and the rapist disappeared—return.

What made a man—any man—want a woman who didn't want him? Andy remembered the old adage that women were like streetcars or elevators. If you missed one, another would come along soon enough. Why would a man kill a woman just to have sex? Surely, there were enough women in the world that one could find a willing partner if one looked.

After Dolores died, Andy hadn't bothered to look for anyone but her killer. He had become so wrapped up in learning forensic science and becoming a cop that he had seldom dated. Every once in a while, he noticed a woman who seemed interested in him, and he had several close friends who were women. He even slept with a few of them occasionally.

Sex, to Andy, meant sharing intimacies that made one vulnerable, and Andy didn't like feeling vulnerable. He had learned his lesson when Dolores was killed. He had allowed himself to fall in love only once, and Dolores' untimely and brutal death had so devastated him that he flinched every time he felt close to a woman. So he had kept his relationships casual. Every time a woman tried to get too close, Andy pulled away.

But he knew not everyone was like him. Some men wanted sex every day and twice on Sunday. Some women, too, he imagined. It took all kinds to make a world, and there was certainly enough diversity to explain sexual assault and even murder.

Andy had studied the deviant mind in abnormal psychology classes, and he had studied it on the street. Sex offenders were often extremely sensitive to rejection, and they had a tendency to act impulsively. Many sex offenders, surprisingly, were married. But whenever they felt rejected by their wives, they impulsively sought sex with a woman who wouldn't reject them. Sometimes, that was a prostitute. Sometimes, it was a small child they could entice with treats or bully with threats. Sometimes, it was a woman they raped at gun point or knife point.

And sometimes they killed the person they had sex with.

But most sexual murders were committed after the fact—after the rape occurred—usually to keep the only witness quiet. Very few murderers had sex with their victims after they had killed them. This guy was different. He killed first, then had sex as if it were an afterthought. Did killing turn this guy on?

Davis was correct about rape being more about power than about sex. After killing, this guy must feel very powerful. If he needed to kill to feel powerful, he'd kill again.

"What else can you tell me about this guy?" Andy asked Linda Davis.

"He didn't like her earrings."

"Why not?"

"They were too large for her face. She had attached earlobes, and dangling earrings made her face look unbalanced, asymmetrical. She should have used diamond studs instead or maybe a jewel like a garnet. She wore a garnet in her navel. But she was young. She thought the dangling earrings were cute. Some of her friends probably wore them and she thought they looked good. They might look good on others, but not on her."

"So he yanked them out?"

"Before he raped her."

"And we know that," agreed Andy, "because we found the earrings in the bathtub and not the bedroom."

"Exactly."

"Thanks, Ms. Davis. You've been a big help. I'm glad you're with us on this."

"You're welcome, Lieutenant."

"Call me Andy. Everyone else does."

"All right, Andy."

He noticed she didn't offer to let him call her Linda. That was okay with Andy. He was new at being a supervisor, and he had a lot to learn about supervisor-employee relations.

And a lot to learn about women that he suspected he didn't even know he needed to know.

Rat was worried about George. The old man hadn't been home for two days, and Rat knew what that meant. George was so wrapped up in thought he wasn't taking care of himself.

Not only was George going without sleep, he was probably going without food, too. Rat imagined the old man stepping outside to smoke his pipe more than usual, that far-away look in his eyes. He had a marvelous mind, but that mind suffered when the body didn't get nourishment and rest. George had gone off the deep-end before. Rat didn't want to see that happen again. Nobody could talk sense into George once he made up his mind. But Rat had to try.

On his way to the Public Safety Building, Rat stopped at Burger King and purchased a couple of Whoppers with fries. He ordered a chocolate shake for George and a black coffee for himself.

George had his eyes glued to a microscope when Rat arrived with sandwiches.

"Time for you to get some fresh air, George," Rat told his friend. "Let's step outside and eat lunch. It's summer. We can sit on the grass and have a picnic. Then you can smoke while we talk about all the evidence you've found from all the overtime you've put in."

"Which case?"

"There's more than one?"

"Three. You already know about the four people killed Wednesday night and the fire on Thursday. A woman was found dead this morning, killed with an icepick."

"The fire? That was an accident, wasn't it?"

"Uh uh. Arson. We found accelerant in the ashes."

"Oh, shit."

"What did you bring me?" George looked curiously at the sack with the Burger King logo.

"Whopper and fries. Chocolate shake."

"I guess I can spare a few minutes."

They took the elevator up to one and walked outside into the bright sunshine. Light still hurt Rat's eyes, and he suspected George was feeling it even worse.

Rat had bought a pair of sunglasses to protect his eyes, but he stopped wearing them when he noticed they made him look like Eddie Moore, the Pickaxe Butcher. Moore had worn sunglasses when he killed because he, too, had lived underground for many years. Residents of the tunnels had adjusted to living in constant darkness. Their eyes became so sensitive to light that they could see in the dark, but they were blinded by sunlight. Light, eventually, proved to be the Butcher's downfall.

After nearly two years above ground, Rat's eyes were adjusting again to living in light. Rat could now see to drive in daylight, he could see to read books, and he could even watch TV and use computers. George could see to use microscopes. He could see to drive. He could even see a future with himself in it.

Rat and George both sat down on the scorched lawn in back of the PSB. Heat radiated from the baked ground, causing the air above the burnt grass to shimmer like a belly dancer's stomach.

"Eighth day in a row over ninety," said Rat. "Remember how we used to complain about the cold last winter?"

"It was the snow I complained about," said George, accepting a sandwich from Rat. "I don't mind the cold, but I hate snow."

"So what have you found so far?"

"Stowe and Andy think we have a serial killer on our hands who killed twice in one week. I have to agree."

"He used the same icepick?"

"No. Same manufacturer, though. Andy brought me a sample from a downtown bar, and it matches the one we found at the scene today."

"Any idea who the killer might be?"

"He's a real sicko, Rat. He killed that woman we found today, and then he raped her after she was dead."

"What?"

"I said he raped her after she was dead."

"I heard what you said. I just can't believe it."

"I *can*. I can believe *anything*," George said, "because anything is possible. But I don't *want* to believe one human being could do that to another."

"I guess that's what I meant," said Rat. "We've seen some terrible things, haven't we?"

"You lots more than me. I know your years in Iraq were pretty damn awful. Then you came back here and saw what the Butcher did to some of your friends. Man's inhumanity to man. It never stops, does it?"

"Doesn't seem to."

"So someone's got to make it stop," said George. "We've got to find out who this guy is."

"That's Andy's job," said Rat.

"But he needs my help."

"He's got a whole team of evidence technicians to help him."

"And they're good at what they do," said George. "But they don't see the big picture."

"And I suppose you do?"

"Not yet. I'm still putting pieces of the puzzle together. But I will."

"You know," suggested Rat, "sometimes it helps to sleep on it. Let your subconscious do the work."

"You think so?"

"I know so."

"Maybe I will," said George, finishing his fries and washing them down with the remains of his chocolate shake. He made child-like slurping noises with his straw as he tried to suck the last drop from the bottom of the plastic cup.

Rat finished devouring his own sandwich and fries while George stoked up a briar pipe. The heavy, cloying, sugary odor of Cherry Blend tobacco filled the air as George puffed like a dragon. That smell always reminded Rat of a cross between dry leaves burning in the fall and chocolate chip cookies baking in the oven. Passersby, however, glanced at George with disgust and disapproval. Smoking, which had once been so socially acceptable that practically everybody did it, was now nearly outlawed everywhere in public places. To see someone sitting on the lawn of the Public Safety Building and brazenly polluting the air seemed like a slap in the face—at least a slap in the nose—of law-abiding citizens.

George ignored the hateful stares. George claimed he did his best thinking while smoking. Rat didn't know how that could be possible. Smoke deprived the brain of oxygen. But then, like George had said, maybe anything was possible.

Suddenly, George's voice emerged from the cloud of smoke like the voice of God from a burning bush. "He goes to the same downtown bar to steal icepicks and to select victims. It's a pattern, a ritual. It's worked for him twice now. He thinks it will work for him again. He knows it's magical thinking, but he can't help himself. That's where I'll find him. He'll be in that bar."

Rat was startled as George jumped up, tapped his tobacco ashes to the grass, carefully ground them out in the dirt, then shoved his pipe in a pants pocket.

"I've got to get back to work," he said. "This guy isn't going to stop killing until we find him. I'm going to find him for Andy."

"How?" asked Rat.

"By watching who goes in and out of that bar."

"You're going there now?"

"No," said George. "I'll go home first to get some sleep. But tonight I'll be watching."

"How will you know the killer if you see him?"

"I'll know," said George.

"Be careful, George," said Rat.

"I'm always careful," said George.

Rat knew that wasn't always true. Often, George became so wrapped up in thought that he neglected to notice what was going on around him. Rat worried that one day George would walk straight into a den of rattlesnakes and fail to hear warning rattles.

But Rat had to be at work by six, and he wouldn't have a day off until Monday. George was a big boy now—sixty-six years old—and he needed to grow up and take care of himself. Rat prayed to God that George would do that sooner rather than later, because later might be too late.

CHAPTER EIGHT

You know you shouldn't go back there, but you can't help yourself. Last night is still fresh in your mind, despite the disappointing day at work. You need to recreate the feeling you had. You need to fall in love all over again.

The cop at the door looks you over real good before taking your money, but you hold your head down so he can't see your eyes. If he continues to look closely at your face, you'll have to take him out here and now. But he decides to let you pass, so you let him live.

You think you'll begin with a cold beer. It's not as crowded in here tonight, and there are only two people ahead of you in line at the bar. Tonight's cover charge is five dollars, half of what it was last night, because the band tonight is supposed to be local. They play here too often to be special.

The bartender, too, looks at you strangely. He may remember you from last night and recall something distinctive about your face. You hold your head down and try to smile as you order a Heineken. Perhaps coming here tonight isn't a good idea. Perhaps you should go elsewhere. It's early yet, and there are other bars just up the street. It isn't as though this is the only place in town where you can hunt.

But you see four girls enter and head straight upstairs to the dance floor, and you take your beer and follow them. Two wear shorts, and two wear short skirts. You get a good view of their legs and behinds as they climb the stairs. By the time they have reached the second floor, you have already picked the one you want.

She's a little older than the one last night. She looks to be around twenty-five. She wears blue softee fold-over-waistband cotton shorts and a red t-shirt. She has a white sports bra evident beneath the t-shirt; you can see it through the sleeves when she moves her arms. She looks very athletic, trim and fit. Her thighs and calves are muscular but feminine. She's very attractive, and she definitely knows it.

It's Saturday night, and the girls are out to have a good time. None of the four wear wedding or engagement rings, but one does have a pale tan line around the third finger of her left hand. Either she took off her wedding band to come to the bar, or she's very recently divorced. It doesn't matter. She's not the one that interests you.

You wander to the back of the room where you'll be less visible. You're a watcher, but you hate to be watched yourself. Tonight's band plays softer and, in your opinion, much better than the one last night. They have a good beat, and the dance floor is filled with gyrating bodies. Two of the girls go out and dance with each other. The other two, the one with the pale line on her third finger and the one in the red t-shirt, stand at the edge of the crowd and watch.

After thirty minutes, you see some guy get up his nerve to ask your girl to dance. She doesn't even think about it, just shakes her head. Either this guy isn't right for her, or she doesn't want to dance. If she doesn't intend to dance, why is she here?

Perish the thought, she may be a watcher, too.

You've never met a female watcher before, because female watchers are so few and far between they're practically non-existent. Women are primarily auditory and kinesthetic—they hear and feel—and they seldom rely on their eyes for sensory input. That's because women have millions more neural connections in their corpus callosum than men. The corpus callosum is the bridge that connects the two hemispheres of the human brain, and women can easily access more than one sense at the same time because of those additional connections. Therefore, women are much better at multitasking than men, because female brains have evolved to use several senses at the same time.

Men tend to process information sequentially—most men don't have enough connections between the right and left hemispheres to walk, talk and chew gum at the same time—plus men rely on visual input much more than women because men, who evolved to hunt, use their two eyes, seldom their two ears, to find prey. Men developed superior hand-eye coordination and greater upper-body strength in order to wield weapons. Women developed better fine-motor coordination because females rely on their superior sense of touch, plus their enhanced sense of hearing, to orient to their environment. Men orient with their eyes.

Both genders use all of their senses, of course, and they normally do; but women use several senses simultaneously while men use only one at a time. Not only have these natural inclinations of the human organism evolved over generations, they are constantly culturally reinforced by a kind of classical conditioning. Men are socially rewarded for tracking and hunting; women are rewarded for gathering and nurturing. Women hold what they love close to their hearts.

Women dance with their eyes closed, hearing and feeling the music as it enters their bodies and moves them to ecstasy. Men dance with their eyes open. They need to see everything around them. What turns men on is not hearing or feeling the beat of the music but seeing the way women respond to the beat.

There are exceptions, of course. The woman in the red t-shirt appears to be an exception. Her ring-less friend is moving ecstatically to the beat, dancing in place, her eyes closed as if mesmerized. She hears and feels the music with her entire body. Her red t-shirted companion pays about as much attention to the music as you do. She is far too busy watching other people to hear or feel. Either she has learned to separate her emotions from her body, or she accesses her senses sequentially. It's as if she's dancing to a different drummer. The beat she hears is not the same everyone else hears.

Your eyes move over her body to make sure she is really a woman and not a man in drag or, heaven forbid, a transsexual.

She is about two inches shorter than your 5′ 11″. She has long, fine brown hair pinned up with polished barrettes. Her face is smooth; her neck is slim and curved, not muscular, with no visible Adam's apple. Her shoulders are not broad but gently tapering, and her breasts are ample and not augmented. She has hips too large for a man but exactly right for a woman, and there is no tell-tale bulge in the front of her shorts. If there is stubble on her legs, it's from feminine grooming. She wears white women's running shoes. She's definitely a woman.

An exceptional woman. A very exceptional woman.

When her eyes come your way, you quickly look elsewhere. Women can actually feel eyes looking at them, and you need to be more careful when you stare. You averted your face so fast you missed catching the color of her eyes. But you don't dare look back. You'll see her eyes soon enough. Close up and personal.

You move deeper into the crowd. You look for a way to watch her without letting her watch you, but it's impossible. If you can see her, she can see you. But why would she want to stare at your face?

Most adults don't look at you long; they don't want to look at you, can't stand to look at you. They turn their heads away as soon as they see your eyes. Children often stare, but then they get scared or bored or their parents tell them it's impolite to stare. Eyes are the windows to the soul, and nothing about your eyes is pretty. In the dark of the bar no one can see what's different about your eyes unless they're standing close and stare directly at you. Everyone is having such a good time that no one bothers to notice you or what's different about you.

With one exception. Did she see your eyes? Impossible! She is all the way on the other side of the dance floor. How could she possibly see your eyes from there?

You know she can't really see you from over there, but she can surely sense. Women's intuition is actually the marriage of all five senses—sound, sight, smell, touch, and taste—something that's incredibly difficult for men. Women merge all five senses automatically, unconsciously, into a sixth sense that can be very powerful. Maybe they can't put a finger on exactly what's wrong, but they realize something *is* wrong. It's like an animal that can't see a downwind hunter hidden in a camouflaged blind, but senses anyway they have become the hunter's prey.

Her friends are oblivious to your presence, but she knows you're here. You know you need to leave right now. It won't be long before she tries to get a closer look at you and realizes what's different about you. Then she'll be on guard. Go now. Don't wait.

You hold your head down as you walk past her to the stairs. Her eyes turn to follow you. She is indeed a watcher.

But you manage your getaway without incident. Neither the bartender nor the bouncer bother to notice you leaving early.

You smell the pipe smoke before you notice the man watching from the shadows. It's the old man from the coroner's office, Harvey Fredriks. You turn around and walk the other way before he can see you.

You have no idea what the old man might be doing down here. Is he waiting for someone? Is he looking to pick up a prostitute? Whatever the reason, it wouldn't do at all to have Fredriks recognize you.

So you walk all the way around the entire block, up to South Street, right to Fourth Avenue, north to West Street, and down West to where you parked your car. You sit in your car and watch Fredriks puff on his pipe. He's observing people entering and leaving Upstairs and Downstairs. Did he see you? The streets are dark, despite the waning full moon. The guy would need to be able to see in the dark to identify you at a distance. You think you turned away before he saw your face.

Fredriks is a bit odd. He began working as a lab assistant in the coroner's office about the same time you came to town and started your current job. He usually works the night shift, coming on duty after you finish work. But lately, he's been in the lab next to the morgue at all hours because the morgue is short-staffed, and once or twice you've actually had to interact with him. His clothes reek with stale pipe tobacco, and his eyes always have a far-away look as if his mind were elsewhere. You, of course, always wear dark glasses during the day when you're out in public. You keep the sunglasses in the glove compartment of the Matrix. Wearing dark glasses at night would attract far too much attention, so you leave them in the car when you go to the bar.

It's nearly midnight, and the girl in the red t-shirt and her three companions will remain in the bar until closing. You have two hours to do what you need to do and get back here.

You didn't try to purloin an icepick from the bar tonight. If the bartender had replaced the icepick you stole last night, it certainly wasn't visible.

You drive all the way out to the suburbs to find a Walmart and purchase a half-dozen icepicks from the housewares section. They are on sale for $2.95 each, plus tax. You also purchase a cheap pair of binoculars and a plain black baseball cap without a team logo. You pay cash.

You return to Third Avenue and park just north of West Street, facing Upstairs and Downstairs. The old man is still smoking his pipe across from the bar. He just stands there on the sidewalk, leaning against the façade of a jewelry store that closed hours ago, partially hidden by shadows.

All four women leave the bar at 1:30. Fredriks seems to perk up and take notice of the women. Maybe the old man isn't as brain-dead as you thought. He follows them with his eyes as they walk to their separate cars.

You put on the baseball cap you have just bought, pull the bill down over your eyes. Then you start your car, wait for the women to pull away from the curb, and follow the girl in the red t-shirt who is driving a beige Ford Fusion.

You feel Harvey Fredrik's eyes on your car as you drive past. Is he noting your license plate number? What the fuck is he doing here anyway at this time of the night? Why isn't he at work?

Coroner assistants get called out at all times of the day and night to collect bodies, and Fredriks probably got called out this morning for the chick you did last night. Unlike your job which has regular hours, he takes time off when he can. *Go home and get some sleep, Harvey Fredriks. You'll be busy tomorrow, too.*

You see the beige Fusion turn right and head west, then turn right again and go north. You follow three blocks behind, close enough to see where she's going but far enough back to be invisible. If she's a watcher, she'll check her mirrors. You fall back another block just to be safe.

She continues north to one of the more affluent subdivisions near the city limits. She uses her remote to open the garage door of a duplex on one of the quiet side streets. She must have money to afford such a place.

You watch the lights come on in the living room, then several of the other rooms. Does she live alone? You park where you can see the house from a block away. You pick up the binoculars you bought at Walmart and focus on each of the windows. She doesn't bother to close the drapes. You see her enter the bedroom and pull off the red t-shirt. She slides the shorts down and walks around in bra and thong.

Either she knows you're watching, or she thinks she's completely safe out here close to the suburbs. Women in the city don't dare parade around like that unless they're deliberately putting on a show.

You see a shadow fill the doorway to the bedroom, and another woman steps into the room. She wears a black lace negligee and nothing else. She takes off the negligee and reclines naked on the bed. She's a real blonde with long luscious hair falling below her shoulders, and a patch of light pubic hair shaved into the shape of a heart.

Your girl slides the sports bra down her tight abdomen and over her hips. She moves both the bra and her thong down her shapely legs with one fluid motion and drops them to the floor as she steps free. She is definitely a female.

Now you know why she lives in such a large place. She has a live-in lover. It also explains why she thinks more like a man than a woman. She watches women the way you do and for some of the same reasons. She wasn't looking at your face in the bar. She was probably trying to see the woman standing behind you or the woman next to you.

You laugh hysterically as you watch them make love. The blonde is soft and seductive, and she's on the bottom. Your girl is aggressive and demanding, and she's on top. Your girl reaches out, opens the drawer on the nightstand next to the bed, and takes out a large rubber toy. She rams the toy in and out of the blonde without mercy. You see the blonde's mouth open wide in what must be a very loud scream. You can't tell whether it's a scream of pain or delight since you can't hear the sound way out here. It could be both, because sometimes it's almost impossible to separate pain from pleasure.

You watch them until they finish. They take turns getting up and leaving the room, presumably to use the bathroom. Then they come back into the bedroom and, both completely naked, climb into bed. They turn the lights out in the living room. Finally, the light goes out in the bedroom.

You give them time to fall asleep before you leave your car and walk around to the rear of the duplex. It's a one-story brick building with a two-car garage on each side of the two separate apartments. The neighbors are all asleep at 3:30 in the morning. You hear air-conditioners working hard to cool both sides of the building because it's still hot outside. Crickets chirp in the grass. The more-than-three-quarters-full moon floats high in the sky, surrounded by a sea of dazzling stars. It's a beautiful night, calm and peaceful. You have just enough light to see to work, but not so much you feel exposed. There's no need to hide.

You find a sliding glass door in the back that opens from a brick patio into the girls' apartment. There are two loungers and two Adirondack chairs on the patio. The door is locked, but you easily slide your ATM card into the thin crack between the door and the aluminum frame and lift the latch with the card. The door slides silently open with only a slight tug.

You carry the new icepick in your gloved left hand, its steel shank gleaming in the moonlight. You walk slowly through the too-dark living room, careful not to bump into furniture or knock anything to the floor. You enter a hallway that connects the living room with the bathroom. There are carpeted bedrooms on both sides of the hallway. The doors to both bedrooms stand open and faint light filters in through windows on the outside walls. You know the bedroom where you saw the two women has to be located on the right. You pause in the hallway to listen. You hear nothing but a clock ticking on the left, deep breathing on the right and an occasional snore. They are both still sound asleep.

Had you encountered a closed door on either bedroom, you would have suspected other people might also be in the house. But both doors are wide open, and you hear no sounds of breathing from the back bedroom. You're good to go.

Moonlight shines through the undraped windows. You can make out two dark shapes on the bed. You assume their feet are facing the foot of the bed, their faces near the head of the bed. You squint to distinguish which shape is your girl and which is the blonde. The blonde is on the right. Your girl is on the left. It's too hot tonight to hide under sheets or blakets.

You have to do your girl first. The blonde poses no problem. She's both docile and submissive. But you know your girl is athletic and aggressive, and she'll try to fight. You need to take your girl out fast, then turn your attention to the blonde.

You move around to the left side of the bed holding the icepick ready, alert to any changes in breathing. You can barely make out her face. Her eyes are closed. You move the icepick closer.

Her sixth sense kicks in just as you are about to ram the icepick into her eye socket. Her eyelids suddenly pop open, and she kicks at you with both bare feet. She can't see any better in the dark than you can, and her feet miss your groin only to put bruises on your hip. At the same time, she jerks her head back, and the icepick sinks into her cheek instead of her eye.

You pull the shank free of her flesh, and blood pours out of the hole. The blonde wakes up and tries to move her butt off the bed, but she is still half asleep and she moves too slowly to escape. You jab the icepick into her chest and feel the shank bend against her breastbone. You pull it out and stab her again. This time the tip enters between her ribs, goes all the way in, and penetrates her heart.

Meanwhile, your girl is still trying to connect with your groin. Her feet and fists flail at your body. She fights like a girl and not like a man. You hear her screaming obscenities and hope her screams don't wake the neighbors. She's trying to hit you but she doesn't have the upper body strength to really hurt you.

As you remove the icepick from the blonde and turn it toward your girl, you notice the shank of the icepick is bent from striking the blonde's sternum. But, fortunately, the cheap steel didn't break. You take another swipe at your girl's eyes, and this time you gouge open her eyebrow and half her forehead.

Her face is quickly covered with a river of blood flowing down the furrow in her forehead, and she's temporarily blinded as blood pools in her eyes. There are copious veins and capillaries throughout the face that gush, but don't spray, blood. It's arteries that spray, and the major arteries are located in her neck. Strike an artery, and she'll bleed out in minutes.

Instead of aiming for the eyes again, you go for the neck. You feel the metal tip penetrate the skin, the shank pass through tracheal tissue, the tip excise the carotid as it comes out the far side of her neck. Now blood sprays out like a guy taking a piss.

Both women are covered in blood, and so are you. Your clothes are completely ruined. And so is your mood. Though the women are naked, their curves no longer look appealing.

So, instead of raping them, you puncture their eyes with the icepick.

Then you insert the icepick into your girl's vagina and ram it up as far as it will go to teach her a lesson. You feel tissue rip and tear. You repeat the process on the blonde.

When you have finished, you step into the bathroom and turn on the shower. You use their soap to wash as much blood from your clothes and body as possible. When you have finished, you spray the walls and tub with Lysol and wipe it down with toilet paper. You flush the toilet paper down the toilet while letting the shower continue to run. You take the towels you used with you. You're not sure if your DNA is on file but why take chances?

It's still so warm, your clothes are nearly dry by the time you reach your car.

Rat was surprised to find George already at home when Rat got off work. George had been putting in so much overtime during the past several weeks that he certainly deserved to take some time off, and Saturdays and Sundays were his scheduled days off anyway. Unfortunately, death seldom took days off. George was always on call, at least until Sally Nolan got back from her honeymoon and the day shift lab tech came back from vacation, or the coroner's office hired replacements for the people who had recently resigned, whichever happened first.

Rat once read statistics that showed the job burnout rate for coroner assistants and similarly-skilled mortuary technicians was even higher than the burnout rate of doctors and nurses. Not everyone was cut out to deal with death every day, to literally handle dead bodies in various stages of decay or decomposition, to pick up pieces of bodies and transport them from one place to another. Finding qualified replacements was next to impossible. People who had the required science courses weren't willing to work the often long hours the job demanded for such little pay. Other jobs paid more for less work.

George, who had two earned doctorates—one in higher mathematics and one in theoretical and applied mechanics—from prestigious universities, had all the requisite science courses plus some. One of the requirements of the job George didn't have when he first applied was a valid state driver's license. George couldn't pass the eye exam until his eyes adjusted to seeing in daylight again. After ten years of living in underground tunnels and only coming out at night, he had terrific night vision but lousy daytime vision. Eventually, his eyes adjusted enough so he could pass the examination for a motor vehicle license, and Sally and Troy Nolan both recommended George for the job.

George had something other applicants didn't have: an insatiable curiosity. He wanted to know how and why everything worked, from the farthest reaches of outer space to the inner reaches of cellular biology and human psychology. George analyzed everything on multiple levels. George was the man who once had mathematically verified Einstein's Unified Field Theory. Unfortunately, no one else was capable of understanding the higher math involved, though there were still astrophysicists and mathematicians mulling over the implications of his twenty-year-old published papers and trying to prove him wrong.

Sometimes, George still went off the deep end and got so lost in thought that he paid absolutely no attention to the mundane world. It didn't happen quite so often anymore since George had cut back on his smoking.

"I know who the killer is," announced George when Rat walked in the door at 6:30 Sunday morning. "I saw him."

"Who is he? Where did you see him?"

"I didn't see his face," said George. "But I saw him walk out of the bar around midnight."

"How do you know he's the killer?"

"He looked guilty."

"Oh, come on, George. How can you say he *looked* guilty?"

"Because he did."

"What made him look guilty?"

"He came out of the bar keeping his head down so no one could see most of his face. Then he switched directions, and walked south instead of north. He turned right on South Street and I lost sight of him as he headed west. And there was something familiar about him. I've seen him somewhere before. I'm sure of it."

"You're letting your imagination get the better of you again," said Rat.

"I watched everyone who went into or came out of that bar from nine until closing," said George. "He was the only one who looked guilty."

"Maybe he looked guilty because he was married and didn't want anyone to know he was in a dance club without his wife on a Saturday night."

"I saw some of those, too," admitted George. "But this guy was different."

"Describe him to me."

"He was about my height, around five-eleven, and he looked physically fit like he worked out. He wore a plain black t-shirt, jeans, a thick black leather belt, and black Reeboks. He had his hair cut really short all over, like he had shaved it a week ago and it had just started to grow out again. His face looked clean-shaven, no beard or moustache. I'd say he was close to your age, maybe a few years older. Not quite pushing forty yet, but several years past thirty. I couldn't see his eyes because he held his head down, so I don't know his eye color. His hair was cut too short to tell his hair color in the dark. My eyes don't see in the dark the way they used to. How about you? Still have your night vision?"

"It's fading as my daylight vision improves," admitted Rat.

"All of life is a trade-off," said George. "Like a zero-sum equation, there are winners and losers. As one increases, the other necessarily diminishes."

"Are you going to tell Andy?"

"Not until I have more to tell him. I made a mental list of all the license plates on cars driving past Upstairs and Downstairs near closing time. I wrote those numbers down when I came home." George held up a sheet of paper with letters and numbers on it. There looked to be more than a hundred entries.

"I thought you said the guy left at midnight. The bar doesn't close until two. Do you think the guy came back at closing time?'

"I think he identified his potential victims inside Upstairs and Downstairs, then either followed them from the bar or left to watch for them to leave the bar. I think he trailed them from Upstairs and Downstairs to the scene of the crime. He had to have a car to follow Barbara Ames to her apartment. She was the 21-year-old victim we found raped yesterday morning. I think the killer left the bar early last night so he could be ready and waiting when the victim walked out of the bar and headed to her own car."

"So you remembered license numbers?"

"Sure."

"You can keep all those numbers straight in your head?"

"Of course," said George, as if it were something everyone could do.

"And what are you going to do with all those license plate numbers?"

"Recognize them when I see them again. If I see them near a crime scene, I'll ask Andy to run the plates through DMV."

"Either you're brilliant or you're crazy, George."

"I'm not crazy," said George.

Rat was sound asleep when their home telephone rang shortly after noon. It was Doctor Stowe calling to speak with George.

Rat found George in his home office, surfing the world wide web. "Why didn't you pick up the phone?" Rat asked. "You have an extension."

"I was busy. I didn't hear the phone ring."

"The call's for you," said Rat.

George picked up the extension and listened while Dr. Stowe gave him instructions. Then he logged off the computer and stood up. The air was a solid cloud of tobacco smoke. Rat didn't know how George could see the computer screen through all that smoke.

"I've got to pick up the meat wagon downtown and then drive almost to the north suburbs. Double homicide. Two women. Stowe's already on the scene."

George had a bad habit of calling the coroner's van "the meat wagon." It was actually a large panel truck. It had two gurneys strapped to the walls, vinyl body bags, and boxes of supplies useful at a crime scene. It had oversized tires and four-wheel drive to negotiate rugged terrain.

George and Rat both had their own personal cars. Rat drove a new Dodge Dart, and George drove a used PT Cruiser. George parked his car in the city garage across the street from the Public Safety Building while he drove the meat wagon.

"Two victims?"

"Both killed with icepicks," George said.

"Were they both in Upstairs and Downstairs last night?"

"I'll let you know after I see them," said George. "If they were, I'll be able to recall their faces."

"Be careful," cautioned Rat as George went out the door. "Remember, you're not as young as you used to be."

"None of us are," said George.

CHAPTER NINE

"Who discovered the bodies?" Stowe asked.

"Neighbors," said Andy. "The husband's grilling steaks on the patio this afternoon. The wife wanted to ask the girls to join them. The patio door was wide open, and the neighbor's first worry was wasted air conditioning. When no one answered her knocks and hellos, she walked in and found both bodies in the bedroom. Her husband called 911. The wife's in shock and being treated at Bryson Memorial."

"It looks like both victims have been dead at least six hours," said Stowe, putting his thermometers away. "I'd estimate time of death between 3:00 and 5:00 AM. Do you have names?"

"The blonde is Lucy Puente, age twenty. The brunette is Sheila Hansen, age twenty-six. The apartment is leased in Hansen's name."

"Puente was stabbed multiple times with a sharp thin-gauge instrument, less than four millimeters in diameter, probably an icepick. Tool mark analysis will confirm that. She was stabbed twice in the thoracic region, twice in the face. Cause of death was puncture of the descending thoracic aorta which led to severe internal hemorrhaging. Both eyes were punctured post mortem. Puente died before Hansen."

"How can you tell?"

"I can't be absolutely certain, but if you look at the pattern of blood spatters, you'll see Hansen bled out on top of Puente. That indicates Hansen's heart was still pumping when the sharp instrument, which I'm fairly certain was an icepick, entered her neck and opened the carotid artery. Hansen had already been stabbed once in the right cheek and once above the right eye, penetrating the eyebrow ridge and tearing hunks of skin off the forehead, prior to receiving the fatal wound in the neck. I would guess she fought with her assailant, and he opened her carotid in desperation when he couldn't get the icepick into the eye itself. Later, while she was bleeding out, he penetrated each of the eyes. The eyes are important to him for some reason. It's the single common denominator connecting all of the victims thus far."

"Don't forget the icepick. He used an icepick to poke out the eyes of all his victims. Why did he use an icepick instead of a knife or something else?"

"It's easy to manipulate. It's lightweight, easy to hide, and inexpensive to obtain."

"He stole the first two icepicks from a bar downtown."

"Did you find a discarded icepick this time?"

"No. We're still looking."

"Obviously, he wasn't afraid to be caught with it in his possession this time. I think he got rid of the icepick last time because he worried someone might see him with it. This time he wasn't worried. Either he's getting bolder, or he doesn't care if he's caught. Didn't anyone hear screams from either victim? Surely, Hansen had time to scream before she expired."

"The neighbors certainly heard plenty of screams. But the neighbors said they were used to hearing screams coming from this apartment in the middle of the night. It seems at least one of the girls became extremely vocal during lovemaking."

"Both victims were penetrated vaginally post mortem. I'll be able to tell more at autopsy, but it appears he shoved the damn icepick in only to add insult to injury. Puente also has recent labial tears that occurred prior to her death. Either the rapist grew in size since yesterday, or Puente had sex with someone else. I see no similar tears on Hansen."

Andy held up an evidence bag with an oversized rubber dildo inside. "I think she had sex with some*thing* else," he told the doctor.

"Every girl's best friend," said Evangelista as Evangelista and Davis walked into the bedroom. "It looks like the perp cleaned up in the shower before he left. Towels and soap are missing from the bathroom, and the shower stall has been scrubbed clean. We found some hairs down in the drain, but they look like they may belong to the victims."

"Any prints?"

"Size eleven men's running shoes," said Davis. "No fingerprints other than the victims'."

"Where did you find the shoe prints?" Andy asked.

"On the floor in the bedroom, the floor in the bathroom, out on the patio. He had blood on his shoes when he left the bedroom, but we found clean shoeprints in sand near the patio, both entering and exiting. He washed his shoes in the shower before he left. He's far from disorganized."

"What else did you find?" asked Andy.

"He opened the lock on the patio door. I think he used a credit card. He must have worn gloves, because there's no latent prints on the door handle or the glass."

Harvey Fredriks appeared in the hallway. "Let me know when you want me to remove the bodies," he said.

"Do we have all the pictures we need?" Andy asked.

Both Stowe and Evangelista said yes. Stowe had taken digital photographs, and Evangelista had taken several rolls of thirty-five millimeter.

"They're all yours," Andy told Fredriks.

"I saw her last night," said Fredriks as he prepared to bag the bodies. "The brunette. She left Upstairs and Downstairs at closing. The other girl wasn't there."

"What were you doing out on the streets at two in the morning, George?" asked Andy.

"Watching," said George. "It was my night off, so I went downtown to see who entered and exited the bar. I saw the brunette, but not the blonde."

"Blonde was only twenty," said Andy. "Not old enough to legally drink. I know the guy at the door. He's religious about carding."

"The brunette went into Upstairs and Downstairs with three other women," said George. "And she left with the same three women. They exited the bar together just before closing."

"Upstairs and Downstairs is yet another common denominator," Andy told Stowe. "I suspect the first two icepicks used as murder weapons were pilfered from the bar there, and the first four victims were seen by the bartender the same night they were killed."

"You think the killer meets his victims in that bar?" asked Stowe.

"I think he selects his victims from women in the bar, then follows them and kills them."

"Tell me how you think the murders went down," Andy asked Davis and Evangelista after Stowe and Fredriks left with the bodies. This was Pearson's scheduled Sunday off. Del was on call, but Del hadn't responded to any of Andy's telephone calls this afternoon. Davis and Evangelista were the only techs on call, and both came running as soon as they heard two woman had been murdered. Davis and Evangelista were young and single. Pearson was older, married, and had a family. Del was even older, and Andy knew Del had left the west coast after his wife divorced him. Del was a good cop, but he didn't want anyone to think he was married to the job.

"Doc says time of death was between three and five," said Andy. "The blonde was killed first."

"Her name was Lucy Puente," said Davis. "Please don't dehumanize Lucy by referring to her as 'the blonde.'"

"This is your first homicide case, isn't it?" Andy asked Davis.

"I competed an internship with a police department in Florida as part of my masters program," said Davis. "I've been at actual crime scenes before. Why?"

"Didn't they teach you in any of your criminalist classes never to identify with the victims? Because that's all those two women are now. They're victims. They're no longer living, breathing, functioning human beings. They're corpses. They're stiffs. They've been victimized beyond repair, and you can't salvage their lives the same way you might salvage rape survivors because these victims are no longer alive. I'm not the one who depersonalized Lucy Puente and Sheila Hansen. The killer did. If we allow ourselves to get emotionally involved with the victims, we'll burn out before we get close to catching the killer. We simply cannot allow that to happen. We owe it to the victims to see justice done. We owe it to the potential victims we might be able to save if we remain objective. And we owe it to ourselves if we want to stay sane. From now on, we'll all refer to Lucy Puente as Victim Number 1, and Sheila Hansen as Victim Number 2. Is that okay with you?"

"I suppose it will have to be," said Davis. She didn't look happy about it.

"So tell me what you think happened here."

"The perp used a credit card to unlatch the patio door," said Evangelista. "He walked through the house to the bedroom."

"How did he know where the bedroom was located? And how did he know the victims were in the bedroom?"

"He watched them go to bed," said Davis.

"And how did he do that? Where was he when he watched them?"

"Outside," suggested Evangelista. "The drapes were open on the window. He must have watched the vics through the window."

"Very good," said Andy. "Take a look out the window and tell me where he must have been when he watched them?"

"There," pointed Evangelista. "In order to see the bed, he had to be somewhere across the street."

"On foot or in a car?"

"He must have had a car. He had to have one to follow Hansen from downtown."

"Did anyone report seeing a strange car?"

"All the neighbors were asleep."

"And why didn't the sound of the car's engine alert the victims? Or wake the neighbors?"

"The air conditioners," offered Davis. "All of the houses have their windows tightly closed and the air conditioners cranked. The sounds of the air conditioning units acted as white noise that cancelled out the sounds of a car passing on the street."

"I agree with everything you've said so far. Please continue."

"So he watches both victims," said Evangelista, "and he must have gotten quite a show."

"Think time-line now. Victim number 2 left downtown around 2 AM. It's probably a half-hour trip from Third Avenue all the way out here. Let's say she got home at 2:30. Doc says she died between three and five. How long did the perp watch before he made his move?"

"An hour?" suggested Davis.

"At least," said Andy. "He would have waited to make sure they were asleep. Let's say he entered the house around 4:00. Were there any lights on in the house?"

"None when we got here," said Evangelista.

"So he made his way in the dark. He walked around the side

of the house to the back, popped the latch, slid the door open. He left the sliding glass door open about thirty inches. That's what the neighbor said. Then what?"

"He walked through the kitchen, the living room, the hallway."

"In the dark," said Andy. "He negotiated furniture in the dark. He had to move slowly so he didn't bump into a table or chair. What do you think? Ten minutes? Fifteen?"

"Fifteen," agreed Davis.

"Okay. Now it's 4:15. He needs to do the deed before sunrise. It's June 21st. The sun comes up early. Maybe five-thirty or earlier. But it's also Sunday morning. Most people will sleep in."

"Unless someone has an early tee-time at the golf course," said Davis.

"He has only an hour to finish what he's started. He wants to be gone while it's still dark. So he's feeling some time pressure. He enters the bedroom. What then?"

"He finds both women naked in bed," said Davis.

"How can he see?"

"Moonlight coming in from the window?"

"Is that enough light?"

"No, not quite," said Evangelista. "That's why he stabbed Hansen in the cheek instead of the eye. He couldn't see well enough to hit her eye."

"Go on."

"He stabs Puente in the chest as she tries to get away, but he misses any of her vital organs," said Davis. "He stabs her again, hitting her heart."

"And what is victim number 2 doing all this time?"

"Bleeding?"

"What else?"

"Fighting like a wildcat?"

"Exactly. Kicking and clawing and screaming."

"That's why," said Evangelista, "he stabbed her in the neck. He couldn't get the icepick in either eye because the eyes were too small a target with her thrashing around. So he went for the soft tissue of her long neck, punctured the carotid, and waited for her to stop struggling before he stabbed both eyes."

"How long did all that take?"

"Ten, fifteen minutes maybe?"

"So now it's four-thirty. Why doesn't he rape the bodies? He has time before sun-up."

"He did rape them," said Davis. "Symbolically."

"So, it wasn't just about sex after all, was it?" asked Andy.

"No," said Davis. "It was about power."

"Very good. I think that's about as close as we're going to get to knowing what happened. Why did he take a shower?"

"He was covered in blood?" suggested Evangelista.

"True. Why else?"

"He felt dirty," said Davis.

"Very good. He felt dirty because Victim Number 2 touched him," said Andy. "He wanted to be in control of all the touching."

"He's really sick," said Evangelista.

"I personally agree with you," said Andy.

"He's killing someone almost every night," noted Davis. "When is he going to stop?"

"When we catch him," said Andy.

You feel physically sick. Not only do you have bruises all over your body, but you now have new scratches added to your face that you didn't notice the bitch putting there last night.

Last night was an anomaly. Only once before had such a thing happened, and you don't want to think about that. During the more than ten years you've been active you have always been in total control. What happened that made last night so different?

It wasn't just that there were two victims instead of one, because you've killed as many as six on some nights without a problem. You move fast, take out one right after the other, and keep moving until you finish.

What was different about last night was the brunette. She fought like a demon. She even tried to take the icepick away from you. She wanted to reverse roles, to make you into the victim, herself into the killer.

It was as if she knew you were watching her, knew you were standing there in the dark, knew what you were going to do next. Her eyes snapped open before you could close them forever. You finally had to stab her in the neck to stop the incessant kicking and hitting and scratching and screaming.

Did she see your face? Did she see your eyes? Did she see your fear in them?

You want the women you honor with your touch to see the love in your eyes as the last thing their eyes see. You look at them with love; they look back with fear. That's the way you want it to be; that's the way it has to be.

But that didn't happen last night. Everything was so perfect until she opened her eyes. She moved so much faster than you, and it surprised you.

The element of surprise has always worked in your favor. You know what you must do and you go ahead and do it without hesitation, and by the time they become aware of your presence and your intention it is usually too late for them to react. They freeze like deer in headlights, rabbits before wolves. It has always been easy because they made it easy for you.

You know from your own personal experience what it's like to acquiesce, to hope and pray you won't be noticed and maybe the horror will go away on its own and you'll be left alone if you do nothing. Fear interferes with rational thinking.

The brunette hadn't reacted rationally but instinctively, and her instincts were to fight if she expected to survive. She didn't need to think. She acted.

Watchers were like cats. They maintained a low profile, conserved their energy, observed their prey, instinctively planned their moves to always stay one step ahead, and pounced when they were ready. Watchers were capable of incredible bursts of speed and strength for short periods of time.

And, like a cat, the brunette had tried to kick and claw you. Fortunately for you, she had trimmed her nails. Had her fingernails been long like the blonde's, she might have done even more damage.

You, too, keep your nails trimmed. You need perfect control of your fingertips, and long fingernails get in the way. So you trim your fingernails every day with the Swiss army knife you keep in your pocket.

You use artificial claws when you hunt. Knives, keys, icepicks. Like a cat that keeps its claws retracted, you keep your claws hidden until you pounce.

You touch the new scar on your face and wince. The pain runs deeper than the surface scratches. Old memories return to fill you with fear. You curl up into a ball and try to hide. You are ten years old again, and you see your stepmother looking at you with disgust. She's going to punish you again for looking at the pictures in your father's books. She found you inside your father's study paging through medical texts from the wall-to-wall bookcases. Your father is an eminent plastic surgeon who specializes in breast augmentation and reconstruction, and he has tons of books with pictures of women's breasts. Before your father traded your mother in for a newer model—your stepmother was actually a young fashion model and one of his patients until your father decided to divorce your mother to marry her—you could go anywhere in the big house without reprisal. But when your parents divorced, your father kept the house and you while your mother took your older sisters, plus alimony and child support, and moved to New York. Life has been pure hell since your father remarried and your stepmom moved in.

Not only does your father have a very lucrative private practice, he is a professor at a prestigious medical college. He's far too busy to spend time with you. When he is home, his wife demands his full attention. You miss your father as much as you miss your mother and your sisters. You are convinced your step mother is a witch who has placed a spell on your father.

And now the witch is coming for you. She tells you it's okay for grown men to look at women's breasts, but it's a sin for children. She's going to punish you for your wickedness. She orders you to pull down your pants. You comply, because it's useless to run or hide. The witch always finds you and punishes you even more.

She beats your butt with her bare hand. You feel her long, red-painted fingernails scrape across your tender flesh each time she hits you. Your cheeks turn red—the cheeks on your face red with embarrassment and the cheeks of your buttocks red with painful scratches—as her hand makes contact. The bruises to your buttocks will fade in a week. The bruises to your psyche will never fade.

She digs her nails in and draws blood. Your blood is the same color as her painted nails. You wish her dead, but you know wishes don't work because you wished your parents wouldn't separate but they did. You see your stepmother's face in a coffin—you know what a face in a coffin looks like because you saw your grandmother's face in a coffin after she died when you were six—and you imagine what you might do to your stepmother's face in a coffin if you had the chance. The dead don't frighten you. The living do.

Fifteen years later you kill your father and your stepmother. You kill your wife and your infant son and your wife's parents. You kill yourself, too.

But the living still frighten you. So you work with the dead, not the living. You have become the artist you were meant to be.

You spend the day in your car parked on the street. There are no parking restrictions on Sunday, and very little traffic downtown. When it gets too hot even with the windows open, you decide it's time to replace the clothes you ruined last night. You drive to Walmart and purchase two brand-new black t-shirts, two new pairs of jeans, and a new pair of Reeboks. You discard the old clothes in the dumpster behind a gas station after you fill the Matrix's tank.

Upstairs and Downstairs is closed on Sunday and Monday nights, and you decide to lay low for a few days. Last night scared you more than you want to admit. Perhaps you should look for a new apartment tomorrow before work, something inexpensive and close to downtown.

You wonder again about Harvey Fredriks. What was the old man doing downtown late at night? You know he's only a coroner's lab assistant and not a police officer, but it still worries you that he was there and may have seen you.

Did he recognize you? How could he, unless he could see in the dark?

You always wear sunglasses when you work, and you usually have a lab coat on when you go to the morgue. Fredriks has never see you without sunglasses masking your eyes. You remember he once asked you about why you wore sunglasses. You explained that you had very sensitive eyes and you needed to keep sunglasses on even indoors. He said he knew what it was like to have eyes overly sensitive to light.

But your shaved head is rather distinctive, and that could be a dead giveaway. You'll know if Fredriks recognized you, or not, when you see him again. If he did recognize you, you'll have to kill him. Accidents happen all the time in a laboratory. Besides, he's an old man. He could have a heart attack. He might even die of fright.

It might be prudent to pick up a morning paper and scan coverage of the recent murders. Have the police tied them all together yet? What do they think of the man who committed the murders?

And, more importantly, has the FBI been called in yet? You have been careful to move around after a dozen or so killings in each state. But you know the FBI keeps track of these things. What clues have you left behind?

You haven't always punctured the eyes, but you have done it often enough to label you. You haven't always raped your victims, either. When was the last time you used an icepick on the eyes? Miami. You used an icepick on three women in Miami.

And Chicago. Five years ago. Boston, three years ago.

You have also killed with a butcher knife, a bread knife, a Boy Scout knife, a Swiss Army knife, a scalpel, a claw hammer, a sharpened stake, and a pointed metal rod.

Perhaps you should leave town before the Feds get here. You think about the cop you saw in Upstairs and Downstairs on Friday night. He looked sharp but inexperienced. What can you do to throw him and the Feds off your trail?

You can kill two birds with one stone by making Harvey Fredriks look like the killer. Fredriks is an odd duck anyway, and it shouldn't be too difficult to throw suspicion his way. He's approximately the same height as you, though he's probably twenty pounds lighter and thirty years your senior. You decide to sleep on it. You're sure something appropriate will come to you. It always does.

You drive south on Third Avenue to the factories and industrial parks near the airport. You find a deserted factory with a weed-infested parking lot. You park the Matrix behind the building. No one will see you here, and you won't need to move your car early in the morning.

You fall asleep thinking of the women you have touched. You don't want to think of the women who have touched you. They're all dead and can no longer hurt you.

CHAPTER TEN

Andy was at his desk when his team assembled at 8:00 AM on Monday morning. He had already updated the spreadsheets with the data on the latest victims, and Stowe had e-mailed Andy the recently-completed autopsy results on both Hansen and Puente.

"Doctor Stowe found blood and skin under Hanson's fingernails that didn't belong to either victim," Andy announced when everyone was seated. "We suspect it came from the assailant."

"Did Stowe send it out for DNA analysis?" asked Pearson.

"Yes. He put a priority on the request, but he still expects weeks to get results back from the state. We now have seven people killed with an icepick in less than a week."

"Same perp?" asked Del Conklin.

"Sure looks like it. Anything new on the arson investigation?"

"We've interviewed most of the neighbors. As far as I can determine, we're one body shy on the headcount for 2306."

"The guy who lived on the third floor?" asked Andy.

"We know the names of the people on the first floor. Fred Gorski was the building manager. Toby Peters was the first floor renter. Both bodies were found in pieces outside the house. Neighbors saw them blown apart when the gas line exploded. There were three men living on the second floor, and one on the third. No one knows their names. The guys on the second floor were older. In their 60s or 70s. The guy on the third floor looked much younger, maybe 30 or 40. But no one can give us a good description except his hair was even shorter than mine. He moved in less than a year ago. One of those four is unaccounted for. We don't know which."

"Has Miller determined a possible motive for arson?"

"Not yet. He has a bunch of arson experts from the state Fire Marshal's office working on motive."

"It sounds like Miller has plenty of help. Let's put the fire—please excuse the bad pun—on the back burner for a while so we can concentrate on the icepick killer. Del, do you see anything else we can do to facilitate Miller's investigation? If not, I'm going to pull everyone back together again. Rich has tapes or digital discs from the security cameras in two buildings, the one where the victim lived and the apartment building directly across the street from the vic's apartment. Doctor Stowe estimated that Barbara Ames died between two and four on Saturday morning. Del, I want you and Evangelista to help Pearson go through those tapes. We're looking to identify some guy playing Spiderman on the drain pipe or the ledge outside the victim's window. Maybe we'll get lucky and glimpse our perp. If they're VCR tapes, convert them to digital discs. We've got the equipment and software. Zoom in and enlarge the images. Also watch the traffic going in and out of the apartment's parking lot during that same time frame. See if you can get make, model, and plate numbers. Davis, I need you to liaison with the lab downstairs. You know Dr. Stowe and Harvey Fredriks. Pick their brains. Meet with the medical technologists and the lab boys going over the trace evidence gathered from yesterday's victims. See if they had any luck on typing the saliva Stowe collected from Barbara Ames. Any questions before we get to work?"

"Yeah," said Del. "Have you seen the morning papers?"

"No," said Andy.

"Here," said Del, handing Andy the folded front section of the morning newspaper. "Not only did we make the front page, but we're all over the editorial pages, too."

The giant headline, all in upper case letters, read: "THIS MUST STOP!" Beneath the headline was a photograph of Dr. Earl Stowe, identified as assistant county coroner, and his assistant, Dr. Harvey Fredriks, wheeling two bagged bodies on gurneys from Sheila Hansen's duplex to the meat wagon. Accompanying sub-heads made it seem that women were unsafe in their own homes because women were being raped and murdered daily all over Riverdale. Another sub-head announced: "Police have no clues." There was a two-page spread on inside pages A8 and A9 with names and addresses of all the victims, including the four from Wednesday night. The lead editorial on page A20 implied local authorities were unable to protect the citizens because they were all either on vacation or totally incompetent. Captain Troy Nolan and Doctor Sally Brightson had left the investigation of these murders to relative newcomers—Lieutenant Andy Sinnott, Doctors Stowe and Fredriks—while they were off honeymooning in the Bahamas. The editorial implied the city was going to hell in a hand basket and no one was safe.

Another editorial, this one bylined by newspaper columnist and local television commentator Joel Hickman, asked: Quis Custodiet ipsos Custodes? Who, in this day and age, watched the watchmen? The police, he said were supposed to be watching out for and protecting the citizens of Riverdale, but they had failed miserably. Hickman promised to expose the incompetency of public officials at all levels, from the mayor down to the patrolman on the streets, in daily columns that would run on page 3. He ended today's editorial with a warning to "Watch out, because I'll be watching *you*."

"Jesus," said Pearson. "That's just what we need. Some asshole newspaper reporter getting in our way all the time."

"Freedom of the press," said Del. "The public has a right to know."

"Refer all press inquiries to Betty Halloran in Captain Nolan's office," directed Andy. "Betty's the department's press liaison, and she can put out periodic press releases. I'll stop down and have a talk with her this morning. Meanwhile, we all have jobs to do. Let's get to it."

Andy and Linda Davis rode down in the same elevator to the basement. Neither spoke until the door opened on the lower level.

"He's right, you know," said Davis.

"Who's right?"

"Hickman. This does have to stop. Women aren't safe in the city. We've failed to protect them."

"What do you suggest we do that we aren't already doing?"

"Warn people," said Davis. "Let them know there's a predator stalking women and teach women how to protect themselves."

"What could any of the victims have done differently to protect themselves?"

"Close blinds and drapes. Put a security bar across patio doors. Be more aware of their surroundings. Fight back if attacked."

"Good. Can you get together with Betty Halloran and craft a news release to that effect"

"Sure."

Betty Halloran had been a sworn officer and Troy Nolan's partner when Troy was a detective in Violent Crimes and Andy was a rookie. After Betty discovered she was pregnant with her first child, she asked for a desk job. Betty worked as the press liaison and assistant to then Captain Carl Erickson's secretary, and Betty moved into the secretary's position when the former occupant retired. Betty now had three children, worked eight-to-five Monday through Friday, and hadn't fired her weapon in years. Andy knew her as a street-smart woman in her mid-forties who had filled out substantially after three children and eight years of sitting behind a desk. Betty probably couldn't get into her old uniform if she tried.

Betty and Linda had met briefly during Davis's initial hiring process, and again during Linda's recent walk-through. Betty was the connection between the Violent Crimes unit and Police Department Administration, and most paperwork filtered through her capable hands. Not only did she have a way of finding out everything that happened in the Public Safety Building, she was connected, via the grapevine, to secretaries of the powers that be over in City Hall.

"I assume you've seen today's papers," she said. "So has the Mayor. The Mayor called the Chief of Police into his office first thing this morning and reamed him a new asshole. So the Chief got on the horn and talked to the state police. He also talked to Cartwright over at the FBI field office. Both state and federal help is on the way."

"What kind of help?" asked Andy.

"Dave Mullins and his evidence techs. Cartwright and another Special Agent from the FBI."

"I've worked with both Mullins and Cartwright before," said Andy. "They're good men to have around."

"I've scheduled a briefing in the conference room at three. The Chief will be there. So will Mayor Walters."

"And you?" asked Andy.

"I'll be there, too. Coffee and cookies are on the agenda."

"Betty, I want you and Linda to put together some press releases.

We need to inform the public we're doing everything we can to catch the killer, and we need people to take some common-sense precautions."

"It won't help," said Betty.

"Why not?"

"Because people expect you to do it for them. That's why they pay us, you know. To serve and protect. It's our job, not theirs."

"That's crazy," said Andy. "We can't be everywhere and do everything."

"People think we can."

"That's the kind of thinking that gets people killed."

"Look, Andy, ordinary people have lives to live. They won't hide behind closed windows and locked doors. They demand we protect them inside and outside their houses because it's our job to make the streets and the city safe."

"We're working on catching the killer," said Andy.

"I know you are," agreed Betty. "That's what you need to tell the people of this city when you send out a press release. Let them know what you're doing to keep them safe, and tell them you're making progress. Do you have a description of the perp?"

"White male, thirties, left-handed, five-ten or eleven, hundred and seventy."

"Anything else?"

"Running shoes. Probably clean shaven and has really short hair because we didn't find any of his hairs at any of the crime scenes."

"Good. Now people know who to watch out for."

"That description could fit thousands of men in this city."

"True. But it eliminates thousands of others. Let people know you have already narrowed the search down. You might even say you are watching several suspects or persons of interest. That will restore confidence in the police department, and it might even give the killer second thoughts."

"You think?"

"It's worth a try."

"You two work out the details and draft a press release. We can vet the press release at the meeting this afternoon. I'm going down the hall to talk to Stowe about autopsies."

Doctor Stowe looked like he still hadn't slept much. He had

recently showered and shaved, and he wore a fresh white lab coat over clean green scrubs. But the bags under his eyes indicated he badly needed rest.

"Don't you ever go home?" Andy asked.

"Sure. I was home yesterday. I had just fallen asleep when I got another damn phone call. Then I had to drive almost all the way out to the suburbs to process the crime scene. I figure I might as well stay here and sleep whenever I can. This way I'm centrally located, plus I don't waste valuable time traveling back and forth between home and here. I have a shower in the locker room, a chair in my office, all the comforts of home. I even have a big refrigerator that stores leftover pizza along with bodies. But I'll be glad when Sally comes back to work. Then I can finally go home, maybe even take a day or two off."

"What did you find under Hansen's fingernails?"

"Skin and blood. Not Hansen's blood. Not Puente's. Hansen's nails weren't very long, but they were heavily lacquered. She dug in and must have left two or three really good gouges in the guy's face. I sent skin samples we recovered to state labs for DNA testing. I've already determined the blood under the nails was type A. Unfortunately, more than 40 per cent of the population has Type A blood. Hanson's blood type, however, was O. So was Puente's. So the blood and epidermis under the nails had to come from the perp and not the victims."

"It takes two weeks or longer to get DNA results from the state?"

"Two weeks, usually a lot longer. I did put a rush on it, but the state is really backed up. Their labs are still processing rape kits I sent them months ago from other cases."

"Other cases? Homicides?"

"Before you became homicide honcho. I think you were doing Academy training at Quantico when those rapes occurred. Two separate incidents about a week apart last January. One woman had her throat slit from ear to ear. The other died from multiple stab wounds. Both appeared to have been raped, though presumptive tests showed no evidence of semen."

"What's taking the state so long to process samples?"

"They're short-staffed like everyone else."

"So you think the killer has a scratch on his face?"

"A deep scratch. And more than one. Hansen ripped off a good chunk of skin with three of her fingernails. She broke the nail on her middle finger, and the nail split in two. The jagged edges of the broken nail ripped deep. It may leave a permanent scar."

Sooner or later all violent perpetrators left evidence—traces of themselves—at or near a crime scene that would inevitably identify and convict them. Sometimes it was fingerprints on a coin or another object that fell from the perp's pocket during a struggle, or DNA in the form of semen or sweat or saliva or pieces of skin. It was the job of forensic experts—crime scene investigators, pathologists, evidence technicians, criminalists—to discover, collect, preserve, analyze, and provide proof of that evidence so prosecutors could present it as argument at trial. Similarly, the victims left traces of themselves on the perpetrators. Wounds or scars, for example. It was the job of cops like Andy to use all available evidence to locate and apprehend the criminal. Knowing that the perpetrator likely had a scar on his face from a victim's fingernail was helpful.

"Doc, what are the chances the earlier rape cases and the icepick murders are related?"

"As I remember, both of the earlier rapes occurred at shopping malls not long after the malls closed at ten. The first victim was a woman who had bought books at a bookstore, and she stayed in the bookstore's coffee shop reading right up to closing time. She was found in a culvert behind the mall's parking lot the next morning, not far from where she had parked her car. The second victim was an employee at a boutique. She had stayed in the store to close out the register and lock the money in the store's safe. She was walking to her car in the employee parking deck about ten-thirty when she was grabbed, stabbed, and dragged into a dark corner near the back of the parking deck. She was stabbed several more times with the blade of a pocket knife. She was likely dead or dying when she was raped. So, yes, there are some similarities. But that perp used a knife instead of an icepick. The guy stopped raping and killing after those two, and Troy couldn't come up with a suspect. I'm sure it's still an open case. If you don't have a file in your office, I can dig up the autopsy reports."

"Would you do that, please?"

"If it is the same guy, why would he stop and then start up again?"

"Good question. Something must have triggered his killing impulse."

While Andy waited for Stowe to locate file copies of the autopsy reports from last winter, he phoned upstairs to Del on the fourth floor and asked him to search the files for open rape-homicide cases. "You think this guy is a serial rapist and killer who goes on sudden sprees?" asked Del.

"Could be," said Andy. "Go over those files and compare the MO to the icepick killings. I want everyone to be at a meeting with the Mayor in the conference room at three. Spread the word. Bring the files to the meeting."

When Stowe handed Andy the autopsy reports and coroner's files on the two earlier victims, Andy couldn't help but notice striking similarities to the rape and murder of Dolores Ledbetter more than ten years ago. Was it only Andy's imagination? Or was the MO essentially the same?

Andy had gone over the autopsy findings and case files on Dolores so many times he knew the details by heart. Not only had he a personal interest in catching Dolores' murderer, but he had used the case as the basis for his master's thesis. Police had theorized that the rapist had not intended to murder any of his victims. Other rape victims had cooperated once they saw the rapist's knife, and the rapist—if it were the same man—had killed none of them. But, police speculated, Dolores had surprised the rapist by fighting with her attacker. Perhaps she had tried to wrest the knife away from her assailant, and he had accidentally stabbed her in the process. She did have defensive knife wounds on both hands. Once her assailant drew blood and she still didn't back off, he got scared and kept stabbing her. Eventually, he killed her.

Police had found skin and blood under Dolores' fingernails, too.

Her rapist's blood type had been Type A.

Dolores died when the rapist slit her throat with a knife, but evidence indicated she had been raped before she died and not after. When she grew too weak to fight him off, he had his way with her. Killing her was the rapist's way of insuring her silence, though she was probably already dead from her other stab wounds by the time he cut her throat.

Was that what the rapist did with twenty-six-year-old Mary

Woodman in January? Mary had been found in a culvert behind the parking lot of an east-side shopping mall. Her jeans and panties, along with her purse and a bag of books, were found nearby. She was wearing a red knit sweater, a white bra, a caramel-colored winter coat, and white socks with red Keds. The coat was open and the sweater and bra had been raised above her breasts. She had suffered multiple stab wounds to her naked chest and abdomen from a three-inch blade, the size and shape of an ordinary pocket knife. Mary was already dead when her assailant slit her throat.

Jean Johnston was also stabbed with a similar weapon. Jean, the assistant manager of a small boutique in a different shopping mall, was raped and murdered in the mall's enclosed parking deck. Jean's assailant had stabbed her multiple times as she was getting into her car, then he dragged her bleeding body to a dark corner of the parking deck where he raped and killed her. Or killed her and then raped her. Doctor Brightson had counted forty-two stab wounds to various parts of the body, many of them made post-mortem. Brightson speculated that the killer continued to stab Jean Johnston while he was sexually assaulting her. The red blouse she had been wearing had been slashed to shreds.

Why was this rapist so violent? Why so many stab wounds? It was almost as if, once he started, the guy couldn't stop. It was more than just overkill. It was obsessive behavior.

And then, as though he had vented all his rage and had none left in him, he stopped killing and raping. But only for six months. Then he killed and raped again, using an ice pick instead of a knife.

What triggered this kind of violent behavior? Surely, something must have motivated the perpetrator to kill and then to kill again. Was it something the victims had said or done?

And was it possible the same person that had killed Dolores Ledbetter more than ten years ago was still raping and killing today? How many other women had he raped and killed in those intervening years? And why hadn't he been caught?

No, thought Andy. That surely couldn't be possible. Dolores died on the state university campus more than two hundred miles away from here. What were the chances that Dolores' killer could have relocated to the same city where Andy was now head of homicide?

Nevertheless, as far as Andy knew, Dolores' killer had never been caught. His DNA had not matched the DNA of any known perpetrator at the time of Dolores' death, and police had no other way to ascertain the killer's identity. The number of reported rapes on campus suddenly diminished, and no other murders occurred on campus while Andy was a student there. If the killer remained in the area, he had assumed such a very low profile that he essentially dropped off the radar. Andy was almost certain the rapist had left the state after raping and killing Dolores. Where he went was anybody's guess.

Had he come back? Was Dolores' killer here now?

The telephone rang on Doctor Stowe's desk, and Stowe answered it. "I'll bring her down," he said and hung up.

Stowe checked his watch. "Harvey isn't scheduled for another hour," he told Andy. "Do you want to give me a hand?"

"Sure," said Andy. "What can I help with?"

"One of the funeral homes is here to pick up a woman killed in a car accident Wednesday night. I finally got around to doing her autopsy. I notified the mortuary this morning that I could now release the body."

"So how can I help?"

"You can clear the way through the tunnels for me."

"What tunnels?"

"The delivery tunnels. How do you suppose we get stiffs in and out of this building? We park the meat wagon across the street in the city's parking garage, take the freight elevator down to the tunnel that connects the garage with the PSB, and come in the back door to the morgue. You use the same tunnels when you bring prisoners in for booking and interrogation. Building services staff use the tunnels for freight deliveries. Trucks unload at the docks in the lot across the street, building services move the deliveries through the tunnels with forklifts, and there are no traffic blockages like there would be with semis trying to unload on the street. Come on. I'll show you."

Stowe led Andy from the offices into the morgue itself. Autopsies were performed in a large sterile surgical suite that looked like a cross between a locker room, a laundry room and a butcher shop. Andy saw several large industrial scales used to weigh human organs, stainless steel sinks with a variety of hoses attached to floor drains and water spigots, high intensity lights on movable arrays coming down from the ceiling, numerous instrument carts with knives, saws, shears, forceps, probes, and some things Andy didn't recognize. Beyond the surgical suite was the meat locker, a few dozen refrigerated compartments where bodies were kept and Stowe stored left-over pizza. Doctor Stowe opened one of the labeled doors and slid out the steel slab where the mortal remains of Toni Fisher, age 48, temporarily resided. Mrs. Fisher, Stowe explained, suffered from a variety of ailments for which she was taking prescribed medications. On Wednesday evening, she had attended a birthday party for a friend who had turned fifty and Toni consumed a large amount of alcohol at the party. She should not have attempted to drive in her condition. The combination of drugs and alcohol proved a deadly combination, and she passed out behind the wheel of her car while driving fifty miles an hour, smashed into a mailbox and then a brick wall. She died, not from the impact, but from the drugs and alcohol in her system and the effect they had on her heart. Her heart had already stopped beating before she sustained massive injuries to the rest of her body.

Stowe raised a gurney to the level of the slab, asked Andy to help him transfer the body, and closed the locker. Andy followed Stowe as he wheeled Mrs. Fisher through one hallway after another to the door that led to the tunnels.

A uniformed officer sat at a desk next to the exit door. Standing next to him was a muscular man with a shaved head, sunglasses, and a white lab coat over a black t-shirt and jeans. He was about five-eleven, a hundred and seventy-five pounds, and he wore black leather Reeboks. He had brought his own gurney.

"Where's Harvey?" asked the man whose face looked like it wore heavy make-up, the kind used to make the face of a corpse presentable.

"He doesn't come in until three this afternoon," said Stowe, handing the man a clipboard to sign.

"Too bad," said the guy. "I'm sorry I missed seeing the old guy. The funeral director sent me to collect Mrs. Fisher so I could start work on her as soon as I got in at noon." He rolled Mrs. Fisher's body from one gurney to the other. "Any personal effects?"

Stowe reached under his gurney and extracted a purse. "Her

rings, earrings, and wristwatch are inside," said Stowe.

The uniformed officer pressed a button on the wall and the large steel door opened, revealing a wide, dimly-lit tunnel that looked like it went on for miles. As the guy from the funeral home pushed his gurney into the tunnel, Andy saw the name "Albertson Mortuary and Crematory" printed on the back of his lab coat.

"Isn't Albertson the name of the County Coroner?" Andy asked Stowe.

"Yeah," said Stowe. "He retired and turned the business over to his eldest son before he ran for coroner."

"Did anything about that guy's face seem odd to you?"

"You mean the makeup? He says he practices on himself so he can get it right on his clients. He's one of the cosmetologists and embalmers at Albertson's. I guess you've got to be a little weird to work on dead bodies all day."

"Are you speaking of yourself, Doctor? You work on dead bodies all day."

"I take them apart to find out what makes them tick," said Stowe. "That guy puts them back together and makes them look presentable."

"Kind of like Doctor Frankenstein?"

"I suppose you could say that. But it's necessary. Families need closure, especially after a tragic event. Seeing their loved ones as they looked in life helps them adjust. Mortuaries provide a valuable service."

"And charge through the nose for it. I remember what it cost to bury my mother."

"That's how Albertson could afford to run for coroner. He made millions before he retired. Albertson's a real slimeball."

"Why do you work for him?"

"I accepted the fellowship before I knew what he was like. Now I need Albertson's recommendation in order to move on. I can't just quit. Most of the time he leaves us alone and lets Sally run the show because he doesn't know diddly about forensics. But he keeps pinching pennies and won't hire adequate staff. Sometimes I think Albertson and the Mayor are stealing taxpayers blind. They sure aren't spending tax money on salaries. My salary is paid for by the fellowship grant. Sally is the only pathologist actually on staff, and the only two medical technologists are a histologist and a part-time microbiologist. We're lucky to have Harvey as a lab tech. He's worth his weight in gold, though he's barely paid enough to live on. We should have six mortuary techs to help move bodies, and we have none."

"That's why you and George are working so many hours?"

"Yeah. There's no one else to do the work."

"And Albertson doesn't help out?"

"He spends his days hob-bobbing with the Mayor. I swear, Jim Albertson is at a political luncheon or dinner every day of the week. I can never catch him in his office, and I have to leave paperwork with his secretary for him to sign."

"I bet he'll be at the meeting this afternoon with the Mayor and the Chief. You'll be there, won't you, Doc?"

"If Albertson is going to be there, I wouldn't miss it for the world," said Stowe.

"Yeah," said Andy. "It'll be the highlight of both our days."

You wheel the body of the woman through the tunnels to the hearse. You open the back and slide the body in. Then you fold the gurney and slide that in, too.

Coming here today was a risk you had to take. You expected Harvey Fredriks to deliver the corpse. That way you would have discovered if Fredriks recognized you outside the bar. Instead, you saw Doctor Stowe and the same detective you had seen asking questions in Upstairs and Downstairs.

Fortunately, you had covered the scratches on your face with makeup before leaving the mortuary. You felt the cop's eyes scan your face, questioning the heavy makeup. You could see his eyes, but he couldn't see yours behind the dark glasses. The next time he sees you, he'll recognize you. Then you'll have to kill him.

You drive 2.7 miles to Abertson's Mortuary and Crematory, back the hearse up to the receiving entrance, and unload. You take Toni Fisher's corpse down the elevator to the workroom, your sanctum sanctorum, and unwrap her like a kid opening a Christmas present on Christmas morning.

She's a real mess. Besides the injuries she suffered in the auto accident, the pathologist made the usual incisions. Doctor Stowe was careful to sew up the incision behind the ears and below the hairline, beneath the occipital ridge, that extended from ear to ear. That incision was necessary to pry the scalp and face from bone in order to open the skull. You feel around to make certain the skull cap is firmly glued in place, and it is. You can barely feel, much less see, the indentation left when the Stryker saw cut through the skull. Stowe had been careful. The "Y" incision of the torso has also been sutured shut, encasing the internal organs from the tongue to the intestines, which had been removed for examination and then placed en masse in the abdomen.

You begin by spraying the body with disinfectant, and then reverently wiping it clean with soft cloths. You examine the eyes, adding cotton and plastic eye caps to give the eyeballs a natural shape. Then you coat the eye caps with stay crème and glue the eyelids shut.

You massage the limbs to remove any residual effects of rigor mortis, gently move the head and neck around for the same reason. Then you sew the mouth shut, adding stay crème and mastic compound. You shape the mouth into what you think looks pleasing.

Now you insert three needles with plastic tubes attached. One goes into an artery to inject embalming fluid, while the other goes into a vein to extract the remaining blood. The third goes into the carotid and acts as a pressure release valve in case pressure in the veins causes swelling. You drain the blood directly into a vent in the floor that carries the blood into the city sewer system.

You sever the bottom of the "Y" incision with a scalpel, remove the organs from inside the body, place them into a viscera bag, and drop them into a chemical bath to soak. You coat the inside of the body cavity with embalming powder. Later, you will place the viscera bag inside the body and sew the body back up.

You remove the embalming tubes. Then you wash her hair, blow dry it, and carefully comb and style it.

Now the rebuilding begins. This is what you live for. You will make her more beautiful than she ever was in life. You have a natural eye for beauty—probably inherited from your father—and the same artistic temperament that made him a truly great plastic surgeon. He wanted you to follow in his footsteps, and, in a way, you have.

You glance from time to time at the pictures Toni's family

provided. You will reconstruct her features perfectly, then embellish them. People will say how natural she looks, how life-like. You are a god who can bring the dead back to life.

You work all afternoon and into the evening. Shortly before nine o'clock, you replace the dried organs inside the body and sew the torso shut. You dress Toni Fisher in the clothes her family provided, and you position her lovingly in the casket they paid for.

Before you leave, you wheel the casket into the viewing room and leave it for the funeral tomorrow. Your work is done. The rest is up to the funeral director and the mortuary assistant. They will arrange the flowers, put out the memorial cards, set up the seating, prop open the casket lid for viewing.

Jack Albertson is the only one who knows you are not a licensed embalmer or a licensed cosmetologist, but he hired you anyway once you showed him what you could do. He gives you free rein to do your thing because you are willing to work cheap. As far as anyone else at the mortuary knows, you are only another mortuary assistant. Albertson takes credit for the work you do. He's a bumbling fool, greedy and egotistical. Someday, before you leave, you'll show Mr. Jack Albertson what you can really do and it will be guaranteed to take his breath away.

Now, as you drive around town in your red Matrix looking for rooms for rent, you turn your thoughts to the game at hand. Wouldn't it be wonderful if Harvey Fredriks were implicated in the rapes and murders? How difficult would it be to frame the old man?

This morning's newspapers said police had no clues. What kind of clue could you give them that would lead to the arrest and conviction of Harvey Fredriks for murders you committed?

You remember the cloying smell of the old man's pipe smoke, and that gives you an idea. Practically no one smokes these days, and far fewer smoke a pipe. If you can get one of the old man's pipes, you could leave it behind at a murder scene. That would be a start.

And you could plant the bloody icepick you have wrapped in a towel on the back seat of your car. You wore gloves when you handled the icepick and the towel. All you need do is find where Fredriks lives and hide the icepick and towel where they might be found by police.

You could follow Fredriks home when he leaves work. He was

scheduled to work three to eleven today. It's now 10:35.

You don't know what kind of car Harvey drives, but he probably parks in the city parking garage across the street from the PSB where you parked the hearse earlier today. You can wait near the exit for Fredriks to drive out, then follow him home.

While you wait for Harvey Fredriks to leave work, you think of other things you can do to implicate the old man. Planting the pipe and the icepick are only the beginning. If you want to hang a man, you know you need to tie a noose big enough to fit around his neck. Harvey's neck is scrawny, and it won't take a lot of rope to hang him.

Dirty old men make natural suspects, despite statistics that show rapists are usually close to the same age as their victims. You know that's true because old women and kids have never interested you. When you began raping on the state university campus so many years ago, you were a medical student who raped other college students. They were targets of opportunity, and you were able to watch them and follow them because they thought you were one of them. Had they seen an old man following them around campus, they would have become suspicious. Old men were always natural suspects for deviant behavior.

And Harvey Fredriks looked and acted strange anyway. He was much too old to be working as a low-paid lab assistant in the coroner's office. All of the other lab assistants you have seen in past jobs were college age. It was supposed to be a stepping-stone job for young people to learn about one branch of the medical field.

Besides, hadn't one of the officers at the morgue's back door told you Fredriks had been a homeless person for ten years before the deputy coroner hired him? The guy was lucky to have any job at all.

But what would be a more perfect place for a rapist and murderer to keep tabs on the murder investigations? Wouldn't it make sense to investigators that Harvey Fredriks had taken a job as lab assistant in order to doctor evidence found at crime scenes?

The more you think about it, the more certain you become that Harvey Fredriks is the perfect fall guy. After all, who in the world would care if the old guy went down for a crime he didn't commit? The cops would have their killer, the crimes would be solved, and you could move on to someplace else and start all over again.

What could be more perfect than that?

CHAPTER ELEVEN

Lester Cartwright was the Special Agent in charge of the FBI's local office. He wore a black business suit, red-and-black striped tie, and Florsheim oxfords. He was in his forties with neatly-trimmed brown hair, had a miniature American flag in his lapel, and a bulge on his hip from a nine millimeter Beretta 92FS.

Dave Mullins was a state police lieutenant assigned to this district, and Andy had worked closely with Mullins when Dave was still a sergeant and Andy was only a crime scene tech. Mullins was an experienced crime scene investigator. Dave was in his early fifties, overweight, wore his salt-and-pepper hair in a military-style crew cut, and carried a Sig Sauer P226. Today he wore a brown sport coat over beige slacks and no tie.

Mayor Samuel L. Walters was also in his early fifties, wore a gray pin-striped designer-label tailored suit with a maroon tie. He was tall, broad-shouldered, and looked a little like a middle-aged Ronald Reagan. Andy could also see facial similarities to Jeff Walters who had tragically died in an auto accident while still in high school. Andy's bad memories of Jeff caused him to dislike the Mayor the moment he met the man.

James Albertson was mid-sixty-ish, balding, short and stocky. He came across as a blend of TV evangelist and slimy used-car salesman. Like Mayor Walters, Albertson was a talker. He hadn't stopped glad-handing and talking since he entered the conference room.

Chief of Police Roger Elway was in his late forties, appointed by the Mayor after the former chief retired two years ago, and Elway appeared quite handsome in his white summer chief's uniform with four gold stars on each epaulette. He was tall, muscular, and looked like most people thought a cop should look. He wore a black tie and carried a Smith and Wesson .44 magnum revolver, Dirty Harry's kind of gun. Elway had been a deputy chief in a smaller city where he excelled in placating the press as the department's spokesperson. He had a masters degree in business management and hadn't worked the streets in twenty years.

Betty had set out two plates of cookies, carafes of coffee, Styrofoam cups, and bottles of water on a credenza next to the conference table. She also had a laptop computer connected to an LED projector ready for Andy's presentation at three. The computer was already logged onto the department's network and Andy's victim spreadsheet was showing on a screen set up in the front of the conference room.

Del Conklin, Rich Pearson, Linda Davis, and Lorraine Evangelista entered together just before three and quickly took seats at the table. Doctor Stowe and Harvey Fredriks came in a few minutes later.

"I'm Lieutenant Andy Sinnott of Homicide," Andy began. "I want to welcome Mayor Walters, Chief Elway, and Coroner Albertson. Also welcome to Special Agent Cartwright of the FBI and Lieutenant Mullins of the state police who have agreed to assist us with this investigation. My key staff are here, including Sergeant Delbert Conklin, Detective Richard Pearson of Violent Crimes, and officers Linda Davis and Lorraine Evangelista of the crime scene team. Doctors Stowe and Fredriks from the coroner's office just arrived. You all know Betty Halloran. We're here today to find a solution to the recent murders plaguing our city. Four people were killed Thursday morning, one Saturday morning, and two on Sunday morning. That's seven homicides in four days. Three of the women were also sexually assaulted. It appears we have an organized serial killer in our midst. I want to share with you factual information about the victims and what little we know about the killer. Betty has drafted a news release to keep the public informed of our progress, and I'd like you all to read it over and offer suggestions. I'll begin now with a briefing, and then I'll ask for your help. Feel free to interrupt with questions at any time. Each of you has special expertise in crime investigation or in dealing with the public. We all need to work together if we hope to catch this killer before he kills again."

Andy aimed a red laser dot at the screen. "The first four victims were Daniel Berger, age 29; Lila Evans, age 25; Paul Rodriguez, age 30; and Sylvia Simons, age 27. They were discovered downtown near the west bank of the river at approximately 2:00 AM on Thursday, June 18. All four had been stabbed in both eyes with an icepick. The perpetrator escaped into the river and was gone when the first officer arrived on the scene. We found prints of size eleven men's running shoes at the scene and on the east bank of the river about a mile downstream.

"The next victim was Barbara Ames, age 21. Ms. Ames was found dead in her apartment the morning of Saturday, June 20. She had been stabbed in both eyes with an icepick and raped post mortem.

"Sheila Hansen, age 26, and Lucille Puente, age 20, were found dead in their apartment the afternoon of Sunday, June 21. Time of death was estimated between three and five AM. Both women had been stabbed multiple times with an icepick and their eyes punctured with the icepick after they died. Both women were sexually assaulted post mortem with the same icepick."

"Are you saying," interrupted Albertson, "that these women were raped after they were dead?"

"That appears to be the case with Ms. Ames. Hansen and Puente were assaulted with the icepick after they died of their wounds."

"What kind of a sick monster are we dealing with here?" asked the Mayor.

"A very dangerous one," replied Andy. "I have reason to believe the same man was responsible for two previous rapes and murders: Mary Woodman, age 26, and Jean Johnston, age 24. Those murders were committed with an ordinary pocket knife rather than with an icepick, and the perimortem rapes—rapes immediately before or at the time of death—occurred outside shopping malls, rather than in homes. So there are both similarities and dissimilarities in the modus operandi."

"Why," asked the Chief of Police, "would a rapist stop for nearly six months and then start up again?"

"Good question. Why would he rape in the first place? Something must have triggered the impulse in him. Perhaps these women reminded him of someone he knew. I suspect he goes on an impulsive killing spree, then stops until something triggers his next killing spree. I think he's been doing this for a very long time."

"Why did he use an icepick?" asked the Mayor.

"I think he uses whatever weapon is handy. In January, he used a pocket knife. In June, he used an icepick. Six months from now, he might use a screwdriver."

"I would hope that six months from now he'll be in jail awaiting trial," said the Chief of Police.

"We all hope that. But this guy is organized, methodical, and smart. He moves fast and he leaves no fingerprints and no living witnesses. We do have impressions of his running shoes from the east riverbank. We have identified the shoe prints as size eleven men's Reeboks. We determined, from the angle of thrust, that the assailant is left handed. We suspect he is a Caucasian male, approximately 5 feet ten or eleven inches tall, weighing perhaps one hundred and seventy pounds. Based on the age of the victims and the speed and agility of the assailant, we estimate his age as early-to-mid thirties. We analyzed video footage from around the Ames residence, but we were unable to obtain images of the perpetrator. We may have collected DNA from the Ames murder and the Hansen murder, and we've sent samples from those crime scenes to state labs for testing. We have determined the assailant's blood type is Type A. That's all we have so far, ladies and gentlemen. Betty, would you please distribute copies of the news release? We want to keep the public informed of our progress. You may have seen this morning's papers. Officer Davis feels it's imperative we warn citizens and tell them how they might protect themselves. Linda and Betty worked on the news release together. I think they've covered everything pretty well."

"When will you catch this guy?" asked the Mayor. "That's all I want to know. That's what the public wants to know."

"We're doing everything possible to apprehend the perpetrator," said Andy.

"But when will we see results?"

"We know the killer obtained two of the icepicks used as murder weapons from a downtown bar called Upstairs and Downstairs. We believe he frequents that establishment and that's where he selects his victims. We deliberately left that information out of the news release because we plan to set up surveillance there when the bar reopens tomorrow. That's the best lead we have, at least at this time, to locating the killer. One other thing we deliberately left out of the news release is the possibility Hansen inflicted a scratch or scratches to the killer's face. We hope those scratches will help identify the killer if we see him in the bar."

"What if he doesn't return to that particular bar?" asked the Chief. "What if he goes elsewhere to select his victims?"

"That's possible," admitted Andy. "But he's been successful so far at finding victims in Upstairs and Downstairs."

"Serial killers," contributed agent Crawford, "tend to be creatures of habit, repeating what worked for them in the past. Once they establish a pattern, they seldom break it."

"Didn't you say he found the earlier victims at shopping malls?" asked the Chief.

"Yes," agreed Andy. "And those murders were committed with a knife instead of an icepick. The killer's MO varies."

"So what if the killer changes locations? What if he looks for victims in another bar? Or a shopping mall?"

"Or," asked Alberston, "stops killing for six months?"

"Sooner or later, this guy is going to slip up. He'll leave behind something that will identify him, or someone will see him that he doesn't manage to kill. When that happens, we'll get him. I promise you, we'll get him."

"It had better be sooner," said the mayor. "Or we'll all be out of jobs."

Rat heard a noise. Old habits died hard, some died very hard, and some never died at all. Rat had been trained in the Army to listen for noises in the dark, and his ears still functioned as his eyes in the dark.

Rat worked four nights in a row at the call center, then he had three consecutive nights off. Because he was used to staying awake all night, he often found it difficult to sleep on his nights off. George had come home shortly before midnight, and George had told Rat all about the meeting with the Mayor. Pressure was mounting to find the killer before he killed again, and George wished he could do more to help Andy locate the killer. He said he was sure the man he had seen outside Upstairs and Downstairs was the murderer, and he tried to remember all he could of the guy. George said he was about the same size as himself, wore jeans and a dark t-shirt, and walked fast. George lamented that he didn't get a good look at the man's face before the guy turned around and walked off in the opposite direction.

"There was something vaguely familiar about him," George claimed. "I know I've seen him somewhere before. But I can't remember where."

"Get some sleep. It will come to you."

Sleep was Rat's remedy for everything that was wrong with the world. After returning from Iraq, Rat had been unable to sleep. He tried drugs and alcohol and they didn't help. His dreams, when he did sleep, were filled with dead bodies and parts of bodies, and the dead accused him of not doing enough to save them. He always awoke screaming and couldn't get back to sleep. It was only after five years of hiding in sewer tunnels beneath city streets that Rat managed to sleep again. The sewers had protected him from the voices of the dead that haunted him, and when he finally did manage to sleep without dreaming and without waking, his body and mind began to heal.

But the tunnels had made him a night person. Night was the time when Rat left the tunnels and searched for food, wandered the city, and breathed fresh air. While his eyes slowly adjusted to living constantly in the dark, Rat had relied on his ears to do much of the work his eyes used to.

His job at the 911 call center was perfect for him. Rat was a good listener. Not only did he hear all that the callers were saying, his mind paid attention to background noises, too.

He worked from 6 PM to 6 AM. He slept from 8 AM to 2 PM. On his nights off, Rat tried to live a more normal schedule. But old habits died hard. Tonight, he had gone to bed sometime around three. He had read for an hour in bed before turning the lights off and trying to sleep. It was sometime around four that he heard the noise.

Normal noises, like the air conditioner's compressor or the ticking of an alarm clock, were routinely filtered out by his subconscious mind. They were not a threat, so they seldom reached conscious awareness.

But the noise he heard now was not a normal noise. It sounded like someone was cautiously walking around downstairs, someone inside the house. At first, Rat thought it was only George. The sounds seemed to be coming from George's study, across the hall from George's downstairs bedroom. Rat's bedroom was up on the second floor, directly above George's bedroom. If George had gotten out of bed, Rat would have known it. But none of the sounds came from George's bedroom. They came from George's study.

Rat lay in the dark listening. He remembered the sounds he had heard in the sewers: rats and possums scratching around, water flowing through the pipes, other people living in various parts of the tunnels. This sound was different: a subtle creak from a hardwood floorboard beneath the carpet as a foot put pressure on a loose board.

There was definitely someone in George's study. Rat heard a sound like wood scraping against glass as if someone had picked up a briar pipe from the big pipe-smoker's style ashtray on George's desk. George kept half-a-dozen different pipes in that ashtray. He liked to switch between pipes to keep the wooden bowls from burning out. When George finished one bowl of pipe tobacco, he set that pipe in the ashtray to cool while he lit up another.

Rat wished he had a weapon so he could confront the intruder. But he had neither the M4 carbine he had carried in Iraq nor the pickaxe he had carried in the sewers. If there were an armed intruder in the house, Rat would be at a tactical disadvantage.

He heard the footsteps slowly retreat from the study. The intruder was in the living room now. Light from the three-quarters moon allowed the intruder to negotiate furniture and find his way to the front door. Had Rat remembered to lock the door before going to bed? Had someone discovered the door unlocked and simply walked in?

He heard the door open and close. Then the house was silent again.

Rat waited until he was certain the intruder was gone, then he got out of bed and cautiously made his way downstairs to the living room. He peeked around and saw no one; nothing looked out of place. He turned on a light and checked again.

Rat walked into George's study and switched on the overhead

light. Nothing seemed disturbed in the study. If there were a briar pipe missing or out of place, Rat couldn't tell.

"Trouble sleeping?" asked George from the doorway.

"Were you just up?" asked Rat.

"No. I woke up when I heard you turn on the light."

"I think someone else was in the house. I heard noises coming from your study."

"Sure you weren't dreaming?"

"I was awake."

"There's no one here now."

"Did you lock the front door?"

"I thought you did."

"Let's check it."

The front door was closed but unlocked. Either someone had managed to unlock it, or Rat had forgotten to lock it before going to bed. He turned the lock and set the deadbolt. The locks still worked. If they had been jimmied, they hadn't been damaged.

"Anything missing?" asked George.

"Not that I know of. I thought I heard someone in your study. Take a look and see if everything is exactly as you left it."

"It looks okay," said George from his study.

"Any of your pipes moved?"

"One may be missing. Let me check my coat and pants pockets. Maybe I didn't take it out when I came home from work."

"Why would someone break in to steal one of your pipes?"

"Nothing special about that pipe. It's a plain straight stem with an apple-shaped briar bowl. I think I bought it for thirty dollars a year ago."

"Think we should call the police?"

"And tell them what? There's no evidence of a break-in. The only thing missing is an old tobacco pipe that I could have lost or misplaced. I am kind of absent-minded from time to time, you know. Maybe I did lose it. Forget it, Rat. Let's go back to bed and get some sleep."

Rat did go back to bed, but sleep wouldn't come. Rat was plagued with the same kind of uneasy feeling he had felt in the sewers when his friends began disappearing, only to turn up later with their faces caved in. Until now, Rat had had felt relatively safe in his own home. He had been raised in a house where his father's drunken outbursts in the middle of the night often sent him or his sisters to the hospital's emergency room. He never had private space nor felt safe in the Army, either, not even when he was in garrison. And when he was in Iraq, violence was always just around the corner. His makeshift home in the sewers, constructed of discarded cardboard cartons, had been subject to invasion by other human residents as much as by vermin. But this house, shared only with a trusted friend, had always seemed safe.

Until now. He was certain he had locked all the doors before going to bed. He made it a ritual to check the front door as he passed it on his way to the stairs that led to his bedroom on the second floor. But the locks were simple brass entry locks that were easy to pick by anyone with tools and experience. Locked doors kept honest people honest; they seldom kept dishonest people out. How easy would it be to get in? Easy enough for someone determined.

But who would break into an occupied house only to steal an old pipe?

Rat suddenly had a sinking feeling as he remembered George tossing his wallet and keys on a small wooden table near the front door right after he came home. Did he see the wallet and keys when he checked the living room? Rat got out of bed again, turned on the lights, and walked downstairs. The wallet and keys were missing.

"George," he called. "Wake up."

"What now?" asked George, rubbing sleep from his eyes as he emerged from his bedroom.

"Your wallet and keys are gone."

"Oh, shit," said George. He stared in disbelief at the empty tabletop. "I put them right there when I walked in the door."

"He got your IDs, your credit cards, and your cash."

"And my car keys and the house keys. Plus my keys to the office at work."

Rat picked up the phone and dialed 911. "Now we're going to report it," he said.

Art Lewinski came to the house twenty minutes later and took a full report of the missing items. Along with his driver's license, insurance cards, a Visa credit card, and about sixty dollars in cash, the thief got George's work ID and electronic access card to the PSB.

He got the key to George's PT Cruiser, keys to the front and back doors of the house, and keys to desks and filing cabinets in the lab.

Lewinski looked around the property and inspected the lock on the front door. If the lock had been burgled, he said, it was expertly done. There were no tell-tale scratches on either of the brass locks.

George's PT Cruiser was still parked in the garage. Obviously, the thief wasn't interested in stealing the car.

After Art left, Rat made a pot of coffee and he and George stayed awake and talked about the theft. Did the thief know what he had on that key ring? Did he intend to use the ID and the keys to break into the offices at the PSB? He certainly could.

Or was he simply a thief who wanted the money in the wallet? If so, why had he taken the keys?

Lewinski said there had been no other break-ins or thefts reported in this neighborhood in years. Rat had purchased the sixty-year-old Cape Cod because it was located in a middle class residential neighborhood of single-family, owner-occupied houses far from the inner city. Why would a thief target this house and not others? It didn't make sense.

"I'll call a locksmith and get new locks installed on the front and back doors this morning," said Rat. "You'll need to stop by the Secretary of State's office and obtain a new driver's license."

"Have you got the duplicate keys to the PT Cruiser?" asked George.

"I do," said Rat. "They're upstairs in my bedroom."

"I'll need them to get around today."

"You need to call Visa and notify them your credit card was stolen."

George made a to-do list while Rat went upstairs to fetch the spare set of car keys. The sun had been up for nearly two hours when the telephone rang. George picked it up in his study.

"I've got to go to work," he told Rat. "There's been another murder. Stowe's already on his way there and he wants me to bring the meat wagon."

"Better call Stowe back and have him meet you at the office," said Rat. "Your keys to the meat wagon were on the ring that was stolen. Stowe has the only other set of keys."

"Oh, shit," said George. "I didn't think of that."

George phoned the Doctor and told him about the stolen keys. Stowe agreed to meet him at the office.

"Who got killed this time?" asked Rat.

"Another young woman," said George. "It looks like she was killed and raped. I'll tell you about it when I get home tonight."

"Be careful, George," Rat said as George opened the door to leave.

"I'm always careful," said George as he went out the door.

CHAPTER TWELVE

Y ou follow the old man's PT Cruiser from the PSB parking garage. He travels east two miles, then south another mile to a quiet middle-class residential area of single-family brick houses with big back yards and two-car garages. You stay a block or two behind him all the way. You stop and park at the side of the road when you see him enter a driveway in the next block, open an over-head garage door with a remote, drive into the garage and park the PT Cruiser next to a blue Dodge Dart. He shoves a briar pipe in his mouth as he comes out of the garage, lights it with a match, closes the garage door, and enters the front door of the house.

You watch and wait. You use the cheap binoculars you bought at Walmart to see through the windows, and you see Fredriks and another man sitting in the living room talking. You look through each of the lit windows with the binoculars, familiarizing yourself with the layout of each room in the house. You see Fredriks disappear into a hallway. Then a light comes on in another room. You see Fredriks sit at a desk with a laptop computer. To the right of the computer is a big round glass ashtray filled with pipes. In the center of the ashtray is a cork knob to dislodge ashes from the briar bowl. Fredriks smokes one pipe, then sets it aside to smoke another.

Shortly before three, he turns the lights out in that room and turns the lights on in an adjacent room. The blinds are closed and you can't see inside.

Lights go out in the living room and lights come on upstairs. You give the men a half hour after all the lights are out. When you are certain they've had time to fall asleep, you put on gloves and a black baseball cap, take the towel with the bloody icepick wrapped inside, and boldly walk to the front door. If anyone sees you, they'll think less about someone going to the front door in plain sight than sneaking around the back.

You open the screen door and examine both locks on the front door. They're cheap entryway locks with only three tumblers. You take the set of locksmith picks from your pants pocket and have both locks open within minutes.

To the right of the front door is a small table with keys and a billfold. You slip keys and wallet into your pants pocket as you gently close the door behind you. Moonlight coming through the windows provides enough illumination to negotiate furniture. You pause and listen for sounds. You hear the air conditioner, the refrigerator, the clock on the mantel. The rest of the house is quiet.

You move through the hallway to the room where you saw the big ash tray. The adjoining door is closed, and you suspect Fredriks is asleep in that room. Your rubber-soled Reeboks move silently across the carpeted floor. You reach the desk and deposit the towel and icepick in a wastebasket on the floor next to the desk. You cover the towel with blank sheets of paper from the HP printer next to the computer.

You pick a pipe at random from the ash tray. Any one of the pipes will do, because Fredriks has smoked each of them. His fingerprints and DNA reside on all of them.

You make your way back to the front door. Within minutes you are in your car and driving away.

Finding a suitable victim at five in the morning is more difficult than you thought. Most of the city is asleep, and there are few places where you can hunt. You drive around looking for lights on in houses, but all are dark. You think about driving downtown to the bike path to search for a female jogger out on an early morning run. Unfortunately, the sun will be up before you get there. It's too risky to attack someone in the open in daylight.

You pass an all-night gas station and convenience store and notice a twenty-some-year old female behind the counter. You think about abducting her from the store, but you see security cameras both inside and out. You find a place to park outside the view of the cameras, and you watch the woman. She has long yellow hair tied up with a red ribbon. She looks perfect. You decide to follow her when she gets off work.

Her relief arrives shortly before six. You wait for her to get her purse and leave. She walks to a silver Chevy Sonic hatchback parked in the convenience store's open parking lot. You follow her as she drives from Denton's Super-Mart to a residential street not too far away. She pulls into a driveway and opens a garage door with a remote. She drives inside.

The sun is already above the horizon so you have to move really fast or someone might see you. You park two doors away from her house and run to catch her before she leaves the garage. She has the driver's door open and is struggling with her heavy purse. You have your gloves on, an icepick in your left hand, and you catch her as she takes her first step out of the car. Your gloved right hand goes over her mouth, the icepick slips inside her eye, and she collapses in your arms.

You lay her on the floor in the rear of the hatchback, then you close the garage door.

"She got off work at six this morning," Art Lewinski told Andy. "Her husband woke around eight, noticed she wasn't home yet, and got worried. The husband went looking for her. He found her in the back of her car parked inside their two-car garage. The garage door was closed, and he saw her body as soon as he opened it to get his own car. The perp must have left by the side door."

"Got a name on the victim?"

"Carrie Yalden. Age twenty-eight. Husband's name is Ralph. They've been married two years this month. He works second shift in a factory, two PM to midnight. She works ten to six at a Denton's Super-Mart. Husband sleeps while she's working, she sleeps while he's working. The only time they have together is mornings. She usually wakes him up when she gets home. Today she didn't wake him so he overslept."

The crime scene team arrived with the evidence van. Evangelista was driving, and the three male techs were passengers. Davis and Pearson came in Pearson's car. Del wasn't here yet, and neither was Stowe.

Evangelista began snapping photos while two of the other techs searched the grounds for footprints and the third tech prepared to dust the front seat of the Chevy for possible latent fingerprints. Davis and Pearson entered the garage and looked around. Parked next to the Chevy Sonic was an older Dodge pickup truck that belonged to the husband. The front driver's side door of the Sonic was open, blood spattered on the inside of the door.

"She was killed getting out of the car," said Pearson. "He must have come up behind her, grabbed her, and stabbed her. She dropped her key ring to the garage floor." Pearson bent down and picked up the ring of keys with gloved fingers and slipped them inside an evidence envelope.

"Keys aren't hers," said Davis, looking through the purse left on the front seat. "Her car keys and house keys are inside her purse. Wallet with ID and credit cards are here, too. Plus four dollars in cash."

"That rules out robbery," said Pearson.

"Someone dropped a tobacco pipe. Looks like it rolled under the car door," said Davis. She reached under the car and retrieved the pipe, placed it in an evidence bag, and labeled the plastic bag with date, time, and location.

"Does the husband smoke?" Andy asked Lewinski.

"I'll go inside and ask him," volunteered the patrolman. "Carson is in the house with him. The poor guy's pretty busted up after finding his wife like that. We didn't think it was a good idea to leave him in there by himself."

Carrie Yalden had been positioned on the cargo floor in the rear of the Sonic, naked from the waist down, her legs spread apart. Her pants, panties, and sandals were scattered on the cement floor of the garage where the killer had tossed them. It was very obvious she had been raped. Finding his wife like that must have been a real shock to the husband. She had died a horrible death while he had been blissfully asleep not more than a hundred yards away. The poor guy was probably kicking himself for not hearing his wife scream. If she were able to scream.

Doctor Stowe and Harvey Fredriks arrived with the coroner's panel truck. "Sorry we took so long," apologized Stowe as he set down his black coroner's case. "Harvey lost his keys and I had to go back to get the truck. What do we have?"

"Carrie Yalden, age 28. Stab wounds to both eyes."

Stowe got out his two thermometers and his camera. He took photos while one of the thermometers measured the ambient air temperature. Then he inserted the rectal thermometer and measured the body temperature. He rapidly calculated time of death in his head.

"She's been dead about two hours," he said, the voice-actuated digital recorder in his pocket picking up and recording his every word. "I estimate time of death between six and seven AM. Puncture wounds to both eyes were made with a long sharp instrument, probably an icepick. Obvious trauma to the vaginal area, indicating she was raped post-mortem. She wasn't killed in the back of the car. She was dragged or carried. There is a visible trail of blood on the floor of the garage leading around the side of the car. There are blood spatters on the driver's door. She was likely killed getting out of the car."

"Husband doesn't smoke," interrupted Lewinski, returning from the house. "That pipe ain't his. It must belong to the perp."

"We found a tobacco pipe and a set of keys on a key ring near the car," Andy told Stowe. "They might have dropped from the assailant's pockets while he was struggling with the victim or moving the body to the back of the car. It's the first time he's been careless."

"Also the first time he's killed in broad daylight," said the doctor.

"The first time we know about anyway," said Andy. "The night club where he usually finds his victims was closed last night. He must have looked all night long to find a suitable victim. He probably saw Carrie at work, followed her home, and killed her while her husband was asleep not a hundred yards from here. That's pretty brazen."

"Or desperate," said Stowe. "He's on a killing rampage. The newspapers are correct. No woman's safe in Riverdale until this guy is caught."

"He chooses his victims for some particular reason," said Andy. "They're not purely random. Something about each of the women attracted his attention."

"They're all in their twenties. They're all white. They're all slim and attractive. Maybe that's enough."

"No. There's more. There's something that I'm not seeing that ties all of the victims together."

"It can't be hair color. Or eye color. No two victims were alike."

"Nor how much clothing they wore or didn't wear. Some of the other victims were dressed seductively. Carrie here was dressed for work. So were Mary Woodman and Jean Johnston."

"We about done here?" Stowe asked. "Okay to remove the body?"

"Go ahead, Doc."

Stowe asked Harvey Fredriks to back the meat wagon up to the garage. Harvey parked about four feet from the opening, and he brought a body bag to wrap the body. When he had Carrie bagged and tagged, Stowe helped him carry the corpse to the truck.

After they drove off, Andy joined Davis and Pearson.

"Where's Del?" asked Rich Pearson. "I thought he'd be here."

"Maybe he got lost," said Andy. "Dispatch said they notified him. He still doesn't know his way around Riverdale. Give him a call on your cell. See where he's at."

"He's here," said Davis as Del Conklin drove up, followed by television crews in broadcast vans and Joel Hickman driving a red Corvette with the top down. "And it looks like he brought an entourage. Thank goodness, the coroner removed Carrie's body before the press got here."

"Art, keep the press behind those crime scene tapes," Andy instructed Art Lewinski.

"Back off!" Lewinski growled as he walked purposefully toward the cameramen climbing out of the vans. "Get back and stay back."

Del walked up the driveway looking frustrated. "I tried to shake them off," he said, "but they stuck to me like stink on shit. Next time, I'm sneaking out through the tunnels."

"How did they happen to latch on to you and not any of the rest of us?" asked Andy.

"They must have picked up the dispatch on their police scanners," Del said. "They were waiting to ambush me as soon as I walked out the front door of the PSB. They recognized me because the department sent out all those news releases when I started work here last month. They thought I was easy prey since I was new. I tried to be polite, especially since they had cameras and microphones. But they wouldn't stop asking questions. Finally,

I had to walk away. They followed me, and I tried to shake them by driving all over town. They're like fucking animals. Once they catch the scent, they don't give up. Reporters in California act more civilized. They let us do our jobs, and we let them do theirs. They never once tried to interfere with an on-going investigation when I was there. These guys don't care. They just want a story."

"This city is a piddling middle market," said Pearson. "Reporters start here right out of journalism school. As soon as crime reporters make a name for themselves here, they move on to bigger markets so none of them ever stays around here long enough to care. They take their broadcast tapes or newspaper clips and move on to Minneapolis or Miami. If they happen to catch a big story, they have a chance at LA or Chicago. Then they're replaced with a new bunch of superstar wannabes."

"Lewinski will handle them," said Andy. "He takes pleasure in dealing with the press."

Andy gave Del the details of the latest murder, including showing him the keys and pipe found near the car.

"Isn't that the old man's pipe?"

"What old man?" asked Andy.

"The guy who works downstairs in the lab. The coroner guy. I see him all the time outside the PSB puffing on that pipe or one that looks exactly like it."

"Harvey Fredriks?"

"Yeah. That's the guy. He's the only man I know that smokes a pipe anymore. I go out sometimes for a cigarette and see him. He's a little strange, don't you think? He stands off by himself. I tried to talk to him once, but he doesn't say much."

"He used to be a college professor," said Andy. "He's always thinking."

"He's pretty spry for an old guy," said Pearson. "He has no trouble picking up bodies and moving them around."

"Oh, come on now," said Andy. "You don't think Harvey Fredriks is the killer, do you?"

"He's the right size," said Pearson. "About five-eleven. He's slim and trim. I bet he wears size eleven shoes. I heard he was homeless and lived in the sewers before he got his job with the coroner. Just because he's old doesn't mean he couldn't be the killer."

Andy called Evangelista and Davis over. "I want you two to process the pipe and keys we found. Don't turn them over to anyone else in the labs. See if you can get prints, DNA, anything you can find. Keep it hush-hush. Let me know what you come up with as soon as you have something."

"You want us to do it in the van instead of the labs?" asked Evangelista.

"Can you do that?"

"Sure. The evidence van is a mobile laboratory. We have microscopes, centrifuge, refrigerator, computers, fingerprint equipment. No scanning electron microscope or any of the heavy-duty stuff. But we can run prints. Give me a half hour and I'll have something for you."

"You can do that right here, right now?"

"That's why we have the van," said Evangelista. "It's a forensics lab on wheels."

Evangelista and Davis disappeared into the van. Andy went inside the house to talk to the husband.

Ralph Yalden was a big man, six-one and maybe two hundred pounds. His black hair was a mess and he hadn't shaved. He wore jeans and a navy-blue muscle t-shirt. He had a red heart tattooed on his left biceps with Ralph written above and Carrie written below.

He sat on a sofa in his living room with his head in his hands. It was obvious he had been crying.

"Mr. Yalden, I'm Lieutenant Sinnott of homicide. I'm sorry for your loss, but I need to ask you a few questions."

Yalden looked up. "Why Carrie?" he asked. "Of all the women in the world, why did he have to pick Carrie?"

"That's what I need to find out," said Andy. "Have you noticed anyone watching your wife? Any one hanging around your house?"

"No," he said. "Carrie and I don't go out much. I mow the lawn, and she has a garden in back of the house that she weeds. But no one has been watching us that I know. Not even the neighbors."

"What about at work? Has anyone bothered her at work?"

"She sits behind a glass partition all night. It's bulletproof, you know, in case someone tries to hold up the store. She takes money through a slot. They have security cameras all over the place. She sees all kinds of people, but they can't get close to her. If anyone had bothered her, she would have mentioned it. But she didn't say anything."

"How was she dressed when she went to work?"

"I work second shift, so I didn't see her when she left. She usually wore a blouse and slacks. Sometimes she put her hair up and tied it with a ribbon, especially when it was hot. I like her with long hair, and I wouldn't let her cut it short even when she complained about it being too hot for long hair." He began sobbing. "She had such beautiful hair."

"We'll catch the man who did this," promised Andy.

"He poked her eyes out, didn't he?" asked Yalden. "Her eyes were all bloody."

"Yes," said Andy.

"And he r-r-raped her?"

"It appears he did."

"Why didn't I hear anything? How could I have slept through all that?"

"We believe she was dead before he raped her," said Andy. "She didn't know what he did to her."

"She didn't scream?"

"She didn't have a chance."

"What will you do to this guy when you catch him?"

"He'll be prosecuted to the full extent of the law."

"Frying him in the electric chair is too good for him."

"They use lethal injection to execute criminals," said Andy. "They haven't used the chair in years."

"I want to see him die," said Yalden. "I want to see him suffer."

"I promise you we'll get him."

"What kind of animal would do something like this? Carrie never hurt anyone."

"Do you have someone who can come and stay with you? A relative? A friend? A neighbor? Clergy?"

"Oh, God, I've got to tell Carrie's parents."

"Officer Carson will stay with you while you call them. We won't leave you alone."

"I've got to make arrangements for the funeral."

"The coroner will release your wife's body to the funeral home after an autopsy. That may take a day or two."

"They're going to cut her open?"

"An autopsy is required by state law in all cases of suspected homicide or violent death. Don't worry, the doctor doing the autopsy will be very respectful of your wife. I'll leave you so you can make your calls. If you think of anything that might help us find the killer, call me." Andy handed Yalden his business card. "You can reach me on my cell anytime day or night."

Evangelista and Davis were waiting for Andy when he returned to the garage.

"We found prints on both the keys and the pipe," she said. "You aren't going to believe who the prints belong to."

"Harvey Fredriks?" asked Andy.

"How did you know? Fredriks was printed when he went into the Navy almost fifty years ago. He has no previous criminal record."

"The prints give us probable cause to get a search warrant," said Davis. "We should search his house and car for trace evidence."

"We know Fredriks was at the scenes of all the homicides," said Andy. "He may have picked up trace at the crime scene."

"Do we get a warrant?"

"Yes. Get a search warrant and execute it. Take Del and Pearson and search Harvey's home and car. I don't think Harvey is a killer, but we need to follow up on the evidence. Just remember Fredriks is presumed innocent until proven guilty in a court of law."

You drive downtown to the familiar parking garage across the street from the Public Safety Building. You know Fredriks leaves his PT Cruiser in the lot while he's working, and you spot the car on the third level of the garage near the elevator.

You take the key you removed from the key ring before you left the rest of the keys at the crime scene, and you unlock the PT Cruiser with the remote door opener built into the key. You place the bloody icepick you used on the girl you killed this morning on the floor under the front seat. Then you lock the car with the remote, get back in your Matrix, and drive away.

It's time to resume a low profile and watch the rest of the game play out. This morning is as good as any to search for a new apartment where you can hide. Perhaps something slightly more up-scale than that last shithole you rented.

But in keeping with your low profile, you need a place that doesn't ask a lot of questions. Every city still has its share of flop houses, rooms that rent by the night or week. The number of old hotels has dwindled with urban renewal of inner cities, but the number of rooming houses has significantly increased as slum lords bought up foreclosures in older neighborhoods and converted large houses into buildings with rooms for rent. There are always plenty of people living from paycheck to paycheck who need places that charge weekly rent and require no security deposit. You can easily pretend to be one of those people.

You drive past the burnt-out houses on Elm Street and continue west. A hundred years ago these were very nice houses, big enough to accommodate large families and elderly in-laws. Most have at least ten rooms that can be rented out. Some, however, have become so run-down that they are unlivable. Some are boarded up and condemned. A few are still tenable and you look for one with a big "Rooms For Rent" sign out front.

You wear your baseball cap and dark glasses when you go inside and inquire. You try three places before you find one that is acceptable. The apartment is on the second floor, the bathroom is right next door, and the landlord doesn't ask you a lot of questions. You tell him you are employed nights, but you don't offer where or what you do. You pay for two weeks in advance with ten crisp new twenty dollar bills from the ATM machine. There is even a parking place in back of the building accessed from an alley. This will do nicely.

You have time to shower and shave before going to work. As you look at your face in the mirror while shaving, you see the long scar left behind by the bitch who tried to gouge your eyes out yesterday. The flesh is still red and festering. Older scars around your eyes are rude reminders that all women can be extremely dangerous when alive. That's why you prefer them dead.

You have a love-hate relationship with women. You want to love them, but they hate you. It is only after they're dead that you are able to show them how much you truly love them.

You have to be careful shaving today because the deep scratch on the left side of your face extends into your beard. She dragged her nails a good four inches from just above your left eye almost to your chin, barely missing the eye itself. You covered the long scratch with makeup that the shower washed away. When you get to work, you can treat it with hydrogen peroxide. Later, after it's had time to breathe, you can cover it again with makeup.

You remember the days before your face became scarred. You were quite handsome then, and women flocked to the young pre-med student at the state university who was the son of a rich doctor and would someday be a rich doctor himself. When you accidentally got one of them pregnant, you did the right thing and married her. Life was good until she had the baby.

Somehow, after the baby was born, your wife and your stepmother became close friends. Your stepmother actually moved in with you, ostensibly to help take care of the new mother and the new baby, and thereafter she was a regular visitor to your home. Perhaps it was because she had never had a child of her own that she devoted so much time to your infant son. Perhaps it was because your father had found a new, younger girlfriend. Perhaps it was simply to taunt you. Did it matter which?

And, somehow after that, sex was never the same for you. Your wife refused your advances when your stepmother was sleeping in the same house, and even when she wasn't staying with you anymore her presence lingered. It was as if your stepmother had stepped between you and your wife and destroyed the beautiful relationship you and your wife once had. It seemed like each time you tried to make love to your wife, she wasn't in the mood.

So you went elsewhere for sex. You began following women around campus. Where before women had seemed naturally attracted to you, now they seemed repulsed. Either the lean and hungry look they saw in your eyes frightened them away or they noticed the gold wedding band on your left hand. Even when you took your wedding ring off, you remained branded by the tan line on your ring finger.

Finally, you simply took from women what you wanted. You wore a ski mask and forced yourself on co-eds at knifepoint. You told them that you would kill them if they said no, so they didn't say no. You had your way with them, and you let them live.

It seemed so easy. The campus was full of young women walking alone between classes or walking home from the library after dark. None of the women ever said no after you showed them the butcher knife you borrowed from your wife's kitchen.

Until you finally met one who fought back and changed your life forever.

She was walking across campus shortly after sunset on a beautiful night in May. She was a petite sophomore or junior, maybe nineteen or twenty, heading toward the apartments where upperclassmen lived on the north side of campus. You were hiding in bushes near the north end of the quad, not far from the student union. You stepped out and grabbed her, brandishing the knife.

And she reached out and ripped off your mask. She scratched at your eyes with red-painted fingernails, barely missing your left eye. Her nails ripped open your cheek and you instantly reacted by stabbing her in the stomach.

She began to scream, but you slapped her face hard, knocking her to the ground. You tried to stick the knife into her again, but she grabbed at the blade with one hand while raking your face once more with the other. You pushed the knife through her hand and into her breast. Bright red blood bubbled out of her, staining her blouse and the grass around her. You stabbed her again and again.

She stopped moving. You pulled her pants down, ripped off her underpants, and plunged deep inside her. There was nothing she could do to stop you.

No one seemed to notice that you were covered with blood as you walked eight blocks to the luxurious faculty residences where your father and stepmother lived. It was the mansion you had grown up in, and you still had keys.

Your father must have had surgery planned for early the next morning because he was already in bed. You found your stepmother in the living room getting drunk on expensive wine. You showed her the knife and told her to be quiet. She saw the blood on your face and your clothes and she knew you meant business. You ordered her to disrobe. She complied. You saw fear in her eyes and it brought joy to your heart.

Her body was no longer young. Her breasts were still unnaturally round from the silicone implants your father had installed so long ago, but now they looked obscene. Her belly was no longer flat, her pubic bush scraggly and unkempt, and her legs looked scrawny.

You forced her to her knees in front of you, forced her to open her mouth and take you in. When you were ready to come, you pulled out of her mouth and ejaculated on her breasts.

Then you slit her throat.

You went upstairs to your father's bedroom and found him asleep on the king-sized bed. You plunged the knife into his abdomen again and again.

Before you left that house with its many memories, you doused the bed with lighter fluid from the can your stepmother used to fill cigarette lighters. You set the bed on fire and watched your father's body burn.

You took your father's Mercedes from the garage, drove to an ATM, and emptied your checking and savings accounts before driving to your own house. Your wife saw the bloody scratches on your face and the butcher knife in your hands and she screamed. You moved too fast for her to get away. You stabbed her once for each of the times she rejected you. Then you found your infant son and mercifully deprived the motherless child of the rest of his life.

You entered the bathroom, stripped off your bloody clothes, and showered yourself clean. You packed your straight razor, shaving kit, and a toothbrush into an old duffel bag you bought at the Army-Navy store. You added a dress suit, a couple of shirts, socks, jeans. You dressed in clean jeans and a t-shirt. You put on the new pair of Reebok running shoes your wife bought you for your birthday.

You left your house for the last time and drove to your in-laws' house. Their house was made of wood, and you stopped at a nearby gas station to fill a two-gallon gas can with unleaded regular. You splashed gasoline on the back and front porches, both sides of the house, and the decorative shrubbery surrounding the house. You walked around the building tossing lit matches. You wrote a suicide note and left it in the mailbox by the street.

You got into the Mercedes Benz and drove away before the house became an inferno.

You often thought about the river that flowed not far from the campus. When you were younger, you had fantasies about diving from the high bridge into the fast-flowing water and letting the water wash away your troubles. Now you head for that bridge at a fast rate of speed, taking your duffel bag with you and jumping from your father's Mercedes before it plunges through the railing and over the edge. You land on the duffel bag and it cushions the collision of your body with the harsh cement. You pick up your duffel bag and walk away from the life you once knew.

You lived in many different cities from one end of the country to the other. You found work as a mortician's apprentice, thanks to your pre-med training in anatomy and pathology and because so few others were interested in that kind of job. You hid the scars on your face behind dark glasses. You never stayed in any one place more than a year, sometimes a lot less.

How many women have you raped and killed? Far too many to remember all of them.

You have lived in Riverdale nine months now, and you have rented four different apartments. You never stay in one place long enough for people to get to know you.

Sometimes you have no desire to rape or kill, and you keep a low profile. Sometimes the urge comes over you and you cannot help what you do.

You dress for work. Work allows you to sublimate your urges in creative ways. You are always in complete control when you work, and you love what you do. Besides embalming and cosmetology, you run the crematorium for Albertson. Today, you have two bodies to cremate. Because the human body has a negative caloric value due to containing sixty-five percent water, incinerating the two bodies will be an all-day process.

You leave your new digs and head for the Matrix parked on the street. Tonight, after work, you will go to Walmart and purchase a cheap television set. It will be fun to catch the news and witness what happens to Harvey Fredriks.

You almost feel sorry for the old man. Almost, but not quite.

You know what it's like to be accused of something you didn't do. Your stepmother was always accusing you of being a sexual pervert and wanting to look at her naked body.

It wasn't true at the time. She made it true.

CHAPTER THIRTEEN

Rat was home when two male detectives and two female evidence technicians served the search warrant. They introduced themselves as Sergeant Conklin of homicide, Detective Pearson of Violent Crimes, officers Davis and Evangelista of the forensic evidence team. George had mentioned their names only yesterday when he had talked about the conference at the PSB.

Officer Evangelista discovered the towel and icepick hidden beneath discarded paper in the wastebasket in George's study. Rat watched as she took photographs, then placed them into an evidence bag and labeled the bag with place, time, and date.

They also confiscated George's tobacco pipes. Rat tried to explain that someone had broken into the house last night and stolen one of the pipes from the ash tray. That same person could have planted the towel and icepick. He told them that officer Lewinski had taken a report. They said they would obtain a copy of that report when they returned to the PSB.

After the police left, Rat tried to telephone George at work. Doctor Stowe explained that George had been taken into police custody after a search of George's personal car turned up the bloody icepick that had been used in this morning's murder. The victim's blood was all over the icepick. George was being questioned by police, but it didn't look good. Not only was George the same height and build as they suspected the killer would be, but George was also left handed. The only thing that didn't match the killer's profile was George's age. However, he was fit enough to have committed the murders.

And even if he hadn't committed the murders himself, he was

caught hiding evidence that belonged to the killer. He was either the murderer, or an accessory after the fact. Either way, George was in big trouble.

Rat couldn't believe this was happening. He was absolutely certain George would never deliberately harm anyone, much less rape and kill innocent women. Besides, Rat suspected someone had deliberately planted that evidence after breaking into the house last night.

Rat wanted to go downtown to the PSB and talk with George. But he couldn't leave until the locksmith arrived and installed new locks on both front and back doors.

It was late afternoon when the locksmith finished his work. Fortunately, Tuesday was another of Rat's days off. He didn't need to prepare for work at six.

He did need to find George a good lawyer. He called several lawyers listed in the phone book, but they were only ambulance chasers and didn't take criminal defense cases. Finally, he called the local bar association and asked for a referral to the best trial attorney in Riverdale. The bar association suggested James Bentley.

Rat talked with the lawyer's secretary and learned that Bentley required a ten thousand dollar retainer. Rat said he would stop at the bank and be right down with the money.

"Tomorrow," said the secretary. "We close the office at five. Come in tomorrow morning at nine, and we'll ask you to sign a contract. Attorney Bentley has court in the morning, but he'll be able to see you tomorrow afternoon."

Rat made the appointments. Then Rat drove straight to his bank and withdrew the money from his savings account before the bank closed. He had the teller make out a cashier's check payable to James Bentley, Esq. George would have to spend tonight in jail. But at least by tomorrow morning George would have a defense lawyer.

Rat drove to the PSB and parked in the garage. He walked around to the front door and took the elevator up to the fourth floor. If anyone knew what was going on, it would be Andy Sinnott.

But Andy wasn't at his desk in the homicide squad room. Sergeant Conklin sat at an adjacent desk where he entered data into a computer spreadsheet with two fingers. Conklin barely looked up when Rat entered.

"I heard you arrested Harvey Fredriks," Rat said. "Can I see him?"

"He's being questioned at the moment," said Conklin, still pecking away at keys.

"Without an attorney?"

"He said he didn't need one."

"Well, he has one. James Bentley."

"I hear Bentley's good."

"When can I see Harvey?"

"Not until tomorrow." Conklin finally stopped typing and turned his chair around to face Rat. "He'll be arraigned sometime tomorrow afternoon over at the courthouse. After that, he'll be remanded to the county jail to await trial unless he's able to post bail. You'll have to check with the jail to find out visiting hours. I don't know what they are."

"Where is Harvey now?"

"Lieutenant Sinnott and some guy from the state police— Mullins, I think his name is— are questioning Fredriks in the interrogation rooms in the basement. He'll stay overnight in one of the holding cells down in the basement, almost next to where he works. He should feel right at home."

"Harvey couldn't have killed those people. Did you read officer Lewinski's report on the theft at our house early this morning? I can verify that Harvey was home all night. He didn't leave the house until after Doctor Stowe's call around eight. Lewinski left around five–thirty, and George and I didn't go back to sleep. We stayed up and talked."

"So you actually saw him there in person? I mean, you were personally with him and didn't just think Fredriks was home and asleep in the other room?"

"That's right. We sat in the living room, drinking coffee and making a list of people to notify about the stolen items."

"Will you sign an affidavit to that effect?"

"I certainly will. I'll swear to it in court, too, because it's true."

Conklin handed Rat a piece of paper and a pen. "Okay. Write your statement down and I'll give it to the Lieutenant."

Rat wrote out a statement that he had personally been with Harvey Fredriks in their residence at 8617 East Fifteenth Street from before Midnight on Monday, June 22, until eight AM on Tuesday, June 23. He dated and signed the statement. Sergeant Conklin dated and signed as a witness to the statement.

"I'll make sure the Lieutenant gets this," said Conklin. "And I will obtain a copy of Lewinski's report. But I gotta tell you we get people all the time who file false reports their guns or cars were stolen, and then we find out later they used those same guns or cars themselves to commit crimes. They file false reports to try to throw us off. So we don't put a whole lot of stock into reports of stolen property. Likewise, you're a personal friend of the alleged perpetrator. Friends sometimes lie to help out friends."

"You think I'm lying?"

"I don't know," said Conklin. "Are you?"

"No," said Rat.

"Good. 'Cause if you are, well find out."

"I'm not lying!" Rat practically shouted, offended.

"Good," Conklin said again. "If you are lying, you committed perjury by signing that affidavit. You can go to jail for that."

"Do you mind if I wait for Lieutenant Sinnott?" Rat asked.

"Be my guest," Conklin said, indicating a chair next to Andy's desk. "But it might be a while."

"I've got time," said Rat.

Andy and Dave Mullins interrogated Harvey Fredriks in Interview Room Number 2. Between interview rooms one and two was a separate viewing room where Special Agent Lester Cartwright and Detective Richard Pearson witnessed everything. The interrogation was video and audio recorded, and Cartwright and Pearson watched on a monitor and listened to the conversation with headphones.

"One more time, Mr. Fredriks," said Andy.

"I already told you twice," said George. "I know nothing about the icepick and towel found in my house, and nothing about the icepick found in my car. I'll be happy to take a polygraph, if you like."

"I suspect you're smart enough to beat a polygraph test," said Andy. "You know how they work, right?"

"I do," said George. "They measure physiological response to questions by recoding fluctuations in pulse rate, blood pressure, respiration, and GSR, or Galvanic Skin Response."

"So you could beat it," said Andy.

"Probably," agreed George. "I've never tried, so I don't know for certain."

"Tell me about how you lost your keys and pipe."

"Someone broke into our house last night. I don't know who. Rat and I discovered the keys and pipe were missing around five this morning. We called the police and officer Lewinski took a report."

"And did he find evidence of a break in?"

"No. The locks on the doors were undamaged."

"So maybe there was no break in. You could have reported the keys and pipe missing just to cover your tracks. "

"Does that make sense to you, Andy? Think about it. I reported my keys and pipe missing around five this morning. They were allegedly left at a crime scene more than an hour after I reported them missing. Didn't Doctor Stowe estimate TOD at sometime between six and seven? So how could I possibly know in advance that I would lose my keys and pipe at the murder scene? As much as I've tried, I've never been able to accurately foretell future events. There's something known as Heisenberg's Uncertainty Principle that prevents anyone from predicting the future, even when one is aware of all precipitating causes. The very act of being aware, according to Heisenberg, affects the outcome in unpredictable ways. Karl Raimond Popper's logic of scientific discovery speculates quantum shifts…."

"How do you explain the items we found in your home and in your car?"

"Obviously, the same person that broke into my house to steal keys and pipe planted the evidence in the wastebasket in my study. He found a key to my PT Cruiser on the key ring he stole from my home. He must have planted the icepick in my car while I was with Stowe at the crime scene. I parked across the street in the PSB garage. He could have gotten into the car anytime."

"How did he know which car was yours?"

"I don't know. How did he know which house was mine? He must have watched me for some time, maybe followed me home from work."

"And why did he pick you to frame? Why not someone else?

Someone younger, maybe?"

"Because I fit the description you released to the press. I'm five-eleven, maybe ten pounds lighter than the one seventy you guestimated, and I'm left-handed. The only thing that doesn't match is my age."

"I suppose we could have been wrong about the age. As you say, it was only a guestimate. So you do agree that you fit the description of the killer?"

"Me, and hundreds of other men in this city."

"Why'd you rape those women, Harvey?" Andy asked.

"I didn't" said George.

"Oh, come on now," said Mullins. "We've got you dead to rights. We know you did it. We just want to know why. Was it because an old guy like you can't get any without killing a girl first? Did the women not find you attractive anymore? Were you trying to prove your masculinity?"

"I'm only ten years older than you, Dave," George said. "Are you projecting your own impotence on me?"

"We're your friends, Harvey," said Andy. "You can tell us what you did and how you did it. It will relieve your mind if you tell us. Besides, haven't you wanted to tell someone? I mean, it was real smart the way you managed to get a job in the labs so you could doctor evidence. You're a smart guy, Harvey."

"I got the job because Captain Nolan recommended me," said George. "I took the job because I wanted to contribute my skills and help you, Andy, find killers. I could have retired on social security, you know. I didn't need that job."

"Right," said Andy. "You didn't need to work. You took this job to monitor what we learned about you. I bet you planned to skip town when we got close. But you slipped up."

"Andy, if I were that conniving, why would I keep the two ice picks and the towel?"

"Souvenirs," said Mullins. "Serial killers like to keep souvenirs. Look at what Jeffrey Dahmer kept in his refrigerator. Or Ed Gein on the lamps in his living room. You're just as bad as any of them, Harvey, maybe worse."

"I didn't do it. I've never killed anyone in my life, not even when I was in the Navy. I'm a scientist."

"Maybe you wanted to learn what happened when a woman died," suggested Mullins. "Maybe you killed for science. You killed your victims up close and personal, Harvey. Did you want to observe life draining out of them? Did you poke holes in their eyes so you could watch their souls leave through an open window? You tell us, Harvey. Why did you do it?"

"I didn't," said George again. "I didn't do it."

"Yeah," said Mullins sarcastically. "That's what they all say."

"It looks like we're going to be here for a while," said Andy. "You could make it easier on all of us and confess."

"I didn't do it," said George again. He was beginning to sound like a broken record repeating the same phrase over and over.

"I need a cup of coffee," said Andy. "You want anything, George?"

"That's the first time you've called me George since I was arrested," said George.

"Yeah, well, I'm getting tired and it just slipped out. Would you like something to drink? A glass of water? Coffee?"

"No, thank you."

"I'll go with you and see what drinks are in the vending machines," said Mullins.

Andy went to the door and knocked three times. Pearson had to come from next door to unlock the door from the outside. All the hardware had been removed from the inside of the interrogation room doors. When the door slammed shut again, it automatically locked. Someone had to open the door who was outside and also had a key.

"What do you think?" asked Andy when they were all in the viewing room.

"He didn't do it," said Cartwright. "His story is consistent. Someone could have planted the evidence to frame Fredriks."

"Why? Why frame Fredriks?"

"Because it keeps us busy concentrating on Fredriks while we should be looking for the killer elsewhere," said Mullins.

"We'll know we got the wrong man if the killer kills again," said Pearson.

"He's not going to kill again," said Cartwright. "Not for a while. He's toying with us."

"This guy has killed eight people in less than a week," said Mullins. "You think he'll just stop?"

"He stopped once before," said Andy. "After he killed those two women last January."

"What are we going to do with Harvey Fredriks?" asked Mullins.

"We have to hold him," said Andy. "The State's Attorney will decide if there's enough evidence to prosecute. Meanwhile, we need to go over everything we have. I don't think Harvey did it, either. But I can't prove it one way or the other."

"What about DNA?" asked Cartwright. "Didn't you recover skin and blood samples from the fingernails of one of the victims?"

"We're waiting for the results to come back," said Andy. "The state labs are taking forever. Dave, can you do anything to hurry them up?"

"I'll try," said Mullins.

"What about blood type?" asked Cartwright. "You said the killer had Type A blood. What's Fredriks' blood type?"

"According to his military records," said Andy, "Harvey Fredriks has Type A blood. But, as I understand it, so does nearly half of the population. Having Type A blood doesn't necessarily mean Harvey is the killer."

"But it doesn't rule him out, either," said Rich Pearson. "Does it?"

"No," agreed Andy. "It doesn't rule him out."

"Are we going to continue questioning him?" asked Mullins. "It seems kind of useless."

"One more time," said Andy. "Let's get some coffee and go at it one more time. If he doesn't change his story, we'll call it a night."

Rat wished he'd brought a book to read. He didn't know he'd have to wait this long. It was nearly eight o'clock before Andy returned to the squad room, and Andy looked too exhausted to talk.

Sergeant Conklin had left Rat all alone in the office when Conklin went off duty at six. Rat wore his PSB picture ID card clipped to his shirt pocket, and he was allowed to go practically anywhere in the building. But, except for a bathroom break, he had remained in the chair next to Andy's desk waiting to speak with Andy. From time to time, he had dozed off.

Today had been a total nightmare. It began with the break-in at the house around four AM, followed by the discovery of the missing wallet and keys, topped off with police officers coming to the door with a search warrant, and George's eventual arrest for murder. If anything else could possibly go wrong, Rat had no idea what that might be. But the feeling of dread he had felt in Iraq and during his last days in the tunnels had returned stronger than ever.

Rat felt small and insignificant compared to the malicious forces at work around him. Rat's father had instilled that feeling in him. Jon was a physically and emotionally abused child. He had grown up always waiting for the other shoe to drop, for his father to suddenly burst into his bedroom and beat him black and blue in a drunken rage. If it wasn't Rat that was beaten, it was his mother or his sisters. Each time Rat had tried to fight back, his father had beaten him badly enough to send him to the hospital. But he had survived.

And then, during two tours in Iraq, watching his friends die one by one from snipers' bullets or roadside bombs, knowing all the time that he could be next, Rat's fear intensified. Finally, when the bullets with Rat's name on them found their mark, Rat had managed to survive. Even when that improvised explosive device blew up his Humvee and killed everyone else in the vehicle, he had survived. And even in the tunnels, when the Pickaxe Butcher killed most of his friends and tried to kill him, Rat had survived.

His body was a mass of scars from the beatings, the bullets, and the bombs. He had artificial knees and artificial hips and two of his vertebrae were fused together. But he was alive, and each time he had been injured he had grown stronger. He had let bad things happen to his mother and his sisters. He had let bad things happen to the men he had served with in Iraq. He had let bad things happen to his friends in the sewers. He wasn't going to let anything bad happen to George.

"George didn't do it," Rat told Andy as soon as Andy appeared in the squad room.

"That's what he says. I want to believe him."

"He was home with me when that girl was killed this morning. There's an affidavit on your desk that I signed and Sergeant Conklin witnessed."

Andy sat at his desk and read the affidavit. "I'll take that into consideration," he said.

"Look, Andy. You know George. You know he's not a killer."

"We found evidence in his home and in his car that proves otherwise," said Andy.

"The real killer is trying to frame him. George thinks he saw the killer outside that downtown bar on Saturday night. He said he recognized the man from somewhere. I think the killer knows George saw him, and the killer wants George in jail so George can't identify him. Or, at least, he wants George discredited so anything George says won't be believed."

"That," said Andy, "is the first thing I've heard today that makes sense."

"So you'll release George?"

"I can't, Rat. Once he's charged, I can't simply drop the charges. Only the Chief can do that, and then only with the concurrence of the prosecuting attorney."

"Oh, no," said Rat. "Isn't there something we can do?"

"Get George a good attorney."

"I'm seeing James Bentley tomorrow."

"Bentley is good. He's expensive, but he's good."

"That's what Conklin said."

"Look, Rat, I'm going to find who did these murders. I don't think it's George. Are you willing to help?"

"Sure. What can I do?"

"Hang around the bars when they're open. You're about the right age, you don't look like a cop, and you can mingle with the crowd. The man we're looking for is George's height and build, left-handed, and he wears Reebok running shoes. If you see anyone who looks like that, try to find out his name or the license plate on his car. Tomorrow night, I want you to pair up with one of my officers. Did you meet officer Davis when she served the search warrant?"

"The short blonde?"

"Her name is Linda Davis. She's relatively new, and she doesn't look like a cop any more than you do. Are you willing to do that?"

"I'm off tonight and tomorrow night. I have to work the rest of the week."

"Tomorrow will be a start."

"I can go there tonight," Rat offered.

"You do that. Upstairs and Downstairs is the name of the dance club where our killer met some of his previous victims. But check out the other clubs, too. The killer changes his MO as often as he changes his socks."

"All right. If you think it will help."

"It can't hurt. Right now, it's the only thing we have to go on. But be careful."

"I'm always careful," said Rat. That's what George always said. The time to be careful was over. Now it was time for Rat to be bold and brave.

George's life and liberty might depend on it.

CHAPTER FOURTEEN

You purchase a television set at Walmart immediately after work. It is a 24-inch RCA LED flat-screen on sale for $149.00. It has both an analog and a digital tuner, and it will pick up local over-the-air broadcasts without a cable connection.

You drive to your new apartment, eager to plug in the television before the late night news comes on at ten. This 10' by 15' apartment came furnished with a sofa that opens into a bed, a small wooden table, and four wooden chairs. There is a worn-out dirty brown carpet on the floor, and the walls are painted what must have once been birds-egg blue but are so badly stained from years of cigarette smoke they now look the same color as the carpet.

You center the television on the table. There is a small hoop antenna on the back of the TV set that brings in three of the local channels. You turn on the TV and adjust the antenna.

Ten o'clock news opens with the story of Fredriks being arrested for the icepick murders. A young female reporter stands in front of the Public Safety Building and says, "Tonight Harvey Fredriks, the alleged rapist and killer, is behind bars. Women can sleep soundly tonight for the first time in weeks."

You switch channels. News anchors banter back and forth about Harvey's employment with the coroner's office. "He has an unnatural obsession with dead bodies," alleges a male anchor.

They show file footage of Harvey Fredriks and Doctor Stowe wheeling a body bag to the coroner's truck. "Fredriks, a sixty-six year-old Navy veteran, was employed as a lab technician in the coroner's office. Prior to joining the coroner's staff last year, Harvey Fredriks was homeless and unemployed for at least ten years. How did someone so obviously mentally deranged get a job in the Public Safety Building? A channel seven news reporter asked County Coroner James Albertson that question."

"He was highly recommended by my chief pathologist and by the head of homicide," said a somber Albertson. "Mr. Fredriks will no longer be in a position to harm anyone because I terminated his employment after he was arrested."

You smile. If Harvey Fredriks saw your face in front of Upstairs and Downstairs on Saturday, no one will believe what he says. Fredriks is definitely not in any position where he can harm *you*. Not anymore.

The weatherman comes on with a forecast of unrelenting heat. "Temperatures for the rest of this week and the next will remain in the mid-to-high nineties, with a possibility of more than one hundred for your Fourth of July," says the weatherman, sweating in a suit and tie in front of bright lights and camera. "Because of the excessive heat, the city opened up the first-floor lobby of the Public Safety Building as an emergency cooling center for those unfortunates who cannot afford air conditioning. Also, a city-wide moratorium has been declared on watering lawns. The water department announced they will carefully monitor water usage, and anyone caught watering their lawns will be fined two-hundred and fifty dollars."

The weatherman promises a full seven day forecast after some brief commercials. You are surprised to see one of the sponsors of the evening news is Albertson's Mortuary and Cremation Services, Inc. "At Albertson's, we care," says the male voice-over as the screen shows a smiling Jack Albertson shaking hands with two older, but still living, customers. "We care for your loved ones, and we care about you. Ask us about our wide range of pre-planning services. Albertson's cares."

Cares about money. That asshole Albertson charges an arm and a leg for funeral services. He loves it when people pay in advance for their own funerals. Albertson can certainly afford to run commercials every night on the local news. Not only does Jack cut corners on everything else, he does things like remove gold crowns from the teeth of people he cremates and sells the gold and personal items like wedding rings. "Who will ever know the difference?"

Albertson argued when you refused to pull teeth for him. But you noticed that the two bodies you cremated this afternoon were missing their gold crowns. Someone had crudely yanked the gold teeth out of their mouths early this morning. Albertson must have done it himself before you came in to work.

You get up and turn off the TV. Tonight is a night to catch up on the sleep you didn't get last night. You pull out the folding bed from the sofa. The mattress is very thin, and it's also very lumpy. You haven't slept in a bed of any kind for more than a year. It feels good to lie down and stretch out. Lumps don't bother you.

You spent all of last night awake, most of it in your car watching Fredriks' house before going inside to plant the towel and icepick. After that, you hunted for this morning's prey. The rest of the day went by fast, exactly as planned. You located Fredriks' car, planted the icepick from this morning's murder under the front seat, then went shopping for a place to stay. You arrived at work a few minutes before noon, fired up the crematorium, and reduced two cadavers to ashes in about four hours.

You deserve a rest. You have been a very busy boy this past week. It's time to lay low for a while.

You close your eyes and watch the blonde in her short red skirt dance across the back of your eyelids. You regret not having a chance to taste her, but there simply wasn't time on Thursday morning. So now you use your imagination to do what you had no time to do then.

Because you are a watcher, your brain records what your eyes see in such vivid detail that you can reconstruct images at will. It's never been really necessary, you realize in retrospect with accurate 20-20 hindsight, to rape and kill. You could do it merely in your mind. But you choose to do it in the real world, to prove that you are in complete control. To prove you can reach out and touch whoever you want whenever you want.

You are gifted with a mind that works so lightning fast you don't need to think before you act. Retrospective introspection makes clear to you how special you are. Your mind and body work in perfect harmony, your muscles sing counterpoint to your vision. What you see is what you get. You have never questioned if you are delusional. If you are, it doesn't matter.

You have gotten away with murder for more than ten years. How many others can say they have done that?

Someone pounds loudly on your door, and you jump up. The window is open and you can grab your duffel bags and be gone in seconds. But you know if it's the police, they'll have the place surrounded and you won't get far.

"Who's there?" you ask through the closed door.

"I saw your lights on and wanted to welcome you," says a male voice. "I'm your neighbor, Pete Smith. You got a minute to talk?"

You walk to the door and cautiously open it. You already have the blade of your Swiss Army knife open and ready. You see a big guy in his early thirties with long greasy hair. His eyes are glazed over like he's on drugs.

"I just want to let you know, man," says the guy at the door, "that I can supply anything you need. You need drugs, man, I got 'em. You need women, I got 'em. Whatever you want, man, I can get. Cheap, too."

You open the door wide. "Come in, Pete Smith," you say, smiling. "Have a seat and let's talk business."

Rat was at Attorney Bentley's office in a high-rise building across the street from the courthouse before nine AM. Bentley had a suite of offices on the eighth floor. Rat handed Bentley's secretary the check for ten thousand dollars. The secretary gave Rat a three-page contract to read and sign.

According to the contract's fine print, Rat agreed to pay all legal fees, photocopying fees, and one thousand additional dollars each time Bentley appeared in court on the client's behalf. Other added costs included research, para-legal fees, and any unforeseen fees that might be incurred. Bentley, in turn, agreed to represent the client to the best of his ability. It was expressly stated that Bentley guaranteed nothing, while Rat guaranteed to pay for everything.

Rat signed both copies of the contract and returned them to the secretary. She said Attorney Bentley would speak with Rat this afternoon following the arraignment. She told Rat that bond was likely to be denied in a capital case such as this. This afternoon's hearing was scheduled for 1:15 in room 403 of the courthouse. Rat could attend, but it wasn't necessary he be present. She assured Rat that George was in good hands with Attorney Bentley as his defense attorney. Rat wanted to believe her.

After leaving the attorney's office, Rat stopped at Denney's for a big breakfast. Last night had been a total bust, a complete waste of time. He had gone to Upstairs and Downstairs around eleven, searched the small weeknight crowd for anyone matching the killer's description, and left around midnight to try some of the other nearby bars. None of the places were crowded on a Tuesday night, and none of the male patrons who appeared to be left-handed came close to the height and weight requirements.

Tonight Rat would go back to Upstairs and Downstairs with officer Davis. It would feel awkward to escort a woman around bars. Rat hadn't dated since high school. He had entered the U. S. Army the week after graduation, his combat units were composed of all men, and he hadn't met any women soldiers he cared to date before being shipped overseas where dating wasn't an option. After he returned from Iraq, he had been too physically and emotionally fragile to think about dating. And, of course, the years he had spent underground in the sewers had offered few opportunities to meet women.

But, even though he knew it wasn't a real date, he found himself actually looking forward to spending time with Linda Davis. She was quite attractive, the perfect size for a guy who was barely five-six, and she had seemed more respectful of Rat's and George's personal property than the other police officers when they searched the house. Rat was glad it was Davis and not Evangelista he'd be taking to the dance clubs and bars. Evangelista didn't seem at all friendly.

Last night had been the first time in more than five years that Rat had tasted alcohol. Like his father, Rat had once been a binge drinker. Drinking was one way of coping with the vicissitudes of life. Rat's father, Earl Bradley, worked a boring and repetitive non-union factory job. He was constantly told that he wasn't worth what they paid him, he could be easily replaced by someone much younger and smarter, and he worried every single day that the next paycheck would be his last. With a wife and four children to support and a mortgage to pay, Earl blamed his wife and children for the anxiety that had taken over his life. He thought alcohol provided a temporary escape from fear, but drinking only made matters worse. As soon as

Earl got off work, he rushed to a neighborhood bar for drinks with co-workers. By the time he staggered through the door of his house, he was already falling-down drunk. Despite the nutritious meal that Rat's mother had ready and waiting, he continued to drink for the rest of the night. Sometimes he would simply pass out in his chair in front of the television and not wake up until morning. More often, however, he woke up sometime during the night and took out life's frustrations on those closest to him. He would go into a violent rage and storm into one of the bedrooms shouting obscenities. He would tell his children how worthless they were, how they were sucking the lifeblood out of him and draining him dry as if they were leeches or little vampires. He cursed the day each of them were born. Sometimes he picked them up by their tiny arms and shook them until their heads rattled. Sometimes he slapped them or hit them.

When Rat's mother tried to intervene, Rat's old man hit her, too. He said he only hit to put everyone in their place. Sometimes, the place he put them was the hospital. The place Earl Bradley worked had excellent health insurance. There was no co-pay for emergency room visits. If there had been a co-pay, Earl might have thought twice before sending his family to the hospital.

Rat's mother had apologized to the children for the actions of her husband. She tried to explain how hard his job was and how hard he worked to support his family. She told doctors and nurses in the emergency room that her children had fallen down the stairs or they had gotten into fights with each other. She said she, too, was accident prone and fell down the stairs on a regular basis. When doctors suggested she take the children and move to a place without stairs, she said she would think about that. Rat was sure she thought about it a lot through the years, but she never did anything about it.

When Rat came home from the Army an invalid, he had confronted his father. The two men had nearly killed each other. Fortunately, Rat's father was very drunk and no match for a much younger man, especially one who had recently been trained in hand-to-hand combat. For once, it was Rat's father who went to the hospital. After that, Rat moved out of the house for good. He offered to take his mother and sisters with him, but they wouldn't leave the old man.

Rat started drinking heavily himself when the pain he felt

became much too much to handle. It wasn't the physical pain as much as the psychological pain that hurt. Rat was still alive and men he had served with—men he knew deserved to live more than he— were dead. Drinking and drugs helped quiet the voices he heard in his head, the voices of the dead, but no matter how much he drank the voices wouldn't go away.

He drank up his disability check before the month was half over, and he'd have to cold-turkey the rest of the month until the next disability check was deposited in his bank account.

Finally, he stopped drinking and doing drugs because going cold-turkey every month was worse than staying sober. Now he felt no need to drink. Last night he had consumed a total of four half-beers, buying a bottle at each of the bars he entered and leaving half of the bottle behind when he left. Whether alcoholism was inherited or was a learned behavior, Rat knew he was at risk of becoming an alcoholic because his father had been an alcoholic. Rat's father had gone into rehab after Rat had sent him to the hospital, and Earl Bradley was now a changed man, thanks in part to regular attendance at Alcoholics Anonymous meetings. So maybe alcoholism was a learned behavior, one that could be unlearned with proper motivation. Rat had no desire to drink, but he proved last night that he could drink in moderation.

After breakfast, Rat went home to change clothes. He put on a suit and tie to attend the hearing at the courthouse. He entered the courtroom at one PM, taking a gallery seat in the back of the room. Joel Hickman took the seat next to him, and several other reporters Rat recognized from television took seats in the gallery.

At one-fifteen, the defense and prosecuting attorneys entered the courtroom and sat at opposite tables up near the judge's podium. James Bentley was an older man, gray-haired and dressed in a double-breasted gray-flannel suit. He had piercing blue eyes and wore a tie that was the same color as his eyes. The Assistant States Attorney was a woman. She wore a dark blue skirt with matching jacket and a pink blouse. She had relatively short hair and wore glasses. Rat couldn't see her eyes from where he was seated.

A bailiff and two police officers—Andy Sinnott and Del Conklin— escorted George into the courtroom. George was dressed in an orange jumpsuit with "Prisoner" stenciled in white capital letters across the back.

The bailiff asked all to rise while the judge entered from a side door. The bailiff recited something about the 17th circuit court of this county was now in session with the Honorable Judge Randall Montgomery presiding. Then he told everyone to take their seats.

The judge said this was an arraignment hearing to advise the defendant of the charges against him and to set a date for trial, and he read the list of charges against Harvey Fredriks. George was being indicted on eight counts of murder in the first degree, and the judge said each count was a capital crime which could result in a penalty of life imprisonment or even death. He told George he had the right to have an attorney represent him, and he noted that James Bentley was George's attorney of record and was present in the courtroom. Then he asked George how he pleaded.

"Not guilty, your honor," said George.

The judge set a date and time for the trial that was more than six months away. He said that because of the egregious nature of the crimes that bail was denied. Attorney Bentley argued that George had no criminal record and co-owned a home in the community, he was not a potential flight risk, and he should be presumed innocent until proven guilty. He asked the judge to reconsider bail. "My client is entitled to bail," he argued. The prosecutor argued against it. Judge Montgomery relented and set bail at three million dollars. Bentley argued that was much too high for someone with George's known assets. The judge rapped his gavel and said his decision was final.

The bailiff asked everyone to rise again as the judge left the courtroom. Andy turned George over to two county deputies who shackled George hand and foot and took him to the county jail to await trial.

Joel Hickman and two of the other reporters rushed to get comments from Andy or Del before they had a chance to exit. Andy pushed past them, but Del seemed reluctant to anger the press. He stayed behind and talked with Hickman.

Rat wanted to hear what Del said to the reporters, but he had an appointment with James Bentley at two-thirty.

Bentley's inner office had a large mahogany conference table with six leather chairs. When the secretary showed Rat into the office, James Bentley rose from behind a matching mahogany desk and shook Rat's hand, then indicated they would sit at the conference table to discuss the case. Bentley brought a yellow legal pad and a thick black Mont Blanc Meisterstuck fountain pen with him to the conference table.

"I noticed you in the gallery," said Bentley. "So you know that bail is exorbitant. Is there any way you can raise ten percent in cash? I didn't think so," he continued before Rat had a chance to shake his head. "I spoke with Harvey briefly before the arraignment. He's upset that they won't let him smoke. Personally, I think that's the least of his worries."

"He didn't do it," said Rat.

"I believe you," said Bentley. "But we have to convince a judge and jury of that. Police found two of the murder weapons in Harvey's possession after executing legally-obtained search warrants. They also found keys and a pipe that belong to Harvey at one of the crime scenes. That might be enough to hang him."

"Someone broke into our house and stole the keys and George's pipe. They also stole the keys to his car. They planted one icepick in George's study and the other in his car."

"George?"

"That's what I call Harvey. He looks like George Washington, doesn't he?"

Bentley laughed. "I suppose he does," Bentley said. "Maybe we can use that to our advantage. But George Washington was a bit taller than Harvey Fredriks. Unfortunately, Harvey matches the police profile of the killer to a T, same physical size, left-handed, smart enough to take a job with the coroner so he could doctor evidence. I don't think the jury will buy that Harvey Fredriks, unlike the young George Washington who reputedly chopped down the cherry tree, is incapable of telling lies."

"He couldn't have committed any of those murders," said Rat. "He was at home with me when the last girl was killed, and he was working when the others were killed."

"An off-duty police officer saw Harvey outside Upstairs and Downstairs on Saturday night watching one of the victims," said Bentley. "On the other nights he was working alone in the lab. I have been told he often leaves the lab unattended. People have seen him take the elevator up to the exit and walk outside when he was supposed to be working. He could have killed the others and returned to work and nobody would have known how long he was gone."

"He goes outside to smoke when he takes breaks," said Rat. "That's the only reason he leaves the lab. He can't smoke in the building."

Bentley wrote notes on his legal pad. "I have a copy of the police report of the alleged break-in at your home. It happened around five AM?"

"Before five. We didn't call the police right away."

"Why not?"

"We didn't know anything was missing."

"There was no evidence of the lock being damaged?"

"No."

"I'll do everything in my power to get Harvey off," said Bentley. "But it won't be easy. He looks guilty as sin."

"I have faith in you, Mr. Bentley."

"That's all I think we'll be able to do today," said Bentley, putting the cap on his fountain pen. "We have six months to prepare for trial. We'll keep in touch, Mr. Bradley."

Rat left the attorney's office and went to the PSB to talk with Andy. Andy and Del Conklin were looking at today's newspaper.

"Goddamn that Hickman," said Andy. He showed Rat Joel Hickman's column on page 3. The column head read, "Killer Hiding in Plain Sight inside PSB."

Hickman blamed County Coroner James Albertson and deputy coroner Sally Nolan, wife of police Captain Troy Nolan, for allowing Harvey Fredriks to work "essentially unsupervised" with the evidence police had recovered at the crime scenes. He alleged that Fredriks was able to doctor evidence—"after all," wrote Hickman, "Harvey Fredriks had an earned doctorate, though a doctorate of higher mathematics and not a medical doctorate"—and he had deliberately thrown police off his trail so he could continue raping and murdering innocent women. Hickman said he also had it on good authority from an unnamed source inside the police department that Homicide Lieutenant Andrew Sinnott was a close personal friend of the killer. He alleged a police conspiracy to protect Harvey Fredriks from prosecution.

Hickman went on to say he would be watching police actions closely, and any attempt to cover up Fredriks' guilt would be exposed in future columns.

"Hickman's trying to pound nails in Harvey's coffin before he's even fried," said Andy. "Hickman's just tied my hands so I can't prove George's innocence, assuming he is innocent. This guy's on a witch hunt."

"Witch hunts sell papers," said Conklin.

"Are we still on for tonight?" asked Rat.

"Yeah. Davis will meet you outside Upstairs and Downstairs at nine."

"What's going on?" asked Del.

"Mr. Bradley here agreed to escort Linda Davis to several of the bars. If Fredriks was framed, maybe they'll spot the real killer."

"You think Fredriks was framed?"

"Some things don't add up," said Andy. "For example, Fredriks reported a break-in at his house and his keys and the pipe missing before the killer could have left them in Carrie Yalden's garage. How did he know in advance that he would lose them or we'd find them? Mr. Bradley claims Fredriks was home with him when Carrie was murdered, and he was willing to sign an affidavit to that effect. The towel and icepick could have been planted at the time of the break-in. We found a murder weapon in Harvey's car. The keys to that car were among those reported stolen from Fredriks' home, but the car keys weren't on the ring we recovered at the crime scene. Frankly, I think that's enough to create reasonable doubt that Fredriks is the killer."

"I don't," said Conklin. "The old man's obviously guilty. You're wasting your time looking for anyone else."

"Maybe," said Andy. "But I don't want to find out after the fact that I've sent an innocent man to the death chamber. The only place I know to look for the killer is in the bars where the killer finds most of his victims."

"You're sending a police officer with a civilian?"

"Yes."

"Not just any civilian, someone who is a personal friend of the accused murderer?"

"That's right."

"I hope you know what you're doing."

"We'll see," said Andy.

Rat met Linda Davis outside the bar at nine PM. Linda wore a blue halter, red shorts, and white deck shoes with no socks. Her short reddish-blonde hair made her eyes look green in the ambient light of Upstairs and Downstairs. She had an upturned nose, luscious lips painted red, and the freckles on her cheeks made her look even younger than she was.

"The bartender's name is Gordy," said Rat.

"How do you know?" asked Linda Davis. Her voice was soft and melodic. Rat had to strain to hear her over the loud music drifting down from the dance floor and the even-louder conversations of all the people around them. Tonight the place seemed crowded.

"I was in here last night," said Rat. "It wasn't half as crowded then. I was able to talk to the bartender."

"Today's hump day," Linda said. "Half-way through the work week. People need a break."

"What will you have? I'm buying."

"I'll have a rum and Coke," she said. "Easy on the rum and long on the Coke. But you'll have to let me get the next round. I don't think it's fair for the guy to always pay."

Rat asked Gordy for a rum and Coke and a bottle of Budweiser.

"You get out much?" Rat asked when they reached the second floor and found a place to watch the dancers.

"I used to. Then I got engaged."

"You're engaged? To be married?"

"Not anymore," she said.

"What happened?"

"I took this job. I wanted to become a police officer, and he didn't want to be married to a police officer. He went his way, and I went mine."

"I'm sorry," said Rat.

"Me, too," she said, seeming genuinely sad. "It was good while it lasted. How about you? You get out much?"

"I work nights," Rat said. "I'm a call-taker at the 911 center. I work six PM to six AM Thursday, Friday, Saturday, and Sunday. I don't have much time to date."

"I'm sorry about your friend," said Linda. "He seemed like such a sweet old guy the few times I met him. Who would have suspected he was a killer?"

"He's not," said Rat. "That's why we're here. We're looking for the real killer."

"Are you sure he didn't do it?"

"Yes," said Rat. "I'm sure."

"So we're looking for a guy who's about the same height as your friend, left-handed, and who may or may not have scratches on his face?"

"Scratches on his face?"

"We found blood and skin under one of the victim's fingernails. It appears she scratched her attacker's face."

"I didn't know that," said Rat.

"We haven't released that information to the general public."

"George—I mean, Harvey—doesn't have any scratches on his face."

"I know," she said. "That's why I agreed to come here tonight with you."

"So you think he's innocent, too?"

"I don't know," she said. "But Sheila Hansen fought back, and she got the skin and blood Doctor Stowe found under her nails from somewhere. It didn't belong either to her or Lucy Puente. Therefore, I think the killer has some deep scratches on his face that he won't be able to hide."

"So we're looking for a man with scratches on his face?"

"Probably on the left side of his face. She scratched him with her right hand. If he was facing her, she gouged his left side. Probably near the eyes. If someone tried to rape me, I'd go for the eyes. I can't understand women who won't fight back."

"They're afraid," said Rat.

"Fear should make them fight back even harder."

"Fear can be paralyzing."

"Fear gets you killed."

"Haven't you ever been afraid?" asked Rat.

"Of course, I have. But I don't let fear stop me from doing what I have to do."

"You're brave as well as beautiful."

She blushed. Her whole face lit up as the freckles on her cheeks and forehead turned scarlet. "I heard you were brave," she said. "I heard you were a hero."

"Who told you that?"

"Andy. Lieutenant Sinnott."

"I was scared every moment I was in Iraq," Rat said. "I've been scared most of my life."

"But you didn't let that stop you, did you?"

"I used to," Rat said. "But not anymore."

They were silent as they glanced around the room at the dancers and the on-lookers. There appeared to be an equal number of men and women in the bar tonight, and not all of them were paired up. Some of the women were gathered in small groups, and many of the men were standing alone watching the women.

"It reminds me of a meat market where men are shopping for steaks to put on the grill," Linda said.

"Lots of hungry people," Rat agreed.

"I can see why the killer came here. The women are on open display, and the men can pick and choose."

Rat watched a big man with long hair and a thin black moustache sidle up to a group of women and begin chatting casually with them.

"I think he's offering to sell them drugs," said Davis. "See his eyes? He's a user. Most users sell to support their habit."

When the girls shook their heads, the big guy moved on to another group of women. He talked with four different groups of women before he found some takers for what he had to offer. Two of the women left with him, following him downstairs.

"I really should follow them and bust all three of them when the deal goes down," she said.

"That's not why we're here," Rat reminded her.

"You're right," she said. "But I haven't seen anyone who matches the description of the killer. Have you?"

"No," said Rat.

"Do you want to try one of the other bars?"

"Let's take one more look around. Then we can try the place across the street."

They walked around the outside of the dance floor, searching the faces of all of the men for tell-tale scratches. One man must have had a bad case of acne because his face was scarred with pock marks. But he was short and chubby, and he was right-handed.

Rat saw three men who appeared to be left-handed. One was too tall, one was too short, and the third looked too fat. None of them had scratches on their faces.

Linda led Rat downstairs and they abandoned their half-full drinks on the bar. After walking through the crowd and looking at all the men standing at the bar or sitting at tables, they headed across the street to a place called Ernie's.

Ernie's was relatively quiet. They did a quick walk-through and advanced farther up the street to a dance club called Stepping Out.

Shortly before two, after visiting every open bar on the strip, they called it a night. If there were a killer still on the loose, he wasn't in any of the downtown bars on a Wednesday night. Tomorrow night Rat had to work at the call center. It would be nearly a week before he could visit the bars again. Davis said she was sorry they had no luck. Rat thanked her for her trouble and he walked her to her car and watched her drive away.

PART II

"Yet I should kill thee with much cherishing. Good night, good night! parting is such sweet sorrow, that I shall say good night till it be morrow."

—William Shakespeare
Romeo and Juliet, Act 2, Scene 2.

CHAPTER FIFTEEN

"You wanted to see me, Doc?" Andy asked. Doctor Stowe had sent Andy an urgent e-mail, and Andy rushed down to Stowe's office next to the morgue as soon as he read his e-mails after Thursday morning's staff briefing.

"I finished the autopsy on Carrie Yalden," said Stowe. "I found something interesting on her breasts."

"What did you find?"

"Opaque cosmetics. A cream foundation and the kind of opaque cosmetics used to hide disfigurement."

"Her breasts were disfigured? She tried to hide scars? Did she have reconstruction after a mastectomy?"

"No. Her breasts were perfectly natural and normal. They weren't scarred."

"Then why was she wearing cosmetics?"

"She wasn't. It was trace left by her attacker."

"Jesus! The guy wore makeup?"

"To hide scars. Hansen must have scratched his face pretty bad. Our killer had to use makeup to cover up the gouges on his face. When his cheeks came in contact with Yalden's breasts, residue transferred from his face to her skin."

"Did you find the same kind of residue on any of the other victims?"

"Yes. There was some, not as much, in the swab I took from Barbara Ames. I didn't pay any attention to it, figuring it was caused by cross contamination. But finding the same kind of residue on Yalden raised red flags."

"Interesting."

"And speaking of red flags, did you notice that most of the victims wore something that was red?"

"No," said Andy. "Yalden wasn't wearing red."

"But she was," said Stowe. "She had a red ribbon in her hair."

"Interesting. Lila Evans had a red skirt. Barbara Ames wore a red t-shirt to Upstairs and Downstairs."

"Sheila Hansen had red fingernail polish and red lipstick," added Stowe.

Andy remembered that Mary Woodman had worn a red sweater and red shoes. Jean Johnston had worn a red blouse.

"Red is a common color," said Andy. "It could be a coincidence."

"It could," agreed Stowe.

"Thanks, Doc," said Andy.

"Have you seen Hickman's column in the morning paper?"

"I haven't had time."

"Here." Stowe handed Andy the front section of the newspaper. "It's on page three."

The headline read, "Police Cover-up in Progress." Hickman reported that Andy Sinnott, head of homicide, had sent a female detective to accompany Harvey Fredriks' roommate to local bars looking for scapegoats to implicate in the murders. "Police are desperate to get Fredriks off the hook, but we won't let them. The days of cronyism in this city, days when people in power can get away with murder, are past. We call upon the Mayor and the Chief of Police to do their jobs. Remember, Mr. Mayor, we're watching *you*."

How had Hickman learned that Linda Davis had gone with Rat to the bars last night? Had Hickman been there himself and observed them? How did he know Rat was George's roommate? How did he know Davis, dressed in civilian clothes, was a police officer? Was Hickman following Davis or Rat? Or had Hickman been in the bar himself and recognized them?

"It looks like you have a leak in your department," Stowe said. "Hickman mentioned in yesterday's column he had a source close to the investigation. Whom do you suspect?"

"It has to be Linda Davis," said Andy. "No one else knew that I ordered her to check out the bars last night. She's new, and I'm not sure I can trust her. She has a mind of her own. She and I have had a few minor disagreements."

"You think she might be trying to sabotage you? Maybe undermine your authority?"

"It's possible."

"Did she say she learned anything last night?"

"No. Del said it would be a waste of time, and it was."

"What about Del? It sounds like he knew that you sent Linda and Bradley to look around the downtown bars. Could Del be talking to the press after hours?"

"No. Not Del. Del's been a cop for a long time. Why would he do such a thing?"

"Who knows? Maybe he believes he's doing a public service. Maybe he wants your job."

"I still think Del's a good cop."

"If it's not Del or Davis, who else?"

"No one I can think of."

"Harvey didn't kill anyone," said Stowe. "The real killer's still out there, and he won't stop killing for long. I think you were right to send Davis to check out the bars. I think you should send someone there every night until the real killer is behind bars instead of stalking women in bars."

"I don't have the manpower to do that," said Andy.

Andy's cell phone vibrated in his pocket and, at the same time, the doctor's desk phone rang. Both men answered their phones. The automated dispatch system gave them virtually identical information. Two women were discovered in the bushes at the public park near the river. Both were dead and naked from the waist down. A woman eating lunch at one of the picnic tables in the park had noticed feet sticking out of the bushes and had taken a closer look. Then she had called 911 on her cell phone.

Stowe grabbed the keys to the meat wagon and escorted Andy through the maze of corridors that led to the tunnel between the PSB and the parking garage. Stowe drove the meat wagon while Andy drove his own car.

A small crowd of onlookers had gathered around the bodies. Andy asked them all to step back from the crime scene, called Evangelista and the forensics team and told them to get down to the park as fast as possible and tape off the area, then he knelt down next to Stowe as the doctor examined the bodies.

Both women looked to be in their mid-twenties. One wore a blue halter and white shorts, the other a yellow blouse and blue skirt. Neither of them wore red.

The bodies were partially obscured by the bushes decorating the north side of the park. The park district had planted a hedge from the river's edge all along the border between the park and commercial properties to the north, but the hedge had been neglected most of the season and allowed to grow taller and cover a wider area than was originally intended. Scraggly branches laden with green leaves protruded from both sides of the hedge line, creating private enclaves where drug dealers and prostitutes conducted business after dark. During the day, downtown office workers enjoyed lunch at tables or benches in the park, and young mothers brought their children to play on the swings or climb on monkey bars. Fortunately, none of those mothers or children had seen the half-naked bodies obscured by the bushes.

The woman who had called 911 was middle-aged and worked as a receptionist at one of the offices nearby. Her name was Nola Winters, and she came to the downtown park nearly every day from noon to one to enjoy the sunshine and eat a sandwich. Today, she was so distressed by what she had seen that she couldn't finish her sandwich.

"I saw the shoes," she told Andy when he arrived at the scene. "Two pairs of sandals that looked practically new. I went to get a closer look and saw the naked bodies. I knew they were dead because of the flies. It's just terrible. Women aren't safe anywhere anymore."

"They don't look like prostitutes," said Stowe. "They were probably here to buy drugs."

"And got raped instead," said Andy.

"They were both raped post-mortem," said the doctor. "It looks like they had shot up with something, probably heroin. A tox screen will tell. They must have overdosed."

"And someone found their bodies and raped them both?"

"Whoever gave them the heroin knew they would overdose," said Stowe. "He deliberately killed them with a overdose of drugs so he could rape them after they expired. He didn't just find them shooting up. He lured them here with drugs."

"Premeditated murder?"

"Neither victim is a regular drug user. I see no tracks on the arms or inner thighs like you'd expect to find on an addict. These are recreational users who wanted to experience a different kind of high last night. Someone injected them. They didn't do it themselves. Each has a single injection prick on their right forearms and ligature marks above the biceps. Do you see a needle or a rubber strap around anywhere?"

"No," said Andy. "Maybe the crime scene team will find one."

"There are probably needles all over this park," said Stowe. "But I suspect the killer took the needle and paraphernalia he used with him."

Evangelista and Davis arrived with the forensics van, followed by Conklin and Pearson. Evangelista spread yellow tape around the entire area while Davis looked for tell-tale footprints.

"Too many people have trampled the ground around here today," Davis said. "We can forget about getting viable footprints."

Evangelista took photographs of both bodies and the surrounding area. Davis found a purse in the bushes that might have belonged to one of the victims. She walked over close enough to compare the driver's license photo with the victims' faces. "The woman on the left is Rita Esteban," she announced. "Age 24. Money and credit cards are still in the purse. If we find the other purse, we might be able to rule out robbery as a motive. By the way, I saw both of those women last night in Upstairs and Downstairs. They left with a man. It looked like they were going someplace to do a drug deal. I wish I had followed them and busted them. If I had, the women might still be alive."

"Can you describe the man?" asked Andy.

"Six feet or six-one. Maybe two hundred pounds. Muscular. Early thirties. He had long black hair and a black moustache. He didn't fit the profile of the icepick killer."

"Look very closely at the eyes," interrupted Stowe, lifting the eyelids of one, and then the other, of the victims. "Both women, both eyes. There's a small pinprick in the right side of the sclera of both eyes of both victims that leaked vitreous fluid. I think he shoved a syringe into their eyes after they had expired. There's some minor leakage, but little or no blood. It's as if, even though they were dead, he didn't want them to be able to watch him. That's the same MO as the other murders. And the needles were inserted into the right side of the eyes, indicating they were held in the killer's left hand."

"Can't be the same killer. The guy Davis described doesn't match the profile. Besides, he used a needle instead of an icepick."

"Could be a copycat then. There has been tons of publicity about the icepick killer's MO. I'll know more after the autopsy."

Television crews began arriving with cameras. Del went to talk with the reporters and keep them on the other side of the yellow tape. Lewinski wasn't normally on duty in the middle of the day, and the patrolmen who had responded to the call were two young guys who seemed too shy to tell the hoards of reporters to keep their distance. Del had more experience dealing with news hounds, and Andy heard Del promise to give them a story as soon as the police and coroner had finished their preliminary investigation, provided they stayed out of the way and let the crime scene team do their jobs. "You let us do our jobs, and we'll help you do yours," Del said.

Stowe took some more photographs, and then he went to the truck to fetch a gurney and body bags. Andy helped him roll the dead women into the bags and lift the dead weight up onto the gurney.

"I really miss Harvey at times like this," said Stowe, strapping the bags to the gurney. "I'll have to speak with Jim Albertson again about hiring replacements. I can't do it all myself."

"How long before Sally gets back from her honeymoon?" Andy asked as he helped Stowe push the gurney across the grass to the back door of the truck.

"Another week. Albertson is blaming Dr. Nolan for hiring Harvey."

"Albertson's totally useless. How does he keep getting re-elected?"

"He has a recognizable name in the community. And he has powerful political allies."

"Like the Mayor?"

"Among others. He contributes lots of money to party coffers, and he's always doing political fund-raisers."

"Why don't we have a medical examiner system like Chicago does?"

"It might be better, but it can also be almost as bad. The Cook County Medical Examiner is appointed by the county chairman and approved by the county board. It's still very political. But, at least, the medical examiner is a medical doctor, once approved an appointed by the board, and he or she doesn't have to run for re-election every four years."

Stowe unlocked the back of the meat wagon and Andy helped him lift the two body bags, one at a time, onto the floor. Stowe folded the gurney and got up into the back of the truck to strap down the gurney and both bodies. Then he hopped out and locked the back door.

"You've got the second set of keys to this truck on Harvey's key ring," he said. "I suppose you need to keep them as evidence until after the trial."

"You'll get them back eventually," said Andy.

As Stowe drove off, Andy walked back to the bushes where Evangelista was still processing the scene and Davis searched around for the missing purse. Pearson and the other techs were combing the other ends of the hedge line.

"I think there were two men," said Evangelista. "One stood over there, off to the side, on the look-out while the other man raped the women. I found three cigarette butts ground into the grass by the pointed toe of a size twelve boot."

"I only saw the women with one man," said Davis. "And the man I saw was wearing cowboy boots."

"He must have had a friend waiting here in the park," said Andy.

"I bagged the butts and maybe we can get prints or DNA off them," said Evangelista.

"I found another purse," shouted Pearson. "It got thrown all the way over here. Wallet looks intact. Woman's name is Elaine Ryan. Age 23. There's also an open pack of cigarettes, a used crack pipe, and a Bic lighter in the purse. When we get it to the lab, I'll check it for prints."

"I was right," said Davis. "The women went with the guy to score drugs."

"You think the guy you saw in the bar is a drug dealer?"

"He's definitely a user himself. He probably deals to support his habit."

"Why did he kill the women and not take their money?"

"He wouldn't."

"So the other guy must be the killer," said Evangelista.

"Makes sense," agreed Andy. "He paid the guy with the moustache to lure the women to the park and keep a look-out while he killed them and raped them."

"Both men are equally guilty," said Davis. "One is a murderer and the other is an accomplice to murder."

"I'm going back to the office and enter the latest data into the victim spreadsheet," said Andy. "You finish up here and see what else you can find."

"I want to go back to Upstairs and Downstairs tonight," said Davis. "Maybe the guy with the moustache will be there."

"I can't let you do that," said Andy. "If Hickman sees you there, it will be hell to pay. Besides, Bradley works at the call center tonight. I don't want you going there by yourself."

"I'm a big girl, and I can take care of myself. I don't need a man to protect me."

"I'll go with you," said Evangelista. "It'll be fun to have a girls' night out."

"I can't authorize it," said Andy.

"Then we'll go on our own," said Evangelista.

"Why do you dye your hair and moustache?" you ask Pete Smith.

"Black makes me look sexy," he answers.

"It doesn't look natural," you tell him. "It looks like you soaked your hair in liquid shoe polish."

"I ain't going to change it."

Smith is an ignorant asshole, but you put up with him because he's useful. He brought you two women last night, just as he promised. And all it cost you was a few hundred dollars so Smith could buy some coke and smack and a few needles. He got to keep half the drugs for his trouble.

Smith supplied the women, the drugs, and the needles. He stood guard while you shot up the girls and waited for the nearly-pure heroin to stop their hearts. He didn't interfere while you examined their bodies and found the bodies suitable. Neither of the women had augmented their breasts, and you took the time to do their eyes before you fondled their still-warm flesh. With Pete watching for intruders, you could take your time and properly appreciate the beauty of the female form. No one was around to punish you for looking or touching.

Pete doesn't work a regular job, but you do. You send him home at four, sleep six hours, shower and shave and get ready to go to work. When you arrive at the funeral home at noon, Jack Albertson asks you to go to the morgue and pick up a new client. Her name is Carrie Yalden, and the assistant coroner has just released her body for burial. Albertson tells you Yalden's husband Ralph has made arrangements for her embalming and burial. He was willing to pay Albertson's exorbitant fees for the deluxe funeral package. He must have loved his wife very much.

Before you leave your workspace, you apply makeup to the scars on your face. The scratches have scabbed over nicely, but they require a heavy application of opaque cream to obscure them from view. With your sunglasses on, you can barely tell the scars are there.

You drive the hearse to the PSB parking garage, walk the gurney through the connecting tunnel to the Public Safety Building, and ask the guard to notify Doctor Stowe that you are here to pick up Carrie Yalden. Ten minutes later, Stowe appears with Yalden's body on a gurney. You sign the papers and transfer the body from his gurney to yours.

You catch Stowe looking curiously at your face, and you wonder what he knows. He is a medical doctor, and he's observant. Should you kill him now? Can you do it with the guard present?

Your hand goes into your pocket and your fingers touch the Swiss Army knife, deftly prying the blade open. One swipe and the guard's throat is opened wide, then Stowe's neck is next.

But Stowe takes his gurney and disappears behind a locked door before you make your move.

You wheel the body across the connecting tunnel to the elevator. Five minutes later, you are on your way back to Albertson's mortuary.

Carrie is still cold when you remove the wrappings from her body. She is also still beautiful, despite the ugly Y-incision from her clavicle to below her navel. You run your hands over her cold breasts and smile. You massage her breasts, her neck, her arms, her legs.

Over the next few hours, you do your best to bring her back to life. You wash the body with anti-bacterial soaps. You make tiny incisions in her carotid and jugular, insert the embalming tubes, and begin the familiar process. You open her up, aspirate her body cavity, soak her organs, and inject preservative chemicals. You wash and style her hair. You even find a red ribbon to tie in her hair, just as you remember seeing her.

When you are finished sealing her eyes and lips, you apply cosmetics. You work your famous magic on her until she looks even better than she did in life. You hope her husband appreciates the love you have given his dead wife.

You wheel her into the viewing room and look at her one more time in the same light where others will see her. She looks perfect.

You close the lid on the casket, return to your workroom, and clean up.

You think a drink would taste good after your long day. Perhaps you should celebrate by going to Upstairs and Downstairs and watching the dancers. After all, what harm will it do to just look?

You drive home, shower again, and change clothes. You take time to turn on the television and watch the ten o'clock news.

Channel seven shows pictures of the police in the park. There are a half-dozen male officers, and two females in civilian clothing. The camera is too far away to see any of their faces. The anchors say the police think the latest murders were done by a "copycat killer" who was trying to imitate Harvey Fredriks.

At ten-thirty, you turn off the TV and drive to the bar.

It's Thursday night, and the bar is fairly crowded for a week night. Singles are looking to find dates for the weekend. One more day at work in the office or factory, and it will be time to party the weekend away.

You order your usual, and the bearded bartender brings you a bottle of cold Heineken. You take your beer and ascend the stairs to the dance floor where the DJ is actually spinning vinyl records on a turntable. Thursday is "oldies" night, and some of the songs are by Jimi Hendrix, the Beatles, and Rolling Stones.

You are glad to see women still dressed for warm weather. Shorts with halters, t-shirts, and short skirts are in abundance.

Shortly before midnight, two new women arrive that you haven't seen before. One is on the smallish side with pixyish reddish-blonde hair, wearing a white halter and red shorts. The other is slightly older with dark hair, slightly taller and heavier, and she has on tight jeans and a blue t-shirt. Neither woman is wearing a bra.

You watch as they go out on the dance floor and get into the music. After two numbers, they retreat to the sidelines and look around at the men. You avert your face as their eyes come in your direction. You give them time to look around the room, and then you stare at them again.

The small one is absolutely perfect. The other one isn't bad, but there's something about her that makes you think she prefers women to men. Perhaps it's the way her eyes keep returning to the younger woman's face and chest. Perhaps it's the mannish way she's dressed and walks.

It doesn't matter to you one way or the other. All women are the same when they're dead.

The two dance some more, and you appreciate the way they move to the music. Music doesn't move you in the same way. Music has never been a big part of your life.

But you enjoy watching others enthralled by the beat. Their eyes space out the same way Pete Smith's eyes space out when he shoots up. It's the look of pure ecstasy, and it turns you on.

You decide you have to have these two women. Which one first? Does it matter?

When they announce last call and the women head downstairs, you follow them. They both have cars—the younger one a KIA Soul and the other one a Dodge Ram pick-up truck—and they hug and go their separate ways. You get in your red Matrix to follow the younger girl driving the Kia.

She lives in an apartment complex on the far east side of the city. Unfortunately, you see security cameras trained on the parking area and on each side of the building. Getting inside will be next to impossible.

Besides, you want to maintain a low profile. If you do another woman in her apartment, you might undo the work you put into framing Harvey Fredriks. You need to wait for an opportunity to take her someplace else.

But her reddish-blond hair and all of those freckles are so enticing, you will remember her forever. Before you leave this city, you promise yourself will have your way with her.

You drive back to your apartment and fantasize about the new love of your life. You wonder if she has a name and what it might be. For now, you will simply call her "little one." You envision having her all to yourself on the embalming table. She is still alive, still warm and pliant. You imagine all the things you will do with her.

Someone knocks on your door, and you recognize Pete Smith's voice as he says, "Hey, man, you in there?"

Smith is becoming a bother. You get up and open the door. "Go away," you say. You can tell he's been drinking. You smell the alcohol as he breathes in your face.

"Last night was more fun than I've had in a long time," he says. "I got off watchin' you nail those broads."

"Go away," you say again.

"Listen, I was thinkin'. We can do it again tomorrow night. No charge. I got plenty smack left. I'll bring you a couple of broads and you do them. Just let me watch. Okay?"

You can't believe that this bozo is a watcher. It almost makes you sick to think that he gets pleasure out of seeing naked bodies. It's a sacrilege. You think about taking out his eyes right here and now. He doesn't deserve to see what you see.

Instead, you say, "Okay. Tomorrow night. I want you to find two women for me. But not just any women. The ones I want were in Upstairs and Downstairs tonight. One is small, short, with short blondish-red hair trimmed in a pixie cut and freckles on her face."

"Hey. I know the one you want. I saw her in there last night with some guy."

"Tonight she was with another woman, a few inches taller than the little one, heavier, with short dark hair. She walks like a man."

"I can get 'em for ya. Both of 'em."

"You do that. There's another hundred in it for you when you deliver them to the park."

"Consider it done."

"Now get lost. I need my sleep."

"Okay. Tomorrow night, then. We'll do it all over again."

"Tomorrow night," you say, as you push Smith out the door.

"Only you can keep the hundred bucks if I can have sloppy seconds."

You slam the door in his face to keep from killing him now. The thought of Pete Smith touching your little one is so repulsive, you have to fight to control your impulse to open the door again and jab your Swiss Army knife into his eyes. He gets to stay alive until he brings you what you want. Then Pete Smith will be history.

You open the couch into a bed and lie down on the lumpy mattress. You close your eyes and see the freckles on her face, the green of her eyes.

You fall asleep, thinking of tomorrow night.

CHAPTER SIXTEEN

"Police Muzzle Press" read the headline atop Hickman's Friday morning column. "Two more mutilated bodies of nude women were discovered Thursday in the center of the city," wrote Hickman. "To keep the public from learning the gristly details of the murders, Homicide Chief Andrew Sinnott sent his lackey, Sergeant Delmar Conklin, to muzzle the press. Conklin promised to give reporters the facts later, but the facts were not forthcoming by the time this column went to press. It is only because this reporter has a secret source within the police department—a concerned citizen who cares about seeing justice done—that I am able to reveal here exclusively what really happens in this city."

Hickman went on to say a "copycat killer" had emerged to emulate the terrible misdeeds of Harvey Fredriks. Hickman even went so far as to allege that Andy Sinnott wanted the public to believe that the icepick killer was still on the loose and that Harvey Fredriks was innocent. "I can assure you that is not the case," wrote Hickman. "Not only were the recent murders done with a hypodermic needle and not an icepick, but there appear to be two men involved instead of only one. If Lieutenant Sinnott thinks he can pull the wool over our eyes and get Fredriks released, he is sadly mistaken."

Hickman called upon the Mayor to "muzzle the police and not the press." He went on to promise he would remain vigilant and report the truth as he saw it, not as the police wanted him to see it. "Thank God," he ended the day's column, "that we live in America where the press is still free to report the truth."

"Hickman's a lying piece of shit," said Del Conklin at the

morning briefing. "I told reporters that we wouldn't give them the story until we had completed our investigation. The investigation is still ongoing."

"I learned a long time ago not to tell reporters anything unless I absolutely have to," said Andy. "And then what I do have to tell them gets vetted by half-a-dozen people before it's finally put out in an official press release."

"Who is Hickman's inside source?" asked Davis.

"Good question," said Andy. "Betty Halloran is our liaison with the press. Maybe Betty can find out for us."

"You don't think it's one of us, do you?" asked Del.

"It has to be," answered Andy. "Someone is feeding Hickman inside information that no one else knows. Betty sent out a news release late yesterday afternoon that gave the names and ages of the latest victims. But she said nothing in that news release about hypodermic needles or two perpetrators. That's something no one but the people in this room knows."

"What about Doctor Stowe?" asked Del.

"He knows about the hypodermic needle, but not about two possible perps. Evangelista discovered the cigarette butts and second set of footprints after Stowe left the scene. Either someone talked to the press or the press overheard us talking among ourselves. We weren't exactly quiet out there in the park, but Del kept the press far enough away I don't think they could have overheard us."

"So what are you going to do about the leaks?" asked Del.

"Nothing," said Andy.

"Nothing?"

"I'm not going to worry about it. Eventually, I'll find out. And then I'll know who I can trust and who I can't. Until then, there's nothing I can do. Our job is to concentrate on finding the killer or killers. If we let the press sidetrack us, we aren't doing our jobs."

"Did Stowe get the toxicology analysis completed?"

"I'll go down and talk with him after our meeting. He was still doing the two autopsies when I went home last night. Harvey Fredriks was the chemical analysis expert, and Stowe depended on Harvey to do tox screenings. Stowe might have to send the blood out to be analyzed, and that can take weeks to get results. Losing Harvey has made Stowe's already difficult job even tougher."

"How come he doesn't have help?" asked Evangelista.

"The Coroner is saving money by not hiring replacements. He says he's waiting for Sally Nolan to come back to advise him before he hires anybody new."

"I thought," said Davis, "the coroner blamed her for recommending Harvey."

"He does. But he depends on Sally to know what kind of help they need in the morgue. Albertson isn't a doctor. He's absolutely clueless."

"Why doesn't he ask Stowe?"

"Stowe is here on a fellowship. Technically, he's not a part of the coroner's office. Doctor Nolan wrote the grant request. Technically, Stowe reports to Nolan and not to Albertson."

"So what do we do now?" asked Del.

"Now we look for the guy Davis saw in the bar night before last. Ms. Davis, would you please describe him for all of us?"

"He's a big guy. I know you probably think all guys look big to me, but this guy is about six-one and two hundred pounds. He must have worked out at one time, because he still looked very muscular despite being a long-term drug user. You could tell by his eyes that he did the real hard stuff, the opiates. Probably pills, too, most likely amphetamines. He had black hair and a black moustache. Neither the moustache nor the hair on his head looked recently trimmed, and the hair was real long but looked too dark to be natural. I think he dyes the hair and moustache. He wore an old muscle t-shirt that was too tight for his torso because the cotton had shrunk from multiple washings. Dirty jeans. And brown cowboy boots with pointy metal toe tips. Real shit-kickers, and I wouldn't want to be kicked with those metal-tipped toes."

"Anything else you can think of?"

"He carried a bottle of beer around with him in his right hand. Dark bottle. Bud maybe. He had peeled the labels off with his fingernails. The guy seemed wired. Probably from the drugs."

"Davis saw him Wednesday night in Upstairs and Downstairs. He approached several women before he found two that would leave the bar with him. Those were the two women we found murdered in the park."

"Any idea about the second guy?" asked Del. "Assuming there was one."

"Evangelista did find some partial footprints in the dirt around the bushes. She compared photographs with prints found on the riverbank a week earlier. She tells me they're almost a perfect match."

"And a close match with prints at Hansen and Puente's apartment," Evangelista said. "I'd say the prints were made by the same kind of shoes, but not the same pair of shoes. The treads on the shoe prints found yesterday weren't as worn down in the heels as the ones from the riverbank."

"Are you saying the women we found yesterday were killed by the same guy who killed all the others?" asked Pearson. "The icepick murderer?"

"I can't say that definitively," said Andy. "But the prints came from the same *kind* of shoe and they look to be the same size."

"That can't be," said Del. "Harvey Fredriks is in jail."

"And Harvey Fredriks doesn't own a pair of Reebok running shoes," said Andy. "But the killer does."

"Just because we didn't find a pair of Reeboks in Fredriks' house when we tossed it, doesn't mean he isn't the killer."

"That's true," said Andy. "But we know the second guy yesterday wears the same size shoe as the previous killer, so he must be about the same size. And he's left-handed because the needles were inserted into the right side of the eyes."

"I thought," said Del, "the evidence against Fredriks was pretty strong. I guess I was wrong."

"We still don't know for certain if Fredriks is the killer or not. But we do know there are two men out there who killed Esteban and Ryan while Fredriks is in jail. If we find those two men, maybe we'll discover the truth. So that's your assignment, guys and gals. Finding two men in a population of a quarter million people will be like looking for a needle in a haystack. But we know the killer selects his victims at the downtown bars. Check with the bartenders and see if anyone knows the big guy with a dyed-black moustache and cowboy boots. We think the killer also looks for victims at shopping malls or convenience stores. Make the rounds and see if you spot the big guy or a scarred left-handed guy wearing Reeboks."

"Evangelista and I will take Upstairs and Downstairs tonight," said Davis. "We can probably hit one or two of the other clubs as well."

"I'll take the convenience stores," said Pearson.

"I guess that leaves me with the shopping malls," said Del.

"All right," said Andy. "And I'll have a talk with Doctor Stowe and get copies of the autopsy protocols if he's finished the autopsies."

Andy took the elevator downstairs and found Stowe asleep in his office chair.

"Hey, Doc," said Andy. "You still alive? You look like one of your own patients."

"I'm alive," he said. "But I need to get a life. This job is wearing me out."

"What did you find out about Ryan and Esteban at autopsy?"

"High concentrations of monoacetylmorphine present in the blood and heroin in the vitreous fluids of the eyes on both victims. Heroin breaks down into monoacetylmorphine almost immediately, and it's hard to find pure heroin anywhere in the body except the gel of the vitreous humor. They died of asphyxiation and massive heart failure evidently caused by a lethal injection of nearly pure heroin. They also had blood alcohol levels of point oh-nine and ten, so they were both legally drunk before they added the heroin to their blood stream. Alcohol and opiates can be a deadly combination anyway, but they didn't have a chance when that amount of nearly pure heroin hit their hearts and lungs like runaway freight trains. They had no idea what hit them when the ligatures were released from their arms and pure heroin flowed through their veins. If both victims were injected at the same time, as I suspect, there must have been two people to administer the drugs, one for each of the victims. Someone had to untie the bands at the same time they pushed the plunger on the needles, and that's a two-handed job."

"We found footprints from two apparently different shoes. Running shoes and cowboy boots."

"Then there were two killers. I thought so."

"Looks like there were."

"I sent samples of the blood to the state labs for a complete screening. They'll confirm my analysis."

"Any word yet on the DNA tests you requested?"

"Nada."

"I asked Mullins to help hurry it along. I can't understand why it's taking so damn long."

"DNA typing takes time. First, it's extracted from the individual cell nuclei in the sample. Enzymes are used to break down cell proteins; DNA fragments are separated by size and grouped into bands; the bands are tagged with isotopes of radioactive phosphorous and exposed to X-ray film; and the unique pattern of bands appearing on developed x-ray film creates the DNA profile. Then that DNA profile is run through the FBI's CODIS database of known samples. Thirteen core nuclei Short Tandem Repeats, or STRs, are compared. A forensic to forensic search is completed, comparing our sample with samples found at other crime scenes nationally, and then a forensic to offender search is initiated to compare our sample to the DNA of known offenders and arrestees. A list of candidate matches is analyzed by a qualified DNA analyst at the state labs. Finally, the results are sent back to us. All of that takes time. And the state is backlogged with samples submitted daily from all over the state."

"Can the DNA found on Hansen be matched to the DNA discovered at a rape and murder committed ten years ago?"

"Only if that DNA is in the CODIS database."

"What about Harvey Fredriks' DNA? Do we have a sample?"

"I assume someone took a swab, along with his fingerprints, after he was arrested. Anyone arrested for a felony in this state is required to supply DNA for testing. If you didn't do it when Harvey was first taken into custody, then someone else probably did at the county jail."

"So, eventually, we'll know if Harvey's DNA matches the DNA from the skin under Hansen's fingernails."

"Eventually, yes."

"Did you see Hickman's column in this morning's paper?" asked Andy.

"I haven't had time to read it yet."

"He admitted he has a source that told him about the hypodermic needles and the evidence of two perpetrators we found at the scene. You didn't tell Hickman anything, did you?"

"I don't have time to go to the bathroom, much less talk to the press."

"What about Albertson? How much have you told him?"

"His secretary typed up the autopsy protocols. I'm sure she'll give him copies."

"So he could have leaked the information to Hickman?"

"I didn't finish the posts until late last night. She didn't transcribe the recorded autopsies until eight this morning. The paper went to press at two AM."

"Then the leak has to come from someone on my team."

"You still think it's Davis?"

"It has to be."

"What are you going to do about it?"

"Talk to Betty. She knows Davis better than I do. Plus, she has contacts at the newspaper. Maybe she can find out who leaked to Hickman."

"Turn off the overhead lights on your way out," said Stowe.

"You don't have any windows. If I turn out the lights, it will be pitch dark in here. You won't be able to see."

"That's the idea," said Stowe. "I'm going to catch some sleep."

"What if Albertson comes down here and finds you sleeping?"

Stowe laughed. "When was the last time you saw Albertson visit the morgue?"

"I haven't," said Andy.

"I rest my case," said Stowe. "Now turn off the lights so I can rest my eyes."

Andy hit the light switch on his way out of Stowe's office. He walked down the hall, turned left, and entered the Violent Crimes office where Betty Halloran sat at her desk studying the victim spreadsheet displayed on her computer.

"Ten murders in one week," she said. "That's a new record. We've never had ten murders in one week before. The closest we came was two years ago when the Pickaxe Butcher was running wild."

"Don't take this wrong, Betty, but I have to ask. Have you told Hickman anything about this case?"

"I sent copies of the press releases to his office. But I haven't spoken to Joel recently."

"You do know him? Personally?"

"I've met him several times at social functions around town, and I've seen him at a few political fundraisers. He's an acquaintance, not a friend."

"Did you see his column in this morning's paper?"

"I read it at home before I came to work."

"Do you have any idea who his source might be?"

"No. It's not me, I can tell you that."

"Do you think Linda Davis is Hickman's source?"

"No," said Betty without hesitation. "If Linda had a beef with you, she'd come to me and file an official complaint. She wouldn't go to Hickman and spill her guts to the press behind the department's back. I know, because she came to me to file a complaint about you being a sexist pig, and I talked her out of it."

"When was this?"

"Her second day working with you. She said Evangelista told her you were a sexist pig, and Linda discovered Evangelista was right."

"Lorraine thinks I'm a sexist pig?"

"Lorraine thinks all men are sexist pigs. She didn't like men much in the first place, and she's been to a few rape scenes too many. To hear her talk, you'd think she'd like to shoot every guy's balls off."

"I don't hear her talk. Lorraine is usually very quiet. She's always impressed me as very efficient and professional."

"You should hear her sound off in the ladies' locker room. And when you asked Davis to check out Upstairs and Downstairs with Harvey's roommate, Evangelista practically went ballistic."

"How did she know I had sent Davis with Rat to Upstairs and Downstairs?"

"Linda probably told her. Come on, Andy. Women talk. Especially to women co-workers. We do it all the time, and just because we're cops doesn't mean we don't complain about what happens at work. You guys get together and talk shop, too. Don't tell me you don't, because I know better. Ten years ago, when I used to work the streets with Troy Nolan and Bill Bowers and Art Lewinski, they'd go drinking every night after they got off duty. Sometimes, I joined them. It seems all they wanted to talk about was how the brass had their heads up their asses and politicians and lawyers were ruining the country. I remember Lewinski liked to bad-mouth the press. Troy always had a gripe about Captain Erickson who was only a lieutenant then and head of homicide. I don't remember what Bill griped about, but I'm sure it was something. They were all good cops, but they blew off steam by complaining about work. Women cops are the same way. Only we don't need a few drinks to loosen our tongues."

"I guess I don't know much about women," said Andy.

"Most men don't," said Betty. "I'm still trying to educate my husband after eleven years of marriage. And my sons are clueless. Maybe when they become teenagers, they'll want to learn a few things. Now all they seem interested in is playing war games on X-Box."

Lester Cartwright of the FBI and Dave Mullins of the state police walked into Betty's office together, both looking very excited. Mullins handed Andy a large packet composed of computer printouts. "Those are the results of the DNA samples Stowe sent to state labs," he said. "I asked our people to drop everything else and expedite the processing. Wait until you hear what CODIS turned up."

"We found matches to samples recovered from all over the country," said Cartwright. "After CODIS came up with hundreds of positive hits, I got a call from the Justice Department. Your icepick murderer is one of the most sought after unknown fugitives we have. I've been asked to provide any assistance you need to apprehend this killer as quickly as possible. He never stays in any one place long enough for us to identify him. He's killed in Florida, California, Oregon, Illinois, New Jersey, Colorado, Texas, you name it. Now he's here, and we want him. If we don't catch him here, who knows where he'll turn up next?"

"There were no matches to known felons in the system," said Mullins. "Only to other crimes. That means the guy's never been arrested for a felony."

"He leaves no witnesses alive to identify him," added Cartwright. "This guy's been killing for at least ten years, and he's still at it. If we didn't have his DNA, we'd never know it was the same guy. He never leaves fingerprints. He's probably never been fingerprinted anyway. I doubt if a guy like him ever enlisted in the armed services. His DNA isn't on file with the Defense Department. CODIS checked."

"Jesus!" said Andy as he leafed through the printouts and found a match to the DNA discovered under Dolores Ledbetter's nails ten years ago. "He's the guy that killed my girlfriend. I've been looking for this guy half my life."

"See the spikes on the graph?" asked Mullins. "All thirteen loci match. It's the same guy."

"I know it can't be Harvey Fredriks. Harvey hasn't been out of this city in twenty years."

"Are you sure?" asked Cartwright.

"He spent more than ten years living underground in sewer tunnels," said Andy. "And half that time he's been living next-door to Rat."

"Rat?" asked Cartwright.

"Jon Bradley. Bradley's Harvey's roommate and he works upstairs in the 911 call center. He won a bunch of medals in Iraq before he got blown up by an IED."

"Wasn't Bradley a suspect in the Pickaxe murders?"

"He was. He helped Troy Nolan catch the real Butcher."

"I met him at Troy's wedding," said Mullins. "He seems like a real stand-up guy. He was Troy's best man."

"If Bradley was in the service in Iraq, we know it can't be him. His DNA would be on file with Defense."

"County submitted a sample of Harvey Fredrik's DNA when he was arrested. Can you expedite that and get Harvey cleared?"

"I'll do my best," said Mullins.

"What are you doing to catch the killer?" asked Cartwright. "And what can I do to help?"

"I have my people watching the shopping malls, convenience stores, and the downtown bars. I think the killer picked up an accomplice. The accomplice is six-one, about two hundred pounds, black hair, and moustache."

"You run that description through the NCIC?"

"No one with black hair turned up locally. We think he's dyed his hair. We don't know what color it was originally."

"No DNA?"

"Wait a minute. We found some cigarette butts at the last crime scene."

"Give them to me, and I'll get them processed ASAP," said Mullins.

"Evangelista bagged them and turned them in to the evidence room. Come on. We'll walk down to the evidence room and get them."

The evidence room was at the other end of the basement. Locked behind a wire cage were rows of steel shelves with labeled boxes, and Andy asked the officer on duty to retrieve the box from yesterday's murders in the park. Andy, Cartwright, and Mullins waited ten minutes for the officer to return with the file box. Andy dug out the evidence bag containing three cigarette butts. Mullins signed a chain-of-custody receipt and shoved the bag into a pants pocket.

"I'll run these back to my office and start the ball rolling," said Dave Mullins.

"I'm going to stop by the morgue and show the DNA printouts to Stowe," said Andy.

"I'll go with you," said Cartwright.

They left Mullins waiting for an elevator. Andy led Cartwright around the corner and down the long hallway, past the labs and other offices where the medical technologists worked next door to the morgue. He used his ID card to open the door to the morgue and walked past the autopsy suite and refrigerators to Stowe's office all the way in the back.

"There's blood on the floor," noticed Cartwright. "They must really be short-staffed to leave blood on the floor. Stowe doesn't seem like the sloppy type. I'm surprised he didn't have someone clean it up or do it himself."

"They are extremely short-handed. Doctor Nolan's on her honeymoon, the day morgue assistant is on vacation, two other assistants quit and haven't been replaced, and Harvey Fredriks is in jail. Stowe is trying to do everything by himself."

Stowe's door had automatically locked when Andy left more than two hours ago to talk with Betty. Andy knocked on the door and waited for the doctor to respond.

"He must be sound asleep," Andy told Cartwright. He knocked longer and harder on the door.

"Can you get in?" asked Cartwright when Stowe still didn't respond.

Andy swiped his key card, and the door unlocked. He pushed the door open. The room was still completely dark. He fumbled on the wall for the light switch.

Stowe's chair was empty, but there was blood on the arms of the chair and on the floor.

"Don't go any farther until you've processed the room as a crime scene," Cartwright warned as the room filled with light. "Let's lock the door and follow the blood trail. I have a bad feeling about this."

Andy telephoned the crime scene techs in the neighboring police lab with his cell phone while he and Cartwright followed the blood on the floor into the autopsy suite. Doctor Stowe was lying naked on one of the stainless-steel dissecting tables, his torso opened wide with a Y incision from his clavicle to below his navel. A bloody scalpel lay on the table next to Stowe's body.

"It just happened," said Cartwright, taking out his Beretta. "The killer may still be close by."

Andy had his Glock in his hand and searched the other autopsy rooms while Cartwright opened the refrigerator and looked closely at each of the toe-tagged cadavers.

Two techs arrived from the labs down the hall, and they put on gloves and booties and one entered Stowe's office to process the scene while the other did a walk-around Stowe's body on the bloody autopsy table. Evangelista and Davis, the tech said, had gone home early because they planned to work later tonight. The two male techs took photographs of the crime scenes and the hall between the office and the autopsy suite.

"I'm not certain," said the guy processing the room with Stowe's mutilated body, "but it looks like several of the scalpels and tools from that table over there are missing. I don't see the Stryker saw either. The scalpel that was used to cut Doctor Stowe open came from that table."

"He's gone," said Cartwright. "I checked the main hallways and the other offices."

"The perp was in and out in less than two hours," said Andy, holstering his Glock 17. "I talked to Stowe between nine and ten. It's," he glanced at his watch, "twelve-thirty now."

"How did the killer get in?" asked Cartwright. "The outer door was locked, the door to Stowe's office was locked, there are people in the hallway and nearby offices. It looks like he knew exactly where he was going."

"And he knew how to make a Y incision with a scalpel," said the tech. "This guy's almost as good as Doctor Stowe was. It's a precision surgical incision. The guy who made this cut must be a doctor."

"Or someone who trained to be a doctor or watched doctors perform autopsies," said Andy. "Stowe said the guy knew anatomy."

"Look at the eyes," said the tech. "Doctor Stowe was killed by the stab wounds in his neck, but both eyes have been punctured. Then the eyelids were closed and sealed with some kind of glue or cement that hasn't completely cured and hardened yet. I was able to pry the eyelids open."

Both eyeballs looked deflated as if the fluid that had given them shape had drained out and left behind only empty bags of flesh. Whatever those eyes had once seen, it was lost.

"He had Harvey's key card," said Andy. "The guy who did this was the same guy who broke into Harvey's house and stole his wallet and keys."

"And no one saw him enter? How is that possible?"

"The tunnels," said Andy. "He came into the building from the parking garage. He entered through the tunnels and the back doors."

"Isn't there a guard on the doors to the tunnels?"

"Yeah," said Andy. "Either the guard knew the guy and let him pass, or the guard's dead."

Andy led Cartwright through the back hallways to the place where the guard usually sat at his small table in front of the door leading into the tunnel between the PSB and the parking garage. The uniformed officer lay slumped over the table, his throat opened from ear to ear.

"They should have a security camera covering this area," said Cartwright, looking around at the walls and ceiling.

"They did at one time," Andy said. "They moved it as part of cost-cutting measures when the Mayor slashed the PSB's budget. They figured having a guard twenty-four-seven was enough."

"It wasn't the Mayor who slashed this man's throat," said Cartwright. "Now we know how the killer got into and out of the building without being seen."

"Obviously, no one else came through the tunnels since the killer," said Andy. He called the techs and told them they had another crime scene to process.

"Why would anyone want to kill the assistant coroner?" asked Cartwright. "What did Stowe know that the killer didn't want revealed?"

"Whatever it was, I don't think Stowe was aware of its significance. Stowe didn't say anything to me before he died. But he's been so overworked, he couldn't think straight anymore. He was half-asleep when I went to his office, and he planned to go back to sleep after I left. He was probably asleep when the killer came in."

"This has to stop," said Cartwright, speed-dialing his cell. "I'm understaffed, too, but I'll get my people down here. "We have a chance to catch this guy if we work fast."

"I'm going upstairs," said Andy, "to tell the Coroner that he had better get his ass down here and do what the county pays him to do. He's run out of people to do his dirty work for him. It's time for Jim Albertson to shit or get off the pot."

"You're late," Jack Albertson tells you when you walk into the mortuary at fifteen minutes after twelve. "I ought to fire you."

Albertson stands at the back entrance with his father. The junior Albertson wants to impress on the old man that he has what it takes to run the family business.

Carrie Yalden's funeral was this morning, and the mourners have already left. There are no other funerals scheduled for today, and Albertson has sent the rest of the staff home to save money. The only ones in the mortuary are the two Albertsons and you.

"But I'm not going to fire you," Jack Albertson says with a smile. "I'm going to dock you one hour's pay for being late. Now get to work before I dock you even more."

"Go to hell," you say.

Albertson's mouth drops open and you envision sewing his lips together, inserting an S-hook through the roof of the mouth and tying off the loose ends of the sutures looped through his nostrils.

Before either Albertson can respond, you open the bag you carried with you from the morgue and stab Jack in the stomach with one of the longer scalpels. You drive the blade deep into his intestines and feel the intestines rip apart. You quickly remove the scalpel and leave him to bleed out on the floor.

James Albertson is backing away, his face as white as a shroud, staring at you in horror. You back him into a corner and slit his throat with the same scalpel you used on his son. Now he looks like he has two mouths: one frowning and sad, the other grinning like a Cheshire cat with bright red lips.

James Albertson's sphincter lets go and he shits his pants.

You stab their eyes because they have seen you. Jack Albertson is still alive when the scalpel slices through the optical nerve of his left eye and enters his brain. He almost manages a scream as he sees the blade coming closer to his eye. The scream dies in his throat as you plunge the scalpel into his brain.

You make certain all the doors are locked, then you take the service elevator downstairs and bring a gurney up to remove both bodies. They will go into the crematorium and disappear forever. Ashes to ashes, dust to dust.

You try to scrub the blood from the floor, but some has soaked into the carpet and the stain won't come out. "Fuck it," you say aloud. Today is the last day you will remain in this city. You don't care what you leave behind to remind people of what you've done. And you sure as hell aren't worried about what the Albertsons will say about spilled blood on their fancy carpet.

You take the bodies downstairs and fire up the crematorium. Gas jets ignite and you feel the flames on your face. You will allow an hour for heat to accumulate before inserting the bodies. Then you can kiss the Albertsons goodbye.

You prepare everything for tonight when you will transport the two women from the downtown park to Albertson's mortuary. You will allow Pete Smith to assist with procuring and drugging the little one and her companion. Then you will kill Smith and have your way with both women. You want the little one alive when you make love to her. You want her to see you, and you want to hear her scream.

The Stryker saw you borrowed from the morgue is for the other woman. You have never removed a brain before, and it will be fun to try your hand at being a pathologist. You will let the little one watch while you take her companion apart and sew the woman back together. You want her to know you are a true artist. For some strange reason, you feel compelled to show off for her.

You want the little one to know that you will take good care of her after you have finished. You have the power to bring her back to life. You are a god that deserves her adoration and worship.

When you are certain the crematorium has reached the required temperature, you place the body of Jack Albertson on one of the steel cremation tables and use the hoist to lift the body up onto the rollers that lead into the furnace. You open the heavy door using asbestos gloves, and shove the table with the body into the inferno. You leave the door open while you repeat the process with James Albertson. When they are both inside the furnace, you close the door and lock it. Then you set the timer.

You remember watching your birth mother cook supper for your family when you were a child. She wore a yellow kitchen mitt when she put the pan with the beef roast into the pre-heated oven, then set the timer on the top of the stove. You wonder if your birth mother would be proud that you remember her. You hope she is still alive and well and living happily ever after.

You have always blamed your stepmother for breaking up your family. You wonder if things would have turned out differently for you if your mother had taken you with her, along with your sisters, when she left. But your father wouldn't hear of such a thing. He wanted a son he could raise to be exactly like him. He succeeded beyond his wildest dreams.

Though you never became a doctor, you do have the same surgical skills your father had. You studied all of his books, and you have practiced your art on hundreds of clients instead of patients over the years.

Your father was a smart man, but he thought with his penis instead of with his brain. You know that is something you inherited from him, and it caused you to have to get married and give up your dreams of ever becoming a real doctor. When your son was born and your wife stopped wanting sex, your penis made you look elsewhere for pleasure.

Tonight, you anticipate the greatest possible pleasure. To have the little one watch you work—to have her know what will happen to her and realize there is absolutely nothing she can do to stop you—will be pure ecstasy. And then to do her while she is still alive and feeling you inside her will be icing on the cake.

At six PM you check the oven and see that the roasted flesh is well-done. You use a long-handled steel rake to break up the white-hot ashes. You switch the furnace off and leave the ashes to cool.

When they are cold enough, you scoop them out and put them into the blender. Then you flush the fine powder down the toilet. Down the tubes and good-riddance for piggish Jack Albertson and his money-grubbing father.

You wash up and apply cosmetic cream to your face to disguise your scars. You want to look your best for your date tonight with the girl of your dreams.

You spend the rest of the time at work dreaming of what you will do with the pretty little pixie with the reddish-gold hair. At nine o'clock, you lock up the mortuary and drive the hearse to the park where you will await delivery of your prize.

If Pete Smith screws this up, you will kill him.

And, if he doesn't screw things up, you plan to kill him anyway.

CHAPTER SEVENTEEN

Rat began work at 6:00 PM, relieving Richard Giolitto who worked the same desk on the day shift. This was Friday night, the start of a busy weekend, and calls were already beginning to come in fast and furious. Many people had left work early today because next week was the Fourth of July. People were so eager to begin their summer vacations that the accident rate was already more than twice what it was on a normal day.

Getting into the PSB tonight had been quite a chore. The tunnel entrance was marked as a crime scene, and Rat had to walk all the way around to the front door of the Public Safety Building where a uniformed police officer closely scrutinized the two pieces of identification he was asked to show. He had to wait in line to get in because two other officers waved hand-held scanners over the front and back of everyone entering. If someone set off the scanner's alarm, he was physically searched for weapons.

"What going on?" Rat asked one of the officers with a scanner, but the officer's only reply was to motion Rat past the checkpoint into the building.

It wasn't until Rat was able to take a fifteen minute break around nine PM that he heard the scuttlebutt in the break room. Doctor Earl Stowe had been killed in his own office and dissected with a scalpel on one of his own autopsy tables. It had happened this morning in this very building, and Andy Sinnott and some guy from the FBI had discovered the body. Also, Coroner James Albertson was missing. He hadn't returned to his office all day nor had he responded to calls on his cell phone. He was supposed to attend a political fundraiser—a pre-4th of July outdoor BBQ tonight at the home of the party chairman—but had not shown up. A man who answered the telephone at Albertson's Funeral Home had said James Albertson had been there sometime around noon, but he thought Albertson had left with his son for lunch and a round of golf at the country club. The employee said neither man had returned this afternoon, and he certainly didn't expect Jack or his father back until Monday or later.

Police had sealed off the tunnels and placed double guards at all the other entrances to the Public Safety Building. The officer guarding the tunnel entrance this morning had also been killed, his throat slashed open with a knife. There had been security cameras at the other entrances and in the lobby, but none in the hallways downstairs or in the tunnels.

Plus, it was rumored that the killer had used an employee key card to enter the morgue. Either the killer was an employee, or he had stolen the key card. The only key card that had been reported missing belonged to Harvey Fredriks. The electronic locks had recorded Harvey Fredriks, or someone using his card, had entered the morgue at 10:15 this morning and left at 11:29. But Harvey Fredriks was still in jail, wasn't he?

Rat returned to work and worried that George would be blamed for Stowe's murder, too. That was irrational thinking, he knew. George was in jail. If anything, Stowe's murder should prove that George was innocent.

For the next hour, Rat was kept too busy to think. The incessant heat was taking a toll on the elderly, especially those who couldn't afford to air-condition their homes. Temperatures at ten o'clock at night were still dangerously close to ninety, and sixteen people had to be taken to local hospitals by paramedics for heat stroke or heart conditions. Several others had difficulty breathing.

A car accident on the north-side bypass resulted in a pile up that blocked one lane and slowed traffic to a crawl in the other lane. Two people were reported dead, and four others were trapped in their vehicles and had to be forcibly extracted.

Police were called to a brawl at a working-man's bar on the far south side near the factories where two men had started a fight and others had taken sides and joined the melee. The bartender reported damage to property and he worried that someone might have a gun and would soon kill one or more of the brawlers.

A frantic woman called to report a female child had been abducted by the girl's father, and the woman said she worried her estranged husband would harm the child. She said she had left her husband because she suspected he had touched the three-year-old inappropriately. The girl's father had simply shoved the woman aside when she answered a knock at the door, walked in and scooped up the sleeping girl in his arms, and ran out before she could stop him. She said she thought the man would try to take the child out of state, and she wanted the police to set up road blocks to stop him. Rat issued an Amber alert, informing all units of the situation and requesting assistance from the state police.

Rat suspected the heat was getting to everyone, and ordinarily rational-thinking adults were behaving totally irrationally. Two more calls of domestic violence came in one right after the other. There were reports of shots fired on the far west side, but responding officers found it was only firecrackers being set off early in celebration of the Fourth.

As the night wore on, there were break-ins reported all over town. Burglars were taking advantage of houses and apartments left empty when people departed on vacation, but neighbors were being extra vigilant because of the recent murders. Two men were killed when they broke into a house that was dark but occupied by a man who had a gun. He shot both burglars in the back when they had attempted to walk out of the house with his 60-inch television set.

There were also the usual armed robberies of convenience stores and gas stations. Every available police officer was already busy, and Rat had to assign low priorities to calls that should have had immediate responses.

Rat had just returned from taking his lunch in the break room when he received a call at 1:38 AM from a voice he recognized. The usually soft-spoken Linda Davis sounded frantic and out of breath as she shouted "Officer down" into her cell phone as she ran. Rat heard shots being fired.

GPS showed her present location in the park near the river. Rat immediately assigned a priority one and sent a ten-double-zero—officer down, all units respond—to the police dispatcher. He also sent ambulances to the same location while he tried to get a response from Davis to his essential questions. "Where are you? What are your injuries? How can I help?"

Rat opened up another line and called Andy Sinnott's cell phone number. "Lieutenant Sinnott," Andy answered.

"911 just got a ten-double-zero call from Linda Davis," Rat said. "GPS shows she's in the downtown park near the river. I heard shots fired."

"I'm on my way," said Sinnott and disconnected.

Rat deferred all other calls to the next available call-taker. Linda's line was still open, and Rat could hear labored breathing and Linda's voice repeating, as if from a distance, "Oh, God! Oh, God! Don't die. Don't die."

"I can help," Rat practically shouted into his headset microphone. "Talk to me, Linda."

But Linda didn't say anything except, "Don't die!" again and again.

Rat could hear sirens through the phone. Help was on the way.

Rat watched the status board as police cars and ambulances accumulated at the scene. He switched to the police channel and listened to the chatter. There was one person confirmed dead, one female police officer critically injured, and another with minor injuries to her hands and arms. The suspect had fled in a late-model dark gray station wagon that might have been a hearse. Suspect was a white male, 30s, medium height and build. He had a sharp knife and should be considered armed and dangerous.

Rat's calls were stacking up, and he had to return to his duties because other people were depending on him. But, from time to time, he monitored the police chatter. Davis and an officer named Evangelista had been transported to Bryson Memorial Medical Center for treatment of their injuries. Davis had kept Evangelista alive by stanching the blood spewing out of her slashed neck. When police arrived, they discovered both women covered in blood. They were surprised to find either of them alive. Paramedics immediately administered plasma to Evangelista and put pressure bandages on her neck. She was in critical condition and might not survive.

Rat wished he could leave the call center and rush to Bryson to be with Linda. He knew what it was like to see your friends critically injured and try to save them. He remembered the sticky feel of blood gushing from severed limbs or bubbling from holes in heads or torsos, the sinking realization your friends' lives were slipping away right through your bloody fingers and there was absolutely nothing you could do to keep it from happening. Every beat of their hearts brought death closer as their life's blood pumped out through those gaping holes. There wasn't a single one that Rat had been able to save. Carson, Churilla, Ford, Jones, Meehan, Nelson, Raditch, Turner, and Wilkes. All dead. And for what?

Death was something that Rat had learned to live with. It had taken a long time to realize that life went on, and the dead—though not forgotten—were gone forever. Perhaps it was God's will. Perhaps it was the fickle finger of fate. It didn't matter. They were gone, and you were still here.

You, Rat told himself, can still make a difference. Just because you couldn't save those who died doesn't mean you can't save others from dying.

So Rat continued taking calls from people in need. He did not desert his post. He did not run to Bryson Memorial to comfort Linda Davis. Instead, he stayed on the phone and was instrumental in saving several lives that Saturday morning near the end of June. When his shift ended, however, he rushed to Bryson Memorial Medical Center to be with Linda Davis and tell her how much he admired her bravery.

But, of course, they wouldn't let him see her because he wasn't family. He sat in the waiting room with the relatives of some of the people he had talked with during the night, though they had no idea who he was.

And, for the first time in a long time, Rat prayed.

Andy arrived at the park ten minutes after receiving the call from Rat. He parked in the middle of Third Avenue because the streets around the park were filled with police cars and ambulances, a big hook and ladder fire truck, and broadcast vans from the TV stations. Paramedics and police officers crowded around the bushes near where the bodies of Ryan and Esteban were discovered less than 40 hours ago. A sobbing Linda Davis sat on the grass with bandages on both hands and a dozen cops surrounding her. Evangelista lay in the dirt near the bushes. She had an IV in her arm feeding her blood and saline as six paramedics tried to keep her alive. Her neck was covered with bandages held tightly in place with metal clamps. Not far from Evangelista lay the bloody body of a man with black hair and moustache, wearing cowboy boots. He was obviously dead, because no one was giving him medical attention.

"What happened?" Andy asked Art Lewinski. Lewinski was always the first on the scene when an officer was injured. He drove like a crazy man and usually got there before anyone else.

"Two female officers, Davis and Evangelista, walked to the park from a nearby bar with that dead guy over there. He had approached them in the bar and offered them free drugs. They pretended to be interested and came here with him with the intent to bust the guy for possession as soon as he produced the drugs. There was another man hiding in the bushes. That guy came at them with a knife, both officers produced weapons, and they told the guy to drop the knife because they were cops. The dead guy, only he wasn't dead at the time, grabbed Davis and forced the gun from her hand. The other guy lunged at Evangelista with his knife and nicked her neck before she could get off a shot. Davis thought sure Evangelista was dead. She thought she was a goner, too, because the other guy came at her with his knife while the big guy tore her clothes and tried to grab her boobs. She struggled, swatted at the knife, and sustained severe cuts to both hands. The knife missed her and hit the big guy instead. It sliced open his throat, tore through the tongue, and punctured the roof of the mouth. When the big guy went down, Davis was able to move the rest of her body. She kicked the guy with the knife in the balls. Then she went for her gun but couldn't find it. How the guy could have run away after being kicked in the balls is beyond me, but Davis said he did. He moved fast, got into a long, shiny gray-colored car that looked like a hearse, and Davis finally found her gun and fired at the car. I guess the knife wounds to her hands spoiled her aim because she said she had a hard time closing her fingers around the pistol grip and squeezing the trigger. She decided it was more important to get help for Evangelista than to pursue the perp, and she called 911 while she fired a few more shots at the car. Then she dropped the gun and the phone and tried to keep Evangelista from bleeding out."

"Is Evangelista still alive?"

"Barely. She lost a lot of blood."

"How's Davis?"

"Pretty shook up. The knife sliced both her hands."

"Have someone set up barricades and string tape. There's already too many people mucking up the crime scene. I don't want reporters in here, too."

"Leave the reporters to me," said Art.

Andy asked the other cops to please step away from the crime scene. After they dispersed, Andy went to Davis and sat down on the grass next to her. He put an arm around her shoulders and let her cry on his shoulder.

"You did good, Davis," he told her.

"It happened so fast," she sobbed.

"It always does," Andy said.

"Will Lorraine be all right?"

"Thanks to you. Now it's up to the doctors."

"He's the rapist," Davis said. "The guy with the knife is the rapist. I saw his face. It was dark, but he was close enough that I could see he had scratches and scars on his cheeks and around his eyes. He tried to cover them up with makeup, but it's hot and he was sweating. Most of the makeup had come off."

"He had a knife? No icepick?"

"It was a scalpel. But it had a long blade."

"Just be glad he missed you and killed the man holding you instead."

"I don't think he intended to kill me."

"What do you mean?"

"It was the way he held the knife. It was aimed above my head. If he wanted to, he could have aimed at my abdomen. Or even my throat. But he came at me with the knife held too high. I had to reach up to grab at it. I had to let go when the blade sliced my fingers. He could have sliced my throat, but he sliced his accomplice's throat instead."

"Why would he do that?"

"Because he wanted me alive. He wanted to rape me while I was alive and could feel him do it. I could tell. I could tell by the way he looked at me. He wanted me alive when he raped me."

Andy felt her shudder.

"You did good, Linda," he said. "Real good."

"I told you I would fight if anyone tried to rape me."

"Yes, you did."

"I think he expected me to roll over and play dead. I don't think he expected I'd kick him."

"You're safe now. I swear to you, we'll get this guy. He'll never be able to harm you or anyone else ever again."

"He got away," she said. "I let him get away. My hands are too small to hold a Glock anyway, and when my hands were cut, I couldn't grip the pistol tight enough to keep it steady."

"That's understandable. Can you describe the getaway car?"

"Gray. Big. A limo with a hatchback. I think it could have been a hearse."

"A hearse?"

"Yeah. Like undertakers drive. You know, the kind they take to the cemetery at funerals."

"Any markings on it? Did you get the plates?"

"No. It happened so fast, I didn't think to look at the plates."

"I want you to take a week off. Go to the hospital and get your hands stitched up. When they're ready to release you, call me on my cell. I'll give you a ride home."

"My car is parked on Third Avenue. Near West Street. So is Lorraine's truck."

"Don't worry about it. When you feel up to it, I'll take you down to get your car."

"We'll get tickets on them tomorrow. I don't want a ticket."

"Don't worry about tickets. I know people in the police department. We'll get the tickets fixed."

Davis smiled. "I was wrong," she said.

"Wrong? About what?"

"About you. You're not a pig. You're really a nice guy."

"And you're a good cop," he said.

"You really think so?"

"I know so. You found the killer—killers—when no one else could. The FBI has been looking for one of these guys for years. You didn't fold under pressure. Your partner is still alive because you made the right decisions at the right time. You didn't faint at the sight of blood. You fired at a fleeing felon even though you were injured. That makes you a good cop in my book. It makes you a good cop in anyone's book."

Andy watched the paramedics lift Evangelista onto a stretcher and carry her to the waiting ambulance. One of the paramedics came to get Davis, and she got up from the ground and walked proudly toward the other ambulance. Andy walked with her, reminded her to call when she was released, and then he went back to look at the dead assailant as the ambulances sped away with their lights and sirens disturbing the night.

The big guy lay where he fell, his arms grasping at his open throat. No one had tried to save him the way Davis had saved Evangelista, though Andy was sure it wouldn't have done any good if anyone had tried. The killer had angrily sliced through skin, muscle, and cartilage as if he hated the big guy. Davis was right. The killer had aimed for this guy's throat, not for hers.

It was as if the killer had wanted Davis all to himself, and he had been offended when the big guy had grabbed at Linda's breasts.

There was something vaguely familiar about the big man. Andy had the feeling he had seen the guy somewhere before. Not recently. Sometime in the distant past.

Normally, Stowe would take pictures of the corpse and so would Evangelista, but neither was able to assist. Nor was there anyone to take the guy's fingerprints. The three male techs were off duty. Andy called dispatch and asked the dispatcher to contact Bryson Medical Center and request their staff pathologists do the autopsy. Bryson could send an ambulance out to pick up the body. After Andy terminated the call, he used his cell phone to take pictures of the crime scene and the body. The pictures weren't as good as Stowe or Evangelista could do, but they were better than nothing.

Most of the cops had left the area to respond to other calls, but Art Lewinski stood watch at the police line tape where reporters and camera crews were congregated. The local stations ran the pile-up on the bypass as their lead story at ten o'clock, followed by a report of the two deaths at the Public Safety Building. It had been a very busy news day, and news sharks were on a feeding frenzy.

"Art," Andy asked Lewinski, "do you still keep a fingerprint kit and forms in your trunk?"

"Sure," said Lewinski. "Want me to get them?"

"Yeah. Take the prints on that stiff and send them to NCIC for me."

"Done."

"Lieutenant," yelled one of the reporters for channel seven, "what's the scoop?"

"Betty will send out a news release on Monday," said Andy. "You know I can't comment on an ongoing investigation."

"Sure, you can," said the reporter.

"Then let me rephrase that," said Andy. "I *won't* comment on an ongoing investigation."

When Lewinski returned, Andy walked around the area to see if he could find anything the patrolmen might have missed. He always carried a 600-lumen LED flashlight on his belt, and he used the light to check for footprints that hadn't been trampled. He found prints in the dirt around the bushes that looked like they belonged to a size eleven Reebok running shoe. He kept the light trained on the prints while he snapped pictures with his cell phone camera.

Andy searched the dead man's pockets and turned up two bags of heroin, a Bic lighter, a spoon, a handful of pills, and two hypodermic needles. There were two rubber straps in his back pockets. Andy went to his own car and grabbed a handful of evidence bags. He bagged the drug paraphernalia and labeled the bags.

The more Andy looked at the dead man, the more familiar his face seemed. Obviously, his hair was dyed black. What if the hair were another color? Would that jog Andy's memory?

Bryson's ambulance arrived at five-fifteen, and Andy was still puzzling over the man's identity. Channel seven had departed without their story, and Art Lewinski had packed up the crime scene tape and barricades and locked them in his trunk. Lewinski directed the ambulance to park close to the body. Andy noticed Art was beginning to look old and tired. He had been a policeman for more than twenty years. Andy wondered what Art would do with his life if he was forced to retire. Unlike most cops with his longevity, Art had never gone on to college and he had never wanted to be anything other than a patrolman. He was divorced because his wife got tired of sleeping alone every night and she had found someone else to keep her warm during the winter. She had given Art an ultimatum: leave the job or I leave you. Art kept the job and never looked for another wife.

The sky had turned yellow and light blue in the east when the hospital orderlies had finished loading their patient. As the ambulance drove away, Lewinski told Andy he was heading back to the PSB to process the prints. Andy did one more walk-around, then he headed for Bryson Memorial to check on Davis and Evangelista.

Evangelista was undergoing surgery, and she was listed in critical condition. Davis showed Andy the stitches in both her hands. Her knuckles had been cut almost to the bone on her right hand. She said her assailant had held the scalpel in his left hand. She had tried to swat the scalpel away from him, but he had such complete control of the weapon that it had been impossible.

It seemed like it took forever for a doctor to sign a release. It was nearly seven when Andy and Davis walked out of the emergency room.

And saw Rat in the waiting room.

"I wanted to make sure you were all right," Rat said. "I was the one you called when you dialed 911."

"Thank you," said Linda, and she hugged Rat.

Andy was surprised to feel jealous when he saw Davis throw her arms around Rat. He remembered holding her in the park, her head leaning against his shoulder. He wished Linda would hug him the way she hugged Rat.

"What about the other officer?" asked Rat.

"We still don't know," said Andy. "She's in surgery. But at least she's still alive. Thanks for calling me, Rat. I really appreciate it."

"I knew you'd want to be notified if your officers were hurt."

"I did. Thanks, again."

"Well, I think I can go home now. It was nice seeing you again, Linda. I'm glad you're not badly hurt."

"Just my hands," she said, showing Rat the stitches.

"Ouch. I bet that really hurt."

"You should see the other guy," she said.

"You got him? You caught the killer?"

"No. But I kicked him in the balls," she said proudly. "Wham.

Right in the gonads."

"Ouch. I bet that did hurt him worse than he hurt you."

"I'm sure it did," said Andy. "Let me get you home, Linda. Then I need to go to the office and check on a few things."

"Thanks for coming down to make sure I was okay," Linda said to Rat. "That was sweet of you, Jon."

"No problem," said Rat.

Andy walked Linda to his Honda and opened the door for her. He saw Rat walk to a blue Dodge Dart and get in.

"Where do you live?" Andy asked Linda as he fastened his seat belt.

"On the far east side. One of the newer apartments not far from where Barbara Ames lived."

The day promised to be another scorcher. They had gone two weeks without rain, and the temperatures had remained in the nineties most of that time. As Andy drove across the river, he noticed the river's water level was significantly lower than it had been only a week ago. If there were another fire, he wondered if there would be sufficient water pressure to extinguish the blaze.

Which reminded him he needed to check with Larry Miller and see if there were any progress in the arson investigation. It was still an open case, and Andy had been too busy to follow up.

Which, in turn, reminded him Del hadn't responded to the call from Dispatch. The police dispatcher was supposed to notify both homicide investigators—the head of homicide and his assistant—when there was a reported homicide anywhere in the city. This was the second time Del hadn't responded to a call. It was especially troubling because two of Del's co-workers were reported injured at the scene. Even off-duty detectives responded to 10-00 calls. Why hadn't Del?

Dispatch had called Andy right after Rat had, so he knew the calls had gone out.

"Where was Del tonight?" asked Linda. "I didn't see him."

"Neither did I," said Andy. "I was just wondering about Del myself."

"Who do you think is Hickman's source in the department?" she asked.

"I have my suspicions," said Andy. "Who do you think it is?"

"I know it's not me," she said." And I don't think it's Lorraine. That only leaves Pearson and Conklin."

"It's not a big deal," said Andy.

"Oh, yes, it is. It means we can't trust somebody we depend on to watch our backs."

"You think it's Del?"

"Yes," she said. "I do."

"We'll see," said Andy.

They were silent the rest of the way, except for Linda saying, "Turn right here" and "Turn left at the next corner."

Linda lived in a modern apartment complex that had security cameras everywhere. Andy saw a camera on the parking lot, one trained on the front entrance, one on each side of the building. He felt better knowing that she had video security.

"Are you armed?" he asked.

"Yes. I have my Glock. And I have a Ruger LCP-PT .380."

"Keep one of them with you all of the time until we get this guy," Andy advised. "Take a gun with you to the bathroom. Make sure you can reach it from the shower or the tub."

"Do you think that's necessary?"

"It would make me feel better to know you were always armed. Probably make you feel better, too."

Andy got out of the car and opened her door. "I'm going to walk you to the door of your apartment and see you safely inside," he told her. "I don't think this guy will come after you again but my mother told me it's always better to be safe than sorry. I've been sorry once before in my life, and I don't ever want to be that sorry again."

"What happened to make you sorry?"

"The same thing that happened to you tonight happened to my girlfriend when I was in college. Only she wasn't as lucky. She fought back, too, but it didn't do her any good."

"Now I'm the one that's sorry," she said. "I'm sorry it happened to her. And I'm sorry it happened to you."

"I think it was the same guy, Linda."

"The guy that attacked me tonight?"

"Yeah. Mullins brought me the DNA results from the residue under Hansen's fingernails. It matched the DNA of the guy that raped and killed my girlfriend ten years ago."

"This guy has been raping and killing that long?"

"Yes. And you're the only person he's left alive to identify him."

"So that's why you seemed so concerned about me. You want a living witness who can point a finger at him when you bring this guy to trial."

"Yes," said Andy. "Of course, I don't want to see anything happen to a good detective, especially one who works for me."

"Of course," she said. Andy thought he detected a change in her tone of voice. It suddenly felt like the temperature had dropped twenty degrees or a dark shadow had passed over Andy's grave.

"I live on the second floor," she said. "But you really don't have to accompany me all the way to my door. Thanks for the ride."

"I insist," said Andy. "Really. It would make me feel a whole lot better to see you safely inside your actual apartment."

"It's really not necessary."

"Really, it is."

Linda used a key to open the front door of the building, walked through the lobby to the stairs, and climbed the stairs to the second floor. She turned right and walked half-way down a long hallway with doors on both sides.

"I live on the back side of the building," she said. "Apartment 212."

At apartment number 212, she inserted her key into the lock and opened the door. "I suppose you want to inspect the bedroom, too, to make sure no one is hiding under the bed."

"It might be a good idea," he said.

"Goodnight, Lieutenant," she said, slipping inside the apartment and shutting the door.

Andy walked back out to his car and drove around the building a couple of times. He wanted to know how difficult it would be to scale the outside wall and enter the apartment through a window.

He counted windows, assuming the numbers began with 200 on this side and 201 on the other side, and located the sixth window. The lights were on but the drapes were closed. Unlike Barbara Ames' apartment building, there were no decorative ledges beneath the windows, and her window was the fourth from the south end of the building. Even if the killer scaled the drain pipes, he couldn't cling to the bricks and get to Linda's window. The only way in and out of the building seemed to be the front and rear entrances, both watched by video cameras.

Andy doubted if anyone monitored those cameras 24/7. They probably recorded to a hard drive or DVD. Unless the killer wanted to appear on candid camera, however, he wouldn't try to go in either the front or back door.

It was after eight when Andy arrived at his office, and Del and Pearson were waiting for the morning briefing.

"Where were you last night, Del?" Andy asked, taking a seat at his desk.

"Home," said Del. "Why?"

"We had another incident last night in the park. Didn't the dispatcher reach you?"

"No."

"Why not?"

"Jesus, Andy, I don't know. What kind of incident?"

"The two killers attacked Davis and Evangelista in the park. Evangelista is in the hospital in critical condition. Davis was wounded, and she's convalescing at home. One of the perpetrators is dead, and the other made a getaway in a hearse."

"I wondered why Davis and Evangelista weren't here this morning," said Pearson.

"Didn't you get the ten-double-zero either, Rich?"

"No. I wasn't on call, so I had my phone switched off. I didn't check my voice mail this morning. I guess I should check it." He took out his cell phone, switched it on, and listened to his voice mail. "I got it," said Pearson.

"Check your phone, Del."

Del reached in his pocket and held the smart phone in his hand. "I...uh...I don't really know how to use this thing."

"You've got to be kidding me," said Andy. "Everyone knows how to use one of those."

"I don't," admitted Del. "My cell phone company made me upgrade to this new fancy-smantzy gizmo. I knew how to work the old one. It was simple. You pressed the on button, and it turned on, you answered a call or dialed a number. You pressed the button for voice mail, and it took you right to your messages. This thing has all the bells and whistles on it and it's more like a computer than a telephone. You've got to touch the screen and scroll to the right menus before you can answer a call or make a call. I tried fiddling with it, and I guess I must have turned off the ringer. I don't know how to find voice mail. I don't know how to text or get on the internet, but I guess the phone lets me do all those things."

"Let me see it," said Andy.

He looked at the Android phone and tapped the screen a couple of times. Del had forty-seven voice mail messages. Sixteen were from dispatch. Twenty-two were from the newspaper where Joel Hickman worked, and four were from Hickman's personal cell phone. Two were messages from Andy.

Andy got out his own phone and dialed Del's number. The phone went directly into voice mail. It didn't ring, and it didn't vibrate.

Andy scrolled through the menus on Del's phone and turned the ringer on. He handed the cell phone back to Del. "Now you'll get calls. It will go to voice mail after six rings. Take some time this morning and listen to your voice mails. You have forty-seven of them."

"Tell us more about what went down last night," said Pearson.

"Davis and Evangelista went to Upstairs and Downstairs last night looking for the man with the moustache and cowboy boots. They found him, or rather he found them. He lured them to the park with an offer of free drugs. When they got to the park, a second guy jumped out with a knife. They drew their weapons, identified themselves as police officers, and ordered him to drop the knife. The guy with the cowboy boots jumped Davis, and the other guy stabbed Evangelista in the neck. Then he came at Davis with the knife. She fought back, and the guy with the cowboy boots got the knife in the neck instead of Davis. Davis kicked the guy holding the knife in the nuts, went for her gun and cell phone, but the guy made it to his car and got away. Davis emptied her Glock. Because she has small hands she carries a Glock 19 instead of a 17. It only holds fifteen rounds. She couldn't aim right because her fingers were cut when she tried to wrestle the knife away from the perp. She may have hit the getaway car, but she's not certain. The guy didn't stop. He was last seen going north in a dark gray late-model limo that might have been a hearse."

"A hearse?" asked Pearson. "Like undertakers drive?"

"Yeah."

"Speaking of undertakers," said Del, "did anyone ever reach Albertson after Stowe got croaked?"

"No. His secretary tried to call him on his cell. He left his office about eleven to have lunch with his son, and he never came back here to the PSB. Someone at the funeral home said he went to the country club, but he never showed up there, either. We sent an officer to the funeral home to check on him, but the place was locked up. If there was anyone inside, they didn't answer the bell or the knocks on the door."

"Don't you think that's odd? Closing the funeral home in the middle the day?"

"Albertson's secretary says they often close early on a Friday afternoon. Jack Albertson sends everyone home to save money, unless there's a funeral scheduled."

"Let me go over there this morning," said Del. "There should be somebody working on a Saturday."

"You guys didn't see either perp at the convenience stores or the malls you checked out yesterday?"

"No," said Del. Pearson shook his head.

"All right," said Andy. "Today you're looking for a gray hearse that may have nine-millimeter holes in the passenger side. Check out all the funeral homes."

"I'll start with Albertson's," said Del.

"I'll do O'Connor," said Pearson.

After the two detectives left, Andy checked his own e-mails. He had a response from the FBI's National Crime Information Center. The fingerprints Lewinski had taken from the mustached man belonged to a parolee named Peter Smith, thirty-three, last known address on West Elm in Riverdale.

Andy was just shy of thirty-two, and now he knew why thirty-three-year-old Peter Smith's face looked so familiar. He was the same Pete Smith Andy had known in third grade. Pete hadn't changed much since high school. His natural hair was sandy-colored, and Andy had been thrown by the bad dye job. Pete had also grown an inch and he was a good forty pounds heavier than Andy remembered, but it was the same Pete who had made life miserable for Andy in grade school. It had been rumored that Pete was using and dealing drugs even back in high school, and he had a juvenile record plus dozens of minor adult busts for everything from possession to aggravated assault. Pete had been in and out of jail most of his life. He was on parole at the time of death.

That e-mail had solved two mysteries: who was the killer's accomplice and whatever had become of Pete Smith. Now, if only Andy could locate the killer, maybe he could solve a few more mysteries that plagued him.

First on the list of things to do was to get a search warrant for Pete's last known address. He'd hand that off to Del when Del got back from Albertson's mortuary. Andy was beginning to have second thoughts about Del's reliability. On Monday, Andy would ask Betty to pull Del's personnel jacket and call the department where Del had worked on the west coast. Maybe there was something that his former co-workers would tell about Del if the inquiry were less official than an employment inquiry. Del had come highly recommended. Andy wondered if Del's glowing recommendation had more to do with his former employer wanting to get rid of a bad apple than a true reflection of his job performance. Andy knew that such things sometimes happened. Bad cops were often shuffled off. It was far easier to make a bad cop someone else's problem than go through the rigmarole of an internal affairs investigation or battling a cops' union, especially if the union threatened litigation.

Andy's cell phone vibrated in his pocket. It was Del. He had learned how to use his cell phone real fast, at least he knew enough to make an outbound call. "I'm at Albertson's Mortuary and Crematorium," said Del. "And can you guess what's parked in the parking lot?"

"A gray hearse," said Andy.

"Complete with a dozen nine millimeter holes on the passenger side. The mortuary is locked up tighter than a drum. I think we have probable cause to get a search warrant. What do you think?"

"Come on back to the office," said Andy. "We need to prepare two search warrants. I'll see if I can get a judge on a Saturday to sign them. And Del?"

"Yeah?"

"That's good work."

"Thanks," said Del, and he switched off his cell phone.

CHAPTER EIGHTEEN

As you speed away from the park in Albertson's hearse, you hear sirens coming your way from all directions. You have killed a cop, and cops don't take kindly to one of their own having her throat slit.

How could you possibly have known the two women were cops? Okay, maybe the bigger one could have been a police officer, but the little one looked way too small. What ever happened to size and weight restrictions for police officers? How did someone as tiny as your little one make it onto the police force in the first place?

Two squad cars rush past you in the opposite direction, followed by an ambulance and a fire truck. They are headed where you have been, and they don't notice that you are exceeding the speed limit. Police wouldn't stop a hearse anyway, but you slow to a reasonable speed.

Your groin aches terribly. When her foot connected with your body, a sharp pain shot through your entire nervous system like a bolt of lightning. You saw stars and nearly blanked out. You actually dropped the scalpel to the grass, but you quickly picked it up and half-ran, half-limped, for the car.

You were already driving away when you heard the first shots and felt the car vibrate from their impact. She fired again and again and again, bullets ripping through the steel passenger doors, shattering the glass in rear windows. Some bullets passed through the vehicle entirely to exit on the other side. If Jack Albertson could see what you have allowed to happen to his hearse, he would instantly dock you ten years' pay.

How could the little one shoot so accurately with her hands practically sliced to shreds? You held a pistol once and even tried to fire it. They taught you all about guns at that dreadful military academy prep school where your stepmother forced your father to send you at age fourteen. Learning to shoot a gun is like learning to throw a bowling ball. It takes lots of repetitive practice to hit where you aim. And a lot depends on how you hold your hands when you aim.

Using a scalpel is much the same way. The more you practice with one, the better your hand and eye coordination becomes. Besides having a natural gift, great surgeons have years of practice. You have had lots of practice with a scalpel.

Police officers carry guns. You have never wanted to use or carry firearms because you prefer to get up close and personal when you show people how much you care. You want to reach out and personally touch them like your stepmother touched you. Firearms are impersonal, meant to keep distance between people.

Now your little one has tried to put distance between herself and you. Not only did she touch you without your permission when she kicked your groin, she tried to shoot you with a gun. As your stepmother once told you when you had accidentally brushed her breasts when you were ten, such insolence must be punished.

You could easily have killed the little one in the park while Pete Smith was still holding her. But seeing Pete Smith pawing at her breasts made you go wild. How dare he touch the breasts of your little one without your permission? But when you brought the knife up to aim at Pete's throat, the little one tried to swat the scalpel away and actually grabbed onto the blade with both of her hands. You felt the blade bite into her fingers and saw blood running down her arms from deep cuts on both hands. You couldn't help but cut her even deeper as you pulled the knife free from her grasp. She had no choice but to open her fingers and release the blade or the sharp blade would have sliced her fingers off.

When she let go, you drove the blade forward as hard and fast as you could, piercing Pete Smith's jugular, ripping his flesh apart, slicing through strands of muscle, easily sliding the blade of the scalpel through trachea, esophagus, and thyroid with a flick of your wrist.

Pete released his iron grip around the little one's mid-section as his hands reflexively flew toward his injured neck. He collapsed to the ground, clutching vainly at flaps of loose flesh, trying to close the yawning opening where severed muscles had spread apart so much they were no longer able to support the weight of Pete's head. Blood pumped from his carotid arteries and jugular veins, staining the grass around him bright red.

You didn't see the kick coming. The little one moved so fast that her knee smashed into your testicles before you could turn away. Breath caught in your throat; the scalpel dropped from your hands. For a moment you were aware of nothing but the incredible pain coursing through your entire body.

Instead of continuing her attack, the little one looked around for the pistol that Pete had pried from her hand when he grabbed her from behind. Still in pain but once again able to see, you discovered the scalpel in the grass and quickly scooped it up. All you could think about was getting away before she kicked you again or found her gun and began shooting.

It hurt to run, but you forced yourself forward until you reached the hearse. Fortunately, you left the doors unlocked and you managed to get inside and get the car started before she found her pistol. You were already driving away when she fired her first shots.

You reach Albertson's Mortuary and Crematorium, pull the hearse into the parking lot, and desert it for your Matrix. Blood smears all over the seat and the steering wheel, but it can't be helped. Some of the blood covering you came from the woman cop, some from Pete Smith, and some from the little one. You drive to your apartment on Elm.

You don't have much time before the police learn where Pete lived and come to the apartment building to search for you. You quickly shower and shave, leaving your bloody clothes behind in the bathroom. You pack your duffel bags and carry them out to the car.

Tonight you will have to sleep in your car in the parking lot of one of the shopping malls. Tomorrow, you will drive to the little one's apartment and watch her until you see an opportunity for revenge.

Killing her, you decide, is too good for her now. Eventually, of course, you will kill her. But before you do, you will make love to her.

And then, while she watches, you will use an icepick on her eyes.

Rat telephoned Linda Davis at her home number before he left for work at the call center. "It's Jon Bradley," he identified himself when she answered her phone. "I saw you this morning at the hospital. I wanted to call and see if you needed anything."

"Oh. Hi, Jon."

"I hope I didn't wake you," he said.

"I haven't been able to sleep," she said.

"Have you heard how your friend is doing after surgery?"

"She's still critical. She lost a lot of blood."

"I wanted to tell you I think what you did was very brave. I was in combat in Iraq, and I know what it's like to face someone who is trying to kill you and your friends. Not only did you face two killers and fight them off, but you saved your friend from dying. I hope you appreciate how special that makes you. Most people would have tried to run away."

"I don't think either of those men were seriously trying to kill me. Not yet, Jon. I think they both wanted to rape me first."

"Then I'm doubly glad you managed to fight them off. I just wanted to let you know that I'm here for you if you ever want to talk about it. Sometimes, it helps to talk. I'm a good listener."

"Thank you, Jon."

"Rat. Please call me Rat. All my friends do."

"Why do you insist on being called Rat?"

"Because I'm small like a rat. And I used to live in the sewers."

"You really lived in the sewers?"

"In the storm sewers, sewer tunnels they used to have downtown beneath all the major streets. In fact, I lived in a tunnel not far from that park where you were attacked. I lived in the sewers for five years."

"Why?"

"Because I couldn't live above ground close to people. I was wounded in Iraq, and I lost a lot of my friends to bullets or roadside bombs. Doctors said I had Post Traumatic Stress Disorder from seeing so much death."

"I'm sorry."

"I'm all right now. It took time for me to heal. Well, I need to get ready to go to work. I just wanted to tell you, I think you're very brave. And I'm glad you're all right."

"Thanks, Rat. I think I'll be okay."

"And, remember, if you ever want to talk, you know where to find me."

"How did you get my phone number, Rat? My home number is unlisted. Did Andy give it to you?"

"No," said Rat. "I used the database at work to look up your home address and telephone number. I hope that's okay with you, Linda. I thought maybe you'd want to keep in touch after we met on Wednesday."

"You don't get out much, do you, Rat?"

"No."

"I guess it's all right. Will you give me your telephone number, since you already have mine?"

Rat gave her both his home number and his cell phone number. "Call me," he said, "if you ever want to talk."

"If I ever want to talk," she said.

Rat went to work early so he could get through the increased security and still be on time to take calls. Richard said the day had been relatively slow, and he hoped the night would be the same.

Saturday nights, however, were usually busy. Drunk drivers accounted for the bulk of the calls, especially after midnight. There were slightly fewer heart attacks than on weekday days, but there were more armed robberies, motor vehicle accidents, and reported domestic violence incidents. Hopefully, there would be no homicides.

Neither James nor Jack Albertson had been located yet. They had abruptly disappeared on Friday. A police officer had discovered a bullet-ridden hearse parked in the lot behind Albertson's mortuary. The man killed in the park yesterday had been identified as a local long-time drug abuser and known felon named Peter Smith. His accomplice had gotten away and was still at large. He had abandoned the hearse at the mortuary.

Linda was very lucky to have survived. Though neither the police nor the press would admit it, Rat believed the man who had attacked Linda with a knife was the icepick killer. George had claimed the killer used icepicks with the precision of a scalpel, and now the killer was actually using a scalpel instead of an icepick. Rat was sure it was the same man.

Rat had taken the time this afternoon to drive by Linda's

apartment. He wanted to know exactly where she lived and how safe the building looked. For some strange reason, Rat felt a personal responsibility for Linda's well-being that he couldn't explain and which didn't seem rational. He cared for her the way he had once cared for his younger sisters and his mother. Rat had tried to defend them against his father, and for more than twenty years he had failed miserably. But, eventually, Rat had succeeded in bringing his father to his senses by sending the old man to the hospital, and now that the old man's secret was out in the open for all to see, Rat's mother and sisters were safe.

Rat had also cared about the old lady in the sewers that he had named Lil, but whose real name had been Dorothy Middleton. Because no one who lived in the sewers ever used their real names, each resident had made up new names for themselves and others hiding in the tunnels. Rat had called Harvey Fredriks George, LeRoy Forbes Sam, Jackson Campbell Ron, and Leonard Gough Pete. The name he had made up for himself was Sewer Rat, Rat for short. Lil, Sam, and Pete had been killed by the Pickaxe Butcher last fall. Rat had been unable to protect them.

Similarly, Turner, Nelson, Wilkes, Jones, Raditch, Churilla, Ford, and Carson had been killed in Iraq. Rat hadn't been able to protect them. Their ghosts had haunted him for years until Rat took a stand against the Pickaxe Butcher and was nearly killed himself. He hadn't heard their voices calling him useless and a coward since he had emerged from the sewers.

Rat knew it had been his father's voice he had heard in his head all those years. It was his father who had called him useless as a child, and he had grown up believing it. He felt he had been a coward because, after his father beat him so severely, he was unable to stand between the old man and Rat's mother or his sisters without feeling debilitating fear. Likewise, he had been afraid all of the time he had been in Iraq. He had hidden behind the protective armored plate of the Humvees while his friends died.

But now he realized he had never been afraid for himself. Dying was easy. It was living that was hard. He had seen many men die, and he had nearly died himself. Rat had been wounded so many times and in so many places that he was no longer afraid of feeling pain, either. His fear had always been for others: that he wouldn't be able to protect them and that they would be the ones who felt excruciating pain or died terrible deaths while Rat survived.

Rat wanted to find a way to protect Linda Davis. Though he had been trained to use all kinds of weapons in the military—the M16A2, the M4 carbine, the M9 automatic pistol, even hand grenades, bayonets and pugil sticks—Rat didn't own any type of firearm. He didn't even own a pickaxe anymore. How could he possibly protect Linda against a crazed murderer and rapist if he had no weapon?

Rat had been trained in hand-to-hand combat by the Army, and he thought he still remembered how to quickly and easily disarm an opponent and then disable him. He even knew how to kill an opponent with his bare hands, but had never done so. To do any of those things, one needed to get close enough to his opponent to literally touch him. That had never been an option in Iraq. The enemy used snipers—men armed with high-powered rifles with scopes—and fired at American soldiers from a distance, often as much as a thousand meters. Most of the time you didn't even see the enemy that shot you, much less have a chance to return fire. If the enemy didn't employ sniper rifles, they used roadside bombs—improvised explosive devices hidden in holes in the road and covered with loose dirt, triggered by tire pressure or remotely by a garage door opener or cell phone—to kill Americans en masse. In neither case did the enemy come close enough to touch. But they could reach out and touch you, seemingly from a great distance.

If this killer intended to kill Linda Davis with a gun or blow up her building with a bomb, there was absolutely nothing Rat could do to stop him. But this killer had never before used guns or bombs. Why would he would start now? This killer preferred sharp instruments like scalpels, knives, and icepicks. And to use those, the killer had to get close enough to touch and be touched.

So Rat had a chance to protect Linda, but only if he remained close enough to her to personally defend her against the enemy. Rat could insert himself between her and the killer. The killer would have to go through Rat first to get to Linda, could only reach Linda over Rat's dead body. Rat could buy Linda time to escape.

Rat couldn't leave work until six in the morning, but then he'd drive by Linda's apartment and check up on her. He wondered what she would do or say if he simply showed up at her apartment door.

Would she mistake Rat for the killer and shoot him? Would she invite him inside for coffee or tea? Would she consider him a stalker and have him arrested?

Saturday night slowly dragged into Sunday morning. A caller reported the theft of his air conditioner. Someone, he claimed, had lifted the portable window unit out of the bedroom window, jerking the electrical cord free from the electrical plug on the wall. The caller and his wife had been at a backyard party until after two, and when they returned home they discovered the air conditioner was missing. Another caller reported that his older window air conditioner that had been running on high constantly for three weeks had overheated and started a small electrical fire that ignited drapes and then the carpet. Rat immediately transmitted the location information to the fire department, and a pumper and hook and ladder were on their way. Rat asked the caller to evacuate his house but to please stay on the line until the fire trucks arrived. "Which do you want me to do?" asked the woman. "I'm calling from the phone in my house. Do you want me to leave or stay on the phone?"

"Get out now," instructed Rat. "Don't breathe any of the smoke from the smoldering carpet. Those fumes can be toxic. Get away from the burning building. Forget about the phone."

Sometime after four AM, calls slowed down and Rat had time to think again. He was scheduled to work again Sunday night, and then he would have three consecutive nights off. Occasionally, Rat's schedule varied, like when one of the other call-takers went on vacation. Sometimes, he was asked to come in extra because one of the other night people was sick or had to care for an ill relative. Rat had accumulated six days of comp time, plus he had two weeks of vacation and ten days of sick time built up after being employed more than six months. Sunday nights were often slow, and Rat felt he could afford to ask for a night off without fear of losing his job. He told his supervisor he needed to take twelve hours of comp time on Sunday night to care for an injured friend. He was granted a night off, and his sympathetic supervisor told Rat to let her know if he needed to take more time later in the week. Rat thanked her and promised to keep her informed of his needs.

Richard Giolitto arrived six minutes late. He had set off one of the hand-held scanners at the security checkpoint, and they couldn't find what had made the alarm sound. After twenty minutes of futile searching, they had allowed Richard to go to work. Richard had a pacemaker implanted in his chest, and he suspected that had triggered the overly-sensitive device. The guards wouldn't believe he wore a pacemaker until they strip-searched Richard and saw the scar on his chest.

"Did your pacemaker set off the same scanners yesterday?" asked Rat?

"No," said Richard. "That's why no one could understand why an alarm went off tonight. I think they had the sensitivity set way too high. It was picking up everything this morning, including belt buckles and keys."

Rat went to Denney's for breakfast, then drove past Linda's apartment. Everything seemed quiet and peaceful at eight o'clock on a sunny Sunday morning. Rat knew Linda lived in apartment 212, but he had no idea which of twenty second-floor windows might be her bedroom window. He assumed she had finally drifted off to sleep by now. Sleep would help her heal.

Sleep had helped Rat to heal, but unbroken dreamless sleep was a long time coming for the wounded warrior. Rat's father had seldom allowed him to sleep a whole night through. Either the old man was yelling at someone in the house or he was beating on someone. During Rat's years in the Army, he had often been awakened by gunfire or bomb blasts or artillery. Some had sounded far away, some much closer. Though he knew it was the one you never heard that got you, those sounds had kept him from getting the sleep he needed. And, after he had been wounded and sent home to recuperate, the voices of the dead kept him awake. It was only after years of relative solitude in the sewer tunnels that peaceful sleep finally came to Jon Bradley and allowed his mind and body to heal.

Now Rat slept fine. He normally slept from eight AM until four PM on days he worked nights, and he seldom had bad dreams. Linda would likely be safe during the light of day. Anyone attempting to do her harm in her apartment would see the cameras and think twice before entering. Besides, there were plenty of people around the building and in and out of the parking lot all day. It was only at night that Rat felt he needed to worry about her.

He drove around Linda's building one more time, then drove

through the parking lot before heading home to sleep.

The Mayor, worried about the fate of party-stalwart James Albertson, had put extraordinary pressure on the police chief. Chief Roger Elway had, in turn, put pressure on Andy Sinnott, demanding answers that Andy couldn't provide. A search of Albertson's Mortuary and Crematorium turned up the Stryker saw missing from the morgue since Stowe was killed, but neither James nor Jack Albertson were found anywhere in the funeral home. It was evident that someone had been practically living in the embalming room until very recently, perhaps even as late as Friday night, and Del had joked in poor taste that one certainly didn't expect anybody to be living in a funeral home. The crematorium had also been used recently, even though no cremations had been scheduled for anytime on Friday.

One of the part-time funeral directors that Albertson employed told investigators that the embalmer's name was Tom Lazar, and Albertson let Lazar do embalming and run the crematorium all by himself, contrary to procedures at other funeral homes and maybe even against state law. Albertson saved money by hiring only part-time people, most of them older and semi-retired, and he used Lazar to do lots of things qualified funeral directors, licensed embalmers, and mortuary technicians were supposed to do. Lazar was willing to work dirt cheap, was relatively young and energetic, and he seemed to do an excellent job. Certainly, none of the people he had worked on had ever complained. But Lazar kept to himself and seemed a little bit strange. "Maybe it was because of the scars," the funeral director had said.

"What scars?" asked Andy.

"Lazar had old scars all over his face, especially around his eyes, like he had been in a terrible accident a long time ago. He usually wore dark glasses and cosmetic creams to hide his scars."

Andy remembered the man he and Stowe had seen picking up Toni Fisher's body at the morgue. That man had worn a white lab coat with Albertson's Mortuary and Crematorium stenciled on the back, and he wore sunglasses and makeup. He had signed a receipt for the body with his left hand.

"Was Lazar left-handed?" Andy asked the funeral director.

"Yes, come to think of it."

Andy mentally kicked himself for being such a blind fool. He had seen the face of the icepick killer and didn't know it. But how could Andy have known at the time that the killer was standing right in front of him?

Lazar was about five-eleven, a hundred and eighty pounds, and left handed.

Andy's three male crime scene technicians uncovered a few viable latent fingerprints that likely belonged to Lazar, although the guy had been smart and worn rubber gloves most of the time he spent in the mortuary. Most of the prints in the basement of the funeral home had been quickly identified as belonging to Jack Albertson or one of the other mortuary technicians that Albertson employed to work part-time. The unidentified prints were run through NCIC and came up empty. Those had to be Lazar's prints.

"We're getting close," was all Andy could tell the Chief.

"Close isn't good enough," said the Chief. "Close only counts in hand grenades and horseshoes. I want Jim Albertson found, or his body found. And if Jim is dead, I want the killer found. Do you hear me, Lieutenant?"

"I hear you," Andy had said.

"Hickman's already after your hide," said the Chief. "Is he correct in calling you incompetent?"

Del had executed a search warrant on the premises where Pete Smith had resided, and a bloody t-shirt and jeans were discovered discarded in the wastebasket of the community-use bathroom. Prints found in that same bathroom matched the unknown prints found in the basement embalming room at Albertson's Mortuary.

The landlord of the rooming house where Smith lived knew Smith fairly well and identified Smith as a resident who had lived there more than a year. Another man—who used the name Tom Jones, had scars on his face, wore sunglasses, and matched the description of the icepick killer—had rented a room in the same rooming house next door to Smith earlier in the week. When the landlord voluntarily opened that man's door at Del's request, the room appeared vacant and devoid of personal effects except for a small television set which looked new. Lazar's prints were found on the television he had left behind.

Every police officer in the city had Lazar's description and copies of his prints and were combing the city for Lazar. Mullins and his state police boys were watching the expressways and interstates. But, unless Lazar made a mistake and got stopped for a routine traffic violation, the chances of finding him in a city this size were slim and none.

James Albertson, a widower who lived alone, had not returned to his expensive home since early Friday morning to judge by dirty breakfast dishes his once-a-week housekeeper found in the sink when she came in on Saturday afternoon. Jack Albertson, James' son, was recently divorced and not yet remarried. But the funeral director's new girlfriend said she hadn't seen the coroner's son since Friday morning. She began to worry only after police inquired if she knew his whereabouts late on Saturday. She had assumed Jack and his father had gone to some big political dinner Friday night and had gotten drunk with cronies afterward. It wasn't unusual, she claimed, for Jack to pass out at parties. A party was, after all, how she had met him. She had been asked to drive him home because he had been too drunk to drive himself. When Jack Albertson woke up the next morning with a hangover and found her waiting at the side of his bed with coffee and aspirin, Albertson had asked her to stay.

Andy went home sometime around 2:00 AM on Sunday morning. He had only been able to sleep two hours in the past two days, and he was having difficulty concentrating and even keeping his eyes open. If he had a confrontation with Lazar, Andy realized, he'd be too tired to think on his feet. His reflexes had already slowed appreciatively. If he expected to function at full capacity, he needed sleep.

By checking mortuaries in a dozen cities where there were multiple unsolved rape-murders, Crawford's FBI agents discovered there had been a Tom Lazar employed at one of the mortuaries in each city during the time-frame those homicides occurred. After Lazar left employment, rape-homicides abruptly stopped in each locale. The only city where Lazar hadn't been employed at a mortuary was the city where the state university was located, the city where Dolores Ledbetter had been murdered and Lazar's DNA had first been found under her nails. The state university seemed to be ground zero, the point of origin for an out-of-control fire that had spread to fourteen states and burned for ten years.

Andy knew he was getting very close to the killer. He knew the killer's name, and he knew what the killer looked like. "Close," as Chief Elway often liked to say and had said again this afternoon, "only counts in hand grenades and horse shoes." Andy knew he had lots of work to do tomorrow. He went right to bed and fell almost instantly asleep.

Andy got out of bed at nine. He showered, shaved, dressed, and drove to the office, stopping only at McDonald's for coffee and an Egg McMuffin.

When Andy checked his e-mail, he found a new message from arson investigator Larry Miller. "Sorry I haven't kept in touch," read Miller's message. "Been extremely busy looking for similarities between the Elm Street arson and others around the state. There were two arson fires near the campus of the state university ten years ago that came up in a database search. The FBI's Uniform Crime Reporting Program lists arson as a property crime, not as a crime against a person or persons, and arson cases seldom get cross-indexed with homicide cases. So I had to do some further searching. Here's what I found that may interest you: Rudolph Eddington, Senior, a university professor and plastic surgeon and his second wife Serenity Eddington, a former fashion model, died in a fire that consumed their home near the campus. Accelerants were suspected, and traces of Ronsonol lighter fluid were found in the ashes and on the bodies. Ronsonol was the keyword that brought up the case. Roger Johnson and his wife Sara also died in a fire the same night. Regular gasoline, and not lighter fluid, was used as an accelerant in the blaze that killed Johnson and his wife. Here's the kicker: Their daughter Ellie Johnson Eddington was married to Rudolph Eddington, Junior.

"Coincidentally, Rudolph Eddington, Junior, a pre-med student at the university, killed his wife and infant son, Rudolph Eddington, III, the same night, and then reportedly killed himself. He drove his father's car off a bridge into a river. Eddington's body was never recovered. A hand-written note that Eddington Junior left in Johnson's mailbox said Eddington Junior killed all of them, and he was going to kill himself.

"But, since Eddington's body was never found, I think he's still alive and committed the arson on Elm Street. The reason I say that is the results of tests of DNA recovered from hairs in a hairbrush at Eddington Junior's house never got entered into the CODIS database. So I entered it this morning. I must have received a hundred hits. Eddington's DNA matched the DNA of the icepick guy you've been hunting.

"Now I suspect," Miller's long e-mail continued, "that the arson on Elm was started to hide a homicide that Eddington Junior had already committed. The body, along with other bodies in the house, was destroyed beyond recognition, and any evidence that Eddington had ever been there was lost."

Miller gave his home phone number and his cell number and asked Andy to call as soon as possible. Andy dialed Miller's home number and a woman answered.

"I'm sorry to disturb you, Mrs. Miller, but Larry wanted me to call him right away. My name is Andy Sinnott. I'm a homicide detective working an arson case with your husband."

"Larry," he heard her call out despite feeble efforts to muffle the microphone with her hand. "It's work calling on your day off."

"You get to take a day off?" Andy asked when Miller came on the phone.

"Have to, if I want to stay married."

"How long have you been married?"

"Twenty-six years," said Miller. "What about you?"

"I'm still single," said Andy. "I can't afford to get married or take a day off."

"I assume you read the e-mail I sent?"

"You just cleared up a whole bunch of loose ends for me."

"You'll clear up a bunch of loose ends for me when you catch this Eddington. Let me know when you search him if you find a Zippo lighter in one of his pockets."

"I thought he left his lighter behind at the scene."

"He did. But I bet he replaced it with a new one, same make and model. The guy would feel naked without a Zippo. Kind of like you without a sidearm or me without boots."

"We're closing in on him," Andy said.

"Do it quick. It looks like this guy doesn't stay around one place very long. Our pigeon is likely to flee the coop. You may have a day or two to catch him before he's gone, but don't bank on it."

"Thanks, Larry. I'll stay in touch."

"And if you don't," said Miller, "I'll call you. Good hunting, Tiger."

Miller was right. Andy had to catch Eddington before he disappeared into another city. But how?

Where could the guy have possibly gone after he left Albertson's Mortuary? Obviously, Eddington-Lazar had his own car and he could be anywhere by now. He could be half-way to New York or California, or driving through Minnesota on his way across the border into Canada. But Andy didn't think so.

Eddington had shown an unusual interest in Linda Davis. If Eddington had wanted to kill Davis, he could have done it while Pete Smith held her helpless. But Eddington had killed Smith instead of Davis. Why?

And hadn't Linda said Pete had come directly up to Evangelista and her in the bar instead of approaching or talking to any of the many other available women nearby? Upstairs and Downstairs was always crowded with available women on Friday nights. Why pick two women who didn't look like drug users to lure to the park?

Andy thought that Pete chose Evangelista and Davis because they were the ones Eddington sent Pete to Upstairs and Downstairs to fetch. Few rapists or serial killers chose their victims completely at random. They usually watched their victims for some time—anywhere from hours to years—before they made a move on them. Had Eddington seen Evangelista and Davis somewhere and marked them for murder? He could have followed them from the bar, possibly even followed them home. If he had been able to follow only one, which one would it have been?

The answer was simple. Eddington chose to follow Davis, not Evangelista, home. If Eddington had been able to enter Linda's apartment building without being seen by security cameras, he would have attacked her in her apartment Thursday night instead of Friday in the park. But the cameras were a deterrent. Eddington waited until Friday when Pete lured her to a secluded location before attacking.

Andy had no doubt that Eddington intended to rape Linda. Whether he wanted to rape her before or after her death was the big question. Linda thought Eddington wanted her alive. Why the change to his usual MO?

Even if Eddington wanted Linda alive when he raped her, he would kill her afterwards. She had seen his face. He couldn't afford to leave a witness alive.

And what about Evangelista? If Eddington discovered Evangelista was still alive and might be able to identify him, would he try to kill her, too? Then, again, how would Eddington know Evangelista still lived? Surely, he must have thought she died from stab wounds.

Besides, Evangelista was perfectly safe in the intensive care wing of the hospital with doctors and nurses constantly in attendance. Just to be on the safe side, though, Andy decided to assign Del to guard her room at Bryson Memorial today and ask Lewinski and Carson to check on her tonight. Tomorrow, Andy would ask the Chief to provide twenty-four hour protection with rotating shifts of patrolmen.

Andy dialed Del's cell phone. The phone rang and rang and then went to voice mail.

Andy looked up Del's home address on the west side. Andy was surprised to discover Del lived in an older rooming house on West Elm Street not too far from where Pete Smith and Rudolph Eddington, Junior, had recently lived. Now why would a homicide detective want to live in a run-down old apartment? He was paid enough to afford something much nicer than a one-room rental. If Davis could afford a decent apartment, so could Del.

Andy decided it was time to answer some questions about Del that couldn't wait until tomorrow to be answered. He left the office and drove to the address where Del reputedly had resided since coming to the city to take his new job.

The place where Del lived looked only marginally better than the place where Pete had lived. It was a three-story old brick building with a big wooden porch on the front. Andy parked and walked up on the porch, opened the outer door, and looked for Del Conklin's name on one of the six mailboxes. Del's apartment was on the second floor, the room on the right.

Andy walked up the old rickety staircase and knocked on Del's door. He pounded harder and harder, but Del didn't answer. The landlord, an old man with unruly white hair and a scraggly white beard, came to see who was making such a ruckus in his building on a Sunday morning.

Andy showed the landlord his badge and ID. "My partner, another homicide detective, lives in this apartment," Andy told the landlord. "I haven't been able to reach him by phone, and he doesn't answer the door. I'm concerned for his welfare."

"He's passed out," said the landlord.

"He's *what?*"

"I said he's passed out. He's an alcoholic like most of the people who live here. Only he tries to hide it and others don't bother. He drinks himself stupid, and then he passes out. He don't harm no one. He don't make much noise. He just likes to drink. I like to drink myself. You a drinking man, mister?"

"No," said Andy. "I'm not."

"Then you don't know what it's like. Most of us ain't got no jobs no more. We drink day and night. Your partner can't do that and keep a job. So he hides the booze at work, maybe takes a little nip now and then and covers it up with breath mints. He waits until he gets home to really start drinking. But then, once he starts, he can't stop. He just keeps drinking until he passes out. That's what your partner does. He's inside there passed out right now, I bet. Here, I'll open up his door and show you."

The old man produced a ring of keys from his dirty jeans pocket, and unlocked the door before Andy could protest or stop him. There were empty bottles everywhere—on the floor, on the tables, on the sofa—and Del was passed out face-down on the floor next to a half-empty bottle of Jack Daniel's. He looked comatose or dead.

Andy knelt next to the prone detective and the alcohol fumes nearly made Andy puke. Del's chest was rising and lowering erratically, and Andy could hear Del's breathing was labored. A puddle of saliva had leaked from his mouth and stained the dust on the floor.

"Now you just leave him alone until he sleeps it off. He'll be all right tomorrow. You wait and see."

"I need to get him help," said Andy, taking out his cell phone to call an ambulance.

"He don't need no help. Now you leave him alone, you hear?"

Andy called 911 and requested an ambulance to the address on West Elm.

"Now you gone and done it," said the old man. "They'll take him and dry him out. He'll be in agony for a month or two, but then he'll be right back here passed out on the floor, only he won't have no job. The job's the only thing that keeps him from killing himself with booze. Do you think drying him out and filling him full of drugs will do that? Hell, no! If he ain't got no job, he'll be dead inside a year. His liver'll give out or he'll fall down and hit his head, split it open like a ripe melon. The job's the only thing that keeps him alive."

"He can't do his job when he's like this," argued Andy.

"Maybe not. But he sure as hell can't do it sober. His body got used to having alcohol in the blood stream. Every day he needs more to keep goin'. Without booze, he'll get the shakes so bad he can't control his hands. He won't be able to remember things. You'll see."

"I'll get him help," said Andy. "He was a good cop once. He can be a good cop again."

"An' I tell you it's too late," said the old man as a siren wailed in the distance.

Two paramedics ran up the stairs, pulling latex gloves over their hands. Two more paramedics followed with a medical bag filled with medications and supplies.

"Whoooee!" whistled one of the paramedics. "This guy is really stinko."

Andy and the old man watched the paramedics work on Del, checking his vital signs before lifting him onto a stretcher and carrying him downstairs to the waiting ambulance. Andy followed them downstairs, then followed the ambulance to Bryson.

"You cops used to just throw these guys in the drunk tank and let them sleep it off," complained the overworked emergency room physician at Bryson, sadly shaking his head. "Now you bring them here and we have to take care of them. Every one of these guys you bring us takes resources away from people who can use them. What good will it do him? He did this to himself, you know. He'll do it again. Only a handful out of a hundred ever kick booze permanently. It's in their blood. They can't sweat it out. Alcohol is more addictive than heroin and just as deadly."

"You have a bad attitude," Andy told the doctor.

"You haven't seen what I've seen. Half of the people who come into the emergency room have severe alcohol or drug problems. Or they're spouses or children of people with alcohol and drug problems. All of them lie about why they're here. They deny there's an underlying problem that they need to do something about. There's nothing anyone can do for them until they're ready to do something for themselves. We treat them, send them home, and we see them come back again and again for the exact same reasons we saw them before."

After Andy signed all the necessary papers required to admit the still-unconscious Del to a 30-day mandatory detox program, Andy took an elevator upstairs to the critical care ward to check on Evangelista. As he got out of the elevator, he saw a man in a white lab coat, whom he and the nurses at the monitoring station on the floor assumed was a doctor, heading toward Evangelista's room. The man in the lab coat was about five-eleven, looked physically-fit, had a bald or shaved head, and wore black leather running shoes.

And then Andy saw the name "Albertson's Mortuary and Crematorium" stenciled on the back of the lab coat.

Andy drew his Glock and began running.

CHAPTER NINETEEN

You read in the morning's newspaper that the female cop you thought you had killed in the park is still alive. She is in critical condition at Bryson Memorial Medical Center, but doctors expect her to survive. She has seen your face. She can identify you.

You leave the parking lot in front of the little one's apartment building where you have watched for the little one to emerge. You head straight for Bryson Memorial. Sooner or later, the little one will certainly leave the safety of shelter and become accessible. You will follow her, catch her unawares in an isolated spot, and take her. It is only a matter of time.

But now there is something you must do first. You park the Toyota Matrix in the huge lot surrounding the hospital. You find the lab coat you keep on the rear seat of your car adjacent to your two duffel bags. You select a scalpel to take with you that will do the job, slip on the lab coat, and walk into the hospital lobby. Anyone who sees you will think you look like a doctor. You know the way doctors look and act, the way they walk. You walk fast, stopping only at the reception desk and then only long enough to learn the female cop's room number. You take the elevator up to the critical care floor. You have to get past the nurses' station in order to get to the cop's room, but that should be no problem. You keep your head down and act like you belong in this building. No one pays any attention to a man who looks and acts like he belongs, like a young resident or hospitalist making Sunday rounds.

You grasp the scalpel in your left hand as you approach the open door to the cop's room. You are almost ready to duck inside the room and loosen the sutures in her neck with a few flicks of the wrist when you hear footsteps rapidly running toward you. There should be no reason for anyone to run in the hospital without hearing an emergency code, and there were no recent codes announced over the loudspeakers in the ceiling.

You glance over your shoulder and you see the detective you saw in Upstairs and Downstairs. He has his gun in his right hand, and he's running fast.

You react instantly, seizing a nearby nurse by the front of her blue scrubs and slitting her throat with your scalpel. Then, with that kind of herculean strength you know comes from desperation, you pick up the nurse's bleeding body as if it's only a rag doll and toss it straight at the running man. The sudden impact knocks the cop to the floor and sends the rather square-looking gun flying from his hand.

Without thinking, your running shoes beat a path for the nearest emergency exit. You hit the breakaway bar with all your might and jump down the stairs, round the landing on the floor below, and jump down another flight. You burst through the outside door into bright sunlight that would be blinding if not for your sunglasses. You race for your car and are inside the Matrix, firing the ignition, before the detective emerges from the stairwell. You speed west out of the parking lot and hope the bright sun hitting the cop's eyes keeps him from a good look at your car or your license plates.

You drive recklessly because you know the cop will alert patrol cars to intercept you as soon as he can dial his cell phone. You only have minutes to get away before the area is swarming with uniforms.

You make it all the way to the North Street Bridge before seeing a squad car racing in the other direction with lights and sirens active. You slow to a reasonable speed and continue east, staying off the main drags and taking side streets the remainder of the way to the little one's apartment. You drive around her building twice to check for squad cars, and when you see nothing that looks suspiciously like an unmarked police car, you park in the middle of the big lot, hiding in plain sight.

How could that cop have known you were anything other than a doctor? You wore a white lab coat; you not only looked the look, you walked the walk. Yet, he seemed to recognize you from the back.

Then you remember where you acquired the lab coat and the

Albertson's Mortuary markings across the back. How stupid was that? Anyone who saw you from the rear could have told instantly that you were no doctor. Maybe that cop wasn't so smart after all. Maybe you weren't, either.

What the hell was a cop doing walking around the critical care ward of the hospital anyway? You didn't see any visible signs of police protection anywhere on the floor or near the room when you got off the elevator. The cop must have arrived on one of the other elevators shortly after you turned the corner and started down the hallway. Perhaps he had been elsewhere in the hospital and merely stopped by critical care to check on the injured officer. Seeing that particular cop so close to you was unnerving. You shouldn't underestimate him. He's dangerous.

You think about forgetting about the girl and leaving town right this minute. There will be other girls in other cities. Why do you have to have her? Why must it be her and no one else?

Because she touched you. Not only did her beauty touch your heart, her knee physically touched your groin. You and she are connected. To leave without touching her back—getting tit for tat, so to speak—is simply not possible. Just as an alcoholic cannot be around alcohol without wanting to drink, neither can you see beauty without wanting to touch.

Hot afternoon sun beats down on the red-steel of the Toyota's roof. You spot an unmarked squad car drive past the front of the girl's building. The squad slows as it passes, but it does not stop. You slouch down in the seat. Your scalpel, wiped clean of the nurse's blood with the useless lab coat, is beneath the front seat within easy reach. You breathe a sigh of relief as the unmarked car disappears from sight. If they were looking for you, they didn't see you.

Afternoon turns to evening, and the heat remains unrelenting. From time to time, you start the Matrix and run the air conditioner full blast. You have less than three-quarters of a tank of gas remaining. Cars regularly enter the parking lot, others leave; dozens of people enter the apartment building and dozens leave the building; but the little one is still ensconced safely inside her own apartment. Soon, you will need to eat something and rehydrate with lots of water. You wish you had thought to bring bottles of water with you. When you stop next for gas, you can buy a few bottles in the Denton's Super-Mart next to the gas pumps. Maybe a bottle of Gatorade, too. You want to keep the gas tank full and be ready to move at a moment's notice. You never know when you may need to make your getaway. Toyotas are good on gas. One tank will take you three hundred or more miles, enough to get you safely out of state. You intend to get as far away from here as you can. But before you can leave, you have a date to keep with the little one.

What if she decides to go out while you are at the store or gas station and you miss seeing her? What if she doesn't come out for days? Is there any way you can enter the building without the cameras picking up your face?

You have no key to the little one's building. Therefore, to enter the building, you will need to pause to pick the locks at the front door. When you do, the two cameras aimed at the front entrance will record your face for posterity. You have been very careful in the past to avoid cameras in the commission of crimes, and no one who ever got a good look at your face lived to describe it. But now there are three people alive who know what you look like. The female cop bedridden in the critical care ward, the male cop who pursued you today, and the little one who saw you the other night. You may have to alter your appearance anyway if you don't eliminate all three eyewitnesses. Perhaps it's time for your current face to make its camera debut.

If you pull the visor of the baseball cap down over your forehead, wear your sunglasses to cover your eyes, and don't look directly at any of the cameras, maybe you can minimize your exposure. You have been thinking for some time about getting facial reconstruction for your scars, and you could get a new nose and chin, too, at the same time. You have enough money to pay for plastic surgery saved in bank accounts you can access by ATM. Ten years of frugal living pays dividends when most of the money you've saved is reinvested in foreign stock markets. Investing is something your father taught you. You transferred the last of Tom Lazar's accounts yesterday to new accounts off-shore. When you emerge from plastic surgery, you will have a whole new identity waiting for you.

So it's decided. If the little one does not come out in the next hour, then as soon as it's dark and the traffic in and out of the building slows, you will make your move.

At eight o'clock, you leave the parking lot and drive to a gas station only five blocks away. You fill the tank, purchase a sandwich, four energy bars, six bottles of water, and two bottles of Gatorade at the convenience store when you pay in cash for gas, and you return to the parking lot before eight-thirty. It's obvious some of the residents of the apartment building have left for summer vacations because the parking lot is half-empty on a Sunday night. The sun begins to sink low in the west. Though there are no clouds in the sky, there are cloud-like contrails streaking east and west between Chicago and San Francisco, north and south between Memphis and Minneapolis, crisscrossing the sky like giant hash-tags on Twitter or sharp signs on a musical score. Perhaps tomorrow you will be on one of those planes.

A blue Dodge Dart enters the parking lot and you duck down so the driver doesn't see you. The driver's a small man, late twenties, hair neatly trimmed. He doesn't look like a cop. He finds a space at the other end of the parking lot, turns off the motor and headlights, and rolls down the windows. He just sits there in the car waiting, as if he were patiently waiting for someone to come out of the apartment building to join him. That's just great, just what you need. Someone to watch you as you go up to the door to pick the lock. You will him to leave, projecting your thoughts at him as if it would do any good. He looks around as if he had heard your voice speaking to him inside his head. You duck down again until his gaze returns to the apartment building.

Another hour passes, and he still sits there in his Dodge Dart watching everyone who enters and leaves the building. Perhaps he is a cop after all, someone sent to watch out for the little one after the attack on her companion in the hospital this afternoon. Maybe you should walk over to his car and let Mr. Scalpel have a brief talk with him. It's dark enough now that you can sneak up on his car without him seeing you. His windows are open. It will be so easy to reach in and slit his throat or stab him in the eye.

But then you see the little one emerge from the brightly-lit lobby of the brick building. Today she wears a faded red t-shirt and white walking shorts with matching white tennis shoes. She is too far away for you to read the entire logo printed on the red t-shirt, but you manage to decipher the word "University" on the front. So she's a college girl, probably a recent graduate. How long has it been since you enjoyed a college girl?

She walks purposefully as if she is going somewhere specific on foot. You will wait until she's a block away before you pull the car out of the lot and follow her.

The man in the Dodge Dart opens his car door and runs past you to catch up with the little one. He is wearing jeans and a dark t-shirt like you. His shoes are gray Adidas Springblade running shoes. He moves fast for a small man.

You watch as he catches up with the little one. She seems surprised but pleased to see him. Obviously, they know one another. He stands only a few inches taller than she, and he has a slight limp when he walks.

You wonder what they talk about as they stroll. The little one has slowed her gait as the man limps alongside her. You look at her bare legs, her cute behind. You know you have to have her.

You start the Toyota and slowly drive out of the parking lot onto the street. They are both headed toward the same gas station and convenience store you just visited. You speed up, drive past them. You see a vacant lot that's overgrown with trees, weeds, and shrubs. It's far enough from the nearest street light to be in sufficient shadow to hide you. You drive around the corner and park the Toyota next to the curb. You wait in the bushes for them to walk past.

Hiding in the bushes reminds you of that night when you killed your first woman, a woman you had intended only to rape. She was a college girl, too, wearing a t-shirt and shorts. It had been slightly cooler, late May instead of close to the fourth of July, and you hadn't sweated so much as you waited for her to walk close enough to grab. When she passed the bushes, you reached out and tried to pull her down, showing her the knife and telling her not to struggle. But she had fought you relentlessly, wriggling and clawing at your face until you were forced to stab her. Yet she continued to fight you, and you had to stab her again and again until she stayed still. You pulled down her shorts and panties, pushed up her t-shirt, and discovered you could touch her any way you desired and there was absolutely nothing she could do to stop you. After that, you regularly killed women before you raped them. You know that is what you should do with the little one. Had you killed her in the park, you wouldn't have to be here now.

But there is something about the little one that makes you want her alive when you enter her. She exhibits a vitality that you wish to savor while it lasts. Seeing her face drained of blood would be nowhere near as pleasurable as seeing her freckled face flushed with fear, looking into dead eyes not nearly as lovely as seeing your own face reflected in living eyes filled with fright.

The man walking with your special girl is a minor nuisance that you will quickly eliminate. You know you have to be quick about it because the girl won't freeze. You have to kill the man and immobilize the girl before either can counter-attack. Should you hit her over the head or grab her in a choke hold? You have nothing heavy enough to render her unconscious by hitting her head, so you decide a choke hold that exerts sufficient pressure on the carotid will have to do.

As you watch them approach, you hold the scalpel in your left hand ready to open the short man's neck with a single stroke of the blade. You can grab the girl's neck with your right arm at the same time, pressing the knuckle of your right thumb into her carotid and cutting off blood flow to her brain. Then you can drag her unconscious body into the bushes, tie her hands behind her with her shoe laces, cut off her clothes, and gag her with a strip of cloth from her red t-shirt. When she wakes up, you will already be inside her. You will look directly into her eyes. When you are finished, you will kill her and puncture her eyes. The last thing she will ever see will be your face.

You hear them getting very close now. Ten more steps. Nine. Eight....

Andy reached Rich Pearson at home and asked him to come to the hospital to remain with Evangelista until Lewinski relieved him at eleven. Roadblocks had been set up around the hospital, but the killer had slipped through them as if he were a ghost.

Andy knew only that Eddington had left the hospital in a small red car. Andy had been unable to make plates or exact model, though he thought the car was an older hatchback. Cops all over the city were stopping red hatchbacks and searching for scalpels.

One nurse was dead from knife wounds, and the others were frightened out of their wits. Andy had asked the dispatcher to call out the remaining crime scene team, and they were busy taking photographs and searching for prints. The killer had left familiar-looking size eleven bloody footprints from the nurses' station all the way to the exit.

"I almost had him," Andy told Pearson when Rich arrived on the floor.

"Where's Del?" Pearson asked.

"Downstairs. He's incapacitated at the moment."

"Drunk?" asked Pearson.

"Yeah. How did you know?"

"I've smelled it on him before. If he drank on duty, I figured he drank a lot more as soon as he got off."

"Why didn't you say anything?"

"Not my place," said Pearson.

"What I can't figure out," said Andy, "is how the killer knew Evangelista was still alive and here in Bryson Memorial."

"Morning papers," said Pearson. "Hickman had the full story about Friday night. Someone must have told Hickman, and Hickman printed it where the killer could see it."

"Del told Hickman. Del's been taking calls from Hickman for weeks. I found dozens of voicemails from Hickman on Del's cell phone. And those were just the calls that Del hadn't answered."

"I thought Del said he didn't know how to use his cell phone."

"He knew how to use it. He just didn't answer calls when he was drunk."

"How is Evangelista? The guy didn't hurt her again, did he?"

"I didn't give him a chance. I spotted him wearing a lab coat from Albertson's. If I hadn't seen that, he would have been in and out of Evangelista's room before I could have stopped him."

"He'll go after Davis next, you know. If he went after Evangelista, he'll try for Davis."

"She's safe in her apartment. There are security cameras all around the building, and Davis is armed."

"Do you think this guy will let that stop him?"

"I don't think he'll try anything until after dark. I'll personally stake out her place tonight. She'll be safe until then."

"I hope you're right."

Chief Elway, trailed by a bevy of reporters, got off the elevator and headed straight for Andy. Elway was sadly shaking his head. "This is totally unacceptable," said the chief as shoulder-held cameras rolled and microphones picked up every word. "Sinnott, you're relieved of duty here and now, and I'm personally taking over this investigation from you. But don't you dare leave until I've had a chance to get everything you know from you. How could you let a nurse get killed when you were here to prevent it? How could you then let the killer escape when you had a gun on him? Total incompetence is why. Who appointed you head of homicide anyway?"

"Your predecessor."

"And I suppose Captain Nolan recommended you?"

"Yes."

"It seems the Nolans have a real bad habit of recommending the wrong people for public jobs," said Elway. "I intend to have a talk with Captain Nolan when he gets back from his extended vacation. Who's your assistant?"

"Sergeant Conklin."

"Where is he? I want to talk with him."

"Sergeant Conklin is ill."

"Ill? What do you mean ill?"

"Sergeant Conklin has been hospitalized."

"Where are the rest of your people?"

"Evangelista is in the room over there," Andy pointed at her room. "I told you yesterday what happened to her. Davis was also wounded on Friday, and she's home recuperating. Detective Pearson is here from Violent Crimes. Today is Pearson's day off, but I called him in and assigned him to guard Evangelista. I have three crime scene techs working their butts off gathering evidence and processing it. If you look around, you'll see them."

"Where are your other people?"

"What other people?"

"Do you mean to tell me you don't have anyone else?"

"Mullins and a tech from the state police, but they don't work for me and I have no authority to call them on a Sunday. Crawford and his Special Agents from the FBI, but they're only able to provide technical support unless you want to relinquish jurisdiction."

"So then it's just you and me and Pearson and a couple of technicians?"

"Yes, sir. I'm already way over budget on overtime. Of course, you and I don't get overtime. But the others do because they're union. I needed Pearson and the techs here today, so I called them in. I'll have to find the money from somewhere."

"Are you saying, Lieutenant," asked one of the reporters catching everything on camera from behind Elway, "that your investigation has been hamstrung by personnel shortages and budget restraints?"

"No comment," said Andy.

"Let's go into one of the empty rooms and talk privately," said the Chief, suddenly anxious to get away from the reporters he had previously asked to accompany him. This conversation wasn't going the way he had expected.

"Betty will put out a news release tomorrow afternoon," Andy told the reporters. "Until then, neither the Chief nor I want to comment on an ongoing investigation."

"That's right," agreed the Chief of Police. "Lieutenant Sinnott is going to fill me in on all the facts I didn't have before. Thanks for your time, Ladies and Gentlemen of the press. I'll talk with you again real soon." Then the Chief turned around and walked into a vacant hospital room, motioning Andy to follow.

"What the hell just happened here, Sinnott?" asked the Chief after Andy had closed the door. "I feel like I've just been ambushed."

"How do you think I felt when you came rushing in to relieve me in front of all those reporters?"

"They followed me. I couldn't stop them. The hospital is a public place."

"Bullshit. You called the stations and asked them to send camera crews to the hospital. This floor is now a crime scene. All those reporters walked over evidence my boys were still processing."

"Why didn't you tell me you were so short-handed?"

"I've been requesting additional personnel for months. Captain Nolan and I put numerous personnel requests in writing, and we also documented manpower shortages in our annual budget requests. I know you've seen them Chief. Maybe you didn't pay any attention to them at the time, but you've seen them."

"Well, the Mayor cut the police department's total budget, so I had to make cuts. I've deferred hiring 70 people this year for previously authorized positions. Every division suffered personnel cuts, and homicide was only one of them. We have to make do with what we've got. Now tell me what happened here."

"The killer—and his real name is Rudolph Eddington, Junior, and not Tom Lazar—tried to kill officer Evangelista again today. I just happened to be coming here to visit Evangelista, and I recognized Eddington by the lab coat he wore. I was about to nab him when Eddington killed a nurse and threw her body at me. He picked her up by her clothes and threw her right into me, knocking me down like a bowling pin. By the time I recovered my weapon and pursued him down the stairs, Eddington had escaped in a red hatchback. I put out an APB on the hatchback, but none of the patrols or roadblocks caught sight of him."

"Maybe I was a little hasty in relieving you," said the Chief.

"Maybe you were," agreed Andy.

"So what do we do now?"

"We?"

"Well, yes," said the Chief. "Forget what I said. You're still in charge of this investigation."

"Now," said Andy, "we go to work. We do what the people of this city pay us to do. We process evidence and we catch a killer."

"How can I help?" asked the Chief.

"Unless you want to interview witnesses and process evidence, stay out of my way," said Andy. "And stay the heck out of my way until I hand you Eddington all wrapped up nice and neat."

"When will that be?" asked the Chief.

"When I catch the son of a bitch," said Andy. "Or kill him. I haven't decided yet which I would rather do."

Rat couldn't believe his luck. Linda had emerged from the front door of her apartment building, and it looked like she was going out for a walk. If he hurried, he could catch her before she had gone too far. Then maybe she would let him walk with her wherever she was planning to go.

He got out of his car and ran as fast as his rebuilt legs could carry him. Both of his knees had been replaced with artificial steel knee caps, and his hip joints were stainless steel pins. He didn't move the way he used to. He never would again, thanks to the IED he'd encountered in Iraq that had shredded so much of his muscle and bone.

But he still could move when he wanted, though it sometimes hurt. Tonight he paid no attention to the pain as he kept his eyes on Linda.

"Linda, hi," he said as he approached her.

"Jon. I mean Rat. What are you doing here?"

"I wanted to see you. I've been waiting for you to come out."

"Are you stalking me?"

"No. I want to talk to you. Maybe help protect you, if that's all right with you. If you'll let me protect you."

"You think I need a man to protect me?"

"No. Nothing like that. When I was in Iraq, my buddies and me would watch each other's backs. Sometimes a person needs someone to watch his or her back."

"I can take care of myself, Rat. I am a police officer, you know. I'm trained to protect myself."

"We were trained in the Army, too. But we still needed someone to watch our backs. Do you mind if I walk with you? If you do, I'll leave you alone."

"No, that's all right. I'm only walking to the store to get some bread. I was going to make a sandwich, and the bread I had was all moldy."

"I hate when that happens," said Rat.

"Yeah. Me, too."

"How are your hands?"

"They hurt. They hurt worse now than they did when he cut them."

"You don't notice the pain right away. I know. That's what happened to me. But when the nerves start to heal, the pain can be unbearable."

"Tell me about your injuries in Iraq."

"Nothing much to tell. I got blown up by a roadside bomb. Three of the other guys riding in the Humvee with me didn't survive. I did, but the docs had to piece me back together. My mind took longer to heal than my body."

"But you're all right now?"

"Yeah. Pretty much. I don't hear voices anymore. I lost some of my actual hearing when the bomb went off right under me. But living in the tunnels, in the dark, my ears learned to compensate for my eyes. Now I can hear as good as normal. Maybe better."

"What about your physical injuries?"

"I lost both knees. They were blown completely off. My hips got all screwed up. I have two separate fusions in my spine. L-something and S-something. Doctors didn't think I'd ever be able to walk again. But I can."

"Yes, you can. If you didn't have a limp, I'd never know you had been injured."

"If you saw my back, you'd know," Rat said. "I'm a mess of scar tissue from my neck down to my knees."

"Can you still function?" she asked, and then, blushing when she realized what she had asked, she tried to retract the question. "I mean, was anything essential injured? I'm sorry. I shouldn't have asked. I don't know you well enough to ask personal questions."

"It's all right," he said. "Some of the other guys lost their private parts in the war, but I didn't. I brought all of mine back with me, and they seem to function the way they did before. I wasn't circumcised before, but I am now. When I meet the right girl, I hope to be able to father children."

"You like children?"

"I had three sisters. All three were younger than me, and I tried to take care of them and watch out for them. Two are married now and have children of their own. I'm an uncle."

"Do they live in town? Do you see them much?"

"No. They live in different states. I get to see them maybe once a year, if I'm lucky. Of course, when I lived in the sewers, I didn't see them at all. I didn't even know my sisters had gotten married until I came back above ground."

"What was it like, living in the sewers?"

"Dark. It took years for our eyes to see in the dark. When we came out of the tunnels, our eyes had to adjust to light again. I still have some trouble seeing in bright light. My friend, George, has more difficulty than I do. He was in the tunnels twice as long."

"You mean Harvey Fredriks?"

"I called him George because I thought he looked like George Washington on the one dollar bill."

"I guess he does. A little."

"George didn't kill anyone."

"I know," she said. "I think I met the real killer the other night."

"You're lucky to be alive. Do you think he'll try to kill you again? Because you saw his face?"

"Andy thinks so. He wanted me to carry a gun with me at all times. I tried to hold one today. But my hands wouldn't let me. I couldn't close my hands around the grip, not even on my small .380. So I left both my guns at home. If I'm not able to shoot a gun, I don't want to have one with me where someone could take it away and use it on me or someone else."

"I'll keep you safe. I'll protect you. I promise."

"Thanks, Rat. I don't think I need to worry while we're just walking to the corner store and back."

Rat didn't want to tell her that he thought she had a reason to worry. He had seen a red car in the parking lot with someone sitting in it. Like Rat, that man had watched Linda's apartment building for some time, evident by the big pool of water that had dripped beneath the parked car from running the automobile's air conditioner. At first, Rat thought the guy was probably a cop that Andy had assigned to surveillance. But when the red car had left the parking lot shortly after Linda and Rat had walked far enough away, followed them for a block or two along the streets of the newer subdivision with its still-to-be-rented duplexes and single-family dwellings, then sped by them, Rat began to doubt the man was a cop. First, the car was an older model. Sure, it could have been something confiscated in a drug bust and used by detectives for undercover work. But Rat doubted that the man was a cop because the man driving the car had deliberately looked the other way when he sped past as if he didn't want anyone to see his face. An undercover cop would have watched the road. Besides, if the guy was supposed to be following them, why had he simply driven by and disappeared?

Rat began scanning his surroundings with his peripheral vision, the way he had been trained to do at night in the Army. His night vision had diminished significantly since he had emerged from the tunnels, but he still had better night vision than most people.

"Slow down a little, but keep on walking as if nothing's wrong," said Rat, lowering the volume of his voice nearly to a whisper. "There's a wooded area in the next block that's perfect for an ambush. That's where I would wait to grab you, if I wanted to grab you."

Linda looked at Rat to see if he was kidding. His eyes were continuously flicking left to right, then moving slowly back again to the far left, then flicking right again as she had seen paranoid schizophrenics do.

"We normally disregard 99 percent of what we see," explained Rat calmly while his eyes continued to move, "because our eyes normally want to focus on only one thing at a time. When we stare straight at something, our eyes tend to go out of focus entirely after perhaps a second or two of concentration. Maybe you've noticed that when you first begin to look around a new place—say, when you've just entered a big room you have never been in before, for example— you take in the big picture in its entirety. You see the whole thing at first glance, and then you narrow your attention down to only what seems most important to you at the moment. You pay attention primarily to one special person or object or detail. Once you narrow your focus, you miss all of the other things that are happening around you. They don't seem important, so why bother to notice them at all anymore?"

"I've never thought about it before," said Linda, as if to placate Rat and keep him calm.

"That's because it's subconscious activity that we do automatically and don't need to think about, like breathing or digestion. I asked several shrinks about it in Walter Reed when I was a patient there. They told me that when you constantly change where your eyes will focus, you pick up peripheral detail again. That's why paranoids look around all of the time. They're using their peripheral vision to search for threats. We learned to do exactly that in the Army, particularly at night."

"You learned to be paranoid in the Army?"

"Sure. You've heard the expression that even paranoids have real enemies? Well, it's true. Believe me, it's a big crazy world and there are real enemies out there that want to kill you. As a police officer, I'm sure you know that. There are plenty of people out there hiding in bushes or just around the corner that will kill you if you let them. We're not going to let them."

"You think someone is hiding in the bushes?"

"There's an empty lot at the end of this next block that has bushes and overgrown shrubs close to the sidewalk," Rat said as they crossed a side street. "It's perfect for an ambush. It's the place I'd pick if I wanted to harm you."

"Then let's not go near those bushes."

"We have to," said Rat.

"Why?"

"Because of George. The only way I can clear George, is to expose the real killer. When I tell you to run, I want you to run away as fast as you can and call for help." Rat handed her his cell phone. "Most of the houses around here look vacant. You'd have to run all the way back to your apartment building to find help. Call 911 and tell them the nature of your emergency and your location. They'll have someone here within ten minutes. I want you to find a place to hide until help gets here."

"I can't just run away."

"You have to. If I can't handle this guy, you certainly can't with injured hands."

Rat saw the glint of light as moonlight reflected off a metal object in the bushes. Rat's peripheral vision differentiated the shadowy outline of a crouching male figure from the surrounding shrubbery where the man hid. The killer waited for them exactly where Rat knew he would be.

"Run!" he told Linda as he jumped straight into the bushes and felt cold steel slide into his right hip.

CHAPTER TWENTY

It was nearly nine PM when Andy finished taking statements from witnesses at the hospital. The dead nurse's body had long ago been taken downstairs to pathology for autopsy, and Andy finally gave the nurses permission to have the bloody footprints cleaned from the floor and stairwell. A bevy of housekeeping staff descended on the critical care unit with sponges and mops. By the time Andy was ready to leave the CCU, the place looked spotless again.

Before Andy left the hospital, he went into Evangelista's room where Rich Pearson sat in a visitor's chair next to Evangelista's bed. Rich dutifully asked each doctor or nurse entering the room to show him a picture ID before he let them anywhere close to Evangelista. He made a point of asking Andy to show ID, too. "Just to make sure you're still a cop on duty after the Chief reamed your ass," Rich said with a smile. "Of course, I also heard you ream him back. You were right next door and you weren't always quiet."

"All you need to know is the Chief authorized you to stay until Lewinski relieves you at eleven," Andy told Pearson. "With the Chief's authorization, you know you'll get paid your overtime. Carson will relieve Lewinski at seven tomorrow morning. Walt Exeter or someone else will take the afternoon shift. Thanks for coming in on your day off, Rich."

"My wife bitched until I told her how much overtime I earned this month," said Pearson. "Why don't they just hire more cops? It would be cheaper."

"It's the pensions," Andy said. "It does work out cheaper to pay time and a half or even double-time than to pay into the pension fund."

"It's already dark. Are you headed to stakeout Davis's apartment?"

"Yeah."

"Then you aren't going to get any sleep, are you?"

"Not tonight," said Andy.

"I'm glad I'm only a detective and not a boss like you. I get to go home and sleep once in a while."

When Andy arrived at the parking lot in front of Linda's building, he recognized a blue Dodge Dart that he knew belonged to Jon Bradley already parked in the lot. Bradley wasn't in the car.

Was Rat inside Linda's apartment? Had Linda invited him in? Andy was surprised to again feel jealous of Rat. He liked Rat. But he was sorry now that he had introduced Rat to Linda and sent them to investigate Upstairs and Downstairs together.

Andy knew that it was highly inappropriate to want a personal relationship with an employee he directly supervised. He needed to stop thinking of Linda Davis as a woman and think of her only as a cop. He tried. But after Andy had held her the other night in the park, Andy wasn't sure that was possible.

Seeing Linda injured and vulnerable and smelling her hair and subtle perfume had somehow triggered emotions Andy hadn't felt since Dolores Ledbetter was alive. After Dolores died, Andy had thrown himself into his studies and then his new job so completely that he had allowed no time to feel much of anything. Dolores had been Andy's first love, and after that love was so tragically taken away from him he had sealed himself off from personal feelings. The deaths of both his parents shortly thereafter only solidified his resolve to feel nothing. It wasn't until the other night, when he had held a sobbing Linda Davis in his arms, that he became acutely aware he had never cried himself when Dolores or either of his parents had died.

Andy Sinnott, the smartest kid in the class, was ignorant when it came to emotions and relationships. And, to be honest, Andy had to admit emotions scared the hell out of him.

It was far safer not to allow relationships. Because his parents were so much older and because Andy had no siblings, he had not learned at home what he needed to know about emotions and how to handle them. His early attempts at forming normal relationships with his classmates had come to an abrupt end when Pete Smith had bloodied Andy's nose and humiliated Andy in front of everybody. Andy had retreated into his private world of books and computers and remained there until he had met Dolores Ledbetter.

Dolores said she admired Andy's mind, and it was she who fell in love with him long before he knew he was in love with her. She had coaxed him out of his shell and taught him how to feel. For two glorious years, Andy had felt like a whole person. She very patiently taught Andy how to love, and he had loved her with his whole body and soul. And then some bastard had taken that away from Andy with a dozen jabs of a butcher knife.

Andy debated whether he should telephone Linda and ask if he could come up to her apartment. The more he thought about it, though, the more Andy felt he didn't really want to know if Rat and Linda had been alone in her apartment together all day. He remembered how Linda had practically slammed the door in his face when he had walked her home Saturday morning. That she would let Rat into her apartment and not him in felt like a slap in the face.

Like the fist that Pete Smith had slammed into Andy's nose in third grade.

Like the knife blade Eddington had slammed into Dolores ten years ago.

Like the dead nurse Eddington had thrown in Andy's face this afternoon.

Andy had been so close to apprehending Eddington this afternoon that Andy had grossly miscalculated and allowed the killer to get away. Eddington was standing too close to three nurses for Andy to risk a shot, but he was still too far away to grab. Andy didn't dare shoot because a stray nine-millimeter round that missed its mark could inflict irreparable damage in a hospital filed with people. Eddington had surprised everyone, Andy included, by moving so fast his motions seemed like a blur. He had grabbed the nurse standing right next to him, cut her throat, and hurled her bleeding body at Andy before Andy knew what had hit him. Andy had lost his gun, been blinded by blood pumping out of the huge hole in the nurse's neck, and by the time Andy had regained his feet and retrieved his weapon, Eddington was gone.

And then the Chief had shown up and slapped Andy in the face in front of all those reporters. What more could possibly go wrong?

Andy's cell phone vibrated in his pocket. Caller ID showed it was a dispatch to all available units from the 911 center. Andy listened to the message and responded immediately.

Linda Davis had called 911 from a location four blocks north of the parking lot where Andy was currently located. She had identified herself as a police officer and told the call-taker that she and Jon Bradley were being attacked on the street. She had requested immediate assistance and then the phone had gone dead.

Andy slammed the Honda into gear and sped out of the lot and headed north. He prayed he wasn't already too late.

Rat felt the blade penetrate his flesh and open his hip. The killer had reacted so incredibly fast, bringing the knife down to meet Rat's onrushing body before Rat could wrest the weapon away, that all Rat could do was twist around so the knife entered his hip instead of his belly. But as the blade penetrated, it bent against the indestructible stainless steel pin in Rat's hip joint, and momentum broke the scalpel's blade in two. When the killer made a swipe at Rat's neck, there wasn't enough of the blade left to do more than scratch his flesh.

Rat swung a fist at the guy's face, but once again the guy moved so very fast Rat's knuckles only brushed the guy's ear but didn't connect.

It had been nearly ten years since Rat had completed basic and advanced infantry training, but some things were so ingrained that they were still second nature to him. He wrapped both of his legs around the other man's torso to keep the guy from getting away. At the same time, Rat jackknifed his midsection and butted the guy's chin with the hard top of his head. He heard the guy's teeth slam together.

The guy was still wriggling like a snake, however, trying to get out of the leg hold. Rat could feel him start to slip away as the artificial joints in Rat's hips gave way. His opponent was five inches taller and at least thirty pounds heavier than Rat. Rat had bitten off more than he could chew.

But this was a fight to the death, and Linda and George both depended on Rat to win. He swung again at the guy's face, and this time he connected, breaking the guy's nose. Blood gushed from both nostrils as the guy doubled his efforts to get out of Rat's weakening leg hold.

Rat swung again, this time hitting only air as the guy wormed completely free and crawled away. Rat scrambled to catch the slippery bastard, but the guy kicked Rat in the face. Rat's own nose gushed blood, and a familiar coppery-iron taste flooded his mouth as he tried to gasp air through his mouth instead of clogged nasal passages. Bleeding from both his hip and his nose, Rat began to feel light-headed. How much blood had he lost anyway?

He couldn't think about that now. His night vision told him the killer had taken a pocket knife from his pants pocket and was opening the big blade. He threw himself straight at the killer and grabbed for the guy's left forearm. He had to make the guy drop the knife before he had a chance to use it. Rat's fingernails caught the arm just above the wrist and dug in.

The guy slammed his right elbow into Rat's jaw, and Rat felt his jaw dislocate. He was losing this battle, but he didn't dare lose the war. His very life depended on winning.

Rat jumped up and did a roundhouse kick that connected with the guy's nuts. The guy doubled up, and the knife dropped from his fingers.

Rat tried another kick, this one aimed at the guy's face. But Rat's wounded artificial hip joint wouldn't cooperate. Rat lost his balance and toppled backwards, hitting the ground hard.

Rat tried to get up, but his legs wouldn't work at all. He rolled over and pushed himself up with his arms. If he was going to die, he would die fighting, not flat on his back. He waited for the dark shadow of death to come for him. He was ready to fight to the death, but death didn't come. Instead, Rat heard receding footsteps.

He heard a car door slam and an automobile engine start up, and he heard that car drive away moments before another car approached from the opposite direction with high beams and flashing red and blue blinkers. Andy Sinnott slammed on his brakes, jumped out of the Honda, and ran toward Rat with his gun drawn.

"He just drove away!" Rat yelled. "Get back in your car and maybe you can catch him."

"You're hurt," said Andy, taking out his cell phone to call 911. He ordered an ambulance. Then he called the police dispatcher directly and ordered patrol cars to intercept all traffic leaving this area. Andy gave a description of the killer and said Eddington may or may not be driving a red hatchback.

"Where's Linda?" Andy asked as soon as he put his cell phone away.

"I told her to run and hide," said Rat, his voice sounding real funny because of his smashed nose and dislocated jaw.

"She's all right then?"

"I kept the killer busy. He didn't have time to chase her."

"Sit down," said Andy. "You're leaking blood from your hip. Let me get some pressure on that to stop the bleeding. You're a hero again, Rat. I can't let a hero die from loss of blood after he saved the girl. Now can I?"

Rat sat. Andy went to his car and came back with a first aid kit. He made Rat lower his pants and drop his drawers enough to slap a piece of gauze over the open wound. "Hold that in place until the paramedics get here," Andy told Rat. "Put as much pressure on it as you can stand."

"The blade broke off in there," said Rat. "It fouled up my mobility."

"The scalpel?"

"Yeah. He had a pocket knife, too. It's on the ground over there."

Andy took out his 600-lumen flashlight and scanned the area for a pocket knife. "I don't see it."

"He must have grabbed it again before he ran off."

Sirens got louder in the distance, and an ambulance appeared with its red lights flashing. A hook and ladder truck followed the ambulance. Two paramedics got out and came over with an equipment bag. Two more brought a stretcher.

Rat let them dress the wound to his hip. Paramedics reset Rat's nose, then stuffed cotton up both nostrils. They said doctors would reset the jaw in the emergency room. Rat climbed onto the stretcher, and two of the paramedics carried him to the ambulance.

"Find Linda," Rat told Andy. "Tell her I'm okay. She shouldn't worry."

"I'll do that," said Andy.

You manage to make it into Walmart's parking lot without being stopped by police. Your body is screaming with pain, and you need time to recover your senses before you do anything else.

Who would have thought that little runt could pack such a big wallop? The face you see in the rear-view mirror is a total mess. Not only is your nose broken, it's still bleeding. Your left eye is beginning to swell and discolor. There are parallel lines of blood dotting the front of your t-shirt where your nostrils dripped blood and snot, and even your pants have blood stains on them from when you cut the short guy's hip with your scalpel. When you stabbed the scalpel at his stomach, you were surprised to feel the blade go in only a half inch, then bend and break off. The blade never had a chance to slice into his intestines. What the hell happened?

The guy had snaked his legs around you and held you in an iron grip that pinned one of your arms. He had leg muscles on him like someone who had done a lot of walking. His knees felt as if they were made of steel. Fortunately, he couldn't hold you like that for very long. His muscles finally gave out and you managed to break free. But the bastard wasn't going to let you go. When he kicked you, he took you completely by surprise. It hurt like a son of a bitch, and it knocked all of the wind out of your sails.

When you recovered, you wanted to kill that idiot for what he did to you. But you had no idea where the little one—the female cop—had disappeared. She was a police officer and very likely armed. You wouldn't be surprised if she were trying right now to draw a bead on you with her weapon. You remembered that she had been able to hit the hearse from a distance of more than fifty feet in the dark, and you didn't doubt she could hit you if she tried. You decided it was better to leave while you were able. It was time to get the hell out of Dodge before the cavalry rode to the rescue.

The place would be swarming with cops in a few minutes more. You had seen the runt hand the little one his cell phone just before he told her to run. Maybe, with luck, you'll get away before cop cars arrive.

Cops would watch all of the roads out of town, and they would alert the state troopers to watch the interstates. Your best bet was to hide in plain sight. It was after ten o'clock, and the shopping malls had already closed.

Walmart to your rescue. Not only does Walmart stay open all night, its parking lot has enough traffic to hide your car among hundreds of others. So you headed for the nearest Walmart. The big problem with Walmart is the security cameras in the parking lot. You can't stay here in your car all night without raising suspicions. Walmart has people who monitor the security cameras 24/7.

You open a bottle of water and use it to wash your face. Your nosebleed has practically slowed to a trickle, and you stuff pieces of Kleenex up inside your nostrils to stanch any remaining bleeding. You can hide the swollen eye with your sunglasses, though it will look strange to wear sunglasses at night. You reach into the back seat, open up a duffel bag, and take out a clean black t-shirt. Now you look presentable. No one will stare when they pass by. The blood stains on your black pants aren't visible in the dark.

Your groin still throbs with excruciating pain. You can't believe you have actually been kicked in the balls twice in one week. Only once before in the entire ten previous years of hunting has anyone managed a lucky kick that connected with your testicles, and that person is no longer alive. But both the little one and her runt friend still live. That, in itself, is enough to frost your balls.

The genital areas of both sexes are rife with somato-sensors and proprioceptors, nerve endings extremely sensitive to touch and physical position of body parts. Because so much of the female genitalia lies safely within the body, women have no idea what it's like to be constantly exposed. The little one might be forgiven for kicking you in the balls. But another man? Never!

When nature evolved males, she gave man an extra awareness of the dangerous genetic vulnerability if testicles are damaged. A hard crushing force applied to dangling gonads often causes genetic defects in offspring or curtails sperm production. Thus, nature made such events so extremely painful that men try to avoid them at all costs.

If the testicles are abruptly struck, a reflexive action automatically causes the male to double over into a protective fetal-like position. He drops anything he may be holding and attempts to cover his gonads with his hands. He reflexively turns away to avoid future blows, and for a moment he is immobilized in a purely defensive posture and cannot attack or counter attacks from foes.

When you found yourself in that very vulnerable position, you knew you had to get away as fast as possible. There was nothing more you could do either time it had happened. You needed time to recover.

So you sit in the parking lot in front of Walmart waiting for the pain to lessen. Now there are four people you need to kill: the runt who kicked you, the detective who is tracking you, the female cop in the hospital, and the little one. You want the little one so bad you can taste it. Why is it that men always want what seems hardest to get? There are millions of women out there completely unaware. Why do you want a woman who is armed and forewarned you will attack her?

Is it the challenge? Do you need to prove to yourself and others that you can do it? Never before have you felt challenged like this. Police officers have chased you in the past, and you always eluded them. Not only is the little one an object of desire, she is also a police officer. That makes the challenge even more interesting and the little one even more desirable.

One part of you—the rational part of you—argues that it is time to get away from here fast, to forget all about them and go elsewhere to hunt. Come back here at a later time when they are unprepared for you and you can easily kill them all. Leave the Matrix in the Walmart lot and take a cab to the bus station, buy a ticket for the east or west coast, and hunt to your heart's content. Practice your art again on the dead who need your skills at embalming and restoration. After a year or two, you can come back and tie up loose ends.

But another part of you argues that leaving now is quite impossible. Not only are there eyewitnesses who might identify you should you ever come to trial, people have touched you and cannot be allowed to live even another day.

You leave your car and walk into the Walmart store. You purchase a reinforced jock strap, a clean pair of jeans, a container of Ronsonol, and four new icepicks.

You use the payphone at Walmart to call for a taxi. You change clothes in the men's room, dropping your soiled jeans in the trash.

You open the blister packs on the icepicks, slide the picks into your belt, and dispose of the packaging.

Then you take the cab to the little one's apartment building, pick the locks on the entrance and the locks to her own apartment and wait for her to return. You are certain she must be at the police station giving her statement to the detective. If you are lucky, perhaps the detective will give her a ride home. Then you can kill two birds with the same stone. If he walks her up to her apartment door, you can stab him in the eye and grab the girl.

When you are finished, you can go to the hospital and take care of the other two witnesses. This time, instead of pretending you are a doctor, you can pretend to be part of the cleaning staff. Hospitals are meticulous about cleanliness, and you can easily enter each of the rooms with a mop and dust cloths. Even if there are guards on the rooms, no one will suspect you until it's too late.

It seems like the perfect plan. What could possibly go wrong?

CHAPTER TWENTY-ONE

Linda came out of hiding when the ambulance turned on lights and siren and drove Rat to the hospital. Andy saw her walking toward him, and he waved.

"Is Rat alive?" she asked. "Is he okay?"

"He has a nasty knife wound on his hip that requires surgery. His nose is broken and his jaw is dislocated. How are *you*?"

"Scared," she said. "It was too dark to get a good look at the perp, but I'm sure it was the same guy who attacked Lorraine and me on Friday. He was hiding in those bushes there, Andy. Rat knew exactly where the guy would wait to ambush me. Rat saved my life."

"I'm glad Rat was here to protect you. Yours is not the first life he's saved. Captain Nolan would be dead now if not for Rat. George, too. Dozens of people Rat served with in Iraq would be dead if not for him. He's a hero. Where's your gun Linda?"

"In my apartment. My hands hurt so bad I couldn't hold it or squeeze the trigger if I tried. I didn't want anyone to take it away from me, so I left it in my apartment."

"Why did you leave your apartment?"

"I needed bread. I thought it was safe to walk to the store. I guess I was wrong."

"Let me drive you home."

"Can you drive me to the hospital instead? I want to see Rat. Please? I need to make sure he's okay. And I want to thank him for saving my life."

"You may not be able to see him. He's going to need surgery. Eddington's scalpel broke off in his hip. Doctors have to remove it, and I want it preserved for evidence. I think it was the same scalpel he used to kill a nurse this afternoon."

"Eddington? Who is Eddington?"

"Rudolph Eddington, Junior, is the killer's real name. Larry Miller thinks Eddington is also the arsonist who torched the buildings on Elm that killed a dozen or more people."

"Just how many people has Eddington killed?"

"Far too many. He's been killing for more than ten years, Linda. We've got to stop him."

"He got away again?"

"Yes. I would have heard if a patrol saw him or a roadblock snared him."

"Will he try to kill me again?"

"He tried to kill Evangelista this afternoon in the hospital. I would have been here sooner but the Chief and I had a little misunderstanding we had to iron out."

"Chief Elway? The Chief of Police?"

"Elway came to the hospital to fire me and he brought a bunch of reporters to catch it on tape for the ten o'clock news. Hickman has been lighting a fire under the Mayor's ass to get something done, and the Mayor blew smoke up the Chief's butt. So the Chief came down on me."

"He fired you?"

"Yes. But when I told him how many people he had left to help him work the case, he decided to keep me on."

Andy opened the car door for Linda, then walked around to the driver's side and got in.

"You're doing everything you can do," Linda said, buckling her seat belt. "Doesn't the Chief realize that? My God, Andy, you've had half-a-dozen murders in a week, not counting the arson homicides. You've lost your criminalist and a crime scene tech to injuries. Just how much does the Chief expect you to do with only Conklin, Pearson, and three techs?"

"It's even worse than that, Linda," Andy said as he started the car and pulled away from the curb. "When I couldn't raise Del on his cell phone today, I went to his apartment, He was out cold and had to be hospitalized."

"What happened?"

"Del has an illness I didn't know about before. He'll be out on sick leave for a month or more."

"Oh, Andy. That's terrible. You can't do it all by yourself. No one can."

"I've got Pearson standing guard at Evangelista's bedside. Actually, Lewinski has probably relieved him by now. Captain Nolan will be back from his honeymoon on the eighth. That's a week from tomorrow. He'll be a big help."

"But you know the killer won't wait another week. He wants me, and he'll come for me again. Maybe not tonight, but tomorrow or the day after. He won't wait a week."

"I know. Linda, please don't take this the wrong way. I need to stay with you in your apartment tonight. Rat would ask to do the same thing, if he could. I'd assign a female officer, if I had one available. I'll talk to the Chief tomorrow and see if I can get a female from Vice or a patrol officer or maybe a rookie. But I don't want you to be alone until Eddington is caught."

"You can sleep on my couch."

"He really did scare you tonight, didn't he? Yesterday, you wouldn't even consider my entering your apartment to check under the bed. Tonight you're willing to let me sleep on your couch."

"Yes. I'm scared. Do you blame me? He cut me, Andy, and I'm scared he'll cut me again. I can't bear the thought of being cut again. I saw what he did to Lorraine, and I saw what he did to the other victims. I know he wants to do that to me, too. When I saw him hiding in the bushes tonight, I ran away. I should have stayed and helped Rat. But I couldn't. I was afraid of that blade slicing into my hands again, or maybe my throat this time. I couldn't face him. I know I said I would fight if anyone tried to rape me. But I'm afraid I'll get cut. If I see him again, I'll run. I'll run like a scared bunny rabbit."

"It's okay to be scared," Andy said. "I'm scared, too."

"But Rat wasn't scared. He's been injured before, and he just jumped right in and tackled that guy. Rat didn't have a weapon. It was the bravest thing I've ever seen."

"I'd give him a medal if I could. He's already got medals for bravery."

"I owe him my life. I'd be dead now if not for him."

"I'll find a way to get you in to see him," said Andy. "You're a police officer. I'm giving you the job of finding out all you can about what happened tonight. You talk with him as long as they'll let you stay with him. I'll be waiting for you upstairs in Evangelista's room. Come up when you're ready to go home, and I'll drive you home."

"Thank you, Andy."

"For what?"

"For being the best boss a cop could have."

Andy drove the rest of the way in silence, lost in his own thoughts. Rat deserved a girl like Linda. Andy had no right to even think Linda might ever be interested in him.

Andy parked in one of the spaces designated for police vehicles near the emergency room entrance, and he escorted Linda inside and showed his badge at the reception desk. Andy and Linda were admitted into the secured emergency room, and they found Rat in one of the beds where he had been treated and now awaited surgery. His jaw had been set, and a strange-looking wire contraption—not unlike the face shield worn by NFL football players—held his jaw in place.

Andy left Linda with Rat, and he took the elevator up to the Critical Care floor. Art Lewinski sat in the same chair next to Evangelista's bed that Pearson had occupied earlier.

"I heard you had some excitement this afternoon," said Lewinski.

"The killer tried again with Evangelista," said Andy. "That's why you're here."

"I meant a different kind of excitement. I heard the Chief paid you a visit."

"That he did."

"I also heard you told the chief off. Is that true?"

"No, Art. I presented the Chief with the facts, and he decided he may have been hasty in his decision."

"You mean, he found out how much work you do and it scared him that he might have to do some work for a change."

"Something like that," said Andy with a grin.

"About time somebody put that big windbag in his place. You know he's the one who's been all buddy-buddy with Joel Hickman, don't you? Well, you do know I don't like the press very much, but I especially can't stand Joel Hickman. The guy will sell out his mother for a story. I hear Hickman stops by the Chief's office every afternoon at four, then he goes straight to his own office and writes his daily column. If you're looking for Hickman's source in the cop shop, look to the top. You have to tell the Chief everything you're doing, right? You send him daily reports? They have to be on the Chief's desk by three?"

"Right. Only we send daily reports by e-mail these days. We don't have to hand deliver them."

"So the Chief prints out copies of your reports to give to Hickman."

"Why? Why would the Chief pass on my reports to Hickman?"

"It seems Jim Albertson was kept book on the Chief for the Mayor. I guess politicians just like to keep book on everybody. When the Chief found out, Elway and the Mayor had a big falling out, and Elway formed an alliance with Hickman to put the Mayor on the hot seat."

"What do you mean by keeping book?"

"Making a list of who the Chief's sleeping around with, who he does favors for, who he lets buy him lunch, anything that can be used to keep him in line. For the Mayor, keeping a list is politics as usual. He keeps book on practically everybody. For the Chief, it was an eye-opener. The Mayor held all of the cards, and the Chief held none. So the Chief brought Hickman into the game. The Chief figures if he's going to go down for his indiscretions, he's going to take the Mayor and Albertson down with him. So he started feeding tidbits to Hickman. If the Chief thinks he can manipulate the press in this town the way he could in the last town he worked, he's badly mistaken. Hickman's a shark. Once he smells blood, he don't care who gets swallowed up when he opens his mouth. He just sinks his teeth in and chews everything up."

"How do you know all this?" asked Andy.

"I keep my nose to the grindstone, and my ear to the wall," said Art. "I've been around the department a long time, and people tell me things. I trained all the deputy chiefs, for example. And the Mayor's administrative assistant is my former sister-in-law. They know I like to keep in the know. They tell me things they don't tell nobody else."

"I thought the leak was Del Conklin."

"Del may be a drunk, but he's a loyal drunk. I hear he used to be a good cop, and maybe he still is. Hickman hounded Del and tried to blackmail Del into talking—threatened to put it in his column that Del was drunk on duty—and Del got scared he'd get fired. But Del didn't talk to Hickman. He just started drinking more. He figured he had nothing to lose by staying drunk."

"How come I'm only now hearing about this for the first time?"

"Because you've been too busy to pay attention to what's going on right under your nose. You're focused on finding the killer. This town's a regular Peyton Place. I ain't talking about Walter Payton or Peyton Manning. You're probably too young to remember the book or the soap opera on TV. And you don't get to hang around the locker room during shift changes like I do."

"I had Del committed to rehab. I found him drunk on the floor of his apartment this afternoon."

"That puts you short another person. You got this lady here hanging onto life by a thread, Davis out with cuts on her hands, the Captain honeymooning for another week. You think you can catch this killer all by yourself?"

"I'll manage," said Andy.

"Be careful. I don't want to have to go to your funeral."

"You can attend the killer's funeral, not mine. I'm going to get him Art."

"Be careful he doesn't get you instead."

Evangelista began to stir at the sound of voices she recognized, although she was still heavily sedated. There were IV drips in her left arm, she had monitors taped to her hands and torso, and her neck was covered with thick bandages and a brace to keep her from pulling the stitches loose. She was catheterized, and her bladder emptied into a plastic bag that hung from the side of the bed. Her face was still very pale from loss of blood, and her uncombed black hair probably made her look more like a corpse lying in a coffin than a live body in a hospital bed. But she was still alive and fighting to remain alive.

"I talked with the docs when they came in," said Art. "They think she'll make it."

"Did you check the doctors' IDs? The killer tried to get in here today disguised as a doctor."

"No one gets in this room without a hospital ID."

"I did," said Andy.

"I know you. I've known you since you was a rookie. No need to show me your ID."

Davis walked in the door and stared at Evangelista. "That could be me in that bed with her throat cut," she said.

"Art tells me the doctors think Lorraine will make it," Andy told her. "She'll recover."

"She doesn't look like she'll recover," said Linda.

"I heard you saved her life by calling 911 and then keeping her from bleeding out," said Lewinski. "Quick thinking for a rookie."

"Thanks," said Linda. "She would have done the same for me."

"How's Rat?" Andy asked Linda.

"Sore. He took a real beating. The nurses made me leave to prep him for surgery."

"Who's Rat?" asked Lewinski.

"Jon Bradley," said Andy. "He kept the killer from grabbing Davis tonight."

"The guy who used to live in the sewers? Works upstairs in the call center?"

"He's the one."

"Jesus! This killer doesn't stop, does he?"

"No. But he's getting sloppy. He left witnesses alive who can identify him. That's why I need you to stay alert, Art. He'll try again to silence Evangelista."

"I'm on the job," said Art.

"And I'm going to take Davis home. I'll stay with her until I can get a female officer to take over tomorrow."

"You remember what I said," said Art. "I went to Bill Bowers' funeral. I don't want to have to dress up for another cop's funeral. Be careful. "

The hospital hallways were deserted except for cleaning crews doing floors with mops and buffers. Andy and Linda took the elevator down to the lobby, then walked around to the emergency room and out to the parking lot.

"Lorraine looked awful," Linda said as they reached Andy's Honda.

"She's got a lot of healing to do," said Andy. "Give her time. It's only been two days."

Linda looked at the stitches in her own hands. "I can only imagine the pain she must feel."

"She's pretty drugged up. I don't imagine she feels much of anything yet."

"She will when she starts to heal. Rat told me I wouldn't feel the cuts on my hands until the severed nerves begin to mend. Which reminds me, I left my pain meds at home. I sure could use one about now."

"There's a bottle of aspirin in the glove compartment. If you reach into the back seat behind you, you'll find a warm bottle of water."

"Thanks," she said. She opened the glove box, found the aspirin bottle, and shook two into her hand. She swallowed them whole without water.

"Yuck. How can you do that?" asked Andy.

"I like the taste of aspirin," she said. "The taste lets me know relief is on its way, like those Alka-Seltzer TV commercials used to say. Plop, plop, fizz, fizz, oh what a relief it is!"

Andy drove around the apartment building, then around the parking lot twice looking for a red hatchback before he parked in the lot. "Just a precaution," he said.

Linda opened the lobby door and led the way up the stairs to the second floor. "Open the door, but let me go in first," whispered Andy, drawing his Glock.

"You going to check under my bed?" asked Linda in her normal voice.

"Under your bed and every room and closet in your apartment," said Andy. "Wait here until I say it's safe."

Linda inserted her key in the apartment door and turned the key. The door sprung open to a pitch black interior.

"Light switch is on your left," whispered Linda.

Andy reached for the light switch and a sharp pain shot up his left arm as something penetrated the back of his hand. The palm of His left hand was pinned to the wall. The sudden shock caused him to drop his gun and reflexively reach to free his pinned left hand with his right. Andy realized too late that Eddington must be inside the dark apartment.

"Run!" he yelled to Linda as he felt Eddington rush past him and through the door in a hurry. Andy's right hand found the wooden handle of the icepick and, with a single rapid motion, pulled the steel shaft free from the wall and out of his hand. Blood sprayed from the holes in Andy's palm and the back of his hand. Andy flung the icepick across the room and heard it bounce off the wall and hit the floor.

He heard a struggle in the hallway and ran out to confront Eddington without wasting time to retrieve his gun. Eddington held Linda tightly around the neck with his right arm, and he held an icepick to her neck with his left hand.

"Back off!" ordered the man with ugly scars on his face. "Back up quietly, or the girl gets it in the neck."

Linda's eyes were filled with fear. Andy's immolated hand dripped blood on the carpet as he took a small step backwards.

"Keep going," said the killer.

Andy knew that if he went into the apartment with Eddington, he was as good as dead. So was Linda. Eddington had no intention of letting either of them live. But what could Andy do without a weapon? His left hand felt like it was on fire. Blood continued to drip from both sides of the hand. He took another step backward.

Eddington pushed Linda a step forward. He towered over her, and his right arm held her head bent back and at an angle. The point of the icepick was pressed against the side of her neck just below where the knuckle of his right hand pushed against Linda's left carotid artery. Andy knew Eddington was perfectly positioned to kill Linda any of several ways: icepick into the carotid; break her neck; break her back.

What Andy could see and Eddington didn't realize was that Linda's left elbow was perfectly aligned with the killer's groin because of the differences in their heights. Eddington had one arm around her neck and the other hand held the icepick to her throat. Linda's arms were free to move.

"Move faster," said Eddington. "Don't take all night."

"I'm going as fast as I can backwards," said Andy. "Do you want me to turn around so I can walk faster?" Andy started to turn around.

"No," said Eddington. "I need to watch your eyes. Turn back around." He used the point of the icepick to make a little circling gesture in the air.

Andy knew it was all Linda had been waiting for. As soon as Eddington moved the icepick away from her throat, she jabbed her elbow into the killer's groin with all of her might. The bony elbow joint connected and something hard bruised her elbow. This time, the effect wasn't as debilitating as the last time she had touched him there. Eddington was wearing some kind of padded protection that blunted the blow.

As soon as Andy saw Linda's elbow move, he made his own move. Already half-turned, Andy spun the rest of the way and dove to the carpeted floor of the apartment to feel around for his Glock. The fingers of his right hand closed around the pistol grip and he came up in a one-handed shooter's stance. His left hand felt numb and useless.

"Drop the gun," ordered Eddington.

"Uh uh," said Andy. "Drop the icepick and surrender."

"I'll kill her."

"You'll kill her anyway."

Both Eddington and Linda looked at Andy as if they couldn't believe he'd just said that. Eddington pressed the tip of the icepick into Linda's flesh and drew a drop of blood.

"As soon as you kill her, you're a dead man," Andy promised.

This time it was Eddington that took a step backward. Andy could tell the guy wasn't yet ready to die.

"Let her go, Eddington," Andy pressed his only advantage. "Let her go, and I'll let you walk out of here. She lives, and you live. Fair trade?"

"You know my name?"

"I know all about you."

"Let me leave the building," Eddington said, "and I'll let her go as soon as I get outside."

"And why should I believe you'll let her go then?"

"Because you have no choice if you want her to live," said the killer. "You stay here. I'm going to walk downstairs now. If I see you coming for me, I'll kill her and throw the body at you like I did that nurse this afternoon. I outran you in the hospital. I can outrun you now."

"You're fast," Andy admitted. "But maybe I'm faster. You think of that?"

"I'm willing to take my chances. Are you? Do we have a deal?"

Andy ran marathons. He felt certain he could outrun Eddington. Besides, Andy could see no other way out of this Mexican standoff. "We have a deal," he said, raising the barrel of the Glock.

"Remember, you stay here until I'm outside the building. Then I'll let her go."

"Get out of here," Andy said. "Before I change my mind."

Eddington didn't turn. He dragged Linda backwards toward the stairs. For a moment, Andy was afraid Eddington would push her down the stairs and take off running, but he didn't. Andy watched Eddington hold on to Linda and manipulate her down the stairs one stair at a time. Both Linda and Eddington disappeared into the lobby. Andy began slowly walking down the stairs himself. His left hand throbbed and continued to drip blood. He thought about holstering his Glock and using his cell phone, but he wanted to keep the weapon out and ready to use. When Andy reached the bottom of the stairs, he looked around the lobby for Eddington. Eddington must have gone outside and taken Linda with him.

Andy saw Eddington running into the parking lot. Eddington was running fast, but Andy knew he could run faster.

Where was Linda? She wasn't with Eddington anymore. Did he let her go?

Andy saw Linda on the sidewalk leading to the parking lot. She was lying in an expanding lake of blood that flowed from her punctured neck like water escaping a hole in a dam.

"Oh, God, no!" he yelled and ran to the body bleeding out on the cement.

You wait inside the little one's apartment for the sound of a key in the lock. You were very careful to lock the door so it would be exactly the way you had found it before you picked the lock. When you hear the little one's key, you hold an icepick ready.

The door opens inward to the right and you can see the detective silhouetted in the doorway. He reaches inside with his left hand to find the light switch, and you ram the icepick through the back of his hand and into the plaster.

He makes a startled grunt, but he doesn't let out a scream. Too bad. You wanted to hear him scream.

While he's pinned to the wall, you rush into the hallway and grab the little one in a choke hold. You pull a second icepick from your belt and press the tip of the icepick to her throat. You can sense her fear. It's exactly the reaction you wanted.

You see the detective emerge from the apartment dripping blood from the holes in his hand. His left hand is useless. His right hand is balled into an angry fist.

"Back off!" you tell the detective. "Back up quietly, or the girl gets it in the neck."

The cop takes a small step backwards. His hand drips blood on the hall carpet.

"Keep going," you tell him, pushing the little one in front of you. You tower over her, holding her head bent back and at an angle that exposes the jugular. You press the point of the icepick against the side of her neck. "Move faster," you tell the cop. "Don't take all night."

"I'm going as fast as I can backwards," says the detective. "Do you want me to turn around so I can walk faster?" He starts to turn around and you stop him.

"No! I need to see your eyes. Turn back around." You use the point of the icepick to make your point with a circling gesture in the air.

But as soon as you move the icepick away from her throat, you feel the little one's elbow jab your groin. This time, however, the effect is completely different. The padded protection that you bought at Walmart blunts the impact. You immediately jerk back on her neck with your right arm, shutting off her air, and returning the point of the icepick to her jugular.

But the momentary distraction was all the detective needed. Already half-turned, you see him spin the rest of the way. He dives down to the carpeted floor to feel for his gun with his good hand. When he gets to his feet, he has the gun in his hand and pointed in your direction.

"Drop the gun," you order, holding the girl in front of you as a shield.

"Uh uh," says the cop. "Drop the icepick and surrender."

"I'll kill her," you say. You're not bluffing. You will kill her. But you don't want to kill her yet. You have big plans for her. Maybe you'll even let the detective watch.

"You'll kill her anyway."

You can't believe the cop just said that. You press the tip of the icepick into the little one's flesh and draw a drop of blood to prove your point.

"As soon as you kill her, you're a dead man," the cop says.

This time it's you that takes a step backwards. You're not ready to die. Not yet. There are still things you want to do.

"Let her go, Eddington," the cop says. He knows your real name. This guy is good. No one else has ever tracked you down and learned your name, but this guy did it in a little more than a week. You know he's not bluffing, either. If you kill the girl, the cop will definitely kill you. "Let her go," he says, "and I'll let you walk out of here. She lives, and you live. Fair trade?"

"You let me leave the building," you tell him, "and I'll let her go as soon as I get outside."

"And why should I believe you'll let her go then?"

"Because you have no choice if you want her to live," you reason with him. He'll listen to reason because he seems like a reasoning kind of guy. "You stay here. I'm going to walk downstairs now. If I see you coming for me, I'll kill her and throw the body at you like I did that nurse this afternoon. I outran you then, I can outrun you now."

"You're fast," the cop admits. "But maybe I'm faster. You think of that?"

"I'm willing to take my chances. Do we have a deal?"

"We have a deal," the cop says, raising the barrel of the gun toward the ceiling and away from you.

"Remember, you stay here until I'm outside the building. Then I'll let her go."

"Go," he says. "Before I change my mind."

You drag the little one backwards toward the stairs, then manipulate her down the stairs one at a time. You reach the lobby and drag her out the door. It's two in the morning. People who work for a living are asleep in bed. There's no one around to stop you. But the little one, as light as she is, is too heavy to carry. She senses what you're going to do before you do it, and she tries to struggle and get away before the icepick goes all the way in. You have no time to waste. The cop will be downstairs any moment now. You plunge the icepick into her neck, penetrating the carotid. If you had a knife, you could have severed the carotid, jugular, and trachea the way livestock are slaughtered. You leave the icepick in her neck as she falls to the ground.

There is no time left for anything else. You have no car and no waiting taxi, so where do you go?

Hiding in plain sight has always worked for you in the past. You remember the blue Dodge Dart the runt was driving earlier. It is still parked in the third row.

You see the cop come out the door of the apartment building with his gun in hand looking around for you. He starts to chase you and spots the girl on the ground.

"Oh, God, no!" he screams.

"You wanted to hear the cop scream. Now you have.

CHAPTER TWENTY-TWO

Andy put pressure on Linda's neck with his injured left hand while he maneuvered the cell phone out of an inside coat pocket with his right. He dialed 911 and ordered an ambulance and all available patrol units to the apartment's address with a ten-zero-zero. He told the call-taker that the officer who was down had already lost a lot of blood and required an immediate transfusion.

The icepick was still stuck in Linda's neck. Blood pumped out from around the shaft. It was a good thing that the icepick remained in her neck. Had the killer removed it, even more blood would have poured out than already had. Linda was unconscious from loss of blood, but she must have felt the icepick going in because her face was frozen in an expression of pure terror.

Andy had no time to think about anything but Linda. If Eddington were still around, patrol cars would have to get him.

Andy's injured hand throbbed and pulsated. He had lost a fair amount of blood himself. There was a hole through the entire hand. Nerves and ligaments had been damaged, and the hand would never be the same again. He had to use both hands to stem the flow of blood from around the icepick stuck in the left side of Linda's neck. What damage the pick may have done to her throat and voicebox was the least of her worries. She seemed to have trouble breathing because of the blood pouring down her throat into her lungs.

But she was still alive, and Andy intended to keep her that way. He held onto her neck and tried to keep as much blood as possible from leaving her body.

He heard sirens in the distance. A patrol car arrived first, and two uniformed officers came running over with a first aid kit. Andy let them wrap gauze around the shaft of the icepick to stifle the exsanguination. An ambulance drove up and paramedics brought plasma to replace some of the blood Linda had lost. They quickly loaded her onto a stretcher and hauled her to the ambulance. Andy jumped into the back of the ambulance with them and rode with Linda to the hospital while paramedics continued the transfusion and administered oxygen. Bryson Memorial Medical Center was the nearest hospital with a Class I trauma center. It took twenty minutes to get to Bryson's emergency room but it seemed like an hour.

Doctors removed the icepick from Linda's neck, pumped blood from her lungs, and inserted a breathing tube. Andy received stitches in his hand. Pain finally hit him like a ton of bricks. He had been too busy trying to keep Linda alive to think about his own injury.

The doctor who stitched up Andy's hand said the wound appeared clean. Andy was given a tetanus shot and antibiotics. He refused the pain pills they offered. As soon as Andy was able, he wanted to chase after Eddington. He had a personal score to settle with that guy. There was nothing more he could do for Linda. Either she would live, or she wouldn't. It was out of his hands.

Was there anything Andy could have done differently? Could he have prevented the injury to his hand or to Linda's neck? How could he have known Eddington was hiding in the apartment?

Once Eddington had captured Linda, he held the upper hand. Any move Andy could have made, other than what he did, would have resulted in Linda's instant death. Andy and Linda were, at least for the time being, both still alive. Letting Eddington remove Linda from the building was a calculated risk, a gamble, that didn't pay off. Andy knew he couldn't trust the bastard, and he was right. But there had been no way to shoot him without killing Linda first. Andy had no choice but to let the killer take Linda and go.

Andy had to wait to be released from the emergency room. Once they said he could go home, he would call a cab and go back to join the patrol officers searching for Eddington. Andy had just received his walking papers when Chief Elway walked into the emergency room.

"You let him get away again?" asked Elway. "And you let him

kill another police officer? How could you let that happen?"

"She's still alive," said Andy. "And, yes, he got away again."

"Didn't you try to stop him?"

Andy held up his left hand and showed the Chief the bandages over his stitches. "Yes," he said. "I tried to stop him."

"This is totally unacceptable," fumed the Chief. "Totally unacceptable."

"How did you hear about what happened?" asked Andy.

"I got the ten-zero-zero call. When there's an officer down, the call goes out to every officer on the force, including the Chief. Usually, I let others handle it. This time I went to the scene. I learned that Davis was injured and you rode with her to the hospital. Do you care to tell me what happened?"

"Eddington was waiting inside Davis' apartment. As soon as we opened the door, he stabbed me in the hand and grabbed Davis. He took her outside the building and stabbed her in the neck. I ceased pursuit to treat a wounded officer."

"Just who is this guy anyway? He doesn't use a gun, but he sends three officers to the hospital? Jesus, man. I don't understand this."

"He's a serial killer who's killed hundreds of people over the past ten years," said Andy. "He's never stayed around anyplace long enough to get caught. The FBI have been looking for him all over the country."

"Maybe we should turn the case over to the FBI and let them handle it."

"It's your call. But think what Hickman will write about you if you do that. He'll say you haven't got the brains or the balls to get this guy on your own, and he'll be right."

"Are you calling me stupid or a coward?"

"If the shoe fits," said Andy.

"What do you think I should do?"

"I think you should give me a ride to the crime scene and join the search for Eddington," Andy said. "It's time you showed some leadership." Elway seemed to think it over for a moment, and then he agreed.

The Chief drove a brand new sapphire-blue-metallic Cadillac XTS sedan the city provided him. Other than a police radio, computer, and red and blue flashers, the car looked like an ordinary luxury sedan a corporate executive might drive. It probably set the city back seventy thousand dollars. That was more than enough, thought Andy, to hire two additional crime scene techs for a year or a full-time detective.

Hickman was right in saying the city had misplaced priorities. Political cronies were paid off handsomely with jobs or business contracts—like supplying squad cars or repairing streets or constructing bridges at inflated prices—and provided drinks and free meals at the best restaurants that were billed to the city. The Mayor and city administrators all pocketed hefty raises every single year. The rank and file were told budget constraints prohibited any raises at all. Andy and Linda and Lorraine all got wounded. Other officers had been shot at or even killed in the line of duty. Andy wondered if Elway had even fired his weapon, much less been shot at or stabbed. Andy thought something smelled rotten in Denmark, and it sure wasn't sardines.

Police had strung crime scene tape around the entire apartment building, and the three techs who had responded Sunday afternoon also responded to the ten-zero-zero call. They had already photographed the area in front of the building, and Andy found them searching Linda's apartment for prints. They had found and bagged the icepick Eddington had rammed through Andy's hand.

Andy showed Elway where his hand had been pinned to the wall. There was a hole and cracks in the plaster. Blood stained the wall and floor.

"He shoved an icepick all the way through your hand?" asked a disbelieving Elway.

"Fortunately, it's not my gun hand. Davis can't hold a gun after the guy sliced up her hands. I can still hold a gun. Next time I see the son of a bitch, I won't hesitate to shoot the fucker."

Elway touched the butt of his revolver with his right hand. "Where is this guy now?" he asked.

"We don't know," said Andy. "None of the patrols have reported seeing him or his car."

"When we arrived, there were patrols driving up and down all the streets around here looking for him," said one of the techs. "The guy got away clean before we got here. He's long gone."

"I don't think he went far," said Andy. "Did you find any prints outside?"

"Size eleven running shoes on the sidewalk," said the tech. "We lost the prints when the ambulances and squad cars drove over and obliterated them. Either the guy headed into the parking lot across the street where he had a car waiting, or he stuck to the street for his getaway. Patrol cars went up and down all the streets. There's no sign of him anywhere."

"I saw him in the parking lot when I came out of the building," said Andy. "But I didn't have a chance to chase him. He didn't go back inside the building or I would have seen him."

"How did he get in?" asked Elway. "This is a controlled access building. It takes a key to get in the front door, and another key to get into this apartment."

"He picked the locks," said one of the other techs. "He used the right kind of tools. I'd say the guy either took a class in basic locksmithing or he read a book. The locks are simple pin-tumbler types. He could get in with a couple of good pics."

"What about the security cameras?" Andy asked. "Have you seen the tapes?"

"The cameras are all Wi-Fi connected to DVD-Rs in the apartment management company offices downtown. We can view them tomorrow when the offices are open."

"That doesn't do us any good now," said Andy. "Maybe the Chief can drag someone who works in those offices out of bed. We need to see what direction the killer went when he left here. How about it, Chief? Think you can do that?"

"At four in the morning?" asked the Chief. "I wouldn't know where to start."

"I can tell you the management company's name and address," said the tech. "Denton Properties on Fourth Avenue. Stan Denton is the guy you need to see. When we call the offices, all we get is a recorded message with the hours they're open."

"I can't disturb Stan Denton," said the Chief.

"You know him?" asked Andy.

"Of course, I know him. Everyone knows Stan. He owns half the real estate in town and he's one of the Mayor's biggest supporters and campaign contributors."

"Then call Mr. Stan Denton. Either call him yourself or get the Mayor to call him. We need to see those recordings. There are cameras all around the building. We need to see those images now. You're the Chief of Police, for Christ's sake! Act like it and get us access to those recordings ASAP."

The Chief looked helplessly at Andy, then at the faces of the techs who were looking at him as if they were waiting to see him do something, then his expression abruptly changed and he took out his cell phone and made a few calls.

"I wouldn't call if it weren't a matter of life and death, Stan," said the Chief into his phone. "It's imperative we see the camera footage now. I don't care if you do get my badge for this, Stan. I've got three wounded officers, and I want the guy who did it. Yes, we can meet you at your office. Forty-five minutes? Make it thirty, Stan."

"Okay," said Elway as he put his phone away. I can take all of you in my car. Let's go look at some home movies."

"Thanks, Chief," said Andy.

"No," said Elway. "I should thank you. You're still on the job after taking a hole in the hand. I've stood in your way long enough. It's time we worked together to catch a killer. You with me, Lieutenant?"

"I'm with you," said Andy.

You watch the ambulance take the little one and the detective away. There must be at least two dozen police cars swarming around the entire neighborhood, looking everywhere for you, and here you sit in the runt's car, almost close enough for them to reach out and touch you, calmly watching them chase their tails.

You see a new bunch of detectives arrive in a police van that looks like a mobile laboratory. These cops string rolls of yellow tape around the front of the building, take photographs all around the building, search the grounds closely with flashlights. You worry that one of the new cops might take a walk around the parking lot and look into cars, but that never happens. They follow your footprints as far as the street and go no farther.

An hour later, a dark blue sedan pulls up in front of the building and two men get out. One of them wears a fancy white uniform with four gold stars on his epaulettes. The other man is the detective you stabbed in the hand. Doesn't anything stop that guy?

They go into the building. Half an hour later, they come out with the three guys you saw string tape earlier. You watch them all get into the blue car and drive away.

You wait until the first rays of sunlight appear in the east. Patrol cars have stopped going past every ten minutes, and it could be safe now to leave. Anyone who sees you will think you are an early morning jogger out for a run before breakfast. No one expects you to be on foot.

You tried to start the Dodge Dart earlier, but the ignition requires one of those special keys with a security chip built in. Stealing a car these days is not a viable option. If you want transportation, you will need to think of an alternative.

The red Matrix is entirely out of the question. Even if they don't have a good description of that car, cops are more likely to stop a red car than any other color. Red always stands out. Why you bought a red car, you will never know. It was cheap and good on gas, and it seemed like a good idea at the time.

Renting a car is also out of the question. If the detective knows your real name, he knows your aliases too. He's probably alerted all car rental places to report Tom Lazar or Tom Jones or Rudolph Eddington attempting to rent a vehicle.

Public transportation is your only option, and you wait at a street corner to catch a city bus. You have no idea of when the buses run, but you know that sooner or later you will see one come by. When one does stop at your corner ten minutes later, you climb aboard and ask the driver how to transfer to reach Bryson Memorial. The bus you are on will take you all the way downtown, the bus driver tells you. And then you can catch the Eighth Avenue bus which will take you the rest of the way to Bryson and drop you a block from the front entrance.

You see several police cars driving slowly along city streets. You suspect there may be roadblocks on most, if not all, of the main roads leading out of town. When you are ready to leave, you can take Continental Trailways west or Greyhound east and avoid the roadblocks. Searching a bus usually takes too long and holds up the line of cars accumulating behind the bus. Cops very seldom take the time to search a bus or train unless they're certain their suspect is on it.

First, however, there are some things you must do. You still have a date with the little one, and you know she will be helplessly waiting for you in her hospital bed at Bryson. The other female cop is still there at Bryson, too. And so is the runt. All defenseless. This time they can't fight back.

You have one icepick left of the three you purchased at Walmart, tucked into your belt beneath your t-shirt. You also have a can of lighter fluid in your left pants pocket and a Zippo in your right pants pocket. Plus, you have your pocket knife.

When the bus lets you out in front of the hospital at seven AM, you enter Bryson Memorial Medical Center as if you were an employee going to work. Somewhere in the massive complex of this modern medical center you will find, if you look, the necessary support facilities every hospital requires: the laundry where bed linens and towels and johnnies and scrubs and lab coats are washed and dried, folded and sorted; the facilities maintenance section where mops and vacuums and buffers are stored; the print shop with presses and copiers; the physical plant that runs the heating and lighting and the air-conditioning; the storerooms where everything from scalpels and needles and bandages to diapers and baby formula are locked away.

You wander the halls until you see the signs for maintenance in the basement of the west wing. You take the stairs to the lower level that most people never knew existed. Workers here are dressed as you are in jeans and sneakers. The only thing they have that you don't is a photo ID badge worn on a lanyard around their necks.

No one seems to notice that you don't have an ID. Turnover is high in this department, and new people come and go. Although some employees last, most are here for a few months only, maybe a year at most. New faces are the norm.

You find a men's locker room and open lockers until you see an ID badge hanging from a hook inside one of the lockers. You snatch it and quickly slide the lanyard over your head. Now you look official.

You find a mop and pail. You fill the pail with water from the tap in the corner, take the mop and pail into the service elevator, and press the button for the Critical Care floor.

The floor looks the same as you first saw it yesterday afternoon, before you killed the nurse. There are nurses at several nurses' stations where they stay busy monitoring patient vitals on electronic devices. Each of the patient rooms has a name written on a chalkboard to the left of the door. You see the room where the female cop is recovering from her neck injury. Her name is Evangelista. As you move the mop past her door, you peek inside to see a young man sitting in a chair next to the bed. He's a uniformed cop assigned to guard her, but he looks bored out of his mind. The television is on and Good Morning America flickers on the tiny screen. You are about to go into the room with your mop and pail to end the cop's boredom when you see a new patient being wheeled from the surgical recovery area to a private room down the hall from Evangelista's room. You recognize the face of the man you wrestled with in the bushes earlier last night as an orderly wheels him past you. You watch as a nurse and the orderly transfer his sedated body from the gurney to the hospital bed. The nurse writes Bradley on the chalkboard to the left of the door as the orderly leaves with his gurney. The nurse hooks Bradley up to monitors and leaves him alone in the room.

Which one should you do first? Bradley or Evangelista?

You are about to enter Bradley's room when residents come by making their morning rounds. You continue mopping and listen as the residents and nurses chit chat before the clinical director reviews patients' charts with them. Evangelista is healing satisfactorily, says one of the doctors, and her sedation should be gradually reduced. The new patient is only here for a day or two at the most, they say. Bradley can be sent home with sutures in his hip and be treated as an outpatient as soon as the anesthetic wears off, provided there are no obvious complications. Another new patient will be arriving shortly, says the clinical director. She is already out of surgery and in recovery, but she's still considered critical. She'll need intravenous feeding and intensive care for several days. She's lost a lot of blood.

The clinical director takes the residents into Bradley's room where they all peek under the covers. The man has, explains the doctor, steel hip joints. The right joint dislodged when a foreign piece of steel wedged between the joint and pelvic bone. The foreign object was surgically removed, the joint reset, and the incision sutured. Full recovery is expected. He should be regaining consciousness shortly.

They move into Evangelista's room, and the cop stops them and examines their ID badges before he lets them close to the bed. You keep your head down and swing the mop back and forth. You had to clean the workroom floors at Albertson's Mortuary. You're an expert at swinging a mop.

You can't clean in one spot exclusively, so you move down the hall away from Evenagelista's room.

Should you take care of Bradley now and then Evangelista? Or should you wait for the little one to be brought up from surgery and do all thee, one right after the other? You decide to wait.

Denton Properties owned the high-rise office building on Fourth Avenue where Stan Denton was already waiting for them when Elway parked his Cadillac in the no-parking zone in front of the entrance. Denton Properties owned or managed real estate all over the city, said Elway, from office buildings and upscale apartments to rooming houses and run-down hotels. Andy had heard rumors that Stan Denton was the biggest slum lord in the state, but no one could prove it because many of his holdings were hidden in secret real-estate trusts. Denton was richer than Midas, and getting richer every day.

Stan Denton was in his early sixties, short, balding, and overweight. He had a small gray moustache shadowing his upper lip, and his sunken eyes were overshadowed by thick bushy eyebrows.

"I appreciate you coming down here this early to open up for us, Stan," Elway told Denton as they entered Denton's office.

"You didn't have to threaten me with obstruction of justice charges when I asked if you had a search warrant," said Denton.

"And you didn't need to tell me to talk to your lawyer when I asked to see the recordings," said Elway. "This can't wait, Stan. Where can we watch the camera footage?"

Denton took them into a large room where hundreds of DVD recorders were organized on labeled shelving units. Each recorder, Denton explained, was connected to a Seagate hard drive where digital recordings could be accessed by one of the three computers on a nearby desk. Denton sat at the desk, entered passwords into one of the computers, and brought up menus. He punched a few keys and the computer screen displayed views of the front, back, and sides of Davis' apartment building. The parking lot was visible in the views of the front of the building.

"What time frame are we talking about here?" asked Denton.

"Between one and two this morning," said Andy.

Denton tapped a few keys. The images fast forwarded until Andy saw his Honda pull into the parking lot and Andy asked Denton to slow things down. He watched Linda and himself emerge from the car, cross the street, and walk up the sidewalk to the front entrance where they were picked up by another camera in the lobby. They disappeared into the stairwell.

"I don't have cameras on any of the floors," said Denton. "I should, but it costs too much."

"Take it forward until you see someone come back down the stairs," directed Andy.

Denton tapped keys again. When two blurred figures emerged from the stairwell, Denton backed up the images until they first appeared, then he tapped a key and the images advanced again.

"He's pushing the girl across the lobby to the front door," said one of the techs.

"Can you get a close up of their faces?" asked Elway.

Denton tapped keys again, and the image enlarged to show Eddington's scarred face and Linda's terrified expression. Eddington held an icepick to her neck as he forced her forward in front of him.

Denton hit another key, and the camera switched to outside as they came out the door and took twelve steps on the sidewalk before Eddington shoved the icepick into Linda's throat.

"My God!" said Denton as rich red blood squirted from her neck.

Eddington let Linda drop to the ground as he looked around quickly for an escape route. Then he ran across the street and entered the parking lot. Andy watched him run down the rows of parked cars until he came to a familiar-looking Dodge Dart. Eddington opened the driver's door and got into the front seat.

But, instead of driving out of the lot and making his escape, Eddington remained in the car as the camera showed Andy emerge from the front door of the building.

Andy and the others watched in amazement as Eddington stayed in plain sight while squad cars converged on the crime scene. Ambulances came and went, cop cars came and went, but Eddington didn't move.

"That guy has balls," said one of the techs. "I walked into that parking lot to look. I must have looked right at that car a dozen times. I scanned the entire lot and didn't see anything unusual."

"You may have seen him," said Andy, "but you didn't think anything of a man sitting in a car in a parking lot. You, like all the rest of us, thought the killer had hightailed it away before the police arrived."

"Good thing you didn't get close to that car," said another tech. "He might have killed you, too."

Denton fast forwarded again until they saw the car door open and Eddington step out. The time was 5:39 AM.

They watched him calmly walk out of the lot and disappear from view. Where he went after that was anybody's guess.

"I want copies of those," said Elway. "And I'll subpoena the originals when we get this guy to trial."

Denton placed a disc into the computer's drive and quickly tapped a few keys. "I'll give you everything from 1 AM to 6 AM," said Denton. "Jesus, Roger, I thought you were shitting me when you said you needed to see the recordings. I want you to know it's legal to have cameras on my buildings. I have signs posted that say the premises are under video surveillance."

"I wasn't trying to shake you down, Stan," said Elway.

"When you started talking about search warrants and subpoenas, I got scared. You understand I have investors to protect."

"I understand a lot of things, Stan. Thanks for getting out of bed and coming down here to meet us. I appreciate you showing us those."

"He killed that girl, didn't he?"

"She's still alive," Andy said.

"I never saw so much blood. How can she still be alive when she lost so much blood?"

"Lieutenant Sinnott saved her," said Elway. "He called an ambulance and administered first aid."

"She's in the hospital?" asked Denton. "I'll pay for her hospital expenses. It's the least I can do since she was injured on my property."

"She's a police officer injured in the line of duty," said Elway. "The department will pay her medical expenses. You don't have to worry about being sued, Stan."

Elway dropped them back at the apartment building. "I'll take these discs to the PSB and get blowups made of Eddington's face," said the Chief. "Then I'll have copies sent to every police officer in the state. Plus the FBI."

"I'm going back to the hospital and check on Davis," said Andy. "Thank you, Chief Elway. You did a good thing today."

"Just doing my job," said Elway, and then he drove off.

"You boys about finished here?" Andy asked the techs.

"Almost done," said one of the techs. "Then we'll go down to the labs and run the icepick we found in the apartment for prints."

"You'll probably find my fingerprints all over it," said Andy. "I pulled it out of the wall and threw the damn thing across the room."

"We'll find his prints, too, if he touched it. Was he wearing gloves?"

"No," said Andy. "He wasn't."

"Then we'll get prints. We have ways to bring out smudged or partial latents."

"You boys need to go home and get some sleep. You've worked double shifts today."

"And we'll keep working," said one of the other techs. "He hurt Evangelista real bad and he's hurt Davis twice. This guy has stepped over the line one time too many. It's personal for us now. We want to make certain this guy's put away for good. Getting his fingerprints from the crime scene will strap him into the chair."

"They don't fry them anymore," said another tech.

"Thanks, guys," said Andy.

"You get him for us, Lieutenant," said the third tech.

Andy drove his Honda back to Bryson, taking a regular parking space in the lot instead of looking for a spot designated for police. He checked the emergency room first, and they told him Davis had been moved to intensive care recovery after surgery. Visitors weren't allowed in the recovery room, not even police officers or immediate family. Once doctors were certain Linda wouldn't need additional surgery, she would be moved to one of the critical care units on the critical care floor. Andy could visit her then.

Andy took the elevator up to Critical Care where he intended to wait for Linda's arrival. The floor reeked of disinfectant. A lone cleaning person mopped at the far end of the hall, and nurses were changing dressings on a patient's head in one of the rooms with the door only partially shut. Other nurses were watching monitors and emptying bedpans, carrying meds to patients' rooms, doing the things that nurses do. The floor looked like it had returned to normal after the tragedy yesterday afternoon.

Officer Carson lounged in the chair next to Evangelista's bed. When Andy entered the room, Carson sat up straighter in the chair. He looked half asleep.

Andy flashed his ID and gold badge. "Are you checking everyone's ID?" he asked.

"Yeah," Carson said, looking closely at Andy's lieutenant's badge as if he had never seen one before. "I know you, Lieutenant. You can put the ID away."

"I don't care if it's your mother who comes into the room," said Andy. "I want you to check everyone's ID. Look at it closely to see if it's the right person. Someone tried to get in here to kill officer Evangelista yesterday. I don't want him to succeed today. If he does, he'll probably kill you, too."

"Gotcha, Lieutenant."

"Everything quiet?"

"Half a dozen doctors have come through. A couple of nurses. No one else until you. Lewinski was fit to be tied when I got here because he had to stay put when there was a 10-00 call. I got the call at two this morning. I drove around looking for the guy before I had to come here. You get him yet?"

"No."

"How's Davis? She going to make it?"

"She's out of surgery. They'll bring her up here in a little while."

"What happened to your hand?"

"The guy nailed me. Almost literally. He shoved an icepick through my hand and stuck my hand to a wall. Don't make the mistake I did and underestimate this guy. He can be sneaky."

"How did he get away? We had half the force out looking for him. No one saw him anywhere."

"He hid in the parking lot across the street from the apartment building where Davis lived."

"In plain sight?"

"In plain sight. He crawled into one of the cars and laughed at us as we looked everywhere but where he was."

"How do you know he was in the lot?"

"We watched the videos from the building's security cameras. Chief Elway's making pictures of the guy's face. Eddington's got scars around the eyes and wears sunglasses to hide the scars. Remember that. I'll get you a picture of him as soon as I can."

"You caught his face on camera?"

"First time. We got lucky or the guy's getting sloppy. Maybe he doesn't care anymore if we know all about him. He feels he has nothing to lose by being seen so he'll be doubly dangerous."

"And you think he'll come here?"

"Yes," said Andy. "I do. I definitely think he'll come here."

Carson touched the grip of his service pistol. Andy saw him unsnap the safety strap.

"You ever faced a killer before?" asked Andy. "Ever shot anyone?"

"No," said Carson.

"I hadn't either before today. I had to face a killer twice today, and I almost shot him twice. Don't think about him being a man, a human being. He's not. He's a target. When it's your life or his, better make it his. Don't hesitate. Shoot the bastard."

There was a commotion at the nurses' desk as the nurses prepared to receive a new arrival. They readied the room right next door. Five minutes later, an orderly pushed a gurney with a patient on board down the hallway and into the next room.

"That must be Davis," said Andy. "We'll give them a few minutes to get her settled in the room, and then I'll go over and see how she's doing."

"Are you going to have another officer assigned to her? Or do you want me to watch both rooms?"

"I'll stay with Davis until we can get someone assigned," said Andy.

"It's too bad about Davis," said Carson. "She seemed like a sweet girl. I only met her a few times, but she impressed me as knowing her stuff."

"She knows her job," said Andy. "She fired fifteen shots at a fleeing felon and hit his moving vehicle twelve times. Can you do that? Not many people can. She kept Evangelista alive until help arrived. She faced the killer and kicked the killer square in the balls. I saw her do something similar today. She's a good cop. She sure didn't deserve what happened to her."

Evangelista moaned, and her eyelids fluttered. "The docs cut back on the sedative today," said Carson. "They think she'll start to come around tomorrow, at least they hope she will. It's been three days since she was cut. They want to hear from her how she's feeling."

"Probably pretty awful," said Andy.

"Davis was stabbed tonight, not cut. Right?"

"Yeah. Her hands were cut on Friday. She was worried about being cut again. She got stabbed instead. I don't know if it makes any difference. She's still in the hospital. The doctors probably had to cut her to repair the damage to her throat."

Andy checked with the nurses to see if it was all right for him to go into Linda's room, and they asked him to wait a few more minutes until they had everything connected and she was resting comfortably.

The man mopping the floor was still going at it with vigor. Andy watched him swing the mop around. He had moved this way about ten feet, his back still facing this way. There was something about the way he moved, the cut of his hair, and the clothes he wore that seemed familiar.

He moved the pail with his mop, walking backwards a few inches at a time. As he passed a room in the next unit, he moved the pail toward the door and ducked inside with his mop.

"Who's in that room?" Andy asked a passing nurse.

"A new patient who just came in this morning," replied the nurse. She looked at a clipboard. "His name's Jonathan Bradley."

Andy drew his Glock and took off running. He knew now where he had seen a man with short hair dressed like that earlier today, a man wearing black leather Reeboks.

A man with scars on his face.

A man named Rudolph Eddington, Junior. A man who was a serial killer who had already killed hundreds of people and who had already tried to kill Jonathan Bradley once before.

The man who had raped and murdered Dolores Lebetter.

Andy had just seen the killer go into Rat's hospital room. He hoped he wasn't already too late to stop Eddington from killing Jonathan Bradley.

CHAPTER TWENTY-THREE

R at hurt. His head hurt, his hip hurt, he hurt all over.

Once again he had awakened in a hospital bed. Rat had been in and out of hospitals most of his life. From the time he was two when his father first broke one of his arms to age twenty-eight when the Pickaxe Butcher had shot him, Rat had undergone surgery dozens of times and had most of his original body parts mended or replaced. He had spent nearly an entire year in the hospital learning to walk again after being blown up by a roadside bomb in Iraq. Doctors had replaced both of his hips and both of his knees, fused several of his vertebrae together, and tried to treat him for Post-Traumatic Stress Disorder. He had been shot once by Troy Nolan when Troy had mistaken Rat for the Pickaxe Butcher, and once by the Butcher himself. And now he had been hospitalized after a close encounter with the Icepick Killer.

Rat's body had long ago adapted to the effects of chemical anesthesia. He had no idea whether that was because of the number of times he had been anesthetized in hospitals or because of the alcohol and drugs he had abused for almost a year, but he rarely stayed under half as long as the doctors expected. In fact, Rat had been partly conscious during the suturing process after surgery, gritting his teeth and bearing what little pain he felt as the needle bound up scar tissue to close the wound on his hip. He pretended to be groggier than he was because he didn't want anyone to administer additional sedatives or give him pain killers.

What he really wanted was to show such rapid improvement that the doctors would release him from the hospital. He needed to get out of here so he could go back to protecting Linda Davis. It never occurred to him that Linda might be right across the hall in the very same critical care ward that Rat was in.

When Linda had paid him a brief visit in the emergency room just prior to surgery, asking him lots of questions about the killer, Rat had realized that the killer wasn't going to stop until someone physically stopped him. Not just slowed the killer down, but stopped him permanently and forever. Linda's life would always be in danger as long as the killer was alive. Rat didn't tell Linda, but he had made up his mind to track the killer down and kill the guy in cold blood. It was the only way to keep Linda safe.

Because Rat had once been diagnosed with a mental disorder, he could not legally acquire firearms in this state. But Rat knew the way guns worked. If he couldn't buy a gun, perhaps he could fabricate one.

The killer had moved much too fast for Rat to effectively use any of the killing moves he had learned in the Army. He had tried to ram the guy's nasal cartilage up into the guy's brain, but all he had managed to do was break the guy's nose. He had tried a killing kick to the solar plexus, and all he had managed was to kick the guy in the balls. And when Rat had tried to kick the guy again, it was Rat who had fallen down and not the killer.

So Rat decided he needed a weapon. Any kind of weapon would do. A butcher knife from the kitchen. An axe or a pickaxe. Even an icepick. Something long and sharp. Something hard and penetrating. Something lethal.

Rat hated to feel helpless, and he did feel helpless now. He was hooked up to monitors that measured his blood pressure, his pulse rate, his body temperature. His body was immobilized beneath heavy blankets and sheets. He felt trapped, and he couldn't stand felling trapped.

He kicked off the sheets, sat up, and removed the electrodes taped to his chest and stomach. He pulled the blood pressure cuff off his biceps and the pulse-taking device off his finger. In a minute, alarms would sound at the nurses' station, and someone would come in to see why his blood pressure had dropped and his heartbeat had flatlined. When they did, they would find Rat out of bed, ready to go home. They couldn't keep him here against his will. They would argue and cajole that he needed to stay in the hospital to get well.

But, in the end, they would have to let him go.

Rat climbed out of bed. All he had on was a hospital johnnie loosely tied in the back. He might as well be naked, he thought, and went in search of the clothes had had worn when the ambulance brought him to the hospital.

There was a narrow wardrobe closet next to the room's bathroom. Rat opened the closet door and saw his shirt and his torn and bloodied pants hanging on a hook. His socks and shoes were on a shelf.

Before he could dress, however, he heard a noise and turned, expecting to see a chastising nurse wagging a disapproving finger at him. Instead, he saw the killer holding a mop in one hand and an icepick in the other.

"Hello, Runt," said the killer, dropping the mop to lunge at Rat.

Both men moved at the same time. Rat was stiff and sluggish, and it hurt to engage his hips. The killer swung the icepick in a wide arc and slammed it into the closet door as Rat leapt aside just in time.

Rat rolled on the floor and reached for the mop handle, grabbing the wooden mop handle and swinging the entire mop around to use like a rifle with a bayonet attached. The mop handle's circumference was significantly smaller than Rat was used to, but he had practiced parrying and thrusting with bayonets, pugil sticks, and pickaxes. He had a weapon in his hands that he felt he knew how to use.

The killer pulled the icepick free from the closet door, and he came right at Rat as Rat tried to get up off the floor. Rat's right leg didn't want to work, but his left leg gave him enough purchase so he could manipulate and control the mop handle with both hands. He knocked the icepick away from his face and out of the killer's hands, reversed the mop and swatted the killer across the face with the damp cloth of the mop head. Then he spun the handle around again and dug the end of the mop handle into the killer's abdomen, forcing the killer to retreat all the way back into the narrow closet. Rat drew back the mop handle in preparation for the killing lunge that would drive the end of the mop handle up beneath the man's breastbone and put sufficient pressure on his heart muscle to burst the heart.

Andy suddenly appeared in the doorway holding a gun. "Police officer," shouted Andy. "Nobody move! Back away, Rat. Drop the mop."

When Rat hesitated, the killer's two hands moved much too fast for either Andy or Rat to react, one hand spraying a stream of liquid from a yellow can and the other flipping open the top of a Zippo and with the very same motion running the wheel against the flint. The killer hurled the lighter at the liquid and the bed burst into flame. The flames leapt higher and higher into the air as the killer continued to squirt liquid at the fire. When he threw the rest of the open container of lighter fluid into the fire, flames expanded to the oxygen canister next to the bed. The oxygen exploded like a bomb.

The impact sent Rat flying hard against a wall, and the blast knocked Andy completely off his feet. Andy fell to the tile floor and his head bounced on the tiles like a basketball. Andy went limp, and the pistol fell from his hands.

All kinds of alarms went off all over the building, and the sprinklers in the ceiling emitted a pink chemical foam over everything instead of spraying ordinary water. The room filled with smoke.

Rat was vaguely aware that the killer, protected from the blast by the sides of the closet, was moving out of the closet and going for Andy's pistol. Rat tried to shake cobwebs from his head and force his eyes to focus.

The killer reached Andy's gun. In a moment he would shoot Andy. Then he would shoot Rat. Rat had to stop him.

Rat's hands felt around on the floor for the wooden mop handle but couldn't find it. His fingers found, instead, the wooden handle of the icepick.

Rat didn't think as his fingers closed on the handle. The killer had raised Andy's gun and was now pointing it directly at Andy's head. Rat pushed himself up from the floor with his hands and his one good leg and, in an act of pure desperation, thrust the icepick as far as he could reach. Because Rat was small, and because he was bringing the icepick up from the floor at an angle, the point only reached the seat of the killer's jeans. But Rat's momentum shoved the point through the denim fabric and the shaft penetrated the killer's anus. The tip entered the killer's rectum, ripped a hole in the tender lining, and punctured the prostate. The killer screamed like a stuck pig, and as the killer's entire body jerked in pain and surprise, the weapon he held in his hands discharged.

Certain that the killer had just shot and killed Andy, Rat's anger knew no bounds. He withdrew the bloody icepick and this time deliberately rammed it in lower. The point again penetrated the denim, but it continued on to penetrate the killer's scrotum and exited the scrotum into head of the man's penis.

As the killer's impaled body slumped to the floor, Rat stabbed him again and again with the icepick, puncturing his back, his ribs, even his heart. Rat was still stabbing the guy when officer Carson and hospital security rushed up to grab Rat's arms and pin Rat to the floor.

While they held him down, a doctor administered a sedative into his arm. He continued to struggle until the doctor gave him a second injection. Finally, the ok hold and the world went dark.

You see the detective come around the corner from the elevators and you quickly turn the other way before he can see your face. He walks straight to Evangelista's room and disappears inside.

You continue mopping while the detective and the uniformed officer are talking. You wish you could hear their conversation, but you are too far away and don't want to risk moving closer. The detective got a good look at you earlier and, now that the detective knows what you look like, he might recognize your face. You can take care of the detective after you take care of the little one. Today you feel unusually lucky and blessed. All the people you intend to kill are together in practically the same place at the same time. You can kill one immediately after the other in an assembly-style rampage. You will be finished and out of the hospital, hiding in plain sight at the bus stop, waiting for the next city bus, before anyone knows what just happened. Cops will be looking for a fleeing killer, not for an employee waiting for a city bus after getting off work.

Your plan is bold and daring. Who else but you could pull it off? No one. You are the best at what you do.

Your father was the best at what he did, and he instilled in you his work ethic. You are thorough and meticulous. And you are fast and efficient. You waste no motions. That was something else your father taught you.

You swing the mop back and forth, back and forth. Most others would be bored with the repetitive motions, but repetition frees your mind and allows you to think clearly. When the little one is brought to the floor, you will choose who to kill first: the little one, the runt, or the detective and the two other cops in that room. You will know from where everyone is located whom you will kill first. You will move fast and efficiently, with no wasted motions.

You have the icepick in your belt under your t-shirt, the can of lighter fluid in one pocket, and the Zippo in another. You intend to use the icepick on the little one and the runt, then the lighter fluid on the cops. You can squirt lighter fluid into the room and toss the lit Zippo and hear them scream as they burn. Then you will make your escape down the same stairwell you used yesterday.

It is another perfect plan. What could possibly go wrong?

They wheel the little one onto the floor and you see she is being placed in the empty room right next to Evangelista. You wait until they get her settled in the room before you make your move.

You are closest to the runt's room, and you decide to kill him first. It will be so easy to slip into the room as if you are going in to clean the floor. He will be in the bed, still out cold or groggy from the anesthesia, and you can do his eyes in a matter of seconds. Then you can swoop across the hall into the little one's room, and do both her eyes while touching her breasts.

Then it's next door to take care of the cops. You spray the detective and the other two with lighter fluid and torch them before they know what you have done. You must move fast. You reach into your pants pocket and raise the closed nozzle on the plastic Ronsonol container. Now all you need do is take it out, aim, and squeeze when the time is right.

You walk backwards, mopping as you go. You drag the water pail across the floor with the mop, inching closer to the runt's room. You are in front of his door. You swing the mop inside and follow it, taking the icepick from your belt with your left hand while moving the mop with your right.

Only the runt isn't in the bed. The covers are thrown aside, the electrode leads dangling from the monitors, the monitors blinking red alerts.

You see him standing next to a wardrobe. He hears you and turns around.

"Hello, Runt," you say, dropping the mop and making your move.

He moves as fast as you do, and the icepick misses his face and lodges in the metal door of the wardrobe. You tug it out as the runt falls to the floor and crawls toward the mop. You jab the icepick at his eyes, expecting him to blink and flinch but he doesn't. He brings the mop handle up and hits your arm so hard it knocks the icepick away from his face and out of your hands entirely. He reverses the mop, spins it around with his nimble fingers, and swats you across your face with the wet mop head, and it is you that blinks and flinches when the dirty mop slaps your face. He spins the handle around again and digs the end of the handle into your abdomen, forcing you to retreat all the way back into the narrow closet. He holds the mop handle like a spear aimed at your heart. He has become the hunter, and you have become the prey.

Suddenly the detective appears in the doorway with that toy gun in his hand. Close up, it looks like it's made of plastic. "Police officer," he shouts. "Nobody move! Back away, Rat. Drop the mop."

While the runt is distracted, your hands move fast. One hand has the open can of Ronsonol spraying lighter fluid into the air and the other flips open the top of your Zippo, runs the wheel against the flint, and tosses the lighter onto the bed. The bed bursts into flame, the flames leaping higher and higher into the air as you continue to squirt lighter fluid at the fire. When you throw the rest of the open container of lighter fluid into the fire, you see the flames expand to the oxygen canister next to the bed. The oxygen explodes like a bomb.

The impact sends the runt flying hard against a wall, and the blast also knocks the detective completely off his feet. His head bounces off the tiles. He goes limp, and the pistol falls from his hands.

Alarms sound all over the building, and the ceiling sprinklers spray a pink chemical foam over everything. As the fire goes out, the room fills with smoke.

You move out of the closet and go for the detective's gun. You will shoot the detective, then turn the gun on the runt. There's still time to get out of here if you work fast. You can come back later and do the others.

You raise the toy gun and point it straight at the detective's head. At this range, you can't miss. Your finger tightens on the trigger.

Suddenly you feel pain, and your hand jerks as the gun goes off. Something sharp has entered your rectum and penetrated your prostate. You scream with pain and dread. When the object is removed from your rear, you try to turn around but now you feel another pain, more acute and debilitating than anything you have ever felt before. This time the pain is in your tender testicles, and then you feel sharp pain move into your penis. You scream again and fall to the floor. As you fall, you jerk the trigger and the gun fires again.

But the pain has only begun. Now you feel excruciating pain in your lower back, your ribs, your stomach, your lungs. You didn't know anything could be this painful. And then the pain goes away and the world slowly goes dark, as all the stars in the sky blink out one by one at the cataclysmic end of the world.

Andy awoke in a hospital bed. Chief Elway sat next to the bed.

"Don't try to move," said the Chief. "You have a concussion. You've been out cold for twenty-some hours."

"Eddington was here," Andy said.

"He's still here. Now he's downstairs in pathology after being autopsied."

"We got him? We finally got him?"

"We finally got him. It was a little unorthodox the way it went down, but he's deader than a doornail. He won't kill anyone ever again."

Andy's left shoulder hurt nearly as bad as his head, and he looked at his shoulder and saw that it was bandaged. "What happened to my shoulder?" he asked Elway.

"You were shot in the line of duty," said the Chief. "A few inches lower and to the right, and you'd be dead."

"I don't remember being shot."

"Well, you were. Two rounds were fired from your Glock. One hit your shoulder and the other must have missed. We recovered the bullet where it chipped the tile floor and ricocheted into a wall. Fortunately, no one else was hit."

"What about Rat? Jon Bradley? Is he okay?"

"He went crazy. He stabbed Eddington forty-two times. He had to be pulled off the guy and sedated."

"But he's okay?"

"He'll live. There will be a coroner's inquest, and he may have to stand trial for manslaughter. Stabbing a guy, even a known killer, forty-two times is rather excessive, don't you think? He admits he wanted to kill the guy. He wouldn't stop stabbing him until he was absolutely certain the guy was dead. The Pathologist said some of the wounds look malicious. He stabbed Eddington in the ass and the balls and even the prick. That's sadistic and unnecessary."

"Eddington deserved it," said Andy.

"Maybe," said the Chief. "We'll let a jury decide. Meanwhile, I want you to stay in bed and take it easy. You're on sick leave for the next two weeks. Rest up and get well."

"Who'll run homicide while I'm gone?"

"I will," said Elway. "I'm still a cop, you know. Besides, I don't expect we'll have any more homicides now that Eddington is dead. It should be a piece of cake to do your job. And I'll see about hiring you some more people to help when you're back on your feet."

"You have it in the budget?"

"Hell, no. Fuck the budget. I'm going to strongarm the mayor and shake loose some money he's hiding for himself. The Mayor knows I have a few skeletons in my closet I don't want to see the light of day, but I know where he's buried lots of bodies. I'll get the money."

Andy closed his eyes. So much had happened that his head was spinning trying to absorb it all. Or, maybe, it was the effects of the concussion that made his head spin like a top. Or was it the world that was spinning around and not his head? Maybe it was the whole world that kept revolving and his head stayed stationary. Did the world revolve around Andy Sinnott or was Andy only one small part of the world along for the ride? Did it matter?

Eddington was dead. That was a big load off Andy's mind and wounded shoulder. Andy would recover, and so would Linda and Evangelista and Rat. Now that it had been proven that Eddington was the icepick killer and not Harvey Fredriks, George would surely be released. As Shakespeare might say, "All's well that ends well."

CHAPTER TWENTY-FOUR

Rat and George threw a party on Labor Day. It was the party they had originally planned for a week after the Fourth of July when Troy and Sally Nolan were scheduled to return from their honeymoon. Unfortunately, George was still in jail on the Fourth; Linda, Lorraine, and Rat were still in the hospital; and Andy didn't feel like partying with his injured shoulder. The coroner's jury hadn't yet absolved Rat, and Jon Bradley was being kept in the hospital, ostensibly for observation, until the inquest was completed. That was perfectly okay with Rat. Linda was just across the hall most of that time, and they got to know each other. Even after Linda was released, she returned to the hospital just to visit with him.

But the coroner's jury did eventually absolve Rat. The fact that Rat had been physically injured and was still likely feeling the effects of medication after surgery, plus his former diagnosis of suffering from PTSD, accounted for the excessive force used to kill Eddington. Most of the jury felt Eddington deserved what he got. The ruling was justifiable homicide.

The State's Attorney dropped all charges against George on Thursday, July the seventh. Sally Nolan, the acting coroner until the county board could appoint a new one, welcomed George back as a lab assistant the next day.

Chief Elway had hired new officers with money the Mayor had found in a contingency fund. Andy got two additional techs and one more homicide detective. Nolan's Violent Crimes Division got two new techs and two detectives. Del Conklin had finished his program of recovery, and he was attending daily AA meetings. Conklin was a good cop when he was sober. Andy put Del on probation for six months. If Del drank again on duty, he understood he would be immediately terminated. Andy told Del he would watch Del very carefully for the next six months. Other than that, Del would be treated like any other cop.

Joel Hickman stopped attacking the police and focused his attention instead on politicians and slumlords. Some unnamed source had revealed to Hickman that the Mayor had instructed city building inspectors to overlook code violations by some of the Mayor's largest financial contributors. Hickman promised to reveal all in future columns. Whoever it was that had once said investigative reporting was dead had spoken prematurely.

Linda and Lorraine had scars on their necks that were constant reminders of the ordeals they had endured. Linda's physical scars were less obvious than Lorraine's. Linda had shown Rat her scars, and he had shown Linda his.

Chief Elway had presented Andy an official Riverdale Police Department commendation for his splendid work on catching the Icepick Killer. Elway had publically thanked Andy for reminding him what it meant to be a good cop.

Rat and George held their Labor Day party in the large back yard of their house at 8617 East Fifteen Street. George tended the grill because Rat had acquired an aversion to the smell of lighter fluid.

Troy and Sally Nolan were the guests of honor at the big party. The newlyweds were looking at houses in the neighborhood, and Rat showed them both around his house and pointed out that the spare bedrooms would make excellent nurseries.

Because Del Conklin also attended the Labor Day party, no alcohol was served. Del had been sober more than sixty days, and he said he had no desire for alcohol any more. Rat still thought it was better not to tempt the man. He remembered his father falling off the wagon numerable times after promising Rat's mother he would never drink again. The old man had been sober more than six years now. But Rat didn't want to tempt either man by making alcohol available.

Art Lewinski and Jason Carson put in a brief appearance. Lewinski told Andy he still wasn't sure about the Chief changing overnight, and when Elway tried to have a conversation with

Lewinski, Art said he had somewhere else he had to be and left the party. Carson stayed a while longer, then he left, too. Both men had to work the night shift on Labor Day. It was one of Rat's scheduled nights off. He worked weekends and had Mondays off.

Rat had no regrets. If he had it to do it over again, he would do the same thing to Eddington. Eddington deserved what he got. Though Rat couldn't legally own a firearm, George could buy guns after being exonerated. George was the proud new owner of two Remington M1911R1 .45s, two Colt AR 15 assault rifles, and two pump shotguns. Rat knew where he could find a weapon if he ever needed one.

While George cooked steaks on the grill, Rat filled tubs with soft drinks and ice. He had bought big thirty-pound bags of ice and stuck them in the basement freezer. When the ice he had put out in the tubs melted under the hot Labor Day sun, Rat dumped out the water and went down the basement and brought up fresh bags of ice. Then he refilled the tubs with chunks of ice.

And, of course, if the chunks of ice had frozen together, he would break them up with a special tool he had purchased at Walmart.

Andy saw Rat's arms moving rapidly up and down, and he came over to investigate. "What do you have there, Rat?" he asked.

Rat showed him.

It was an icepick.

AN AFTERWORD FROM THE AUTHOR

Macabre Ink and Crossroad Press published a new digital edition of Claw Hammer in 2014 and has just published an original digital edition of Pickaxe. Icepick is an original publication from the same publisher. This is Icepick's first edition. I hope you enjoyed reading this novel as much as I enjoyed writing it.

Claw Hammer was my first published horror novel, and since its original publication in 1989 I have written nine additional novels set in imaginary Riverdale, Illinois, which is a combination of my native Rockford and Aurora and Oak Park, plus images from a dozen other northern Illinois cities where I've lived and written novels. Carl Erickson, the homicide detective from *Claw Hammer,* also appears in *Pickaxe, Icepick, Sledgehammer, Box Cutter,* and *Pinking Shears.* After Carl retires, Troy Nolan and Andy Sinnott take over Carl Erickson's roles, both appearing in *Pickaxe, Icepick,* and *Meat Cleaver.*

I have ventured out of my comfort zone six times already in the first three days of this week, and I expect I'll venture out at least six more times before the week ends. My comfort zone is sitting at my keyboard inside my own house writing novels and short stories or reading novels and short stories for review. When Gretta died three years ago, I abandoned the real world for multiple fantasy worlds where I could control the outcome of human interactions. Writing kept me relatively sane. Andy Sinnott is a lot like me. But you already guessed that, didn't you?

I write not only for me and to maintain sanity, but I write for people like me—and like you, dear reader—who love to read. I try, first and foremost, to tell a good story because I love good stories. Some of my stories get really weird, and many of my characters bleed and feel pain and some die. I view the world as a dangerous place where bad things happen to good people. Not all of my stories have a happy ending. I hope you're as glad as I am that *Icepick* does end happily for most of the characters. You'll meet many of them again in other novels.

ABOUT THE AUTHOR

Paul Dale Anderson loves to read and write horror, dark fantasy, thrillers, and science fiction. He's an active member of SFWA, HWA, and ITW, and was previously represented by Barbara Puechner of the Peekner Literary Agency. When Barbara died with his breakthrough novel still half-finished, he switched to writing non-fiction. Paul went back to college and earned an MS Ed. and most of a doctorate in Educational Psychology and earned an MA in Library and Information Studies from the University of Wisconsin. He taught creative writing for Writers Digest School (both Novel and Short Story) and for the University of Illinois at Chicago.

He returned to fiction writing with a vengeance in 2012, completing his breakthrough novel and seventeen other novels, and began writing fresh fiction that crossed genres.

Two of his published novels, *Claw Hammer and Daddy's Home* sold very well, and several of his anthologized short stories have reappeared from major publishers. One of those short stories adapted to graphic novel format was recently re-released in hardcover and paper in J. N. Williamson's Illustrated Masques.

He is also a Certified Hypnotist and National Guild of Hypnotists Certified Instructor.

Curious about other Crossroad Press books?
Stop by our site:
http://store.crossroadpress.com
We offer quality writing
in digital, audio, and print formats.

Enter the code FIRSTBOOK
to get 20% off your first order from our store!
Stop by today!

"That's why," said Evangelista, "he stabbed her in the neck. He couldn't get the icepick in either eye because the eyes were too small a target with her thrashing around. So he went for the soft tissue of her long neck, punctured the carotid, and waited for her to stop struggling before he stabbed both eyes."

"How long did all that take?"

"Ten, fifteen minutes maybe?"

"So now it's four-thirty. Why doesn't he rape the corpses? He has time before sun-up."

"He did rape them," said Davis. "Symbolically."

"So, it wasn't just about sex after all, was it?" asked Andy.

"No," said Davis. "It was about power."

"Very good. I think that's about as close as we're going to get to knowing what happened. Why did he take a shower?"

"He was covered in blood?" suggested Evangelista.

"True. Why else?"

"He felt dirty," said Davis.

"Very good. He felt dirty because Victim Number 2 touched him," said Andy. "He wanted to be in control of all the touching."

"He's really sick," said Evangelista.

"I personally agree with you," said Andy.

"He's killing someone almost every night," noted Davis. "When is he going to stop?"

"When we catch him," said Andy.